He started to turn back, but a blur of movement caught his eye. Then he saw the figure clearly, sprinting away from the house toward the seawall. He wore dark clothes and something—*a stocking?* —over his head. McCleary sprang from the shadows like a rapacious animal and tore across the yard. The man saw him coming and flew over the seawall. McCleary followed, jumped the seawall, and half slid down the damp hill. Just as the man reached the dock, McCleary hurtled himself forward, tackling the guy at the knees.

They both went down, smacking the hard wood. The man wiggled free, turned, and an instant before his knife sliced through McCleary's shirt, he saw the gleam of metal and feinted.

But he wasn't fast enough. . . .

Also by T.J. MacGregor
Published by Ballantine Books:

DARK FIELDS

KILL FLASH

DEATH SWEET

T.J. MacGREGOR

BALLANTINE BOOKS • NEW YORK

for my husband, Rob
& my editor, Chris Cox

Special thanks again to
my agent, Diane Cleaver

"We are so accustomed to the apparently rational nature of our world that we can scarcely imagine anything happening that cannot be explained by common sense. The primitive man confronted by a shock of this kind would not doubt his sanity; he would think of fetishes, spirits or gods."

—Carl Jung
from MAN AND HIS SYMBOLS

PART ONE

Labyrinth

1 The Kill

January 24,
Miami

HE HAD MADE an art of murder.

He had studied its anatomy, its colors, nuances, and techniques the way other men studied law or astronomy. He knew that the preparation and aftermath of a kill were nearly as important as the act itself. Like any work of art, a murder had to be able to withstand scrutiny.

The details of this kill, for instance, had taken him a long time to work out. He wanted his victim to feel terror, but it had to be a certain type of terror. He had labored for days over what type of weapon he would use, how he would enter the house, and how long the kill would take. He had deliberated over the kinds of clues he should leave. They had to be the right kinds of clues. After all, part of the thrill lay in the subsequent hunt.

He stopped at the sliding glass door at the back of the house and removed a flat-edge screwdriver from the pouch at his belt. Inside his gloves, his hands were as cool as the moon that had traversed three-quarters of the sky, its journey as solitary as his own. Its light covered the yard in a thin, beer-colored membrane, and seemed to ripen the damp, cool air with the trenchant fragrances of honeysuckle and brine from the nearby canal. The grass felt like sponge cake against his bare feet. The chirr of insects was music to work by as he wedged the screwdriver between the edge of the door and the jamb.

The lock gave easily. The locks on these sliding glass doors usually did. He parted the curtains with his hands and stepped into the kitchen, closing the door softly behind him. A light shone over the stove. A clock ticked in the silence. The refrigerator hummed. The house slumbered noisily, like a child caught in a nightmare.

It wasn't a large place—just two bedrooms, a bath, a family room, the kitchen, and a one-car garage. It was the sort of house a woman alone could draw around her at night and feel as snug as a snail.

He didn't turn off the stove light. He moved left, through the darkened living room, the carpet smooth and cool against his bare feet. He had discovered some years ago that it was best to do his work in bare feet, if the situation allowed. It gave him more control.

The light spilled far enough into the living room so he could see Jessie, the woman's cat, curled on the couch. In one kill, he had slaughtered a cat. It had sickened him. He still wasn't quite sure why an animal elicited such a response in him when a human being didn't. Perhaps it had something to do with animals being like children, trusting and defenseless. Whatever the reason, he—like any artist—had learned his own parameters that night, his limitations.

He stroked Jessie, then unsnapped the pouch at his belt. He withdrew a pair of scissors from a leather case. These were special, as sturdy as garden shears, but with sharper, narrower blades. He slipped the case into his pocket and advanced toward Joyce's bedroom.

Starlight splashed through the window over her king-size bed. She slept sprawled on her back, her hair a wheat-colored tangle across her pillow, mouth slightly open. His deep affection for her seemed inevitable, an avocational hazard. This happened sometimes with his victims, even the men. Of course, Joyce wasn't exactly a stranger; that was part of it.

He moved over to the bed. Since she slept in the center of it, he had to lean toward her to clamp his hand over her mouth. She screamed into his glove a second later, but by then the tips of the scissors were against her throat.

4

"Don't move and don't scream," he whispered.

Her eyes widened. She bit his hand and when he yanked it away, she screamed again. The scissors nicked her neck. He slammed his hand over her mouth. "Don't," he hissed. She remained as motionless as a meditating yogi. With his left hand, he reached into the pouch on his belt again. He brought out a roll of duct tape. The edge was already folded back, and he took it between his teeth, pulled, tore off a strip. He set the tape on the nightstand and pressed the scissors a little harder against her neck. He told her he was going to remove his hand from her mouth. If she screamed, if she made even the smallest movement, the tip of the scissors would poke into her carotid artery. Did she understand? *Yes, yes*, shouted her stricken eyes. A trickle of blood bloomed against her neck.

He removed his hand and taped her mouth shut.

Tears leaked from her eyes.

His heart beat a frantic little rhythm as he reached into the pouch a third time and drew out two nylon stockings. With his left hand, he tied one stocking to the bedpost and with his right, pressed the scissors harder against her neck.

"Now I want you to lift your left arm."

She lifted it and cried harder.

"Drop it a little lower." He stretched out the nylon so her wrist fell into it as if into a sling. He secured the end to the bedpost.

He moved closer to her on the bed as he repeated his instructions for her right arm. There was no need for the scissors now. Her terror had inundated her. Behind the tape that covered her mouth, her sobs sounded strangled, as if she were drowning in her own mucus.

He peeled the sheet off her, brought out two more stockings, and tied her ankles to the baseboard. Her eyes were squeezed shut, her head turned to the side, so her cheek was squashed against the pillow, sinking into it. He almost felt sorry for her. He wished she would struggle, fight back, kick, something.

With the tip of the scissors, he slid her nightgown up her legs, over her thighs. She had beautiful legs, Joyce did, a dancer's legs, like Juliette Prowse. Or Tina Turner. He complimented her on her legs, but it just made her whimper like a wounded animal. A horrible, pathetic sound that annoyed him. Why couldn't she be a little braver?

He brought out a baggie with powdered sugar in it. He dampened the tip of his finger and dipped it into the bag. Then he touched the sugar to her stomach. He kept talking to her, softly, gently, making lazy designs in the sugar with his finger. It reminded him of being a kid, when he used to draw designs in wet sand with the end of a stick.

He dabbed some more on her knees, her arms. In the starlight, she looked like a dappled pony. He stroked her thigh and worked the scissors, snapping them in the air just above her stomach. He watched her face, the nuances of her terror. This was what he had come to learn.

He touched the pulse in her neck, felt it leaping beneath his fingers, racing faster than he thought possible. He noted the sweat that erupted on her brow. It sparkled. He memorized how the muscles in her thighs and stomach quivered when he pressed the flat, cool edge of the scissors against her warm skin. He licked at some of the sugar. It tasted less sweet than it should have, almost as if her terror had altered its chemistry, transmuted it.

She taught him well, this woman, and perhaps tonight he would take a small memento, something to remember her by. He did this with certain victims, his best victims. It was an honor. He told her as much, explaining what he would like to take, and she screamed into the tape.

He smiled and got down to business.

2 The McClearys

HUNGER PURSUED QUIN with a mugger's diligence and made the day look good enough to eat. Cirrus clouds flaked like biscuits against the thin blue February sky. Trees were giant stalks of damp, crisp celery. The bright red blooms on the hibiscus hedge in front of the firm glistened as moistly as strawberries. It wasn't fair that her stomach governed her life, she thought, especially when she'd just eaten breakfast two hours ago.

She parked her Toyota behind McCleary's car and reached for the airline tickets on the dashboard. *Goodbye, Miami, and Happy Birthday, McCleary.* His birthday wasn't until May, but spring was usually their busiest time, and it would be hard to get away. By next week they would have tied up their major cases and could be basking on a Venezuelan beach, winging over Angel Falls, or sampling restaurants in Caracas. Seven days, that was all she wanted.

She moved briskly up the walk, her thick umber hair loose, falling almost to her shoulders. She stood five-ten and tipped the scales at 108, a weight she'd held since she was fifteen and which never changed, despite her enormous appetite. Her eyes, an eerie ghost blue, darted like hummingbirds through the yard at either side of the walk, alighting on the blooming gardenia bushes, the sparges of geraniums and zinnias, the ferns. A cool breeze spilled through the surrounding pines, redolent with fragrances. It was better than strolling through the perfume aisles at Bloomingdale's.

Her shadow hugged the ground to her right like the

specter of a forgotten childhood playmate. It was as short and squat as a dwarf and followed her up the front steps to the porch, which was bathed in sunlight. She became fixated on it.

The shadow dwarf mimicked her when she slid the tickets in a side pocket of her purse. It reached for the doorknob just as she did. She flicked her hair off her shoulders and it copied her. She laughed. She turned ninety degrees and held up her hand, splaying the fingers. She waggled them; the dwarf's fingers waggled back. "Nice to meet you," Quin said, just as the front door opened.

McCleary stepped outside, pausing on the welcome mat that said, ST. JAMES & MCCLEARY, PRIVATE EYES. She grimaced. It was one of her superstitions that neither she nor McCleary should ever step on the mat because something bad might happen. It was silly, but she couldn't help it. McCleary must've read her expression correctly, because he moved aside and glanced around. His smoke-blue eyes wrinkled with mirth. "Invisible friends, Quin?"

"Very funny." She pointed down. "My shadow dwarf. Even *he* doesn't step on the mat, Mac. Where're you off to? I thought you and Bean were meeting some people for breakfast."

"We already did. C'mon, ride with me and I'll explain on the way."

He touched her elbow, urging her toward the steps. He was only two inches taller than she, with chocolate-colored hair graying at the temples and a mustache the same color also laced with gray. Whenever he stood close to her like this, she had an urge to run her fingers through his hair, as if to make certain he was more real than her shadow.

"Ride with you where?"

"To talk with a guy named Ross Young."

"Who's he?"

"Someone who was recommended to us by Tim Benson."

8

Benson meant Metro-Dade homicide. Homicide meant trouble. "Is this about a case?" They moved along the sidewalk, the breeze playing tag with the hem of Quin's skirt.

"Probably."

"Oh." She touched her hand to the side of her purse, where the tickets were.

"You don't want another case?"

"Well, sure. We can always use the money."

He unlocked the door to his silver RX-7 and she slid inside. The car was three years old and still smelled new. Unlike her Toyota, it had remained spotless—no crumbs on the floor, no abandoned paper bags stuck between the seats, no thin layer of dust on the dash, no overdue library books in the back. McCleary, her orderly husband. Sometimes she envied him.

He opened the door to the driver's side and got in. "You don't sound very enthusiastic. About a new case."

She held out the tickets. "Happy birthday."

He looked at them, then up at her, then down at the tickets again, surprise and delight limning his face. "Caracas? Angel Falls?"

"For next week. We can change the dates," she added quickly. "The travel agent said the fare is good through April."

"Let's change them for today. We'll just drive to the airport. Now. This minute."

She laughed. "Sure."

"I'm serious."

"Oh, c'mon."

"Really."

"We'd have to go home first and pack and get someone to look after the cats."

"Okay, fine, but then we'd just go, Quin. Let's do it. Before we have too much time to think about it."

"What about this appointment with Ross what's-his-name?"

"I'll call and tell him I've changed my mind. We'd

keep driving to the airport, with a detour by the house first."

"You're fooling."

"I'm not."

Delighted with his sudden whimsy, she laughed again. "Maybe we should at least see what the guy has to say. It *is* income, Mac. And I just paid fifteen hundred bucks for these tickets."

He winced, shifted in his seat so he was leaning against the door. "I don't know for sure that it's a case. He didn't say much over the phone, except that Tim had recommended he call us."

"Maybe he just wants advice or something."

"Right." He started the car and pulled away from the curb. "We'll talk to him and then head for the house, call the airport, and see when the next flight to Caracas is."

"Okay."

She returned the tickets to her purse, not quite believing they were going to get away with it. They'd been married a little over three years and hadn't had a vacation since their five-day honeymoon in Trinidad. Of course, it had taken them almost that long to get the firm back on its feet after her former partner, Trevor Forsythe, had almost catapulted them into Chapter 11. McCleary, in his usual orderly fashion, had revamped the firm and was largely responsible for its present prosperity.

In the last six months they'd expanded their staff by hiring several new detectives. They also had added five hundred square feet to the back of the building that housed the firm and now had half a dozen computers that did everything but dance. Life was infinitely better than it had been when she'd met McCleary.

He'd been a homicide detective for Metro-Dade at the time and the investigating officer in the murder of Grant Bell, the man she'd been living with. It hadn't been the most auspicious beginning. But considering how things had turned out, she had no complaints.

So how come she felt this creeping certainty that Miami was holding them hostage? That the cosmos was about to rearrange the furniture in their lives and turn her complacency inside out like old laundry?

Because Mac stepped on the mat.

Ridiculous.

But she reached into the glove compartment for a bag of peanuts to allay her anxiety.

Ross Young's office in Coconut Grove was set back in a thicket of Melaleuca trees that muted the din of traffic and softened the February light. Even if Quin hadn't seen the sign that said YOUNG & ASSOCIATES, ARCHITECTS, she would've guessed his profession because of the building. It looked like something out of the twenty-first century. Made entirely of glass and wood, it was split into three levels that ascended sideways. The levels were connected by glass-enclosed suspension bridges. The area around the building had been landscaped with grassy hills, a jungle of plants, a stream, a labyrinthian pebble path.

McCleary parked Lady next to a Mercedes. He leaned forward, hands draped over the steering wheel, his gaze on the building. "I have a feeling I should've called Tim first to get some background on this guy."

She peered out through the windshield at the Melaleuca trees captured in the dark glass. "I think I'm underdressed."

They got out and followed the wending pebble path through the garden. The murmur of the stream followed them. The crisp morning breeze whined through the eaves. The entrance was at the side of the building, and when they stepped into the lobby, Quin felt as if she'd stumbled into a glass bubble. There were no right angles in this room. It resonated with light and soft music. The walls were the color of thick cream, Persian carpets dappled the pine floors, the furniture was colorful high-tech stuff with rounded curves like the walls.

A pleasant-looking woman behind a computer glanced up. "May I help you?"

"I'm Mike McCleary. I've got an appointment with Mr. Young."

"Go straight down the corridor there and then up the steps. His office is the second door on the right."

Except for the pine floor, the corridor was like a hollow glass chute. It disoriented her. She kept wanting to touch the walls on either side of her just to make sure they were really there, that they weren't a trick of the light. The corridor began to narrow and sloped gradually upward to a set of four stairs.

The second floor was no more conventional than the first. Instead of the usual rectangular doorways, there were arches made of burnished cypress, at least a half dozen of them on either side. The air smelled faintly of wood. Several men hurried along in front of Quin and McCleary, their footsteps echoing.

They stopped at the second archway and McCleary knocked on the door. A voice inside called, "Come on in."

Everything in the office was white and blue—the rug, walls, furniture, the frames that surrounded the blueprints on the walls. It was like walking into an August sky. Even the wall of glass that overlooked a forest of green and opened onto a deck seemed to be tinted blue. A man Quin assumed was Young was seated on a stool at a drawing board, juggling three eggs. He slipped off the stool, never missing a beat, the eggs rising smoothly, slipping down, sighing against the palms of his hands, rising again. He caught them finally, one by one, and set them aside.

"That was terrific," Quin exclaimed.

"Thanks. It helps keep my thoughts focused." He strode across the room, a bear of a man who stood about six-three, and introduced himself. He was as blond and fair-skinned as McCleary was dark, with eyes almost the same shade of blue as the room. His smile was quick, refulgent. It brought a boyish dimple to his right cheek, and exacerbated the pinched sadness at his eyes. Quin guessed he was no older than forty, but he looked ten years younger, almost as if his last name had endowed him with perpetual youth. He was dressed simply —in jeans and a pale gold pullover sweater that matched the color of his hair.

He picked up a folder from the nearby counter and suggested they sit on the deck. On his way out, he picked up the three eggs he'd been juggling with and placed them in a pint-sized refrigerator against the wall. "I forgot to put them in the fridge one Friday," he explained, opening the porch doors. "And on Monday morning the stench was incredible."

"How long have you been juggling?" Quin asked.

"Oh, a couple of years, I guess. I find that whenever I get stuck on a design, juggling seems to get rid of the block. And it's riskier when you use fresh eggs. Makes you concentrate harder."

He gestured toward a square, chrome and glass table set for three with huge blue and white mugs and a matching coffeepot. As he sat down, Quin noticed that he wore red socks. She must've been staring, because he laughed and extended his foot. "I've become a compulsive sock buyer. Every year it's something different. Last year it was shirts. This year it's socks." He shrugged. "At the end of the year I weed out my closet and a lot of the stuff goes to the Salvation Army."

McCleary chuckled. "That's what we need at our place. A weeder. Quin's a pack rat."

"And Mac's not."

Young touched her arm and in a commiserating voice said, "The secret is to become a compulsive buyer, Quin, because when you start running out of room, you have to toss stuff."

McCleary shook his head. "She wouldn't. We'd have to move to a bigger place."

"Yeah, I like that idea better," she replied, and both men laughed.

Young poured coffee. As soon as he started to talk

about why he'd asked them here, Quin understood the pinched look in his eyes and said good-bye to Venezuela.

"Two weeks ago, my stepsister was murdered. A Sergeant Martinez was initially in charge of the investigation, then he was moved to another department and Lieutenant Benson took over. That was yesterday. By then I'd decided to hire a private investigator, and Tim suggested I contact you."

"Why do you feel you need a private eye?" McCleary asked.

Young sat back, a leg thrown over the arm of the chair. Beyond them, leaves rustled in a susurrous breeze. "With all due respect to Metro-Dade and Tim, I think a private eye would increase the odds of this guy being caught and convicted."

"Does Tim have any leads yet?" McCleary asked.

"No, not really. She—Joyce—was killed at home, in bed." His leg dropped from the arm of the chair and he sat forward, reaching for the folder. He passed it to McCleary. "Tim gave me copies of these last night when I told him I intended to meet with you today." He paused. "They're photographs from . . ." His voice faltered. "Well . . . from the house when she . . . when she was found."

"Who found her?" Quin asked.

"Her maid. She had a woman come in once a week to clean and do laundry and ironing."

McCleary opened the folder. He passed the photographs one by one to Quin, and her stomach pitched like a ship on stormy seas. She wondered how police photographers maintained their sanity.

The woman's limbs had been tied to the four posts of the bed with nylon stockings, splaying her against the sheets like a frog. There was so much blood, she looked as if she'd been subjected to a vivisection experiment. Her tongue had been lopped off while she was still alive, Young explained in a slow, pained voice, and she'd been sliced open with what the coroner believed was a pair of scissors.

14

I don't know about this, Quin's eyes whispered to McCleary.

Let's hear him out, his shrug replied.

She slid the lurid photos back into the folder. "Was she raped?"

"No." He sat there with his large hands folded on the table, gaze fixed on the knuckles. Despite his size, he seemed small and uncertain now.

"What was the official verdict on cause of death?" McCleary asked.

He raised his eyes, which were stricken, faded as old cloth. "She bled to death."

"What sort of work did your stepsister do, Mr. Young?" McCleary asked.

"She owned a clothing store here in the Grove. She was also taking graduate classes at night at the University of Miami, working toward her MBA. She'd gotten divorced about ten months ago, after a six-year marriage, and felt the need to do something different, so I suggested the graduate classes."

"Was she younger or older than you?" McCleary asked.

"Younger. Four years younger. Thirty-four." His voice still sounded strangled, as though he had something caught in his throat.

Quin asked about Joyce's ex-husband: who was he, where did he live, what did he do, why had they gotten divorced. Nosy questions, she thought, except under these circumstances. Murder invariably changed all the rules.

Young explained that Joyce's ex, Neal Schloper, lived in Coral Gables and worked at the Miami airport as a mechanic for Eastern. "They didn't part under the best of terms. Joyce was involved with someone else, Neal found out about it, and that ended the marriage."

"Was she still involved with the other man?" Quin asked.

"Off and on. His name's Gene Travis. He calls himself a financial counselor, but actually his income comes

15

from two adult bookshops and a topless club that he owns. He and his wife are separated now because she also found out about his affair with Joyce.''

These details seemed to embarrass him. It was bad enough, Quin thought, to lose someone you loved to murder, but even worse to have to lay out the person's indiscretions like a bad poker hand.

"My stepsister wasn't a pristine woman, and she had remarkably poor sense when it came to men. But I can't believe anyone would hate her enough to kill her.''

"She may not have been killed by anyone she knew," McCleary said. Besides these classes she took, Mr. Young, was there anything she did regularly? Maybe a bar she frequented? Or a particular restaurant where she ate a lot?''

"We both belonged to the Grove Fitness Club. She swam there every day. Other than that, I don't know.''

The pained look had returned to his eyes, and behind it was something else, something she couldn't decipher. "We didn't socialize together that much. She found my big-brother routine irritating, I think.'' He smiled sadly. "You have any sisters, Mr. McCleary?''

"Four.''

"So you must know what I mean.''

McCleary nodded. He glanced over at Quin. *So what do you think?* asked his eyes.

Okay, she signaled.

"Mr. Young, we'd like to take the case," McCleary said. "But we're going to need some things from you. Lists of her friends, addresses, phone numbers, where her store is, the classes she was taking, anything that might help us.''

His relief was almost palpable. "I'll give you whatever you need.''

An hour later, Quin and McCleary were sitting on the terrace of a café in the Grove, several blocks from Young's office. Their table overlooked a courtyard spraddled with sunlight and saturated with ferns, geraniums, and short, bushy Aralia trees.

16

"Well?" McCleary asked after the waitress had brought their coffee.

"I kind of wish we'd driven to the airport."

"Then let's drive back to his office now and tell him."

"That'd be a lousy thing to do since he's already paid us two weeks up front. We might as well see it through, Mac."

"On one condition."

"What?"

"That we leave for Caracas right after the case is finished."

"Twist my arm." She extended her arm.

He laughed, a sound as clean as the air, and his fingers tiptoed along the backs of hers. Then he lifted her hand, kissed the knuckles quickly, almost surreptitiously. It was as if they were lovers married to other people, she thought, and he was afraid someone might see this public display of affection.

The analogy would haunt her in the coming weeks, when Sylvia Callahan reappeared in McCleary's life. But at the moment, infidelity was as remote from Quin's thoughts as the possibility of a vacation in Caracas.

3 Crack in the Egg

1.

"THIS IS IT?" McCleary asked.

"Yup." Benson leaned forward, peering through Lady's windshield at Joyce's home. "You were expecting something else? Like maybe a place designed by Young and Associates?"

"Yeah, I guess so."

There was nothing *wrong* with the house. It was simply an ordinary South Florida concrete block house. There was a one-car garage, a pair of large front windows, and a yard thick with plants and bordered by hibiscus hedges. It was on a wide, umbrageous street that paralleled a narrow canal in a neighborhood that was neither affluent nor poor, just old. McCleary pulled into the driveway, and he and Benson got out of the car.

The air was dulcet with birdsong, and cooler than yesterday when he and Quin had taken this case, even though it was close to noon. McCleary zipped up his jacket. "Let's go around back," Benson suggested. "I want you to see how he got in."

Benson had recently gotten contacts, and it made his eyes seem abnormally wide, as if they were frozen in perpetual astonishment. The breeze tousled his chestnut hair, so he looked like he'd just rolled out of bed. He was about McCleary's height, six feet, but thinner. Off and on during McCleary's decade in Miami homicide, they'd been partners. While Benson—like most cops —went through his burnout periods, he seemed oddly suited to homicide, especially since his promotion to lieutenant and head of the department.

"The doc estimates that she'd been dead between six and eight hours when the maid found her that morning at ten. That places her time of death between two and four in the morning. So the main suspects have alibis. They were sleeping. Nifty, huh. How the hell do I disprove that?"

"Your main suspects being Gene Travis and Neal Schloper?"

"Yeah. The porn king and the ex-husband."

"What's Travis' wife have to say?"

"The lady," said Benson, "found out about his little tryst with Joyce about a month before she was murdered. She moved out and went to the Bahamas and has been there ever since. She took their son with her. But Travis' maid swears he was home around nine-thirty after going out to dinner with Joyce that night. She was staying with his son, Sean, by his first wife, and claims he would *never* leave without someone to watch the kid."

"And Joyce's ex?"

"Eastern Airlines mechanic. Smart-ass. He's now living in the Gables. He claims he was sleeping. Maybe he was. Like I said, how am I supposed to prove otherwise?"

"What do you know about Travis?"

"Not much, except that he doesn't have a record and his wife, who's in the Bahamas, is the second Mrs. Travis. I've been racking my brain, combing through old cases for someone who might be able to give us some additional information on Travis. You know, an insider."

Benson remembered old cases the way other people recalled the titles of books and plots. "And?"

"I finally thought of Sylvia Callahan."

McCleary's heart literally skipped a beat. He looked blankly at Benson, who evidently thought the expression meant McCleary couldn't remember who she was.

"You know, Mac, the woman who owned that bar-disco whose sister was murdered about five years ago. You got stuck with the case and it—"

"I remember her, Tim." *Too well.* "Why do you think she'd know anything about Gene Travis?"

"All these bar owners in Miami know each other. Anyway, I checked out the disco and it's under new ownership. She sold out about three years ago and is living up in Lauderdale now. Retired with her millions, apparently. Anyway, why don't you give her a call, since you knew her better than I did."

He didn't feel like explaining that a call to Sylvia Callahan might open a Pandora's box. Benson hadn't known about them. And there had never been a reason to tell Quin, since the Callahan part of his life had happened long before he'd gotten married. "Okay, if you think it'll give us some leads."

They paused at the gate that opened into the backyard. Benson brought out a set of keys. "Ross made me copies." He fiddled with them, looking for the one that fit the gate. "There's something I was always kind of curious about, Mac. Were you and Callahan involved with each other?"

So much for secrets. "Yeah, for a while." He chuckled. "Is there anything you don't remember, Tim?"

"Yeah, what she looks like."

McCleary wondered how anyone could forget what Callahan looked like. "Like Candice Bergen."

A wooden fence ran along either side of the property to the narrow canal, where a small dock jutted out into the still waters. The kidney-shaped pool wasn't screened, and dried leaves and pine needles floated on the surface of the water. Mold had turned the edges of the pool a deep green.

"Ross got the lock fixed on the sliding glass door here, where the guy got in," Benson said, and unlocked it.

McCleary could still detect the indentation in the metal where something—probably a screwdriver—had been pressed hard against the jamb for leverage. They stepped into the kitchen. The air was cool but stale. He could hear the hum of the fridge, the crackle of the ice maker inside it, the whir of the electric clock over the sink. The kitchen was almost painfully neat—glass jars filled with rice and flour and sour ball candies along the counter, colorful pot holders lining the wall behind the stove. A round wooden table was set with two burnt orange place mats. Each had a bowl, small glass, spoon, and knife on it. It was as if the owner had just stepped out and would be back any moment.

"Ross was going to have a cleaning service come in, but agreed to delay it for a while just in case the lab people needed to come back. So anyway, a couple of men came down and cleaned up the mess. The lab took the sheets. Otherwise the bedroom's just as it was. Everything is. Except for the cat. The cat's gone. Ross has got it."

"Was her tongue found?" McCleary asked.

"No. Her mouth was taped shut. Did Ross tell you that?"

He nodded. It was the sort of detail that disturbed him almost as much as what the killer had done to her tongue.

As they walked through the living room, the hunch spot between his eyes blazed fiercely. He rubbed it. Benson noticed. "A burning hunch, huh?"

"I think so."

Over the years, Benson had always asked this question with a thin, sardonic smile, as though McCleary were an eccentric relative who claimed he'd been abducted by a UFO. Benson said he didn't believe in hunches. But for a man who didn't believe, he seemed inordinately interested.

"About what?"

"I don't know."

Which was precisely the problem with a hunch. You couldn't read it like a computer printout. It was a game of blindman's bluff—hot if you were close to the target, cold if you were way off base. The tricky part was determining just what the target was.

They stopped in the bedroom doorway. His head began to throb. The room possessed a quiet hollowness, the stillness of death. Light fell through the venetian blinds over the window, chopping up the bare, blood-stained mattress. In his mind, McCleary saw Joyce Young as she was in the police photographs, limbs tied to the brass posts and baseboard. His eyes swung through the room and locked on the message scrawled on the wall to the bed's right.

"That wasn't in the photos you gave Ross."

"I know. I just didn't see the point. We kept it out of the papers, too."

The large, uneven block letters had been scrawled with Magic Marker: GREYHOUND, LOCKER 31.

"What'd you find in locker thirty-one?"

Benson ran a hand over his thinning dark hair. "That's just the problem. Nothing. We checked Miami, Kendall, Miami Beach, every Greyhound station in Dade County, and turned up squat, Mac."

"What about Broward County? And Palm Beach?"

He shook his head. "Nothing. There's something else I didn't tell Ross and that we kept out of the papers. There were traces of powdered sugar on her body, like the guy had been eating powdered doughnuts or something in here while he was killing her." He jammed his hands in the pockets of his jacket, his eyes fastened on the bare mattress. "I ran the MO on this murder through the computer, Mac, and there's nothing in Florida in the last five years that fits it exactly. I mean, with the mutilation, the teaser on the wall, the tape on the mouth, the scissors."

"But maybe there is elsewhere. I'll run it by Bob Summer and see what he can come up with."

"The LAPD guy?"

"Ex-LAPD. He's now specializing in unsolved homicides, some of them twenty and twenty-five years old. He's been teaching criminology at the University of Miami the last couple of years. I'll check with him and see if he can come up with anything. He deals with cases across the country, so he'll have access to information we don't. This has got all the earmarks of a repeater."

Benson's head bobbed in agreement. "But in two weeks we haven't found even the first lead. Without leads, without *something*, how're we supposed to figure out where he might hit next?"

"What about this health club in the Grove she belonged to?"

"So far I haven't turned up anything except that she swam there every day."

McCleary poked around the room, inside the closet, and went through the bathroom cabinets. He looked under the bed. He opened the drawers in the nightstand and bureau, and the only thing of any interest he found was a photo album. The pictures, interspersed with things like pressed flowers and childhood notes, chronicled Joyce Young's life. After the age of five, when her mother had married Ross Young's father, Ross was in most of the pictures, smiling, fussing over her, the solicitous stepbrother.

In one of her wedding pictures, a lovely Joyce was flanked on one side by her husband and on the other by her stepbrother. Neal Schloper looked like a dashing young aviator with his tinted wire-rim glasses, the tails of his tux flowing behind him. Ross Young looked as grim as a reaper.

After this, for a period of seven years, there were only half a dozen pictures or so of Young. It was almost as if he'd become incidental to his stepsister's life after her marriage, a postscript. The album ended abruptly with a picture of Joyce in which someone—probably Schloper— had been cut out. It was dated a year ago, roughly two months before their divorce.

The album depressed him. There was something infinitely disturbing about perusing photographs of a murdered woman's life. In some ways, it troubled him more than the pictures of her death. He returned the album to the closet shelf. "Let's get outa here, Tim."

Once they were outside, the ache in McCleary's head diminished. He breathed deeply of the cool February air. It was definitely getting colder. It brought back quick, vivid flashes of his boyhood in Syracuse, New York: snowdrifts ten feet high, the sound of plows after a storm, the clean, sharp smell of winter.

As they passed through the gate, McCleary asked about Joyce Young's neighbors. Benson shook his head. "They didn't hear anything. As far as we know, the last person to see her alive was Gene Travis, and that was supposedly around nine when he left her at home after dinner. You or Quin might want to talk to the maid again."

"I think the courthouse and Travis are first on my list. I'd like to check out Travis' real estate holdings."

They stopped at the car. "I hope Quin got somewhere with Schloper, because I sure didn't."

"Knowing Quin, she probably has."

Benson chuckled. "She probably got him to break bread with her."

2.

The only person Quin had broken bread with since breakfast was Zivia Tuckett, one of the new investigators they'd hired six months ago, and then it was just a stale ham and cheese sandwich from a vending machine that had wadded in her gut like chewing gum. Now the two of them were standing inside the Wynn Aviation building at the southern edge of the Miami airport, waiting for Schloper.

They'd found out from a mechanic at the Eastern hangar that he was off today and was probably at Wynn, where he taught flying. When they'd asked for him, the woman behind the counter had stabbed her thumb once toward the ceiling and informed them he was with a student but would be landing shortly. That had been fifteen minutes ago.

Quin supposed there were worse places to wait for someone. Although the aviation office was noisy and chilly and the air stank of burned coffee, the maps on the walls fascinated her. There were detailed maps of the U.S., South America, the Caribbean, Canada. They were all marked by retes of blue lines that were airways, hundreds of them crisscrossing continents and seas, cities and deserts and mountains. It was like looking at the world as layers of interstates and turnpikes. For an instant she felt a kind of pressure against the top of her head, as if one of the layers *up there* were sagging with the ineffable weight of the Miami airport traffic.

She moved away from the maps and strolled over to the window where Zivia smoked and paced. She was a thin, impatient woman five inches shorter than Quin, with ear-length bourbon-colored hair that exploded around her head in artless curls. She had high cheekbones, honey-colored eyes, and, as McCleary had pointed out, an actress's mouth, expressive, both petulant and gay. She was the sort of woman who drew second glances wherever she went. At the moment, though, the only second glances she was getting came from the woman behind the desk, who seemed disturbed by Zivia's relentless pacing.

"Relax, will you?" Quin chided.

Zivia stabbed out her cigarette in a nearby ashtray, stopped pacing, and pushed her sunglasses back into her hair. "When my first ex and I were being hippies and living in New Mexico, I had so much patience I got fat. When we got divorced, I became impatient and got skinny. The moral of the story is that patience is fattening."

Quin laughed.

Zivia dug her hands into her suede jacket and brought out three nugget-sized beanbags, which she began to juggle. Her movements were as smooth and quick and polished as Young's had been when he'd juggled the eggs yesterday in his office. She moved backward and forward, still juggling.

The woman behind the counter was watching, her eyes flitting up, down, around, following the movement of the beanbags. When Zivia finally slipped them back into her pockets, the woman clapped. "Hey, you're really good."

Zivia bowed deeply at the waist. "Thank you, thank you. My assistant here will be around to collect tips."

The woman laughed and informed them that Neal Schloper was on final approach. Quin and Zivia stepped outside.

"I think you should meet Ross Young," Quin remarked. "He's a juggler, too."

"Single?"

"Apparently."

"I hate blind dates, Quin, if that's what you've got in mind. I met my first husband on a blind date, did I ever tell you that? Well, it was *sort* of a blind date. A bunch of us were into Castaneda back then, see, and we wanted to do some mescaline and talk to cactuses. So we drove out to this desert north of Taos and we dropped our mescaline and then some more people showed up and this friend of mine says, 'Hey, Ziv, meet Pete, the guy I've been telling you about.' Then she splits and there are Pete and I, zonked outa our skulls. So he introduces me to his cactus—real heavy-duty stuff—and I showed him mine, and we proceeded to tell each other the stories of our lives. The next day, I couldn't remember anything he'd said, which is too bad because I probably wouldn't have married him if I'd been able to remember."

"I don't think Ross Young is into mescaline," Quin laughed. "So I wouldn't worry about it."

"Well, I'm still not into blind dates."

"Actually, I was thinking that maybe Mac and I should have a party or something."

"Booze, mescaline, what's the difference. But what the hell, I'm game. Have your party and let me know what I can do to help."

A few minutes later, a single engine Cessna landed and taxied toward the hangar. The plane sputtered as the engine was switched off, and two men got out. As they neared, it was easy to figure out which man was Schloper: he was talking about flaps and airspeeds. He looked to be in his mid to late thirties, had a square, stubborn face, husky shoulders, and fawn-colored hair that looked as soft as a baby's. A young Charles Lindbergh.

"Mr. Schloper?" Quin said.

Distracted from what had apparently been part of his student's lesson, he frowned as he glanced over. Quin could see shadowy depictions of herself and Zivia reflected in the blue lenses of his wire-rim glasses. "Yes?"

"We'd like to talk to you a minute. About Joyce."

The mention of his ex-wife stiffened his spine. He murmured something to his student about next week, and then walked over.

"I've already spoken to the cops."

"We're not cops," Zivia said. "We're private investigators. This is Quin St. James and I'm Zivia Tuckett."

Schloper's eyes slid the length of Zivia's body, then fastened on her face. His mouth dimpled when he smiled. He combed his thick fingers through his hair. "Oh? And who hired ya?" He was chewing gum, and he cracked it now, once, noisily, and reached inside his jacket. He brought out a pack of More cigarettes and lit one. It was thinner and longer than a cigar, but the smell was the same. "Gene? Yeah, I bet Gene hired you. That way the cops would be thinking that he couldn't have killed her because why would her killer hire a private eye? That's the way he thinks, you know. For Gene, there's always an angle."

"Why do you think Mr. Travis killed her?" Quin asked.

He laughed. "Lady, if you gotta ask that, then you don't know anything about Gene Travis and you'd best go do your homework and stop bothering me."

"Why don't you save us the time, Mr. Schloper," Zivia said, smiling her best *we-ain't-got-all-day* smile.

He regarded Zivia again and sucked at his cigarette; smoke drifted between his teeth. "She'd become an albatross for Gene. His mistresses always become cumbersome sooner or later. Hell, until Joyce he had a neat little gig for himself—a wife and kids, a million-dollar lifestyle, and a couple of women on the side who never made too many demands as long as he paid them well. Joyce was different. She was educated. She didn't want his money. She wanted his kid. She'd already gotten pregnant once by him and miscarried." His mouth twitched into a pucker. "Gene had a fit when he found out." He tossed his cigarette away from him, slid his hands into the pockets of his leather jacket. "He got rid of her the only way he could. By killing her."

"And I suppose she told you all about her pregnancy," Zivia said.

"As a matter of fact, she did. She sure as hell couldn't go to Ross about it. He couldn't stand Gene. He couldn't stand me, either, for that matter." He rocked forward onto the balls of his feet; his mouth did another little weird number, a kind of lopsided smile. "The funny part is that it wasn't Gene or Joyce's pregnancy that broke up our marriage. That was just the proverbial straw, you know? It was Ross that split us up. He meddled right from the start."

"Meddled how?" Quin asked.

"Meddled. Like an overprotective father or something. He would slip Joyce money. He bought the store for her. He used to stop by all the time. On Sunday mornings, he would come by and he and Joyce would sit in the kitchen getting sloshed on Bloody Marys. That sort of meddling." Then he smiled, as if he'd suddenly understood something. "He hired you, didn't he. Ross hired you. That shit. She's dead and he can't stop meddling, can he."

Quin neither confirmed nor denied anything. Schloper shook his head and gazed at something just over Quin's left shoulder. He sniffled and wiped his hand across his nose. It might have been from the cold—or from a surge of intense emotion. Quin couldn't tell which because she couldn't see his eyes through his tinted glasses.

"Do you belong to the Grove Fitness Club, Mr. Schloper?"

She'd apparently said something amusing, because he laughed. "If you've talked to Ross, then you must know I belong. Ross bought Joyce and me five-year memberships. Wasn't that a generous thing for Big Brother to do?"

"When was the last time you saw her?" Zivia asked.

"Three nights before she died. We had dinner together. She wanted to try to patch up the marriage. She said she was scared of Gene. That he was involved in some things that frightened her. Not that it's any of your goddamn business."

Schloper's anger swelled like a wave of sudden heat; Quin could feel it. "Look, Mr. Schloper. We're just trying to find out who killed her, that's all."

"I already told you that. Go talk to Gene Travis and leave me the hell alone."

Then he sauntered off through the chilly air. "Reminds me of my first ex," Zivia remarked. "If I weren't working on three cases that have me squeezed into a corner, I wouldn't mind working with you and Mac on this one. I think it's going to be a humdinger, Quin."

But there were humdinger goods and humdinger bads. Quin had a feeling this one was the latter; homicides usually were. She said as much.

"If you don't like working on homicides, then don't take the case."

Zivia uttered it as if the choice were as simple as buying rye bread or white, and Quin smiled. "It isn't the sort of thing you say to an ex-homicide detective who'll go right on working on murders whether you do or not." Besides, she'd gotten used to being a team, and if that included homicides, so be it. The problem was that murder wasn't like other crimes. You could investigate an insurance fraud, she thought, and forget about it when you went home in the evening. But a murder investigation had a way of clinging to you, and if you weren't careful, it could crack your life like an egg.

And somehow, she couldn't quite shake the feeling that the crack had already begun.

4   Stalking

THE SECRET OF disguise lay within, he thought. It was an attitude. If you believed that you would blend into a particular milieu, believed it down to a cellular level, then you acted accordingly.

Today's excursion to the University of Miami, for instance, had required him to slip into his student persona. He'd donned khaki slacks and a sweater and carried several books. He was prepared to debate the issues of human rights or nuclear disarmament. He'd eaten cafeteria food. Jesus, that alone would qualify him. Now he sat at a table in the cafeteria, less than six feet away from Bob Summer.

He was close enough so he could hear Summer explaining to one of his female graduate students how he investigated old homicide cases. His transparency was nauseating. It was obvious that Summer's objective was to get the young woman into bed. He would probably succeed, too. Now and then she leaned toward him, touched his arm, asked another question. And Summer, basking like a seal in the heat of her rapt attention, laughed or touched her arm in return.

Summer wasn't a particularly handsome man. In fact, he looked like the ex-cop that he was—burly shoulders, thick arms and hands, thick legs. A muscular bear. But he radiated a kind of presence that seemed to appeal to women. In the weeks he'd observed the criminologist, there had been half a dozen women Summer had bedded and then discarded like dirty Pampers, women who should've known better. The man had come to his attention when he'd been listening to one of the late-night radio talk shows, where Summer had been discussing his views on investigative techniques.

Like Joyce, Summer was annoyingly opinionated, one of those people who thought *his* way was the only way. He was between thirty and forty years of age, in his prime. He was an exercise nut. He was a Taurus. He fit the criteria.

Joyce had been the first in his Taurus kills. He hadn't decided yet how many there would be. The numbers fluctuated in each sign. There had only been two Capricorn kills, in Atlanta and Macon. His three Aquarian kills had taken place in Birmingham and Dothan, Alabama. The Pisces kills had numbered four because Piscean people aggravated him. They were generally sappy, romantic idealists. Those had happened in Tallahassee, Jacksonville, and Melbourne. His two Aries kills had taken place in South Florida, the last one six months to the night of Joyce's death. It was the longest he'd ever waited between kills. He'd had to wait because of an odd configuration in his chart where Mars and Uranus were transiting his eighth house, indicating unexpected mishaps.

He would never wait that long again, even if the stars weren't in his favor. In the weeks and days before the kill, he'd felt as if he were going through withdrawal from a drug addiction—the sweats, shakes, cramps in his gut, insomnia. He was addicted to the kills, to the adrenaline high, the thrilling flush of accomplishment at seeing his meticulous planning become a reality. He needed the lightness of being he experienced afterward, the certainty that he had shoved his own death farther into the future by spilling the blood of another.

One of his victims, the Capricorn in Atlanta, had called him a vampire in the moments before she'd died. Although he didn't drink his victims' blood, he supposed there was some truth to it: their lives for his. He wondered what, if anything, Bob Summer would say to him before he died.

The criminologist and his student were pushing away from the table now. She laughed softly, intimately, as Summer leaned toward her. It didn't take a genius to figure out he was about to score, that they would now go to his place or hers.

Enjoy it while you can, Bobby Boy.

He waited until they'd left the building, then he followed. The temperature had plummeted, and the wind had picked up. A damp cold penetrated his bones, the kind of cold he imagined death would be.

He shuddered, zipped his jacket to the throat, and drew warmth from his thoughts of the impending kill.

5 The Find

DADE COUNTY'S COURTHOUSE, symbol of that grand mistress of corruption called justice, had one thing going for it as far as McCleary was concerned: it was home to the public records. Here you could uncover any number of interesting tidbits on a person—from the specifics of his marriages and divorces to the value of his house and business to who had sued him and for what.

He discovered that the two adult bookstores Gene Travis owned were under different corporate names. The topless club was under the corporate name for his financial consulting firm. His home in Coral Gables was appraised at $150,000, which meant it was probably worth over two hundred grand. He had a son by his first marriage, of whom he had custody, and a son by his second. By cross-referencing, McCleary found out that Wife Number One, Teresa, owned a beauty salon four blocks from the courthouse. He jotted down the address. Ex-wives were usually avid talkers.

Four years ago, Travis had been named in a paternity suit by a woman named Suzanne Mellon. The suit was eventually settled out of court, which was as good as saying that Travis was guilty, McCleary thought. About the same time, there was a divorce petition filed by the present Mrs. Travis, which was later dropped. He scribbled down Suzanne Mellon's address.

"Imagine meeting you here," said a voice close to his ear.

McCleary dropped his head back and smiled. He gazed into the underside of Quin's jaw. "Your perfume gives you away, you know."

"I'll remember that."

She sank into the chair beside him, her stockings rustling together as she crossed her knees. He thought she looked good enough to nibble on. "How come you're not out snooping with Zivia?"

"She had an appointment, so I left her back at the office. The beeper service said I would probably find you here. What've you turned up?" She gestured toward the microfilm machine, then reached into her purse and brought out a bag of peanuts. She munched on them as he gave her a brief rundown on Gene Travis.

"No wonder he didn't like the idea of Joyce being pregnant," she replied, and explained what Schloper had said about Joyce's miscarriage. "His theory is that Travis knocked her off because she'd gotten to be an albatross, 'just like all his mistresses eventually do.' "

"What's he like?"

"Not very friendly. He teaches flying on his free days. When're you going to talk to Travis?"

McCleary turned off the machine and replaced the microfilm reel in the box. "His secretary says he'll be out of town until late tonight, but I can probably find him at the health club tomorrow morning between nine and ten."

"Schloper belongs to the club too, Mac. Apparently Ross bought him and Joyce five-year memberships."

"Then we're on the right track."

"Yeah." She grinned. It was a wicked little grin, one that usually meant she'd been up to something. "I went by to see what it costs to join. I found out that if you sign up for one of their six-week aerobics classes, you get to use the facilities during the course of the class. What do you say?"

McCleary flashed on John Travolta in that movie where Jamie Lee Curtis was an aerobics instructor. Tutus and leg warmers and gyrations. No thanks. He shook his head. "*You* go to the aerobics class."

"We don't have to *attend*, just register. Besides I signed up for meditation."

"Meditation? What's that got to do with a health club?"

"This isn't your typical health club. It's owned by a couple of guys from California who figured the Grove was due for a dose of the West Coast. They took the typical health club concept and combined it with classes in meditation, astrology, visualization, vegetarian cooking, things that five years ago were fringe weirdo stuff. They've got the largest membership of any health club in Dade and Broward."

She wadded the empty peanut bag, and McCleary watched with dismay as it vanished into her purse. The one time he'd gone through her purse trying to find a pen, the experience had frustrated him. Like her desk drawers and her closet, her car and the space on her side of the bed, her purse was a black hole where all sorts of things disappeared forever. She noticed the expression on his face and zipped her purse shut with a flick of her wrist.

"You'd rather I throw the peanut bag on the floor?"

He held up his hands in defense. "I didn't say anything."

"But you were thinking it."

He shrugged. Her disorganization was a sore spot between them, one of those small complaints that threaded through their marriage, underscoring their fundamental differences. It was best to joke about it. Or feign indifference. Or try to ignore it. "I was thinking I would've enjoyed a peanut."

"Ha." She glanced to either side of them quickly, saw no one was around, and covered his crotch with her hand. "Tell the truth. Or I'll squeeze."

McCleary laughed. "You wouldn't."

"I will. I swear I will."

He waited.

She didn't move her hand.

They both started to laugh.

Someone came around the corner where the machines were and Quin quickly removed her hand. "Stubborn

Taurus," she griped. "Okay, item two. I spoke to Bob Summer and explained what we needed. He said he'll stop by the house tonight. And guess what? He belongs to the health club too. He says it's the very *in* place to belong these days."

"He should know." Summer, after all, stayed on top of the current fads. When James Fixx's book on running had hit the bestseller list, he'd become a passionate and dedicated jogger. When vegetarian meals crested in popularity, Summer stopped eating meat and became a gourmet vegetarian cook. And so on.

"Anyway, since I signed us up for these classes, we're in the club for at least six weeks, Mac."

"For whatever good it will do. We're starting on this case with next to nothing, you know."

"That'll change. It always does."

The words had the ring of a portent, and reminded him of the note on the wall in Joyce's bedroom. Another sort of portent. He told Quin about it. "That's all it said? Greyhound, locker thirty-one?"

"Right. And nothing turned up at the Greyhound stations in the tri-county area."

She had a funny look on her face, as if a piece of food had gone down the wrong way. She stood abruptly. "C'mon, I've got to show you something."

"What?"

"It's not the Greyhound *station*, Mac."

He picked up the microfilm reels, left them on the counter, and hurried after her. "What is it, then?"

"Greyhound, dachshund, shepherd, poodle, Great Dane . . . The lockers at the fitness club are divided into sections named after dogs."

McCleary thought of the Grove as Miami's version of Soho, an artsy community where buildings like Ross Young's were the norm rather than the exception. There were outdoor cafés, expensive boutiques, cops on horseback, even a Coconut Grove Playhouse. It lent itself to pedestrians and should've been closed to traffic. Instead, cars snaked through the now deeply shadowed streets, horns blared, exhaust plumed in the chilly air.

He followed Quin's Toyota toward the western end of the Grove. She turned right and pulled into a sweeping field of concrete, the sort K Mart was famous for. Or bowling alleys. The Grove Fitness Club was, in fact, a former bowling alley that now looked like a discotheque. It was pale blue and pink with lavender trim and crowned with a purple neon sign. There was valet parking for those who desired it, a path for golf carts and bicycles that wended along the periphery of the cresent-shaped property, and ramps for the handicapped.

Next door to the club were several small businesses: a health food grocery store and restaurant, an acupuncturist's office, a bookstore. McCleary parked next to Quin's Toyota and shivered as he stepped outside.

"Like Syracuse, Mac?"

"Not until it snows."

"Cuddle weather," she murmured, and slipped her arm through his. He gave it an affectionate squeeze.

At the door, Quin had to show a membership card, then they went through a revolving door into a huge tiled lobby where the air smelled faintly of soap. There were lines painted on the floor in various colors. "What're those for?" he asked.

She gestured toward a billboard that spelled out the color code: black for the gym, blue for the Jacuzzis, yellow for the pool, red for massage, purple for the jogging area. It covered every conceivable form of exercise. Next to it was a posted schedule of the various classes, with their times and locations.

Quin led him through a maze of hallways and stopped outside the men's locker area. His heart began to samba as he stepped inside. *Poodle, Doberman . . .* "Why dogs?" He glanced over at her, she'd paused at the door and drew looks from several of the men at the lockers.

"How should I know?"

He hurried along the gunmetal lockers until he reached "Greyhound" and locker 31. It was padlocked.

"Does the club provide the padlocks?" he asked.

"No. It's a free-for-all. You claim a locker and bring your own lock. No administrative paperwork that way."

He spun the dial on the lock, pulled, spun it again. Nothing happened. "I guess there's only one way we're going to get that sucker open."

"Wire cutters?"

McCleary smiled: Quin and the late movies. "I was thinking Benson would be a lot simpler."

When Benson arrived half an hour later, the McClearys were waiting just inside the front door. The woman at the front desk took Benson to see the manager. The manager, a young man who had probably never done five minutes of exercise in his life, whose bones looked as if they'd never ossified, fiddled with the lock, spun the dial, fiddled with it some more, then finally said he'd be right back. Five minutes passed. McCleary heard Quin's stomach growl. Her presence in the men's locker room elicited a few annoyed looks and amused remarks. Ten minutes ticked by. Benson grumbled.

When the manager returned, he was accompanied by a man built like Arnold Schwarzenegger. McCleary figured his chest measured probably fifty or fifty-five inches across, and his upper arms were the size of McCleary's thighs.

"There, get that loose," the manager said.

The giant nodded. "Sure thing." He took the padlock firmly in one hand, yanked once, yanked so hard McCleary thought for sure the rows of lockers were going to tumble like a house of cards, but the padlock didn't give. The giant shrugged an apology and wandered off. The manager finally located a hammer and a chisel, got the padlock open, then hovered nearby like a mosquito as Benson removed the padlock and the locker door swung open.

There were two dark plastic Tupperware containers inside. Benson whipped a handkerchief from his pocket and used it to reach for the smaller container. He pried the lid off. Inside was a note scrawled in the same childlike letters they'd seen on the wall in Joyce Young's house. It said: *She bellowed like a bull, but not for long.*

Alarm pricked the back of McCleary's neck.

Benson fixed the top back on, wrapped it securely in his handkerchief, and handed it to Quin as though it were a sacred oblation. She slipped it inside her purse.

"You got a handkerchief, Mac?" Benson asked.

"Here's a scarf." Quin pulled one from her purse like a magician embarking on an act.

Benson used it to bring out the second container. As he pried the lid off, a fetid stench permeated the air. Quin pressed a hand over her nose. McCleary stepped back. Benson turned his head to the side, coughing. Then he took a deep breath and popped the lid free.

It took a moment for McCleary's brain to translate what he was seeing, to place an identifying tag on it. And by then, his body had already reacted. His knees had gone as mushy as grits, his hunch spot blazed, his stomach lurched wildly. He was looking at the rotting remains of Joyce Young's tongue.

His eyes rolled back in his head, his knees buckled, and he passed out.

He walked among the dead. He couldn't see them, but he could feel them in the dark, could hear them hissing at him, beckoning. He wanted to run, but his legs wouldn't cooperate. He wanted to scream, but his mouth was bone dry. He stumbled and then suddenly he felt himself rising, rising toward the damp moon in the sky, a gibbous moon that suddenly dimpled with dark spots like eyes.

The eyes blinked.

The eyes grew hoods.

Unseen hands peeled away the hoods like skin and McCleary stared into twin mirrors. He saw himself inside the dark, swirling glass, saw his haunted eyes, his mouth opening silently, closing, opening again. Things crawled down his tongue. He tried to claw them off and his tongue came loose in his hand. He shouted and suddenly there were hands everywhere, holding him down, and voices saying, "Hey, it's okay, Mac. Take it easy, Mac. You're fine, Mac. Lay back, Mac."

He flung the hands away and sat up, slowly, his head throbbing. He rubbed his eyes. Quin and Benson stood over him. The manager flitted about behind them. He was on a couch in an office, and when he tried to stand, his legs still felt weird and he accepted Quin's outstretched hand. Her eyes fastened on his face, coruscating anxiously with all sorts of private messages he was too groggy to decipher.

"Would you please say something, Mac? Are you okay?"

His head pounded fiercely when he moved it. "Yeah, I think so."

"Leave your car here and we'll pick it up tomorrow."

"I'm fine, really. I can drive."

"You smacked the floor pretty hard."

"I'm okay."

She bit at her lower lip. Her expression said she didn't want him to drive, that she thought he was just being stupidly heroic. But she acquiesced without another word. Benson mumbled something about getting his prizes over to the lab, and they left.

The illumination in the parking lot gobbled up the February darkness. The cool air licked at his face and the inside of his eyes, but it revived him. He exhaled; his breath billowed in front of him. Blood rushed through his legs; he no longer felt disembodied. He had never passed out in his life, not even in ten years in homicide.

It wasn't just the severed tongue; he'd seen worse before. Any Miami rookie cop saw worse. It was something else that had struck him like a hot poker in the center of his chest, that had knocked him to his knees. It was as if the woman's tongue had established a conduit between him and the killer. For just an instant, a door had swung open and McCleary had peered inside the obsidian dark of the man's mind. The utter blackness had sucked at him, tugged, struggled to pull him in. Had he not passed out, it would have claimed him.

Benson and Quin stood on either side of him while he unlocked Lady. They were like sentries, patient, solicitous. He looked from one to the other. "Hey, I'm fine. Okay?"

Quin smiled. "Now *that* sounds like you."

Benson said he would talk to them tomorrow and hurried off toward his Honda with his prizes. McCleary gazed across the dampness beaded on Lady's roof and watched the cold breeze combing Quin's hair as she unlocked her Toyota. "Quin?"

She turned up the collar of her jacket when she glanced around. Light from the street lamp limned the worry in her face.

"What he wrote. About Joyce bellowing like a bull, but not for long. It means something."

"It means he cut off her tongue."

"No, something other than that."

"Like what?"

He shook his head. He didn't know. Not yet. But he would.

6 Bob Summer

COLD LIGHT FROM the street lamps curled like mist through the pines and banyans that lined Poinciana Drive. To Quin, it seemed eerily deserted, as though it had been evacuated in their absence. Their road had never been heavily traveled, since it was a dead end with half a dozen homes on one side and a park on the other. But tonight, in the aftermath of what they'd found at the fitness club, the lack of cars spooked her.

McCleary had stepped on the welcome mat at the office; that was why all this was happening. The thought roved through her mind, as lazy as a sloth. More than three years ago she'd padded over that stupid mat one evening, and less than half an hour later she'd found Grant Bell's body.

McCleary called her superstitious. She thought of herself as an empiricist.

She turned into the driveway. Her headlights sliced through the dark, exposing like a photograph the thin pines in the front yard and the banyans at either side of the house. The place was built from redwood and pine and looked as if it belonged in California, not Florida. Quin had lived here five years, but it was only since she and McCleary had gotten married that it really seemed like home.

She reached under the dash and pressed the button on the remote control device that opened the garage. The door rolled noisily upward and she drove inside. A moment later, Lady pulled in beside her Toyota, and the garage door descended, cutting off light from the street.

The absolute dark bit down, and she thought momentarily of Joyce Young, mutilated in the silent, chasmal blackness of her own home.

Not now, Quin. You will not think about it now, here. You're off work.

She would ignore the cold chill at the back of her neck. She would concentrate on the sound of Lady's car door opening and closing. Her hand found the light switch. The dim bulb flickered on. She opened the door to the utility room and turned on the light here, too. She left a trail of lights like bread crumbs from one side of the house to the other.

In the kitchen, she stepped out of her shoes, set her briefcase on the counter, and greeted the Kitty Brigade—a black cat, a calico, and a Persian. They rubbed up against her, fussing for dinner. Then Merlin, the black cat and the aloof one of the crew, evidently decided this was undignified behavior for a cat named after a magician, and strolled over to McCleary as he walked into the kitchen.

"I forgot to take out something for dinner," announced McCleary, who usually cooked.

"I'll fix leftovers."

He looked at her as if she'd just announced she had herpes, and laughed. "I'm not an invalid just because I passed out."

"Who said you were? I'll fix leftovers and you clean up. And you can feed the cats, too."

"Okay, guys," McCleary said, opening the pantry door. "What'll it be?" The felines crowded around him. "Tuna and scrambled eggs? Kitty stew?" He opened a can of food and dished it into their bowls. "What time did Bob Summer say he was coming by?"

"Seven-thirty or so." She emptied a container of leftover noodles and tuna casserole into a pan on the stove and consulted the time. It was now twenty of. "I'll set a place for him."

McCleary came up behind her, arms embracing her at the waist, and submerged his face in her hair. Quin

44

leaned back into him. "We could be sitting at a sidewalk café in Caracas now, you know."

"Or be stuck in customs."

"Or be en route to Angel Falls."

"Or be lost in Caracas traffic."

"Doomsayer."

He laughed. "Look at it this way, at least now we'll have the money to pay for the tickets." He kissed her neck, raising goose bumps on her arms, then moved his hands up under her sweater. They were cold against her skin; she yelped and turned in his arms.

"Don't start what you can't finish," she said softly.

"Right. Bob Summer."

He reached behind her, switching off the stove, then kissed her, softly, gently, a kiss that said Bob Summer could just wait outside if he showed up early. His hands at her hips slowly worked her skirt up. The fabric brushed against her panty hose, sending an erotic chill along her spine. His mouth cruised down the curve of her neck, liquifying her insides. Her skirt was bunched up against the edge of the counter and his hands moved over the curves of her buttocks, peeling away her panty hose, leaving a river of fever behind. Her blood bubbled like soup. She unfastened his belt buckle, unzipped his slacks.

They stumbled into the family room, laughing because the panty hose clung to her knees and his slacks were puddled near his feet and neither of them could move properly. They fell back onto the couch. Her head sank into the tropical-colored pillows, into the circles of light from the lamp. She lifted her hips, wiggling out of her panty hose and underwear. She dropped them on the floor, with her sweater following quickly. McCleary, orderly even now, scooped up her clothes and draped them and his own over the back of the chair.

The couch wasn't really wide enough for them both, so they opened it, unfolding the queen-size bed inside. They rolled into the sagging middle, into the wrinkled sheets, and reached for each other. Time became a skein of sensations, of small murmurs, of quick, urgent rhythms, as if they each sought to obliterate the dark, moiling vestiges of the health club find. His mouth and hands re-created her, imbued her with levity. She became lighter than clouds, brighter than aluminum. Her skin was a membranous sail that filled with wind, lifting her into a bone-white sky. Somewhere far below her, she heard her own soft cries.

Afterward, they lay in the half-light, her leg scissored between his, talking as if this case were wrapped up and by tomorrow they would be on their way to Caracas. She thought of the travel poster of the city snuggled into a valley so green it seemed blue, and of the clouds that hugged the surrounding mountains at the waist. She thought of romance beneath a black-domed sky dusted with stars, and of Venezuelan food.

She lifted up on an elbow and planted a kiss on McCleary's chest. "I'm starved."

He groaned. "What else is new?" He threw back the covers. Quin reached for her clothes, and he lifted the back of her hair and touched his mouth to her neck. "I wish we had the night to ourselves," he whispered, his arms folding around her waist. His thumbs slid over the swell of her breasts, bringing a warm ache to her groin. "The shower?" he murmured.

"The shower," she agreed, and off they went.

By the time Quin had showered and changed clothes it was past seven. She stirred the casserole and added a little more water to the pan so the stuff wouldn't burn. She shredded lettuce for a salad, chopped up radishes, onions, carrots. She'd done the unforgivable and switched on the heat, and now it poured out of the overhead vent, rapidly abrading the chill in the room. But her neck prickled. She glanced around. She'd neglected to lower the blinds, and the implacable black swam in the windows. It possessed weight, this blackness. She could feel it pressing against the panes of glass with the exigency of something living. Funny, she had always loved this room, with its Mexican-tile floors and high ceilings, its butcher block table and counters, and all the windows. But now the windows terrified her.

She thought of herself and McCleary leaning against the stove here awhile ago and in her mind's eye saw someone watching them through the window. Quin hurriedly lowered the blinds over the sink. Then she stood at the windows that overlooked the backyard and on impulse hit the switch for the floodlights. The yard blazed. Pines swayed in the breeze, the water in the swimming pool shimmered, she caught sight of a raccoon scurrying into the bushes. *But no boogeymen, Quin, no stalkers.* She laughed nervously at her paranoia, turned off the floodlights, and lowered the blinds. There, now she felt protected, sealed in.

Ten minutes later, just as she set the casserole on the table, the doorbell pealed. "I'll get it," McCleary called from the stairs.

Bob Summer's stentorian voice preceded his entrance to the kitchen. He swept in like a jovial Santa Claus, his tea-colored curly hair tousled by the wind, his cheeks pink from the cold. He stood just under six feet. Although he wasn't lean, neither was he fat. His bulk was muscular, thick, dense. McCleary had known him since his days at Metro-Dade, when Summer had helped him out on a homicide, and he remained one of Quin's favorite people. He bussed her on the cheek, then held her at an arm's length and shook his head. "Where do you put all the food, Quin? C'mon, you can tell me. You slip it to the cats, don't you?"

"Family secret. I hope you haven't eaten dinner."

"I never eat before coming over here. If I did, I'd weigh three hundred pounds before I left."

"You're picking on me, I can tell."

"Just jealousy, Quin, that's all." Summer shrugged off his jacket and rubbed his hands together, blowing into them. "Jesus, it's colder than Alaska out there. Maybe it'll snow. It hasn't snowed in South Florida in ten years, and the last time it happened it threw the state into panic."

"I remember," Quin said as they settled at the table. "Icicles on the trees."

"Schools closed," McCleary added as he dished casserole onto a plate and passed it along.

"People scraping ice off their windshields. Almost a sacrilege." Summer paused long enough to take a bite of his food, his bushy eyebrows knitting together. One of his thick hands plucked a roll from the basket. "I ran that information you gave me through the computer, Quin. I need more specific details before I can get a close or perfect match on an MO."

"Since I spoke to you this morning, we uncovered a couple of other things."

"He left a message on Joyce Young's bedroom wall," McCleary said, and explained.

Summer nodded as McCleary spoke and scooped more salad into his bowl. "That'll help. The more stuff I can feed into the computer, the closer we get." He whipped a small notepad out of his shirt pocket, added several items to his list, tapped the pad thoughtfully with the end of his pen. "Okay, we've got the scissors, not your usual murder weapon. We know how the killer got into the house and the approximate time of Joyce's death. We know he tortured her first by taking his little trophy, and then left a clue on the bedroom wall, which led to the discovery of the trophy and another clue."

"The note in the locker?" Quin asked.

"Yeah. 'She bellowed like a bull, but not for long.' It's a clue, all right, even if we don't have the foggiest notion what it means, other than the fact that she didn't bellow for long because he cut off her tongue. So we can safely figure that for whatever reason, this guy's playing with the cops, leading them on. The hunt is a sort of game for him.

"The other elements concern Joyce herself. She was divorced, living alone, owned a small business, and was thirty-four years old. Parents are both dead. She's survived by a stepbrother. No kids, right?"

McCleary shook his head. "No."

"She was involved with a porn king," Quin added.

Summer thought a moment. "Okay, we'll add that." He jotted it down on his notepad. "Also, her ex is an airline mechanic as well as a pilot. That might be important. And she was a devout exercise nut and belonged to a health club. What else?"

"She was blond," McCleary noted.

"Yeah, I've already got that." He studied his list, then pushed away from the table. "I've got my computer and a modem out in the car. Let me get it and I'll run this new stuff through."

"Through what?" Quin asked.

"I work with two other criminologists—one out of New York and another out of L.A. Among us, we've got access to, oh, probably five thousand unsolved homicides that stretch back as far as twenty-five years. We've got another three thousand homicides that also involve other crimes like rape or robbery or whatever. They've been broken down by weapons used, times of death, mode of death, gender of victim—dozens of factors. Of course, if this guy hasn't killed anyone before, we're going to strike out. But I'm betting he has."

"You need some help getting that stuff?" McCleary asked.

"Nope, be back in a jiffy."

They set up the computer and modem in McCleary's den. The neatness in here always astonished Quin, especially when she compared it to her own study upstairs. The desk wasn't strewn with papers. The deep blue couch and matching chair didn't have books or folders stacked on them. The filing cabinet was meticulously organized, each drawer labeled. Six of McCleary's acrylic paintings hung on the pine walls—four vibrant landscapes and two portraits—and neither the frames nor the glass was sheathed with an inch of dust.

Summer connected the modem and booted up the computer as McCleary and Quin looked on. He entered the new information about Joyce. "Oh, one more thing. I need to put in her birth date."

McCleary consulted his copy of the investigative report. "May twelfth."

"A Taurus," Summer murmured, typing in the birth date. "Like you and me, Mac. Okay, let's see. Our initial key search words will be: scissors or knives, mutilation, trophies, Southeast, and teasers."

"Why add in knives?" Quin asked.

"Because they're similar to scissors."

"And the teaser is . . ."

"The little clues he's left."

"What about the traces of powdered sugar found on her?" McCleary asked.

Summers shook his head. "Sorry, but sugar is one variable we never included, but I'll note it in her case."

He entered SCISSORS/KNIVES, punched a button, and sat back. The computer whirred.

"Do you enter the birth dates of all the victims?" Quin asked, sitting on the armrest of the couch.

"Yeah, as well as the date the person was killed. But that's strictly for my own information. At one time, I was trying to determine if the frequency of homicides increased at certain times of the year and if people born in particular months were more prone to being murdered."

"What'd you find?" McCleary asked.

Summer shrugged. "That in the northern states fewer homicides happen during the winter, and that no birth month is exempt from murder." The computer stopped whirring, and the screen scrolled a list of a 2,116 victims, with their birth dates, death dates, and the state in which they lived at the time of their death. "Here're the people who've been killed with scissors or a knife. Out of these, we'll see how many have involved mutilations, then how many have involved trophies, and finally, how many have involved teasers."

Something nagged at the back of Quin's mind, but when she tried to coax it out, focus on it, she drew a blank. The computer whirred again. After a few minutes, another list scrolled on the screen, but with fewer names. Each subsequent list diminished until they ended up with 512 cases that included at least one element they were looking for.

"Okay, now let's enter a couple of other variables: the health club and fitness angle, a range for the age, let's say thirty to forty, and a divorced marital status."

"What about gender?" Quin asked.

"Serial killers don't necessarily stick to one gender or time of day. Let's see what we get first with these." He hit the ENTER button again. They waited. The final list contained 105 names spread across five southeastern states and twelve years. "Now what?" McCleary asked.

Summer rubbed his chin. "Let's narrow this down a little more by confining it to the last six years. Then we'll access the cases, print them out, and see what we have."

This cut the number to 21. Summer printed out a summary of each of the cases, then they divided them and perused them for those that had the majority of the variables Summer had entered into the computer. They narrowed the choices even more by discounting murders in which there had been mutilations but no trophies or in which trophies had been personal objects but not body parts or in which there had been mutilations and trophies, but no teasers. In the end, they were left with 15 homicides in Georgia, Florida, Alabama, Mississippi, and South Carolina. None of the MOs matched Joyce Young's perfectly, but all were near enough to warrant close scrutiny, and in each, the killer had left a teaser. Six of these had taken place in Florida over the last three years in Jacksonville, Melbourne, Miami, and Juno Beach, with two in Tallahassee. Summer printed these out in their entirety.

"Benson said he ran a check like this for Florida and couldn't find anything that matched with Joyce's MO," McCleary said.

"None of these is a perfect match, Mac," Summer replied. "But all of them have elements of what we're looking for. State computers aren't broken down into as much detail as our program."

"So this is our guy?" McCleary asked.

"Maybe," Summer cautioned. "But since the match in MOs isn't perfect, that leaves room for error."

Quin, sitting cross-legged on the floor, her back against the couch, said, "Why didn't we just narrow it to Florida to begin with?"

"Because the trick to tracking serial killers lies in looking at the larger picture."

"We'll need copies of the investigative reports," McCleary noted.

"No problem." Summer tapped his computer. "I'll make backups for you of these cases and you can go through them."

It was now past one in the morning. Quin's eyes burned from fatigue, and all she wanted to do was fall into bed. She started to stack the packets alphabetically by the victims' last names, then decided to do it chronologically, according to the dates of death. She spread them out across the floor of the den, arranging them from past to present. She stared at them, only dimly aware of the drone of the men's voices, her eyes skimming the identifying information on each of the packets. Something bothered her about them, but she didn't know what it was.

She decided she would be able to think more clearly if she had a bite to eat.

She went into the kitchen and fixed a munchie plate of cheese, crackers, and raw veggies, then returned to the den. The men were still making backups and talking about law enforcement. She set the plate on the coffee table, dropped some goodies into a napkin for herself, and stretched out on the floor, nibbling at a carrot, perusing the names and birth dates on each of the packets. She separated the Florida victims from the others. Six deaths, and the victims had been born in either March or April.

Significant or just coincidence? She reached for Joyce Young's file. *Born in May. Taurus. The Bull.*

"That's it." She sat up. "Hey, Mac. Bob. 'The bull

bellowed . . .' Joyce was born in May. She was a Taurus. The bull. The bull bellowed."

Summer grinned and slapped his thigh. He and McCleary joined her on the floor as she leaned over the files and quickly went through them. There were less than six months between the four murders among the March (Pisces) victims and less than six months between the murders of the April (Aries) victims. The last Aries murder had happened six months to the day of Joyce's death. Pisces to Aries to Taurus. *There's your pattern, Quin. Follow it.*

Her fingers reached for the Mississippi and South Carolina killings. No, wrong. The dates of the deaths didn't coincide, and the birth dates didn't fit. She was looking for Aquarians, then Capricorns—February and January. Yeah, she was onto it, the pattern, she could feel it, feel the rush of hot wind in her head as though a door had suddenly swung open inside her. Okay, here it was, two Aquarian kills—one in Birmingham and the other in Dothan, Alabama. Now: the Capricorn kills. They had to be at least six months before the last Aquarian kill.

"Here. Here it is," she said, breathlessly, rocking back on her heels. "Two Capricorn kills in Georgia. In Atlanta and Macon. Eleven in all over roughly a four-year period. He was smart about it. He spread them out. Different states and cities. Not all the variables matched except for the teasers. This is the guy. Here."

"An astrology buff," Summer said, rubbing his jaw again, shaking his head. "The bastard's working his way through the zodiac."

McCleary's eyes glossed as though he had a fever. "Then he either knows his victims or observes them long enough to find out their birth dates and that they're health or fitness nuts. He *plans*."

Summer's grin suddenly vanished. "This is great stuff, but how the hell are we supposed to figure out who he's going to hit next? And where? The only solid lead we've got is that the guy either belongs to the Grove Fitness

Club or has a friend who does. So what? They've got about four thousand members on their roster, if you include the people in their various classes."

"Doesn't matter. That's where we start." Quin stood, and floated in the currents of her elation toward the kitchen—and more food.

7 After Hours

HE SHIVERED.

His teeth chattered.

Sweat drenched his sheets.

His gut cramped painfully.

The symptoms proliferated like mice, symptoms that might have fit the incipience of the flu or mumps or mononucleosis or, Jesus, even AIDS. But he knew what was happening, knew because he'd experienced the same thing during the weeks before Joyce's kill. But it wasn't possible. How could he be going through withdrawal when it had only been a little more than two weeks since Joyce's death? *How?*

He squeezed his eyes shut as a shudder whipped along his spine. In his mind, he saw Bob Summer turning onto Poinciana Drive earlier this evening. He saw himself driving into the park, then hurrying through the trees on foot until he reached the edge of the road. He had waited there a long time, watching. Once, Summer had come out of the house, removed something from his car, and gone back inside. Shortly afterward, he'd crept across the road and had looked at the name on the mailbox. *McCleary.*

By then, he was cold and hungry and had rushed back to his car and home. For the last hour, he had lain here, his addiction controlling him.

He wanted desperately to feel baffled by his need to kill. He imagined himself in front of a psychiatrist, explaining his terrible urge, his belief that the spilled blood of another would magically prolong his life. He heard the shrink asking him when this urge had begun and saw himself shrug. *It's a complete mystery, Doc.*

But, in fact, he knew precisely the moment when the urge had rooted in him.

Eight years ago his mother had been diagnosed as having liver cancer. During the six months she had lingered, he'd watched her waste away. He'd watched her retching after chemotherapy treatments, had listened to her begging him to kill her when she was in pain, he had treaded the scabrous landscape of her disease with her, and bled for her. When the end had come, he'd been sitting beside her, gripping her hand, trying not to weep, knowing that if it were in his power, he would kill someone else so that she might live.

Two months later, during a five-hour layover at the Dallas airport, he'd carried out his first kill. There had been no preparation. He hadn't known the woman's birth date or even her name. He had simply picked her up in a Dallas bar and knifed her in an alley three blocks away and then he'd fled. For several days afterward, his terror at being discovered had been equaled only by his self-loathing. He went over and over the killing in his mind, reliving the details, staring at his hands, appalled.

But gradually he realized that the kill had somehow eased the pain and loss of his mother's death, and more, that he had liked it. He had liked the feverish throbbing in his body at the moment he'd stabbed the knife through her chest. The sight of her blood had fascinated him. He had felt like a god.

But he wasn't addicted; not then. In the beginning, he could go as long as nine months or a year without killing. But by his third kill, an unemployed actor whom he'd met on a flight to L.A., he was developing a taste for it.

The actor had been an important lesson, a classic example of Murphy's Law. Everything possible had gone wrong with the kill. So he established standards for himself, as any artist must. He began choosing his victims, studying them, learning their birth dates, rekindling his teenage interest in astrology, which he had learned from his grandmother. He'd immersed himself in the reticular maze of astrological transits and squares, conjunctions and oppositions. He'd learned that in his own natal chart, the Saturn and Pluto conjunction in his eighth house, the house of death, had conferred on him a thirst for murder. He drew up charts on his chosen victims and compared them with his own chart for the day of the kill. He had discovered how to read omens and the propensity for triumph in the stars.

By the time he killed his first Capricorn in Atlanta four years ago, he was hooked—not just on the kill, but on the preparation and aftermath as well. By varying his techniques, by spacing his kills and their locations, he had kept the police as nonplused as clowns. Although he preferred knives and scissors to guns, his collection allowed him to vary his weapons. And yet, he'd been fair. He had always left a sweet. The problem, of course, was the addiction itself. Never in all these years had he gone through the shakes so shortly after a kill. Never.

He sat up, clutching his arms against him, and swung his legs over the side of the bed. He shuffled into the bathroom, splashed cold water on his face. What he needed was a hard game of squash, a five-mile run, physical activity. Exercise purged. But it was too late to go running; he might draw attention to himself. And the fitness club was closed.

What you need is a kill. Now. Tonight.

He leaned into the wall as a violent shudder burned the surface of his flesh. His body had needs. His body demanded. His body was no longer his own.

I'm dying.

Like his mother, he was slowly dying. He felt his cells breaking down, melting like ice. His blood moved sluggishly through his veins; old blood, used up. He pressed his fingertips to his neck; his pulse fluttered erratically.

Feed me, whispered his body.

"It's not time, not time." He couldn't kill Summer yet; the stars weren't right.

Anyone.

Like the old days. He pressed his face into a towel, inhaling the sweet fragrance of detergent, of cleanliness. A random kill, like his first. No preparation, no trophies, no clues, no sweeteners. Swift and simple. *Yes, all right.*

He felt himself growing hard at the thought of killing a woman like the one in Dallas.

He stopped shivering. The cramping in his gut loosened. The sweat on his skin dried in a flash. The thought had triggered the release of endorphins in his brain, and relief coursed through him. Released from the clutch of his terrible need, he rubbed his hands over his face, smiling. He was tempted to simply crawl back into bed, to cheat his addiction. But his gut twitched hard, hurting him, reminding him that cheating was a punishable transgression, that if he cheated, his body would torture him, incapacitate him until its needs were met.

He dressed quickly, scooped his gloves and keys from the dresser. Then he dug down deep into his dresser drawer and brought out his old Boy Scout knife. It was the first he'd ever owned, the beginning of a collection that now included fifty-some-odd knives. It was small, thin, but sharp and powerful.

He hurried outside, into the cold night air. A gibbous moon gleamed in the obsidian sky. Stars winked at him. The night infused him with power; it always had. With the exception of his first kill, all of his chosen had died at night.

He drove to west Dade, to the After Hours Club. The building had once housed a Piggly Wiggly supermarket. Now it was painted lavender and pink and was crowned by a glowing purple neon sign. The parking lot was jammed. Strains of music dipped into the cold air. He left his car some distance from the nearest street lamp, got out, and walked toward the entrance, hands deep in his jacket pockets.

He felt no trace of his earlier malaise.

He paid the ten-dollar cover charge and stepped into

the re-created world of the fifties. A red 1957 Thunderbird, as shiny as a polished apple, was raised on a platform just inside the door. The walls were tiled in deep blues and lavenders and reflected the soft lighting. In the center of the room, waiters and waitresses were rock 'n' rolling to an old song by the Shirelles. The air thickened the farther inside he went: perfume, spilled beer, smoke, sweat, sexual arousal—distinctive, separate aromas that immixed like ingredients in a recipe, South Florida style.

He ordered a beer and stood at the railing that circumvented the dance floor. His eyes searched for a face, the right face. His heart pulsed to the music's beat. Dancing feet pounded the floors. Voices rose and fell in a tantalizing cadence.

He was waiting for the ineluctable signal from his body that would tell him which woman he should choose. That was how it had happened in Dallas, the first time.

The song ended. Another began. Couples drifted toward the dance floor. His eyes searched, paused, searched some more. The beer was deliciously cold; he felt each sip all the way to his toes. His skin tingled as he watched one of the women on the dance floor, her hips undulating, jerking, sliding into a beat all her own.

But she wasn't the one.

There. There she is, his body whispered. His eyes followed the internal nudge, skimming the faces at the railing, then stopped. The woman held a glass of something red to her mouth and sipped cautiously, slowly, as though she had already had too much to drink. She was remarkably unremarkable, except for her hair, which was luxuriously black, and her eyes, which seemed to be a luminous blue, like gems.

Perfect.

He moved away from his spot at the railing and made his way slowly toward her. He squeezed through the crowd until he was next to her, so close their shoulders brushed. An electric chill swept through him. She felt it too, because he sensed her glancing at him quickly, almost surreptitiously.

59

The inside of his mouth tasted coppery, like blood. A spasm of anxiety squeezed at his heart. *Now what?* He waited for his body to direct him, guide him, but nothing happened.

His beer was half gone.

The smoke in here bothered his eyes.

His head began to ache.

He lacked the necessary polish for a pickup routine. He felt like a neophyte.

She moved to his left side and leaned on the railing, and her perfume was a cloud, enveloping him. *A scent like Joyce's.* Jesus, yes. The fragrance triggered a visceral response in him. He thought of Joyce's body, her thighs, her perfect legs opening to him, admitting him. Joyce, who was always tight and hot.

He lifted his hand to his face, lifted it too quickly, and his elbow hit the woman's hand. Her drink splashed over the side of her glass.

"I'm sorry. Oh God, how clumsy of me," he said, holding out a napkin.

"It's okay," she murmured, accepting the napkin and dabbing at the front of her dark brown leather jacket. "No harm done. Really."

"At least let me buy you another drink, then," he said.

Her smile was quick, lovely, as luminous as her eyes. "Thanks. I appreciate it."

He bought her another drink, a Bloody Mary, and they exchanged the usual small talk. He introduced himself as Bert; her name was Lois. "Like Superman's girlfriend," she said with a laugh. She was a schoolteacher in Hialeah, a community north of Miami, and she hated it. "In fact, tomorrow I'm calling in sick," she confided.

She was one of those women who enjoyed talking more than listening, which suited him just fine. The less he said about himself, the better. He would've preferred not knowing her name, but now that he did, he took the next step and asked her what month she was born in.

"November. I'm a Scorpio."

Sensual. Perhaps a little fey. She stings.

"Why?"

"Just curious. I dabble in astrology."

"What sign are you?" she asked.

"Pisces," he lied.

"My last roommate was a Pisces."

"She moved out?" he asked, wondering if he sounded too hopeful.

"She got married. I've been renting the apartment by myself for the last couple of months."

As she talked, she kept sipping at her drink, getting progressively higher. His hand dropped from his glass to her thigh. It rested there lightly, unobtrusively. He could feel the heat of her skin through her navy blue slacks. He stared at her mouth as she spoke, a slightly pouting mouth, he thought, infinitely kissable. Her nails moved lightly over his knuckles and he began to caress her thigh. His heart pounded; spicules of sweat broke out across his forehead. *How long since you got laid, Bert ol' boy?* Not since he and Joyce . . .

He shifted in his seat, touched her chin, lifted it, kissed her lightly on the mouth. Her tongue danced against his, then she drew back a little.

Her eyes searched his face. "Listen, you're not gay or bi or anything, are you?"

"What?" He laughed.

"I mean, you have to be careful these days, what with AIDS and all."

You're almost home free, pal.

No, he told her. He wasn't gay or bisexual and had never shot up.

Her relief was palpable. "Me neither. You never know who a person's been with, though. That's what I don't like."

An awkward moment ticked by. They didn't speak. He glanced out over the room. It was still crowded with people. He turned back to the woman, to Lois. "Let's go somewhere," he whispered, his breath warm against her ear.

"I don't live too far from here. I could fix us breakfast or something."

He kissed her again, and this time there was something desperate in the way she clung to him. He smiled. His body had not betrayed him. It had chosen the right woman.

He followed her three miles to a huge apartment complex. There was no guardhouse. Dozens of cars lined the lot. His car would simply be one among many. No one would see him arrive—or leave.

Her apartment was on the first floor. It was small, tidy, sparsely furnished. "God, it's so cold out," she said, hunching her shoulders for warmth as she fiddled with the thermostat on the wall. The heat clicked on. He followed her into the kitchen. She threw open the refrigerator door. "So what would you like to eat? Breakfast? Dinner?"

He came up behind her and rested his chin on her shoulder. He spotted a plastic Honey Bear container in the fridge. He reached for it.

"Honey?" She laughed. "That's all you want to eat?"

He turned her around, squeezed several drops of honey onto his fingertip, and spread them on her lower lip. She giggled; her tongue licked at the stuff. "Save some for me," he said, his tongue darting out at the honey on her lip. Then he kissed her. His free hand slid under her sweater, against the smooth curve of her spine. He set the Honey Bear down, drew the sweater over her head. She wore no bra, and the sight of her breasts, larger and plumper than he'd thought, delighted him. *Like Joyce's.* He cupped one of her breasts in his hand, reached for the plastic bottle again. He hesitated before he touched it.

A little won't hurt. Honey isn't powdered sugar.

Besides, he would lick it all off.

He squeezed a drop of honey onto her breast, and sucked it off. She made noises deep in her throat and pressed her body against his, murmuring something he didn't hear. "Hold this," he said, handing her the Honey

Bear, then he picked her up. She was lighter than helium. She laughed and directed him to the bedroom.

Moonlight filtered through the curtains. He set her down on the bed, removed his jacket, and draped it over the back of a nearby chair, making sure the knife was still inside. Then he shucked his clothes, placing them neatly over his jacket. From his wallet, he withdrew a condom, which he set on the nightstand, next to the Honey Bear. He moved toward her. She was struggling with the zipper on her slacks.

"I'll do that," he said quietly, urging her back against the bed. She giggled again and stretched back, arms over her head. The zipper was stuck. He yanked on it, the thing popped, and she lifted her hips. He slid the slacks off her like silk. Her pale blue underwear shimmered in the moonlight. She reached down to remove them, but he shook his head. "I'll do all the work." He kissed her, touching her, liking the feel of her damp heat against the silk of her underwear. He slid two fingers inside the elastic band, then drew them off. He told her to bend her knees; she did. That was good. She was hungry enough for obedience.

She followed him with her eyes as he moved over to the nightstand and picked up the plastic bottle of honey. "You're not." She was laughing softly.

"I am," he said, pressing her legs apart. He covered his fingertips with honey, then drew his fingers delicately along the inside of her thigh, up behind her knee, down to her foot, then along the inside of her thigh again, spreading the honey as his hand moved. She squealed.

"Hey, it's cold, Bert."

He laughed. "Won't be for long." He began to lick the honey from the inside of her thighs, behind her knee, from her foot, and she kept giggling and sighing, giggling and sighing, as if she couldn't make up her mind whether it tickled or felt good.

He held the honey jar between her legs and, squeezing it, watched the glistening drops ooze through the moonlight and over the dark hair. "That feels . . ." she began, her voice a murmur, then she gasped sharply when he spread the honey between her legs. "Good . . . oh God, that feels good," she whispered, moving her hips against his hand.

He could see the way her eyes fluttered closed, and how her hands gripped the underside of the headboard. Her chest heaved. Her nipples tightened. The muscles in her tummy quivered. He would please her, and then in return she would surrender her life. It was only fair. After all, she would be his first honey sculpture.

As he squeezed more honey onto her stomach, he wondered how many bees had worked on just this single jar of honey. Hundreds? Thousands? There was a certain rightness about a honeybee's life, he decided. It was born with its singular purpose, and that purpose directed everything it did in its life. In some ways, he was like the bee.

She held out her arms. He had a sudden, truculent urge to slap them away. But he didn't. Instead, he reached for the condom, opened it, put it on. Then he stretched out beside her, his hand limning the curve of her hip, his mouth in the hollow of her throat. She clutched at him; he teased her. He sucked and licked at the honey until she began to pant, until she cried out, and then he thrust himself inside her.

She was narrower and hotter than Joyce. *Claret. Joyce was purple.* He took his time. He savored her. He played her. She came again, twitching, her cry muffled against his chest, her nails digging into his back like tiny daggers. He sank his teeth into the curve of her shoulder as his insides tightened and then exploded, and when he tasted honey and blood in his mouth it took him a long moment to realize it was her blood, that he had broken the skin—and she, in her frenzy, had not even felt it.

She clung to him, and after a while the cool air in the room made him shiver and he rolled away from her. She touched her shoulder. "You bit me." She spoke with a note of awe in her voice, and giggled again. The giggling irritated him, but he pressed his mouth to the bite, kissing it, cooing over it as though she were a child with a skinned knee. His tongue licked away the trickles of blood.

Salty.

It intoxicated him, this taste. His body sang. He kept sucking at the bite, marveling at the mingling of blood and honey. He licked at it, sucked again. *Like a vampire.* The thought jerked his head up. He rolled away from the woman. "Where's the bathroom?" His voice shook.

"First door on your right in the hall."

He practically ran and barely made it before he fell to his knees at the toilet bowl and retched. *You're going to be all right. You are. Just go back in there and get the knife and do what you came here to do and that will be that. No more withdrawal symptoms.*

Yes. Okay. He knew what he had to do. He flushed the condom down the toilet. The taste of her blood lingered in his mouth. He squeezed toothpaste from the tube at the sink edge onto his finger and coated his teeth with it. Then he rinsed. Better. No more blood taste.

Vampire.

It was the word more than the idea of what he'd done that frightened him. It was one of those archetypal words with power. It conjured childhood ghosts, fears of the dark, of life as a walking dead.

He wiped off everything he'd touched, dampened a washcloth, and returned to the bedroom with it. The moon had slipped lower in the sky. He could see it through the window now, a damp glowing face as blank as a baby's conscience. He reached into his jacket pocket for his Boy Scout knife. The rustling of his clothes caused Lois—*like Superman's girlfriend*, he thought—to lift her head.

"Are you leaving, Bert?"

"No. No, not yet."

"I've got to wash this honey off myself."

"I'll do it."

He moved the damp cloth over her body, the knife snuggled against the palm of his left hand. He flicked it open, its blade cold against his skin. His heart hammered. The cloth moved across her tummy. He kissed her lightly on the mouth, caressed her shoulder. His thumb rested on the bite mark. *Ted Bundy bit his victims on the ass, and that was what nailed him.*

But there would be nothing he'd done here to connect him with Joyce.

"Again?" Another giggle bubbled from her mouth. He was getting to hate that giggle.

He smiled; the washcloth continued to move across her skin in light, circular motions. She stretched her arms over her head again. He leaned forward as if to kiss her and plunged the knife into the left side of her neck, directly into the carotid artery.

"Your life for mine," he murmured.

Blood spurted, spraying him. She made a terrible gagging sound, her hands grappled for the knife, she tried to sit up, her eyes bulged in her face. He watched her dispassionately, felt her blood warm against his chest, his arms. His heart thundered in his chest, his ears. Adrenaline whipped through him. For a moment, he felt as if he could lift his arms and rise toward the ceiling like Peter Pan. This was the source of his addiction. This incredible lightness of mind. This surfeit of energy. *This.*

He pulled the knife from her neck. Her life flew out of her like a panicked bird. He could hear its wings beating the air, and he opened his arms wide and dropped his head back, the moonlight cold against his face as her life osmosed through his skin like a mist, like gas.

He trembled as he wiped the blade on the sheets and stood. He looked down at himself, at her blood drying on his skin. He picked up the washcloth, hurriedly wiping away the remains of the honey from her body. Still clutching the knife, he rushed into the bathroom, dropped the washcloth in the shower, and yanked a towel from the rack. He used it to flick on the overhead light and turn on the shower. He stepped under the sharp, warm spray, watching her blood swirl pink down the drain, holding the knife up against the shower head like a corban. He couldn't stop smiling. The years were dropping away from him. Like Dorian Gray, he would remain young and vital while the people around him grew old and died.

When he was clean, he used the washcloth to turn off the faucet, then wiped down the walls and the glass door in the shower. He spread the cloth out to dry over the top of the door, then dried himself with the towel, draped it over his shoulder, and padded back into the bedroom. He returned the knife to his jacket pocket. He drew the curtains closed over the window and switched on the bedside light. He averted his eyes from her and got down on his hands and knees, looking for the package the condom had been in. He found it, shoved it inside his jacket pocket with the knife, and got dressed. Then he thoroughly wiped off the Honey Bear bottle and returned it to the fridge.

He came back to the bedroom and took one final look around. He scooped her clothes from the floor, wiped off the zipper on her slacks, tossed her clothes in the hamper just inside the closet. He switched off the light. He bunched the towel up under his arm and left, locking the door behind him. Gray light oozed against the horizon like pus as he stepped outside. The cold struck his face and damp hair. He felt marvelously alive, invincible, as ubiquitous as a Greek god.

8 Connecting

1.

THE FULGENT TUNNELINGS of Quin's thoughts sought a label, a category, perhaps a word from a pop psychology book that would clarify what she was seeing. She needed something quick and unequivocal like *paranoid* or *obsessed*, which couldn't be misunderstood. Hell, even *out of it* would do. Yeah, McCleary was *out of it, bonkers, zippity do dah*.

It was 6:02 in the morning and she stood at the door of his den, where she'd been for a full minute, peering through the crack, watching him. He was sitting on the floor in his running shorts, his back against the couch. His legs were spread apart, creating an isosceles triangle whose lower line was composed of certain items: a Tupperware bowl, a piece of paper with something written on it, a little hill of sugar, a pair of scissors, four strips of nylon from one of her stockings. It didn't take a shrink to figure out that McCleary was engaging in a kind of sympathetic-magic brainstorming.

Quin nudged the door open, and McCleary looked up. His eyes, though deeply circled and puffy from lack of sleep, shone brightly. Color flushed his cheeks. He looked at her as if he couldn't remember who she was, as though he were suffering the effects of a petit mal, a momentary fugue.

"What're you doing?" she asked.

"I couldn't sleep." As if that explained everything.

His voice sounded small and tight; he resented her

intrusion. She followed his gaze to the objects on the floor. Dread chimed in the back of her mind.

"What's all this stuff?" she asked, even though she knew. She moved over to the couch and sat at the edge.

"The killer's MO. I had to improvise some, but it's close enough." McCleary rubbed his jaw, which was shadowed by a dark stubble, and drew his legs up against him. He rested his chin on a knee and continued to gaze at the items. They reminded her, in a way, of religious icons. She saw that the scrap of paper with writing on it was a duplicate of the message the killer had left in the Tupperware dish. The letters were black, sloppy, not at all like McCleary's handwriting. Her alarm bit deeper, turning her mouth dry and sour.

"So what's the point?"

He raised his bright eyes. "Just to see it laid out, that's all."

"How long have you been down here?"

He shrugged, dropped his eyes once more. "I don't know. A couple of hours, I guess."

A couple of hours? They hadn't gone to bed until almost two.

He ran a hand over his hair. "I feel like I'm getting a handle on this guy, Quin. Earlier, I was sitting here looking at the powdered sugar, trying to figure out why there would be traces of the stuff on Joyce. I went through the other eleven cases and found no mention of powdered sugar. Instead, in all of them, traces of various types of sweets or sweeteners were found: globules of maple syrup, bits of saccharin, a spot of jam, a piece of candy." McCleary rose in a single, fluid motion and reached for the stack of files on his desk. When she'd gone to bed, there had been no files—only packets of computer printouts. He set them down to his left and rifled through them. "Here. The Dothan, Alabama, homicide. A sugar cube was found in the dead man's pocket."

"Where was he killed?"

"In his car. The cops found it alongside the road and

the guy was inside. They figured he'd picked up the wrong hitchhiker." He set it aside, picked out another file. "The Tallahassee coed. A spot of strawberry jam was found on the inside of her thigh. There was no sign of sperm, no sign of rape, but there were bruises on the inside of her thighs. They think the guy used a condom." He whipped out a third file. He spoke rapidly now, as though his mouth were trying to keep up with his mind. "The Macon lawyer, the second Capricorn killing. Saccharin was found in his hair. He was killed in the sauna at his health club." Out came a fourth file. "And here. The Melbourne, Florida, flying instructor. No evidence of rape, but she'd recently had sex and beads of maple syrup were found on her breasts."

"A death sweet," Quin said quietly. "He leaves a death sweet."

"Yeah. For the most part, he gets the women in bed and does weird things to them with fudge and jam, and he gets the men in their health clubs or while they're out running or in their cars or whatever. But he didn't mess around sexually with Joyce or with . . ." He swept through the files. "Or with this women, the librarian in Jacksonville. No sex, but from both of them he took trophies." His hands tapped the files into a neat stack and he set them on the couch and sat back. Fatigue etched deep lines at the corners of his eyes. "A pattern. Even in the most careful murders, there are always patterns. You just have to keep digging, trying to connect facts." He said this as if he were a teacher giving a lecture. "I've probably missed some stuff, but we'll just keep going through these, breaking them down into components, into—"

"Not now we won't," she said. "Right now, I'm fixing us breakfast." She started to get up, but McCleary reached for her hand.

"Wait." He stood and plucked a piece of paper off his desk. "Here. I made up a list of things we need to do related to this case. I thought if we divided them up it'd be quicker."

McCleary and his lists, she thought. How did someone as disorganized as she was end up with a man who
was so maddeningly the opposite? She glanced through
the dozen items. They ranged from talking to Gene
Travis and his first wife, speaking to the maid who'd
found Joyce, taking a look at the topless club and talking
to someone named Callahan.

"Who's Callahan?" Quin asked.

"A source I had when I was working homicide."

"What kind of source?"

"She's familiar with the whole world that revolves
around clubs like Gene Travis owns."

"She?"

"Sylvia Callahan."

"She's a topless dancer?"

"No. She owned a disco-bar in the Grove. Her sister
was a waitress in one of these clubs, and about five
years ago she was killed and I investigated the homicide.
Benson seems to think she may know something about
Travis and suggested I talk to her. Now, which of these
things do you want to do?"

She picked out the tasks she would tackle and McCleary
placed neat little Qs next to them. "I thought we'd hit
Travis' little den of iniquity either tonight or tomorrow
night around eleven or twelve, when things are rolling."

Quin smiled. "You sound like an expert."

"For the eight months I worked on the Callahan case,
I was."

There was some quality to his voice or in his expression, an ineffable nuance, that told her there was more
to the story. She leaned against the doorway. "So did
you catch the person who killed Sylvia's sister?"

"Yeah. He's doing thirteen years at Raiford."

"And Sylvia?"

"I hear she retired on the profit she made from the
sale of the club."

"She lives in Miami?"

"In Lauderdale."

"Oh." She picked at her thumbnail. She felt like an

uncertain teenager plagued with acne, small boobs, and rejection by her peers, and for what? Because McCleary was going to talk to a woman he'd known five years ago who might be a potential source? So what? Nothing like a little paranoia, she thought, then blurted: "So did you have an affair with her or something?"

McCleary leaned into the other side of the door and chuckled. "So *that's* what the third degree was about?"

"What third degree? I was just curious, that's all."

"Yeah, we had an affair for a while."

"How come you never mentioned her before?"

He entreated the ceiling with his eyes. It was one of those looks that said this conversation was veering into the absurd, but that he would go along with it if it was so important to her. "I never think about it, that's why."

"Oh." She looked down at her hands, at the cinnamon color of her nails against the blue of her robe, and wondered why she'd never learned what her sister called 'the art of silence.' Or what Zivia referred to as *the keep-'em-guessing game*. During the course of their marriage, she'd recited the litany of every relationship she'd ever been involved in. For some reason, she'd assumed the same was true for McCleary.

"I can't believe it. You're actually jealous of someone I knew five years ago."

"Jealous?" She laughed. "How can I be jealous of someone I've never met? Of someone I didn't even know existed until two minutes ago?"

"Then what is it?"

She shrugged, feigning an insouciance she didn't feel. "Suppose I hadn't asked who she was? Would you have mentioned it?"

"I guess so. If it seemed relevant."

Relevant? He intended to consult an ex-lover as a source and that might not be *relevant*? She said as much and knew he didn't have any idea what the big deal was.

"It was five years ago, Quin."

"Forget it." His obtuseness exasperated her. She could stand here the rest of the morning, stating and re-stating her case, and he still wouldn't understand. It was one of those finely delineated areas where men and women differed. An important area. "I'm starving. Let's eat."

But as she walked out into the hall, she wondered if McCleary had been in love with the woman, and wished she had asked.

On second thought, maybe it was better that she didn't know. The adage about a little knowledge being a dangerous thing fit her like a shoe. Already, her imagination was seizing on this new information, working away at it, spinning tall tales. A renewed affair. Clandestine couplings. Paroxysms of passion, pleasure. Herself being the last to know. Divorce.

Wonderful.

She should have known. She should have known by the way the morning started that today had all the earmarks of a bad day.

She'd gotten stalled for forty-five minutes in traffic on the interstate because a produce truck carrying hundreds of dozens of eggs had overturned. Had it been warmer, the eggs would've scrambled. As it was, by the time she'd inched past the catastrophe the road quivered with egg yolks.

She hurried into the office shortly after nine. Ruth Grimes was typing up a storm at the IBM Selectric, her sprayed gray hair so perfectly motionless that it looked like it might be fake. "Quin, honey, where's Mike? That Mr. Young is waiting for him in the staff kitchen."

Swell, she needed this. "He won't be in until later. I'll take care of it."

"And Zivia wanted me to buzz her as soon as you got in."

"Okay, let me just take care of Mr. Young first. Anything else?"

"Not that I can remember." Ruth smiled and went back to her typing. Ruth, who had been with the firm when it was still owned by Trevor Forsythe's father, was a fixture, as perdurable as religion.

Young was at the table, paging through the morning *Herald*, sipping at a cup of coffee. Quin's eyes dropped quickly to his socks. They were burnished orange. She laughed. "Hey, I like your socks, Ross."

He looked up, his resplendent smile almost blinding, and chuckled. "Bloomingdale's. I couldn't resist them." Despite his smile, his eyes still possessed that pinched, pained look, as though he were hurting bad inside. "I hope you don't mind my waiting in here, Quin."

"Not at all. Did Mac have an appointment with you or something, Ross?" She poured herself a cup of coffee.

"No. Nothing like that." He reached inside his jacket and brought out a check. "I just wanted to drop this off."

"You paid us a retainer already." She sat across from him.

"But this should cover expenses."

She stared at the check. It was for $3,500. *Nearly two and a half trips to Venezuela.* "But . . ."

"I spoke to Tim Benson this morning. He told me what was, uh, found. At the fitness club." His huge hands curled around his Styrofoam cup, dwarfing it, almost engulfing it. He gazed into it as he spoke, as if a part of him hoped the riddles of his stepsister's death could be divined there. "I understand the club will probably become something of the focus of your investigation, so I don't want you all to put out any of your own money."

It was a refreshing switch from their usual clients, and she accepted the check gratefully. "We usually bill for expenses, Ross, if you'd rather do it that way."

He shook his head. "It makes me feel useful, so indulge me, okay?"

"All right. You'll get a full accounting of expenses at the end of two weeks, how's that?"

"Fine."

"While I've got you here, what else can you tell me about Gene Travis?"

He sat back, combed his fingers through his sandy hair, and shrugged. "Not much, really. I only met the man once."

"Did you know Joyce had gotten pregnant by him and miscarried?"

"*What?* When?"

"I don't know when, exactly. That came from Neal."

"Oh. Well. Neal. Who knows if it's even true, then." He rubbed a hand over his face. "Pregnant. She never mentioned it to me. I think she would've said something. I'm sure she would have." His head bobbed. "Yeah, she would have." Quin had the impression he was trying to convince himself as well as her.

She started to tell him what they had managed to put together through Bob Summer, but changed her mind. Now was as good a time as any to begin learning the 'art of silence.' Something McCleary did adroitly, she thought.

"What'd you think of Neal?" he asked.

"He's not very friendly."

Young laughed. "Yeah, that's an understatement. He was rude to me from day one. He . . ."

His voice trailed off, and his eyes darted toward the door. Quin glanced around. Zivia stood in the doorway. "Oh, I'm sorry, Quin, I thought . . ."

"C'mon in. Zivia Tuckett, Ross Young."

Ross stood, and didn't take his eyes from Zivia's face. They shook hands; he held on to hers a little longer than was necessary. "We heard wild and unmentionable things about you yesterday from your ex-brother-in-law, Mr. Young," Zivia said with a smile.

He laughed; it was a quick, limpid sound. "Yeah, I'll bet."

"Zivia's one of our investigators," Quin explained. "She was nice enough to ride out to the airport with me yesterday to talk to Neal Schloper."

Young's eyes finally left Zivia's face and slid reluctantly toward Quin. "You should've had an armed guard."

"He was tame enough, just not very friendly," Zivia said.

Quin sensed the immediate chemistry between them. It heated the air. It brought a flush to Zivia's cheeks and a broad smile to Young's face, a real smile, without ghosts.

They chatted for a few moments, the three of them. Then Quin, feeling like excess baggage, said, "Ross, I hate to run like this, but I've got an appointment. We're having some people over Saturday night, why don't you come?"

"Thanks. I will."

She started out of the room, then paused. "Oh, Zivia. Ruth said you wanted to talk to me. Can it wait?"

She waved a hand; a mischievous grin claimed her face. "It was just about a cactus, Quin. Sure, it can wait."

Quin laughed.

2.

The two-mile running trail behind the Grove Fitness Club was a landscaping marvel, McCleary thought. It looped through sweet-smelling pine, jacaranda bushes, and sparges of bright lavender Mexican heather, and over the arch of a bridge that crossed a man-made stream. The run chased off the incipience of a fatigue that had been growing like cobwebs in a corner of his mind. It also gave him an opportunity to observe Gene Travis, who was jogging at a swift clip on a curve of the path to his right.

McCleary had expected Travis to look either undernourished—effete—or like a gorilla. He was neither. He faintly resembled David Letterman, and looked like any ordinary businessman who, at the moment, was pounding hell out of his legs and shoes. Gray laced the chestnut hair at the temples. Sweat streaked his square face. His dove-gray running suit was dappled with perspiration. If McCleary had to pick a porn king out of a room of a hundred men, Travis would have ranked somewhere near the bottom. He blended with Middle America.

Travis rounded a second curve and McCleary lost sight of him for a moment. He ducked as he passed under an integument of branches, then saw Travis just ahead, walking briskly toward the door to the club, a towel draped around his neck. McCleary slowed, then followed Travis after he'd disappeared inside the building.

The royal-blue hallway led to the locker rooms. Travis passed through the double doors, and McCleary paused at the drinking fountain just outside. The water was so cold it hurt his teeth. But never had anything tasted so good.

His thirst sated, he pushed through the double doors. This locker room was one of the two for men in the club, and there weren't many people inside. He spotted Travis headed toward the sauna. McCleary opened his locker, which was a free-for-all like the ones in front where they'd found the killer's trophy. He shucked his running suit, wrapped a clean towel at his waist, and went after Travis.

He remembered that one of Death Sweet's victims had died in a sauna. It was not a particularly pleasant thought.

Only the two of them occupied the wooden box, Travis on a bench just below McCleary. Steam hissed. McCleary's pores opened like flowers. The heat sucked out the vestiges of his fatigue and his earlier malaise over the stupid business with Quin concerning Callahan.

He didn't understand women.

He wondered if Travis understood women.

"Do you understand women?" he asked aloud.

Travis, his face as moist as a leaf, glanced around. He looked at McCleary with his deep gray eyes, looked at him like he was wondering who the hell this jerk was, and then he laughed. "No. Never. I've been married twice, have more than twenty women who work for me, and I still don't understand women. Never will."

"My wife . . ." He changed his mind. "Well, I live with her, actually, we aren't married, is pissed because I never told her about a woman I was involved with two years before we even met."

Travis swung around on the bench and sat with his back against the wall, legs stretched in front of him. He wiped the sweat from his eyes. "That's nothing. My first wife used to roll outa bed some mornings all bent outa shape at me because of something she *dreamed* I'd been doing. Dreamed, right?"

McCleary laughed. "I figure I should make a list of the women I was involved with before she and I met and pin it to the bulletin board in the kitchen. That way she can never say I withheld information."

"How long have you been together?"

"Three years."

"Me, I'm just separated from my second wife. Any kids?"

"Nope. Just three cats."

"Cats." Travis chortled, then leaned forward and held out his hand. "Name's Gene Travis.

"Mike. Mike West."

"Don't believe I've seen you around before. You just join?"

"Janet and I signed up for a couple of classes, so we've got the six-week membership. Thought we'd try it out first and see how we like it."

"It's a unique concept for South Florida, combining health and exercise with classes in yoga and meditation and so on. Which classes are you taking?"

"Jan signed up for meditation, so I thought I'd try astrology." He almost choked on the word. *Me, astrology: righto.*

"They're both good. My wife practically had to drag me to the astrology course when we took it. *Astrology*, right? I was totally embarrassed. But hell, it turned out to be one of the better investments I've made. The course is designed with practical application in mind. It comes complete with a computer program. I use it in hiring employees."

And in choosing your victims?

"And the meditation course is great for learning how to reduce stress through biofeedback. Comes in real handy in my line of work."

"What do you do?"

"I own a couple of bookstores and a bar and do some financial consulting on the side."

Bookstores and a bar: slick, McCleary thought. "Tough businesses."

"Sometimes." Travis blinked, and perspiration flew off his lashes. He wiped his face with the edge of his towel. "What line of work are you in, Mike?"

McCleary played his trump. "I find business investments for foreign clients. In fact, one of my clients is interested in your nightclub, Gene."

For a long moment, McCleary couldn't tell whether Travis was amused or angry. Then he laughed, a full laugh that echoed in the wooden box. "I like your style, Mike. C'mon, let's get outa here and go have a glass of carrot juice or something with a shot of vodka."

McCleary felt absurdly proud of himself.

9 Terry & Neal

1.

THE INSIDE OF Terry's Place, the hair salon that belonged to the ex-Mrs. Travis, had black tile floors, pale pink walls and sinks, and rust-colored furniture. A tune from the Miami Sound Machine ripped through the perm-scented air, competing with the noisy sound of blow-dryers. Three movie posters decorated the wall behind the receptionist's desk: Bogie in *Casablanca*, Hepburn in *African Queen*, and Barbara Stanwyck in *Double Indemnity*. No appointments were required, so Quin walked over to the desk and asked the receptionist if Terry was available for a cut and blow-dry.

The woman, whose mascara was so thick it seemed miraculous that she could even keep her eyes open, cracked her gum and consulted the schedule book opened in front of her. "Be about ten minutes. She's just finishing a henna. What's your name?"

"Quin."

Next to the 10:00 A.M. slot, the woman scribbled: Gwen.

"It's Q-u-i-n."

The woman cracked her gum again. The lavender dust on her eyelids sparkled. "Whatever. It'll be about ten minutes."

Fifteen minutes later, a redhead in her early to mid-thirties bopped—not walked—out to the desk, conferred with the gum cracker, then strolled over to Quin. "I'm Terry." She offered her hand and Quin shook it. Her grip was surprisingly strong, considering she stood only about five-four and was shadow thin. "What'd you have in mind, hon?"

"Just a trim."

She combed her fingers through Quin's hair, lifting it. "Hon, whoever cut your hair before must've been stoned."

Quin laughed. "*That* bad?"

Terry smiled. The ginger-colored freckles on her cheeks and across the bridge of her nose gave her a kind of innocence. "But we'll see what we can do. Let's get you shampooed."

As Quin followed her to the shampoo area, Terry Travis spoke nonstop. ". . . so we're going to do a little trim on your hair, and how about if we shape the front just a bit different? I mean, you've got a broad forehead, and we should try to soften it a little. Not with bangs, I hate bangs. Maybe we'll just have some strands or something across your forehead." She combed her fingers through Quin's hair again. "Some gray. Maybe you should think about having a henna done. It'd bring out the reddish highlights in your hair and cover the gray."

She pressed a pedal on the chair and it went back, with Quin's neck fitting in a depression in the sink. As she lathered Quin's hair, she kept chatting, almost as if she were frightened of silence.

When Quin was seated in a chair in front of a mirror, Terry perused a glass jar filled with combs and another filled with scissors. Her eyes drew together with concentration and her tongue moved slowly along her lower lip. Then she plucked out one of each. "So what kinda work do you do, Quin?" Terry asked, dividing her hair into sections.

"I'm a private investigator."

In the mirror, her reflection's ginger-colored eyebrows shot up. "Really? How neat. That must be pretty interesting work. You carry a gun?"

"Sometimes."

"I'm scared to death of guns." *Snip, snip*, went her

81

scissors. "My ex-husband always had guns and knives around the house. Used to make me real uneasy. I figure that if you have stuff like that around, you attract people you might have to use them on, you know?" *Snip, snip.* "But I guess in your line of work, it's sort of necessary. What kind of cases do you take?"

"Right now my husband and I are working on a homicide."

Terry wrinkled her nose. "Plenty of those in Miami, that's for sure." *Snip, snip.* "Must be kinda depressing, though."

"Your ex-husband is one of the suspects."

The scissors slipped. A *big* chunk of Quin's hair fell into her lap. She touched it with dismay, imagining her new hairstyle with a gaping yawn at her temple. Terry stared at her in the mirror, her scissors poised at the side of Quin's head. "Gene."

"Yes."

"Figures." She seemed to have recovered from her initial surprise and continued snipping at Quin's hair. "If you deal with scum, sooner or later things backfire." She lowered her voice. "Must be a woman, huh?"

Quin nodded.

Terry gave an indignant snort. "He was always dipping his prick where it shouldn't have been. That's why I walked out on him. I got sick of it. And *no* one walks out on Gene Travis, so he paid off a judge to get custody of my boy. Nice guy, Gene. Yeah, a real prince of a fellow." She was working away at Quin's hair with a vengeance now.

"Uh, I wanted the length pretty much the same."

"I'm only taking bulk, hon, don't worry about it." She lowered her voice and eyed Quin in the mirror. "Was it one of his girls? Is that who was murdered?"

"His girls?"

"The airheads who dance in his club. You know he owns a topless place, don't you?"

"Yes. But the woman wasn't a dancer. It was a woman named Joyce Young who he'd been having an affair with."

Terry glanced around. There were four women waiting, and the chairs around them were filling up now. "Let's go in the back room. I'll finish cutting your hair in there."

The room was small but pleasant, with mirrors on two walls, a rust-colored chair like the ones in front, and a pint-size fridge and table under the window. Terry motioned Quin to the chair and shut the door. "Listen, do you have any ID that proves you're a private eye? No offense, it's just that I've got to be kind of careful. I mean, for all I know, you might be one of Gene's girls."

Quin smiled. "Hardly." She fished inside her purse and brought out a copy of her private eye license.

Terry examined it carefully, then nodded and handed it back to her. "Okay. But this stuff is strictly between you and me. I want you to understand I've got no intention of ever testifying against Gene or anything else. If the cops come around here asking questions, I'll deny I said a word, understand?"

"No problem."

"I don't want to lose visitation rights with my boy."

"I understand. Really."

She returned to Quin's hair. "Okay, so you're saying this Joyce woman wasn't one of his dancing girls." *Snip, snip.* "But I'm telling you she was involved somehow in his business. All of his mistresses have been at one time or another. Gene has two lives—his wife and kids, his *normal* life—and then his *businesses,* his *sick* life. Now in this *sick* life you've got the bookstores, the club, his girls, and his, uh, videos."

"Videos?"

"Yeah, for his special customers."

"What kind of videos?"

She set the scissors aside. "Pornographic videos, what else?" She combed out Quinn's hair and began blow-drying it.

"Sold just to private customers?"

"More like special orders for particular types of videos from private customers. Gene's mistresses and some of his dancing girls, of course, usually end up in these videos."

"Describe what you mean by pornographic," said Quin. "*Hustler* magazine type porn?"

She laughed. "Hon, these videos make *Hustler* look like Walt Disney."

"Kiddie porn?"

"No. Not *that* bad. Gene, believe it or not, has certain standards. Ain't that a joke. Shit. Standards. But it's true. He loves kids. These things include everything *but* kiddie porn. Usually when a customer places an order for a video, he has some idea what he wants in it. Maybe he's even got a vague story idea. S and M, for example, involving two busty women and a guy built like a weight lifter. Maybe the customer wants it shot on an island. Maybe the female lead has a fetish for dolphins. Maybe the whole thing's supposed to be shot in a Jacuzzi. Whatever. Then Gene shoots the video according to the customer's specifications."

"And the women in all these are either his mistresses or the girls who dance at the club?"

"No. Not all." She turned off the blow-dryer and combed her fingers through the mass of curls that now covered Quin's head. "So, how's it look? You like it?"

Quin leaned forward, studying her reflection in the mirror. All the curls and wisps would take some getting used to, but yeah, she liked it. Her face *did* seem softer, somehow, and her hair actually looked longer, not shorter. "It's great, thanks."

Terry pulled out a chair at the table next to the window and lit a cigarette. She dropped her head back and blew smoke into the air. "Some of the women in these videos are referrals he gets from other people. Most of them are young and hungry and stupid. But he pays them well. He can afford to. These special orders begin at fifty grand."

Quinn swiveled around in her chair. "You didn't know any of this stuff when you married him?"

She stabbed out her cigarette and lifted her feet onto

the opposite chair. Sunlight burned pathways through her hair. Softly, she said, "I knew some of it. I just didn't know the extent of it." She paused. "I met Gene when I, uh, applied for a job at the bar. Back in those days, you had to 'audition' for him, like he was Cecil B. De Mille or something. So I did my little routine, and he liked it, and said he'd pay me fifteen grand to make a video. For his *private* collection. Well, I figured if I had that much money, I wouldn't have to dance. I could go to cosmetology school."

She stopped again, rubbed her hands against her skirt. "God, this is hard to talk about." She lit a second cigarette and continued to keep her gaze fixed on the wall, as if she were embarrassed to look at Quin. "So I made the video. It was a soft-porn thing, pretty tame compared to the stuff he's doing now. Then I took my money and went to school. About four months later, Gene shows up at my apartment one evening, and we started dating. A few months after that we got married." She let out a curt, ugly laugh. "I'm still not sure why he decided I qualified as wife material instead of mistress material. Anyway, when I filed for divorce and custody of my boy, he threatened to use the video against me in court to prove I was an unfit mother. Well, hell, I knew I didn't have a ghost of a chance. There was Gene with his millions, and here I was with my shop. And I don't care *what* anyone says, hon, money talks. So he paid off a judge to make sure he was awarded custody and I settled for visitation rights, and here I am. Like I said, he's a prince of a guy."

"How many video customers would you say he has?"

She shrugged; smoke drifted out of her nostrils. "Who knows? The only time I see him is when I go by the house to pick up my son. But I'm sure the numbers are still small. The customers are repeats. And you've got to be referred by one of the customers to even place an order. There're code words—don't ask me what 'cause I don't know—that you gotta use. I suppose that since the attorney general's report on pornography came out he's gotten even more careful about the whole thing."

"Does he keep duplicates of these videos?"

Terry's blue eyes turned as pale as ice. "Hon, if Gene ever found out that I even *spoke* to a private eye about him, he'd—"

"He's not going to find out."

"Christ." She sighed and ran a hand through her red hair. "He keeps copies, yeah. If this Joyce person was in one of his videos, you'd find it in the dupes."

"Do you know where he keeps them?"

She pressed the heels of her hands into her eyes. "I must have rocks in my head," she murmured. "Yeah, I think so. I didn't know when it could've done me some good, but I think I know now." She dropped her feet to the floor and leaned forward, her arms resting on her thighs. "But only because my son happened to mention that his daddy has a secret room. He evidently walked into Gene's den one night and the closet door was open. He peeked inside and saw a kind of trapdoor, I guess, that led to what he calls a secret room."

A sharp rap at the door interrupted them. The receptionist peeked in. "There're three customers waiting outside for you, Terry. Should I assign them to someone else?" She cracked her gum once.

"No, I'll be out in a second. Thanks."

As the door whispered shut, Quin said, "I've taken up enough of your time. I appreciate your candidness, Terry." She touched a hand to her hair. "And I love my haircut."

"Let me know what happens, okay?"

"You bet."

They stepped out into the hall, which smelled of perm and hair spray. "Quin, if you, uh, decide to do anything about those dupes, I might be able to help you out. I know the layout of the house and all. Besides, I have a personal interest in those tapes."

Her mischievous grin made Quin laugh. "I'll remember that."

For a day that had begun so poorly, things were shaping up rather nicely, Quin decided. With any luck at all, they'd have this case wrapped up in a couple of weeks and they'd be basking on a beach somewhere in Venezuela.

Just the thought of it made her stomach growl.

2.

Over the years, McCleary had found that his first impressions of people were usually correct. Quin had been the exception; he knew Neal Schloper was not.

They sat in the lunchroom at an Eastern hangar at the airport. The air stank of stale smoke and weak coffee, vending machine coffee that tasted as bad as it smelled. Schloper, waving a skinny black cigarette in the air as he launched into a vitriolic attack on Gene Travis, might have looked like a young Charles Lindbergh, but that was where the similarity ended.

His language was punctuated with obscenities about what sort of man Gene Travis was. About what he had done to Schloper's marriage, about what he'd done to Joyce.

"What *did* he do to Joyce, besides get her pregnant?" McCleary interrupted.

Schloper shifted in his chair. Sunlight streamed through the venetian blinds at the window and bratticed his face. "He ruined her, that's what he did. He terrified her."

"How?"

He shrugged and studied the end of his cigarette. "She never said. But three days before she died, we had dinner together, and she was telling me then that she was scared shitless of the man."

Which was, McCleary thought, exactly what Schloper had told Quin. *Tell me something I don't know, pal.* On top of it, McCleary sensed that Schloper was lying about not knowing *why* Joyce had been scared of Travis. If, indeed, she had been. He said as much.

"You dicks kill me, you know? I mean, what gives you the right to come traipsing around here with your stupid questions? Huh? You oughta be glad I consented to talk to you."

Yeah, it's a real pleasure, Neal. "You were married to the woman a long time, Mr. Schloper. I think it's odd that you aren't more concerned about who killed her."

Schloper tapped his long, skinny cigarette against the side of the ashtray. His demeanor slid from bellicose to something that might have been contrition. "I *am* concerned about who killed her. That's why I'm sitting here." He raised his eyes. "That's why I'm telling you Gene is behind this."

He leaned forward. McCleary noted that Schloper's mouth was too small, not proportionate to the rest of his face. *A secretive mouth.* "If I were a different sort of man, Mr. McCleary, I would probably do something like beat the shit out of Travis in an alley. But I am what I am, and I know that Travis would figure out it was me and send one of his lackeys to work me over, and frankly, I don't need it." He sat back, twirling the end of his cigarette against the ashtray, putting it out in such a way that he could smoke the rest of it later. "Something happened to Joyce not too long before she died. Something that made her afraid of Gene. I don't know what it was, I just know that it changed her."

McCleary couldn't rid himself of the feeling that Schloper still wasn't spilling all he knew. Schloper's unctous smile deserved to be erased, McCleary decided. "I'll tell you something, Mr. Schloper. I've been in this business a long time, and it's been my experience that when one suspect heavily maligns another, it usually means the first suspect has something to hide. That maybe he's guilty of something. Now why don't you save us both time and energy and tell me what it is you're hiding."

"Friend, you got it all wrong." He stabbed a finger at his own chest. "I have an alibi for the night of Joyce's murder."

"Being asleep at home alone isn't an alibi."

Schloper opened his mouth to say something, but just then the PA cut in, announcing that a 727 had arrived outside the hangar and would all mechanics please report on the double.

"That's me." Schloper pushed away from the table, plucked his half-smoked cigarette from the ashtray, and lit it.

"I'll walk out with you."

The man's small mouth cockled. "I'd rather you didn't, if you don't mind. Next time you want to see me, give me a call at home." And he rushed off, leaving a trail of smoke behind him.

McCleary sat back down and finished the terrible coffee and glanced at the posters on the walls of biplanes and seaplanes and 747s and wondered why he bothered. Maybe it would be easier to make a living as an artist. On the Left Bank. Yeah, he could be the aging American *artiste*, drinking anisette in cafés, living in a five-story walkup, selling an occasional painting to buy more supplies. The suffering eccentric. How sickening. It was almost as sickening as the general belief that private eyes were alcoholics.

Maybe the majority of them were. Who could blame them.

He dropped his Styrofoam cup in the garbage on the way out, and wished he and Quin were in Caracas.

10   The Past

1.

ALTHOUGH IT HAD been three years since McCleary had resigned from Metro-Dade, every time he stepped into the station it was as if he'd never left. The tang of the air remained the same—smoke and stale coffee mingled with the frail scent of perfume; the walls were still gray, the carpets plum-colored; and the computers still clacked and hummed like energetic tap dancers.

As he exited the elevator on the fourth floor, he almost expected to see the ghost of his old self, chief of homicide, a burned-out case, passing him in the hall. Instead, he spotted Wayne O'Donald, the department shrink, moving down the hall away from him. McCleary sneaked up behind him and tapped him on the shoulder.

O'Donald glanced around and grinned. "Mike, good to see you. You shaved off the beard. I like it. You look less eccentric or something."

McCleary chuckled. If anyone looked eccentric, it was O'Donald. Behind thick glasses, his small black eyes shone like marbles in a face so white it probably hadn't seen sunlight in a decade. He was short and growing a bit plump at the middle. His mouth possessed a unique language of twitches and jerks, probably the result of his fifteen years or more picking apart the psyches of cops and criminals.

He wagged the file he had in his hand. "Benson handed me this last night. On Joyce Young. He wants me to try to put together a profile on the sicko who ripped her apart. I get the feeling sometimes that Benson thinks I enjoy my job."

"You don't?"

He rocked forward onto the balls of his feet. "Listen, Mac. *My* shrink thinks I'll be in analysis another ten years if I don't get outa this line of work. But *his* shrink told *me* not to pay any attention to anything he said. You figure it out."

"Well, I've got some additional information for you. It looks like Joyce's killer has gotten a number of other people in Florida, Georgia, and Alabama. He seems to choose his victims according to their astrological signs."

"Another zodiac killer? Doesn't he know that's already been done?"

As though murder had to have an advertising gimmick, a hook like a newspaper story, McCleary thought. "As nearly as we can figure, he's worked his way from Capricorn to Taurus—January to May. Joyce was a Taurus. He also leaves a sweet at the scene of his kills."

"The powdered sugar they found at Joyce's—that kind of sweet?" His eyes sparkled with interest.

"Or a sugar cube or a globule of maple syrup or a bit of fudge. It varies."

O'Donald snapped his fingers. "I knew it. I knew that was significant. What else?"

"His little clues, his *teasers*, and then his trophies —tongues, the tip of a finger, a toe. But he only seems to take them from women, and only when no sex has been involved."

"Well." O'Donald passed a hand over his thinning dark hair and shook his head. "That's practically a textbook case you've just described, Mike."

"For what?"

"An obsessive-compulsive person."

Speak English, Wayne. "Which is . . . ?"

He started down the hall and McCleary fell into step beside him. "There are two distinct but closely related symptoms in this particular neurosis. The obsessive symptom is an intrusion of particulary intense thoughts or desires. The person doesn't understand why he has these thoughts, but it's difficult for him to *not* dwell on them. An example would be a person who's always thinking about Christ. Or about breasts. Or about blood. Or about murder.

"A compulsive symptom is an uncontrollable urge to act in certain patterns. Take someone who washes his hands two dozen times a day, for instance. He doesn't know *why* he does it, but feels uncomfortable if he *doesn't* do it. Your killer leaving sweets and teasers at the scenes of these murders would be an example of that. Or taking his trophies." They stepped into the staff kitchen. "What bothers me, though, is why the pattern isn't consistent."

McCleary smiled. "That's the problem with labels."

"Sometimes." O'Donald leaned against the counter, the file tucked under his arm. "But maybe your killer is bright enough to make it *look* like he might be a particular type of personality." He paused and regarded McCleary with his black marble eyes. A smile twitched at the corners of his mouth. "Got any gut feelings?"

"Yes."

"And?"

McCleary hesitated. O'Donald, unlike Benson, believed in hunches. But even so, McCleary wasn't sure how to explain what he'd experienced last night at the fitness center before he'd passed out, and early this morning in his den. For the hours he'd been going through the other cases, piecing together clues, he'd felt a sharp awareness of the killer. It was almost as if he could follow the man's scent like a dog or, with concentration, slip under the guy's skin, slide into his bones, wiggle down inside him. Then Quin had come in, distracting him.

"I can't explain it exactly. It's the sort of thing you feel when someone you care about is in trouble. No. That's not quite right. It's . . . well, just a sense of him, Wayne. That's the only way I can describe it."

O'Donald poured them each a cup of coffee and they sat down. "The feeling you're talking about happens a lot in combat and in police work and in any profession where the sharpness of your instincts can spell the difference between life and death. Part of what happens in a hunch or a gut feeling is a result of the brain combining facts in new ways. You've been in the investigative field for—what? Fifteen years?"

"More or less."

"And most of it's been in homicide, Mike. By now, when you read an investigative report, you probably know instinctively what's right or wrong about the report. If you're in a dangerous situation, you get a hunch that someone's behind you because your brain has learned to read the ripples in the air around you. Or the smell of the air. Or shadows on a pavement."

"That's a fine theory, Wayne, but it doesn't explain why someone like Benson never has a hunch. He's been in this game just as long."

"He isn't open to it. You are. You believe in your instincts. If you didn't, I guarantee you they'd disappear this fast." He snapped his fingers. "Our experiences tend to support our belief systems."

"I hope you're wrong about that, Doc," said Benson, standing in the doorway with his arms crossed. His face held an unhealthy pallor. He looked beat. "Because honest, I don't believe in murders. But I keep attracting them." He looked over at McCleary. "I just got a call on a homicide in west Dade. A woman. Stabbed. At home. In bed. You want to ride out with me, Mac?"

McCleary was already rising. "Sure thing." He rapped his knuckles once on the table in front of O'Donald. "Thanks, Wayne."

"Don't mention it. And hey, Tim, the key word is sweet."

"What?"

"I'll explain," McCleary said.

Lois Dwight's apartment complex lay about five miles west of the Miami airport. As McCleary and Benson drove up, two police cars were already in front, blue lights dancing. A dozen or more people were gathered around, watching, waiting, drawn to the smell of death like hyenas. A sergeant stood guard at the entrance and motioned them into the building.

Heads poked out of doorways as they hurried through the bottom hallway toward the apartment at the end. They followed the sergeant into Lois Dwight's living room, where the forensics people were busy dusting for prints.

"Who found her?" Benson asked.

"A neighbor. She was so freaked out, one of the officers took her back to her apartment."

They stopped in the bedroom doorway. The air held the resolute odor of death, an acrid smell of feces and urine and blood. Sunlight poured through the window over the bed, where the blind had been raised, and fell across the woman's forehead and shoulders. Her skin looked like marble.

Her eyes were wide open, vacuous, fixed on the wall to her left. Blood had crusted at her neck, in the hollow of her throat, and seeped into the white of her pillow. McCleary approached the bed, where the sheet covered her only to the hips. For a moment, it seemed that her eyes pursued him. He touched her eyelids and closed them gently. His gaze latched on to her neck. *Stabbed through the carotid artery.*

His hunch spot blazed. He rubbed it; his head began to throb. He wanted to look away but couldn't. It was almost as if someone were holding his head and forcing him to look. "A bite on her shoulder." He motioned to Benson, who leaned closer for a look. "You think forensics can get an impression?"

"I don't know. I'll ask."

McCleary pulled the sheet back, carefully, looking for . . . what? Evidence of mutilation? Of a struggle? There was no sign of either. The acescent taste in his mouth made his lips pucker, as if he'd been sucking on dry ice.

A sparkle of light in her navel caught McCleary's eye. Frowning, he moved closer, leaning over her. He bent the woman's leg. The sheet fell away. He saw a spicule of the same substance on the inside of her thigh. He brought his fingertip to his tongue, wetting it, and touched it to the stuff. Sticky. *Like syrup*.

"What is it?" Benson asked.

He tasted it, and raised his eyes. "Honey."

Three hours later, McCleary and Benson sat in a coffee shop across the street from the station. Mc-Cleary's tuna fish sandwich on rye tasted like dust in his mouth. His head throbbed; he was bone tired. And he wished Benson would stop shaking his head and murmuring, "I don't like it, Mac. Too many things could go wrong."

"Not if we plan it right. I'm supposed to meet Travis at his club tomorrow night. Just to take a look at the place. For my 'client.' My 'client,' although she doesn't know it yet, is going to be Quin. He's got our answering service number. Okay, so there are probably ways he could check on who the hell I am and so on, but I think it's worth the risk."

"We may not be able to establish a connection between Travis and this Lois Dwight woman. She was a schoolteacher. She—"

"Establishing the kind of connection you're talking about is irrelevant. A connection's already been established between Joyce's death and this woman's, Tim. Powdered sugar and honey."

"But no mutilations, no trophies, no teaser scrawled on the wall."

"Which fits these other cases we dug out of Summer's files. *All* of the elements aren't always present, except for the sweets. But some of them are. I just want a stab at getting to know Travis' operation from the inside out. Some of our answers lie there."

Benson shrugged and peered miserably into his coffee cup. "I certainly can't stop you, Mac." He raised his eyes. "So how can I help?"

Quin sat glumly at her desk, picking at the snack she'd prepared for herself: a bunch of dry-roasted, unsalted peanuts, slices of an apple, sections of an orange. *Like I'm someone's pet rabbit*, she thought.

She and McCleary had agreed to meet back here, at the office, at four-thirty. It was now five-thirty. She was starved, tired, and aggravated that he was an hour late and hadn't bothered calling. For a while she'd been worried that something had happened to him. Her imagination, naturally, had clutched at the idea and blown it up like a balloon. She'd visualized Gene Travis locking McCleary into the sauna at the health club and the cops finding him hours later, sizzled like overdone pork chops. Then she'd thought about six-car pileups on the interstate, a shot through the heart, muggers, thieves—the list had been practically endless.

Now she was angry. Fuming. She was always on time for things. For that matter, she was usually early. He could have at least called.

She stared at the oil painting on the wall. One of McCleary's. One of the few abstracts he'd ever done, a violent weird thing that might've been the inside of a tornado, except that it was laced with vibrant, striking colors that seemed to undulate, ripple, as if the hues possessed sounds.

In fact, in the silence within her office, within this old house they had refurbished with such care, she could almost hear those sounds. Heartbeats. Gunshots. Traffic. Screams.

Jesus. How morbid.

The phone rang, as if on cue. Most everyone had left the office, so she let it peal five times before picking it up. "Hello."

"Quin, it's Mac."

"It's five-thirty."

"I know. I'm sorry. I was tied up in traffic. Listen, we're going to have to change our plans somewhat.

We're meeting with Travis tomorrow night," he began, then hurried on, and explained. Her anger fell away from her. As soon as he'd finished his story about Travis and the Lois Dwight murder, she told him what she'd learned from the ex-Mrs. Travis.

"Then we're on the right track. Great. I should be home by eight, and we don't have to meet Travis until tomorrow, so tonight we'll create a history for you as my client."

"Suppose in the meantime he's checked you out and discovered you're not who you say you are?"

"If he finds anything on a Michael J. West, then good for him."

It sounded like a movie star's name. "Where're you now?"

"On my way to Lauderdale."

Where Callahan the mysterious lives. She needed this. "Oh."

"I'll be home by eight, eight-thirty."

"Okay."

He hung up. She sat there, fingers resting lightly on the receiver, an image of Sylvia Callahan taking shape in her head. *Slinky. A dynamo.* She popped peanuts in her mouth. *Blond or brunette? Probably a blond.* She munched angrily on a slice of apple. *If she's married, McCleary would've said so. Okay, not married. Fantastic figure.* She bit into a section of orange. *He wouldn't have told me about her if I hadn't asked.* More peanuts vanished into her mouth.

"Quin?"

The voice jerked her head up. Zivia laughed. "Sorry, I didn't mean to startle you. Your hair, something's different. I like it. Really."

"Thanks."

Zivia sank into a chair, eased off her shoes with a sigh, and brought her legs up, crossing them at the ankles on the corner of Quin's desk. "What're you doing here? I came by to pick up some papers and saw your car in the lot."

"I *was* waiting for McCleary." But she didn't want to talk about that. "Hey, what do you think of Ross?"

Zivia smiled and leaned back in the chair, lacing her hands together behind her head. "He knows all about talking to cactuses."

Quin laughed. "Oh, c'mon."

"Really. He spent some time in New Mexico, studying the Hopi culture when he was an undergraduate student. That included peyote buttons and finding desert spirits. Anyway, I think it's safe to say he's the most interesting man I've met in Florida in two years."

"You've only been here two years."

"Yeah, well." She laughed. "Did you know his firm is involved in the Art Deco restoration project on Miami Beach? And he's personally designing a community in northern Florida? A beach community? He showed me the plans. I mean, Quin, this guy knows what he's doing when it comes to design. So he asks me out to dinner for Saturday night before your party, right? And I hem and haw because I'm thinking about how he's got these long hands just like my first husband did."

Quin decided she must've missed something. "Long hands? There's something wrong with long hands?"

"It's been my experience that men with long hands are usually possessive."

Quin groaned. "That's ridiculous."

"Yeah." Zivia giggled. "So I said sure I'd go to dinner with him."

This brief mention of food triggered a splanchnic reaction in Quin. "Speaking of dinner, if you haven't eaten, how about going out for a bite? McCleary won't be home until later, and I don't feel like cooking for myself. I'm a lousy cook, actually."

And at the moment, I don't want to be alone.

"Sounds great." Zivia leaped up. "Where's Mac, anyway?"

"With a woman named Sylvia," Quin replied, and slung her purse over her shoulder, picked up her brief-case, and headed for the door.

3.

As McCleary turned onto A-1-A in Fort Lauderdale and headed north, he thought back to the last time he'd seen Sylvia Callahan, four years ago, about eight months after her sister's killer had been apprehended.

It was sunrise on a Sunday morning, he remembered. He hadn't been able to sleep and had driven up to a place on the New River for breakfast and to snap a few pictures he could later use for some of his paintings. He was standing on the balcony, adjusting the light meter on his camera, and caught a blur of movement to his left. When he glanced up, there was Callahan, dressed in a long pearl-colored gown, a breeze combing her blond hair. He remembered the peculiar light, how it seemed to turn her hair a blond that was nearly white, and the way it spilled from her nose to her lovely mouth.

"I always dress this way for breakfast," she said without preface, holding the sides of her gown out from her body like a petticoat.

He laughed and looked down at his shorts and T-shirt and sandals. "Me too."

"You alone?"

He nodded. "You?"

"Absolutely solo."

"In that case," he said, taking her arm, "I think we should order some champagne."

They sat at a table under the awning, Callahan in her pearl gown, McCleary in shorts, and sipped champagne with their breakfast, picking up where they'd left off eight months before, as if there had been no lapse of time. They got pleasantly buzzed and went back to her mansion on Harborage Isle and spent the next three days in bed.

They had parted then as they had always parted, without promises, plans, with no regard for the future. It had not been his choice but hers. Even at the height of their affair, it had been like that. They would come together for a few hours, a weekend, a night, locked in a breathless passion, and then they would retreat to their separate worlds. Worlds, she used to say, that were too vitally different for permanence. But her sister's murder had provided a bridge between those very different worlds, and each of them had known, McCleary thought, that when the killer was apprehended, the affair would end. And it had. What had not ended was his feeling that when he walked back into her life after four years, it would be as if he'd never left. His pulse would quicken into somersaults, and the skein of his unresolved emotions toward her, their affair, toward that era of his life, would unravel as surely as Indian madras. That worried him. He was married. Happily married.

But he needed something only Callahan could provide.

He turned west on Harbor Beach Parkway, took a right on Lake Drive, and wound through a paradise of waterways, striated with late afternoon shadows. He passed gracious homes, yards with pastiches of bright flowers, hedges trimmed with almost geometric precision, and boats as large as houses. A little Venice, he thought, then pulled to a stop outside the black iron gate that separated Harborage Isle from the rest of the world. Beyond it lay eight homes.

There was a phone on the brick wall to the right of the gate. He picked it up, consulted the list of names on the billboard, found Callahan's. Next to it was a three-digit number. He dialed it. Suppose she wasn't home? Suppose she was out of the country? He should've called first, set up an appointment. But they had never done things that way, and why start now? His finger tapped the edge of the phone as it rang.

On the third ring, a woman answered. "Callahan residence."

"This is Mike McCleary. I'm at the gate."

"Is Sylvia expecting you?"

"Yes."

"Please don't hang up until the gate opens."

A moment later the gate creaked and swung inward. McCleary hopped back into Lady and drove inside.

He took a right at the end of the road and pulled up in front of another gate. A moment later it also swung open, admitting him. He drove inside a courtyard shaded by the umbrageous folds of a red oak. Acorns littered the ground. The house, with its twin white pillars, was directly in front of him. To his right lay an open area with a swimming pool, and beyond it, the shimmering blue of the New River.

As McCleary got out of the car, he noticed that even the air here smelled different. Sweeter, somehow, as if it had been perfumed. The breeze coming in from the river was cool, pleasant. The sky overhead seemed as lovely as a promise.

An older woman dressed entirely in white approached him. "Hi, Mr. McCleary. I'm Nancy, Sylvia's secretary. She'll be up in a minute. She's down on the boat with the captain. Sit out by the pool if you like. How about some coffee?"

"Thanks. I'd love some."

She walked off toward the house, and McCleary strolled over to the kidney-shaped pool. The yard was thick with seagrape trees, hibiscus, jacaranda, aralias, orchids. And it seemed that each held a forbidden memory, memories that haunted, that shadowed the back of his mind like portents of things that had not yet happened. Time melded here. Past, present, and future oozed together like hot wax, creating a kind of magic.

He heard footsteps on the wooden stairs that descended sharply toward the river to his left, and then Sylvia's blond head appeared, pushing up into a puddle of waning sunlight like something leviathan. Her eyes were lowered. She wore loose-fitting lapis-colored slacks. Her blouse was a much darker blue and set off the color of her hair. She raised her eyes and stopped dead. Her mouth opened. It was obvious no one had told her *who* her visitor was, and she simply stared, frozen in the February sunlight, her hand on the wooden railing, incredulity etched into her features.

"I know, Callahan. You thought I'd gone the way of the dodo bird, right?" McCleary said.

She laughed. It was a full, rich sound, like music, and floated through the cool air, spiriting away time. "Something like that." Then she trotted up the steps, a razor-thin woman several inches shorter than Quin, a Candice Bergen doppelgänger, and hugged him hard.

His arms jerked up around her, hugging her back. Her perfume swam around him and the fabric of her blouse was cool against his hands. It was as if he'd never left.

11 Research

THE HOUSE WAS completely dark.

There were no cars in the driveway.

From his vantage point at the edge of the park across the street from the McClearys' house, he had seen no one arrive or leave. It was time. His body had given the signal: a release of adrenaline. Not a lot, not like during a kill, but enough to tease him, prod him, make him dizzy.

He wore dark clothes, and as he moved away from the shelter of the trees, the early night took him into itself like a lover. It tantalized him with rich, limpid scents: pine, earth, the infrangible aroma of winter, Florida style. His senses swelled and burst like pods as he darted across the road into the McClearys' yard. To understand your opponent—and McCleary was definitely that if he was consulting Summer—risk was necessary.

He sprinted around the side of the house to the back. A porch light sent shoots of pale illumination across the patio to the pool. The susurrous song of a breeze through the pines beyond the pool stirred a pang of longing inside him for . . . what? He didn't know. He was afraid to think about it too deeply, afraid he might stumble on some dark unknown within himself. But after all these years, these kills, what could possibly be so dark and so unknown?

When he was on the porch, he sidled its length, testing the screens that covered the four windows facing the backyard. With a screwdriver, he coaxed the screen of the last window off, then slipped the flat edge of the tool

103

into the crack at the top. He felt the latch give, but when he tried to push it up, the damn thing wouldn't budge. He inched the screwdriver along until he felt the obstruction. He guessed it was a steel pin and that all the windows and doors were equipped with them. He brought out a second tool, a long slender pick with a hook at the end. It took him a few minutes to work the steel pin out of its hole, but the window then gave easily and he climbed inside, onto a butcher block table.

A light shone over the stove. *Like at Joyce's.* He slid off the table and stood absolutely still, listening to the house.

It speaks, this house.

If he listened very closely, he would hear the ghost sounds of the McClearys' lives. But there wasn't time. He moved toward the doorway in his bare feet, stopped when two cats peered at him from the shadows in the living room. One of them, a calico, hissed, scampered across the room, and dived under the couch.

As he walked down the hall, he switched on his flashlight. He shone it on the walls, noting the paintings that hung there, and their signatures. An aesthetic man, this McCleary. Good. That made him a worthy opponent. He stopped in a den. The beam of his flashlight darted across the folders lined up neatly on the floor, leaped onto the desk, fell to the couch, climbed the wall to more paintings. He crouched in front of the files and perused them.

Familiar names leaped out at him: *Evelyn Parker, Atlanta . . . Arthur Janos, Birmingham . . . Stephanie Ansel, Melbourne . . .*

His tongue turned dry and thick, as if he'd just shoved a handful of oatmeal in his mouth. For the first time in eight years, since he'd killed the woman in Dallas, a white panic seized him, squeezed at his heart, rendered him motionless.

This happened because of Summer because of his goddamned computers because . . . His gut cramped. Sweat sprang across his back. He shivered. His vision blurred as his eyes swept from page to page, folder to folder, sealing his doom. *He's onto me. He is. He can smell me. He can almost visualize me.* He could imagine McCleary sitting in here, poring over these files like a medieval alchemist scrutinizing an esoteric text, fitting together clues as if they were formulas.

You've been myopic, his body whispered, and he felt a quick, terrible stab of pain through his chest. He doubled over, his eyes tearing with pain, fear. An atavistic superstition coursed through him. *If I have something of his, I will be connected to him.* Yes. He would be like a good Catholic with icons. But instead of crucifixes and pictures of bleeding hearts, he would have something of McCleary's. Something personal. Something that would give him power over the man. *A painting.*

Excited now, he fixed the files, straightening the papers, resisting the urge to linger over them, read them in detail. He looked again at the paintings in the den, but none suited him. He moved into the hall. As the flashlight's beam skimmed the paintings here, his eye was drawn to one in particular—the white naked back of a woman lying on her side in a field of periwinkles, her hair a bourbon river behind her.

That one.

He would get it on his way out, he thought, and quickly ascended the stairs for a look around.

He was drawn as if by a magnet to the door at the end of the hall. He hurried toward it. A black cat curled at the foot of the bed lifted its head as he entered, yawned insouciantly, and curled up again. The nightstand to the right of the bed and the floor just beneath it were littered with magazines and books. The left nightstand and floor were spotless. Who was the slob, wife or husband?

He opened the left nightstand drawer. Inside, a Magnum and a pair of toenail clippers rested on top of several letters. *McCleary is the neat freak.* Good. He would've been disappointed if it had been otherwise. He examined the other items: a blank notepad and pen, additional ammo, an address book. He shut the drawer and examined the books on the shelf. They ranged from novels by Arthur Conan Doyle and Dean R. Koontz to a book on drawing and one of true crime stories.

He slid open the closet door to the right of the bathroom and wrinkled his nose at the mess: shoes turned every which way, some lacking mates, slacks hanging with blouses, skirts draped carelessly over hangers, the shelf piled high with junk. But the other side of the closet bore McCleary's ineffable mark of organization. It even smelled organized. Shirts hung together, slacks were arranged by colors from dark to light, the things on the shelf were stacked with an almost painful neatness. He ran his fingers through the clothes, waiting for a signal from his body on what he should take. But he felt nothing.

He moved over to the bureaus. He opened the top drawer of McCleary's and removed one of the neatly folded T-shirts. His body signaled that this was what he should take. He tucked the shirt under his arm and touched his hand to the pouch at his belt, where the Parfait mint candies were. He wanted to leave his calling card, but when he opened the pouch and dipped his fingers inside, he experienced a sharp discomfort in his bowels.

"Okay," he said softly. "Okay. Not this time."

He returned to the downstairs for the painting. He removed it from the wall, examining it more closely. It was beautifully rendered, with a kind of Wyeth simplicity about it, he decided. He could almost feel the frame heating up in his hands, connecting him to McCleary. The painting was a manifestation of the man's soul, better than a lock of his hair or a piece of his clothing. Yes, this was the right choice.

He tucked it under his arm and went into the kitchen. He replaced the pin in the window, unfastened the chain on the back door, unlocked and opened it, and stepped out onto the stoop. He closed the door behind him and scampered into the yard. Just as he was skulking around the side of the house, a car pulled into the driveway.

Hc pushed back into the hibiscus hedge, his heart hammering.

He heard the garage door opening and the car driving into the garage.

Move, buddy boy, move.

But his legs felt like they had lead weights attached to them. A twig poked him in the back. A rush of adrenaline coursed through his veins, brought a wave of sweat to his skin. The cool night air made him shiver.

He heard the garage door closing.

Move, you fool. Move.

A light came on.

Then another light. And another. A silhouette passed in front of the shaded window just above him. *The wife.* He pushed himself farther back into the hedge. A hibiscus bloom tickled his nose. His eyes fastened on the woman's shadow. *It's not you I want, it's your husband.*

Funny, he hadn't thought of McCleary in exactly those terms before. But yes, if he fit the criteria, maybe McCleary would be the first of his male victims from whom he would take a trophy.

Now *that* was an intriguing thought.

12 Callahan & Quin

As McCleary told Callahan the story, the light faded. Twilit shadows melted across the tile around the swimming pool and filled the space between them. A vespertine stillness claimed the air. Callahan didn't interrupt. Now and then she nodded, shifted in her chair, crossed or uncrossed her legs.

It got dark. Stars poked through the black skin of the sky. A lamppost at the far end of the pool blinked on. The phone at the poolside bar rang several times, but someone inside the house evidently took the calls. When he was finished, Callahan lit a cigarette, dropped her head back over the edge of the chair, and blew smoke into the air.

"Well?" he said finally.

"Well," she echoed, and lifted her head again. Light from the lamppost fletched her hair, dissolved onto her forehead, her nose, her lovely mouth. "First of all, if you'd like to live long enough to collect Social Security, Mike, then if I were you I'd drop this case. Gene Travis is not a man to mess with." She smiled and leaned toward him, arms parallel to the round, white metal table that separated them. She was close enough so that despite the exiguous light, he could see flecks of different shades of blue in her eyes. "But I don't suppose that's what you want to hear, is it?"

"Not particularly."

She crossed her legs at the knees; her right foot moved slowly back and forth, back and forth. She smiled. "Yeah, I figured as much."

"Tell me what you know about Travis."

Callahan sat back, combing her long fingers through her hair. She stabbed out her cigarette. "Okay, Gene Travis. When I still owned my club, we were competitors, even though I catered primarily to a much younger crowd. It was tough finding good help, but it seemed like when I did, I lost them after a couple of months to Gene, who pays twice the minimum wage. Anyway, it was through one of these ex-employees that I found out about the video service Gene runs. You know about that?"

He nodded. Quin had told him about it over the phone. "For his special clients, right?"

"Yeah. Anyhow, according to this gal, he'll make any type of video, except for kiddie porn, if the price is right."

"Can you be more specific?"

"She says he'll even make snuff films, Mike."

Wonderful, McCleary thought. Murder on camera. No special effects. No fake blood. Only the real thing. "Had you ever heard that from anyone else?"

She shook her head. "But then, I wouldn't have, since I kept out of his way for the most part. Oh, occasionally he'd ask if I could recommend someone who might be interested in doing porn, but I just told him no."

"So it's hearsay."

"Yes. But not improbable, if you know anything about Gene. There's apparently some elaborate code system he uses so he's sure his clients are legit."

"Joyce Young was terrified of Travis. Or at least that's what her ex-husband claims."

"Smart lady."

"Do you know if he's got a fetish for sweets?"

"Not that I've heard about, but nothing about Gene would surprise me."

"What's his opinion of you?" McCleary asked.

She lit another cigarette. The smell of smoke mingled with the scent of salt from the river. The breeze had grown cooler. She hugged her arms against her. "You want me to vouch for you as Mike the business broker, is that it?" She smiled thinly when McCleary nodded. "I think you're nuts getting into this, but okay, I'll vouch for you. Gene knows I own a hotel in the Caicos. I'll tell him you're the one who arranged the deal."

"You're a peach."

She rolled her eyes. "I don't feel like a peach. I feel like I should be ranting and raving at you. I feel like I should get on the phone and call this wife of yours and let her know what I think of this whole deal." She paused. "When're you supposed to meet with him?"

"Tomorrow night."

"With your fictitious client?"

"I was thinking it should maybe just be Travis and me initially."

She gave a nod of agreement. "It's too early to introduce your client. If you're going to play this game, play it right. Lure him with the promise of a big deal. Ask him what price he would like for the place and then tell him you'll have to speak to your client and get back to him. Where're you supposed to meet him? At the club?"

"Yes. At eleven. Tomorrow night."

"Eleven. Okay. Let's see. Tell him you've asked a friend to join you who knows something about the business. Then I'll arrive around eleven-fifteen or eleven-thirty. Who'd you have in mind to play your client?"

"My wife."

"Good God, Mike, don't get her involved."

About the only thing McCleary had said about Quin was that they'd gotten married almost three and a half years ago. It had seemed inappropriate somehow to discuss his wife with Callahan. But now he smiled and said, "Quin and I work together, Callahan. She's been a private eye for more than ten years."

This seemed to surprise her. "Doesn't that get difficult? Working together?"

"Sometimes. But it has its advantages, too."

"Well, anyway, she should play her client routine

after Gene's had a little time to think about things. But a nice twist to this would be if she arrived at the club with another man and sat at the bar or something. That way she can later tell him that she's already seen the club, and name the night. It's the sort of thing Gene would appreciate. Also, if things seemed to be going particularly well, you could always bring her over to the table."

They talked awhile longer about how McCleary could make his role as Mike West the business broker more credible. He absorbed the information like a sponge, prodding her, coaxing out her memories of Travis, seeking the essential thread of the man's personality.

By the time he got up to leave, it was past eight. They walked out into the courtyard, where the moon struggled through a magma of clouds. Callahan's perfume wafted around him in the cool air, stirring old memories, inchoate yearnings. The patina of the past embraced him. He remembered standing beneath this very oak four years ago, on a night like this, holding her. He remembered the feel of her against him, the sharp protrusion of her bones, the sweet scent of her hair, how her mouth had tasted. He remembered loving her. The smallest details stood out in stark relief in his mind, and made him feel as if he were betraying Quin. He pushed them aside and tried to concentrate on what Callahan was saying.

". . . a couple of last-minute tips." She leaned against the side of the car, her hands lost in the pockets of her slacks. Light from the lamppost created an amber nimbus around her head. She gazed at the ground. "Don't drink tomorrow night when you're with him. Gene's practically a teetotaler. If you're going to be armed, make sure it's a small weapon, preferably one that can be strapped to your ankle. He's got bouncers all over that club, and if you get down to any serious discussions and leave the main area, you'll be frisked. It's okay if his lackeys find a weapon as long as it doesn't look like a *police* weapon. Dress casually. And do *not* arrive with a bug on you. He's got some pretty sophisticated debugging devices that he sometimes uses. My vouching for you is going to relieve most of the suspicion, but he may still want to check you out."

"Anything else?"

She thought a moment. "Yeah. When I walk in, Gene's going to naturally assume that we're lovers. Let him. It might strengthen your position."

"Why?"

She chuckled, brushed strands of hair from her cheeks. "Gene and everyone else in his clique have always thought of me as a frigid bitch—cunning, smart, but frigid, maybe even queer. I definitely fed the image, nurtured it, because it made the business easier to manage and kept the hyenas away. The idea that you might have scored and he didn't is going to make him see you differently." She raised her eyes then. "I realize it might be difficult to do with your wife there, Mike, but I really think it would add veracity to your cover."

"Right, I understand."

He just hoped Quin would.

When he walked into the house thirty-eight minutes later, Quin was sitting in the family room with a plate of food in front of her. Two of the three cats were curled on either side of her on the couch. The TV was on, but without sound. A paperback book lay face down on the coffee table in front of her, and beside it rested a 9mm Walther.

"I went out to dinner with Zivia, and apparently while I was gone we had a visitor," she said without preface. "He took one of your paintings. I think he got in through one of the kitchen windows, then left by the back door." She ran her hands along her slacks, a slow, repetitive motion. "I think I would like to move. Preferably to someplace like Kansas. Or Iowa. I think that in lieu of that, I would like to have the entire house outfitted with alarms. Or maybe we could build an electric fence around it." She stood. "C'mere, I'll show you."

He followed her into the hall. The lacuna on the wall between two of his paintings seemed to jape him.

112

"Is anything else missing?"

"I don't think so."

Her face had lost color. "It was him, Mac." She whispered this, as if she were afraid the man might still be in the house.

"Maybe."

They went into the den. The moment McCleary stepped through the door, the skin between his eyes tightened, then burned. *He was in here, too. He went through the files. He knows I'm onto him.*

He crouched in front of the files, lined up neatly on his den floor. He picked them up, one by one, and set the stack inside his closet. His head throbbed painfully as he looked around. *His eyes touched everything in here.*

"We're going to meet with Travis tomorrow night. I'll ask Joe Bean to help us out."

"Bean? What's Bean got to do with anything?" *And what happened with Callahan the mysterious?* her eyes inquired.

McCleary explained his plan over warmed-up leftovers as he and Quin sat at the kitchen table. Like Callahan, she was a good listener. She didn't interrupt. But she looked at him, her chin cupped in the palm of her hands, as if he'd lost his mind. When he was finished, he expected her to comment on the part about Callahan; she didn't. He expected her to say she would like to drop the case; she didn't. Instead, she said, "If Gene Travis is the killer, Mac, if he's the guy who came in here tonight, then he's going to know who you are. Who I am."

"How? There aren't any photographs of us around. And that painting he took didn't show your face, Quin. Besides, you could wear glasses. Change your appearance."

"Yeah, I could." Her hands dropped away from her chin, and she rested her arms along the edge of the table. The overhead light gleamed against the gold of her wedding band. "But if Travis isn't our man, then we're going to a hell of a lot of trouble."

"And if he *is* the guy, Quin, then this is a good place to start."

She dropped her head forward and massaged the back of her neck. After a long few moments, she said, "I'll go call Bean."

Steam drifted around McCleary's face. The heat from the water in the tub seeped into his bones. Behind his closed eyes spread a gloam of melting images, but none that he could distinguish clearly.

After a while, he stopped trying to see anything and his mind floated out into a pleasurable darkness. He came to with Quin sitting at the side of the tub in just her robe, holding out a clean, fluffy magenta towel. "It's almost nine-thirty."

Still groggy, McCleary rubbed his face with the towel, pulled the plug, and stood. The now-cold water burped as it swirled down the drain. "What'd Bean say?"

She rolled forward onto her knees and laughed. "I already told you."

"You did?"

"You were half asleep. He said no problem. He'd be by for me tomorrow night at eleven. I need your opinion on what sort of clothes your fictitious client would wear. Come take a look."

They went into the bedroom. Two outfits were laid out on the bed—a lavender sweater with dark, tailored slacks, and a black skirt with a white sweater and a black jacket. "Which one is the sort of thing your client would wear?" she asked, filliping her thumbnail against her front teeth.

"Black. Definitely black."

She looked over at him, her expression oddly coy, as though they had just met and were standing in a crowded, smoky bar somewhere, each of them trying to decide if things should go farther. And if so, just how far. Her robe had slipped off her shoulder, and McCleary kissed its curve and untied the sash at her waist as her fingers worked at his towel.

114

He combed his fingers through her hair, noticing that she'd done something different to it. He complimented her on it. "Handiwork of the ex-Mrs. Travis," she said, turning away to fold back the covers on the bed.

Her robe had fallen open. She had nothing on underneath, and he stole glimpses of a breast, a hip, the long line of her leg. Familiar sights, and yet always her body seemed infinitely mysterious to him, a tawny, secretive continent that yielded new wonders every time they came together.

It had been the same with Callahan, who had improvised endlessly.

"Be right back," he said, and went downstairs to the kitchen. When he returned, Quin was stretched out in the middle of the bed, head propped up in her hand, the sheet covering her to the hip.

She saw the jar of honey in his hand.

She frowned. "You're hungry?" She asked even though he knew she knew the honey had nothing at all to do with hunger. The apprehension in her voice was the same he'd heard the morning she'd come into his den and found him with his icons.

"Starved," he replied, sitting at the edge of the bed as he unscrewed the top of the jar. Once with Callahan, there had been honey. . . . But he told himself this had nothing to do with Callahan. This was what the killer had done with Lois Dwight.

He dipped his finger inside the jar. *Is this how you did it, you bastard?*

"Me, too," Quin said, sticking her finger in the jar, then licking the honey off as her eyes held his, eyes that whispered, *I know what you're doing and forget it.*

But he touched his sticky finger to her lower lip, smoothing it out. Her tongue flicked at it. He kissed her, a long, slow kiss. She rolled onto her back, away from him.

"No," she said.

"Please," he said.

Her cheeks reddened with agitation. "It's like inviting this guy into our bedroom, McCleary."

He said nothing. He stared at the jar, noting the way the honey absorbed the light from the lamp. He poured some into the top and set the jar on the nightstand. He held the top out, proffering it. "The nectar of the gods. One taste and you'll live forever."

"You're impossible," she replied, but dabbed at it with her fingertip and sucked it off.

He did the same.

Quin started to laugh. She dipped her finger into the top again, touched the honey to the end of his nose, kissed it off. He mimicked her. In moments, they were both laughing, dabbing honey on each other. It was no longer connected to the killer in her mind, but had become a game, erotic foreplay, safer ground for her. He proceeded slowly, carefully, gently, loving her as he always had, despite the stirring of something darker in himself.

The taste of the honey mixed with the taste of her skin and struck that darkness in him. His finger moved down across her chin, throat, up either arm, leaving trails of honey. He dampened his fingers again and this time let the honey drip off his fingertips as his hands moved several inches above her body, traveling in a straight line down her tummy, up the inside of either thigh. Her skin rippled seconds before a drop struck home. The orbs of honey glowed.

The skin between his eyes burned fiercely. *This is what the killer does. Like this.* His tongue followed the trail of honey, dawdling, savoring, tasting. In his mind, her body became a smorgasbord of different sweets: knees made of fudge, a mint thigh, a shoulder that tasted of powdered sugar, a breast as cool as a popsicle.

He does them with his mouth and his hands and then he kills them.

As he followed the sweet scintillas, her body tightened like a bow. She clutched the sheet. She purred as softly as a cat. The darkness opened inside him. He could feel it elongating, lengthening like a tunnel, then melting into something else, something outside him. He asked her what she felt, wanted her to describe it. She rasped, she wiggled, she murmured and the darkness widened. It tugged at him like gravity. He sank into it. An exquisite tension enveloped him. The weight of the darkness, its mass, turned him inside out like a sheet. The burning between his eyes had spread to his temples, the sides of his face, his shoulders. He was being consumed.

Now the hunger swelled inside him, huge and ugly, a ubiquitous hunger that controlled him, drove him, thrust him inside her. He barely heard Quin's muffled cry. He barely felt her shudder. His hunger had effaced everything but the need to feed. Then her nails dug into his back like white-hot daggers and his insides exploded and his mouth opened in a groan against the white curve of her shoulder. He felt the heat of her skin against his lips, his teeth, and he wanted to sink his teeth into her shoulder, wanted to

Something snapped inside him. He could actually hear it, a loud and frightening *pop*. McCleary rolled away from Quin and sat up so quickly he was dizzy. *The bite on Lois Dwight's shoulder.*

He understood now that the killer had bitten the Dwight woman's shoulder as he came. He had tasted her blood.

Behind him, the bed sighed as Quin got up. He glanced around. She picked up the jar of honey, the top, her hair falling around the sides of her face. She set the jar down hard on the nightstand, then yanked at the spread where honey had spilled. She balled the spread up in her arms. She threw open the door to the laundry chute and shoved the spread inside. Then she scooped her robe up from the floor and marched toward the bathroom. In the doorway, she turned, holding the robe against her as if stricken with a sudden modesty. Mascara had smudged beneath her eyes. When she spoke, her voice was utterly quiet, too quiet, as if it were an effort to form words.

"I don't think that kind of research is such a great idea." She hurried into the bathroom and slammed the door.

McCleary sat at the edge of the bed, staring at the door until he heard the pipes clatter in the walls as she switched on the shower. His knees felt stiff as he stood. He walked over to the door, opened it, pulled back the shower curtain. Steam billowed toward him. Quin glanced at him as her hands scrubbed the honey from her skin.

"Why?" he asked.

She blinked. She dropped the soap. Her hands fastened on to the faucet and she shut it off hard, so the pipes clattered again. "Because it was like . . . like being with a stranger, that's why. Because I . . . I kept asking you to stop and you didn't. Because . . . " The word seemed to catch in her throat. "Because it frightened me," she finished softly, then her face squashed up and she snapped the curtain back into place and turned on the faucet again and he knew she was crying. The drumming water pounded against the inside of his skull, and the pounding followed him as he weaved unsteadily, almost drunkenly, into the bedroom.

13 The Pink Slipper

1.

FOR MOST OF the next day, banalities vied for Quin's attention with all the aplomb of spoiled brats. There was, for instance, the broken sprinkler head outside Ruth Grimes' window that the gardener must've inadvertently broken when he'd mowed the lawn yesterday. Water spurted from the thing like blood from a punctured artery and splashed in through Ruth's open window, ruining two files that were on her desk. One of the computers went on the fritz. She spent an hour reviewing an insurance fraud case with Zivia. She fielded a call from an irate client who demanded to know why her bill was so high.

By early afternoon, she finally got around to making an appointment with Joyce Young's maid for tomorrow. She also called Suzanne Mellon, the woman who had brought a paternity suit against Gene Travis several years ago. She had a squeaky nasal voice that sounded as if she'd never had her adenoids removed. Or as if she'd done so much coke that the membrane between her nostrils had rotted away. She informed Quin that her name was Suzi with a Z-I, and that she wasn't interested in talking to no private eye, thank you very much. Quin offered to pay her for her time, and although she hemmed and hawed, she finally agreed to speak to Quin for $50. They set a time for tomorrow.

She fussed with her files and fretted over the honey business that had happened last night with McCleary.

She finally went outside and removed the welcome mat from the front step and slipped it under the couch in her office. In her mind, it meant that the bad luck precipitated by McCleary stepping on the mat would now be buried. It was, of course, the same sympathetic-magic stuff McCleary was doing with his honey and his weird little icons. It exacerbated her mordant mood and propelled her out of the office.

She stopped by Joyce Young's clothing store in the Grove, a trendy place where everything was overpriced. She spent ten minutes talking to the manager, a rather bovine, plodding woman who knew zip about Joyce's life, except that she signed the paychecks and did most of the buying herself. By four-thirty Quin was at home, soaking in the tub.

When all else failed, a hot bath usually did the trick. Today was no exception. The recrudescence of her annoyance about this Callahan woman seeped from her pores. The steam eased the racheting anguish of constricted muscles which stress sometimes inflicted on her neck. *Tonight will be a pain in the neck: illness as metaphor,* she thought, her toes breaking the surface of the water like tiny pink balloons. *Pop Psyche 101.*

Nothing like doing a job when your heart wasn't in it.

At eleven on the button that night, Joe Bean picked up Quin and they headed toward the Pink Slipper, where McCleary already was. Bean was one of those men whose name fit him like a glove. He was tall and lanky and thin as a string bean. He reminded her of the scarecrow in *The Wizard of Oz,* except that his face and hair were the color of bitter coffee. He'd joined the firm when McCleary had, after Quin had bought out her former partner.

As they got out of his black Datsun and walked toward the entrance of the club, music swam around them. Bean snapped his fingers to the rhythm and suddenly broke into his Fred Astaire routine. He ended with a pirouette, a clap, a slide onto one knee, and his arms flung out in front of him.

Quin laughed, grabbed hold of his hand, and pulled him up. "You'll get us arrested, Bean."

"Please. The name's Joe Piscopo." He flicked at invisible lint on the front of his navy blue slacks. "Consort of Ms. Anise Rochelle." He glanced at her. "You don't look at all like Quin, you know. You could fool your ma, take it from me."

She didn't feel much like herself either. A lugubrious pall covered her mind like gauze and chivvied at her. She kept thinking of how a part of McCleary seemed to be stuck in the dark mentality of the killer. It was almost as if the stolen painting, the incident with the honey, the icons, had established a nexus between them. It was ridiculous, a sort of medieval superstition at its worst, but she couldn't shake it.

At the door, Bean paid a cover charge, then asked the cashier for a receipt. "Business deduction," he murmured when the woman gave him a funny look.

"Sure." She laughed and handed him a receipt.

The inside of the Pink Slipper was comfortably large. The stage at the far end was empty at the moment, but everything seemed to radiate from it. An S-shaped bar was to Quin's right, and most of the stools were taken. The tables and chairs in the sunken area in the middle of the room were crowded. The long, elevated strip just beyond it, filled with tables interspersed with plants, looked like an outdoor café. Waitresses in skimpy outfits weaved around the tables, serving drinks. Oddly enough, there was nothing sleazy about them. In fact, there was nothing sleazy about any of it. The clientele were mostly well-heeled couples, people in their late thirties and early forties who, for a reason she couldn't fathom, chose a topless club for their night out.

Bean steered her toward the end of the bar closest to the stage. The music, a sixties tune blasting from a jukebox, made her head pound. They found two chairs and ordered, and only then did Quin swivel around, looking for McCleary and Gene Travis. She spotted them at a table smack in the heart of the sunken area, and her first sight of McCleary struck her in the chest like a meteor. He was sitting with a man she presumed was Travis and a woman who she knew was Sylvia Callahan.

Callahan was blond, just as Quin had imagined. That she was also as lovely as a painting was disconcerting. At the moment, her head was thrown back as she laughed, then she leaned forward, her hand on McCleary's knee, and said something to Gene Travis across the table. McCleary's arm, Quin noticed, rested possessively along the back of Callahan's chair, his fingers brushing her shoulder. What she felt most in that moment was an acute disorientation. It was as if she'd stumbled into an alternate universe, a probable reality where she and McCleary had never married, perhaps never even met, and yet she had somehow retained memories of what might have been. She turned around and gulped at her drink.

Bean touched her arm. "That's straight Scotch, lady. Go easy."

Quin nodded miserably. "I'm not cut out for this, Bean."

"Hey, all we gotta do is sit here. Mike's got the hard part."

She glanced back at McCleary. Yeah, he looked like he was suffering.

The jukebox music suddenly went off and the stage lights blinked. An expectant hush fell over the crowd momentarily. From somewhere, a drumroll beat a steady pulse in the air. The stage went black, then a platform rose out of the floor. On it was a five-piece band.

"If this doesn't beat all," Bean muttered.

A blue spotlight blinked on, illuminating a woman in tight khaki slacks and a khaki shirt unbuttoned enough to see the swell of her breasts. She stood as still as a hummingbird. Her arms were raised in the air, her head tilted back slightly, and her black hair cascaded down her back. She looked as if she were offering oblations to the jungle gods, Quin thought.

A second spotlight came on, shining on a shirtless

man in khaki slacks. He wore a pith helmet. His chest gleamed as if it had been oiled. He stood with his arms extended toward the woman. Behind them was a green scrim impaled with shadows that suggested a jungle. Insect sounds chirred in the air. A noise like a brush being rubbed against a washboard reverberated around them, amplified through speakers so powerful it seemed the sound was inside her. Onstage the woman twitched. Her right arm fell to her side. It was like watching a doll being wound up, coming to life.

This was not going to be what she had expected either, she thought. No sleazy striptease. This thing had been choreographed. Maybe it even had a story.

Her eyes slid toward McCleary's table. Travis was ordering from a waitress who looked to be about a 36D, and Callahan was whispering something to McCleary. His hand was now firmly on Callahan's shoulder. A worm of jealousy burrowed through Quin; her hands, resting in her lap, clenched tightly.

This is a role we're playing. This is not real life. She repeated this silently, like a prayer, and gulped again at her drink, the Scotch burning a tunnel through her throat as it went down.

On stage, the man and woman circled each other as if enacting some strange mating ritual. Her hips undulated; his matched her rhythm.

Quin averted her gaze and peered the length of the bar as she brought her glass to her mouth, sipping at the Scotch, no longer tasting it. And that was when she saw Neal Schloper, sitting by himself, his eyes riveted on the stage.

What was Joyce's ex-husband doing in *here*? In the club of the man he'd fingered as Joyce's killer?

His obvious concentration was broken when a short, rotund guy with a punk haircut tapped him on the shoulder and whispered something to him. Schloper nodded, left some bills on the bar and got up. He followed the short man, and the two vanished through a doorway off to the left.

Quin nudged Bean. "I'll be right back."

"Where're you going?"

"Snooping."

She slung her purse over her shoulder, acutely aware of the weight of her .38 inside, and wended her way through the crowd, now three deep at the bar. The swinging wooden doors through which Schloper had vanished reminded her of doors in a western saloon. Rest room signs were posted on the wall to its left. Quin pushed through the doors into a vibrant pink, empty hallway. The ladies' room was to her right, the men's room to her left. There were two other doors ahead of her, both unmarked.

She strolled past the ladies' room to the first door, her heart doing flip-flops, her hand inside her purse, fingers against the cool metal of the gun. She pressed her ear to the wood, listening. Just then, the door to the ladies' room opened and two women strolled out, chattering, smoking, trailing perfume. Quin dug into her purse as if she were looking for something, but one of the women stopped. Quin felt eyes on her back.

"Something wrong?" the woman asked.

Quin glanced around, leaning into the wall as if she'd imbibed too much and needed support, slurring her words. "Gotta make a call. Y'know where the phone is?"

The woman—an employee, Quin guessed—said, "The phone's in the ladies' room here. The two doors are for personnel only."

"Oh." Quin giggled. "Thanks. I guess I got a little turned round."

The woman smiled. "Yeah, I guess you did."

Quin walked toward them, past them, went through the doors into the ladies' room. The stalls were empty. Only two women stood at the sinks—one washing her hands, the other carefully applying lipstick. Quin walked into one of the stalls, waited until both women had left, then hurried back into the hall. This time she listened only briefly, heard nothing, turned the knob. The door was unlocked. She opened it and stepped inside a blackness so deep, so vast, it was as if she'd been swallowed.

She closed the door softly behind her and removed her shoes. She stuffed them in her purse, found her penlight, and held it toward the floor. Its thin, opaline beam slid across glossy Mexican tiles, climbed over a desk cluttered with papers, glided above a filing cabinet, and paused on a door. A slice of light shone from beneath it.

She could still hear the music from the club, but it seemed distant, almost unreal, like the memory of music. What she heard more clearly was the murmur of voices coming from somewhere in the dark ahead of her. Voices and footsteps.

She scurried toward the wall, pressing herself against it. The footsteps got louder. Keys jingled. The door swung open, so she was now behind it. Her heart leaped into her throat. Through the crack to her left she could see the short, rotund man whom Neal Schloper had followed. Then he strode out of her line of vision. She heard him cross the room, moving toward the door where she'd entered. He opened and shut it, and locked it behind him. His footsteps retreated. She waited until her heartbeat felt almost normal, then stepped out from behind the door, her .38 drawn.

She moved slowly along a dimly lit hall with walls so deeply red, so oppressive, she had trouble breathing. It was like a miniature gallery, this hallway, decorated with dozens of black and white photographs. Pornographic photos. Grainy photos. *Stills*. They depicted positions and acts she had never known existed. She didn't feel revulsion so much as curiosity, and moved from one to the next and the next until she'd reached a black iron staircase.

Here, too, photographs covered the walls. But it wasn't until she was near the bottom that her eyes were drawn to one in particular, a five-by-seven. In it, a woman lay sprawled over the edge of a swimming pool, so she was half in and half out of the water. Her hair floated on the surface like bleached moss, her arms drifted at her sides; they were like sticks of bamboo. Her legs were spread open on the grass. Two men were doing things to her. Quin couldn't have said what things, because she was staring at the woman's face.

It was Joyce Young.

Terry Travis was right.

She took the photograph off the wall, but had no place to put it because her purse was bulging. She yanked her shoes out of her bag and stuck one in each of her jacket pockets. She slipped the photograph inside her purse, descended the last two steps, and stopped. She was in a long, royal blue hallway with probably half a dozen doors. At the very end was a red exit sign.

Make it fast, kiddo.

She hurried to the first door, listened, heard no voices, moved on. The second door wasn't a door at all, but an archway through which she passed to another set of stairs that led up to a room like a small theater, with tiered, red velvet seats. The front wall was glass and overlooked a cozy makeshift stage with scenery and props that depicted a bedroom. A guy with a video camera was recording what appeared to be Neal Schloper's sexual fantasy, involving himself and two women. There was no sound, except for groans and small sighs of pleasure and an occasional direction from the cameraman for someone to do something specifically graphic.

Once, the guy lowered his camera and Quin got a good look at him: a face pocked like the surface of the moon, black hair as tightly curly as a Brillo pad, a nose that was squashed like rotten fruit at the end. Then he shouted another stage direction.

She'd seen enough, thanks.

She hurried back down the steps from the little theater and nearly panicked when she heard footsteps just beyond the archway. *Two people.* She looked about frantically for someplace to hide, but there were no doors, windows, nothing except a narrow space under the concrete stairs. She ducked into it and huddled, arms clutching her legs, face buried in her skirt.

A man said, "You know what Neal likes. Just be inventive, sweetie."

"What Neal likes," replied a woman, "isn't something money could buy."

Their footsteps resounded on the concrete steps. Quin's head pounded. The moment she heard their voices recede, she moved quickly from her hiding place. Too quickly. One of her shoes slipped out of her jacket pocket and fell to the floor. She heard the man say, ". . . you hear something?"

Quin scooped up her shoe and tore down the hall toward the red EXIT sign. Her hands pressed the cool bar inward, the door swung open, and she fled into the dark of an alley that emptied into the parking lot. She leaned against the wall to catch her breath and slip her shoes back on. She combed her hair with her fingers, then strolled around the side to the door, her heart beating an erratic tune. *Travis also lets certain customers star in their own videos. Good customers like Neal Schloper.*

She had to pay another cover charge, and as she entered the smoky club she saw Bean standing at the end of the bar, looking around.

Alarm manacled his features as she approached. "Christ, where the hell *were* you? I was about ready to call the cops. McCleary's gone."

Quin sank into the chair. "I need a drink."

"Coming up."

The band was playing now, the stage was empty, and couples were dancing. Not only was McCleary gone, but so were Travis and Callahan. "Where'd they go, Bean?" she whispered.

"They left."

"Together?"

"Yup."

"Wonderful. Did they look around for Mac's client?"

"Nope. Here's your drink. Now tell me what happened."

He set a Scotch-on-the-rocks in front of her. She sipped at it, then pushed it away. "Let's get outa here. I'll tell you what happened on the way back to the house."

2.

They were inside Callahan's black BMW, speeding away from Travis' penthouse on Biscayne Bay, his *business* penthouse, where they'd spent the last hour. Now that it was all over, McCleary's eyes begged to close and his body screamed for sleep. Callahan, however, looked as fresh and pristine as when she'd entered the club.

"You think he bought it?"

"Yes. He wouldn't have invited us back to his place if he hadn't. You're in, Mike. I think your next step is to introduce Gene to your 'client' and then go from there."

He hit the button for the electric window. The cool night air against his face revived him somewhat and alleviated the crescive pressure in his head caused by Callahan's perfume. They were rising over a bridge, and the thick scent of salt filled his nostrils. The dark waters had seized the reflection of the moonlight, holding it hostage. Distantly, he heard the mournful whistle of a boat.

As the BMW whispered down the other side of the bridge, Callahan pulled off into a holt of thin pines around a deserted picnic area. "I've *got* to use the bathroom," she said. "Be right back."

He watched her hurry off toward the rest rooms at the far end of the picnic area, moving through the thick moonlight like a ship through water. Her perfume lingered in the car, triggering a parade of old memories. Dangerous memories. He got out and walked down to the edge of the bay. The tide was low; rocks and twigs protruded in the shoals. A faint breeze carried off the vestiges of Callahan's perfume. Away from her, from that haunting scent, the puissant radiance of the memories diminished.

His thoughts turned, instead, to the more immediate past, to the way Gene Travis' face had registered surprise when Callahan had appeared. She'd played her part like a trooper, all right. Her mouth had brushed McCleary's cheek as she'd greeted him, then she'd hugged Travis hello as if they were old friends instead of ex-competitors. Just as Callahan had predicted, Travis had assumed she and McCleary were lovers, a role that had been distressingly easy for him to play.

There was no question that he loved Quin. But the old yearnings for Callahan had surged like an errant tide, demanding resolution. He was and always had been essentially monogamous. So how could he feel deeply for two women?

In the stillness, sound traveled with almost painful clarity. He heard the click of Callahan's shoes along the walk, then crunching toward him through the pine needles. She stopped beside him. Moonlight oozed from the water's edge to the tip of her shoes. "Pretty, isn't it."

"Peaceful. It doesn't seem like Miami."

"If you pretend you have blinders on, it reminds me of that place we stayed on Pensacola Beach when . . ."

She stopped abruptly, almost as if the cessation of words could halt the memory, and dug her hands in her jacket pockets. A side of her face was hidden in the umbra of the trees. But he didn't have to look at her to know that she, too, had been slipping in and out of the past as though time were a tapestry which could be rewoven. The place on Pensacola Beach she'd referred to was where they had stayed for a week during the investigation of her sister's murder. It was when McCleary had first realized he was in love with her.

For several long moments, neither of them spoke. The air tightened uncomfortably. "We'd better get going. It's late," she said finally.

The moment he slid into the car beside her, that scent clamped down over him again. She was saying something about her keys, fumbling in her purse for them. Her elbow brushed his, an electricity leaped from her arm to his, and then she was leaning toward him. Her hand cooled the side of his face, her mouth heated his, and his arms went around her.

What am I doing?

She tasted of bourbon, of burned August skies, of a past sweetened by the passage of time. His heart soared and plummeted, his bones sang and wept, he became a battleground of contradictions.

The past is dead.

The past was now.

You'll lose Quin.

This had nothing to do with Quin.

You'll regret this.

He would stop it. Now. This instant.

But his body wasn't listening to his mind. His mouth found the hollow of her throat, where a pulse leaped against his lips. His hands moved with a will of their own, inside her jacket, up under her blouse to the warmth of her skin. He wanted her now as he had for that week on Pensacola Beach when they had played at marriage.

His fingers counted the ridges along her spine, ridges like steps, and his hands moved from her ribs to her breasts, and she murmured his name, her voice soft, musical. His other hand slid her skirt up her thigh, and it rustled against her nylon stockings.

Enough, whispered a voice in his head. *Enough.*

But she threw off heat in waves, and it thickened the scent of her perfume, pulling at him as she leaned into the door. Her hands were in his hair, at his neck, her mouth soft, as hungry as his own. He kissed her cheeks, her eyes, and groped like a horny teenager. Except that this was no teenage lust he felt. It was larger, deeper. The weight of the past was crushed against his back like a bushel of damp flowers. He was sinking, giving in, capitulating to a galvanic response whose source lay five years back.

Then suddenly everything inside him went flat. He

pulled away. His heart thudded so loudly it seemed to fill the car, crowding out the fragrance of her perfume, of her skin, shoving aside the lure of the past.

He ran his hands over his face. "I can't, Callahan."

She didn't say anything. She shifted in her seat. He looked over at her. In the moonlight, her face gleamed damply, her fingers worked at the buttons of her blouse, fastening them, and she tucked the blouse back inside her skirt. "I know." She said this quietly, as if he had voiced something she'd already known. She found the key, inserted it in the ignition, started the car.

"I'm sorry, I . . ."

"Don't apologize. Please." She gripped the steering wheel, biting at her lower lip, struggling not to cry. She brushed strands of hair from her cheek with the back of her hand. "I understand. Really." She sat back, her shoulders sagging as if beneath the weight of a soul fatigue. "I think I would've been disappointed if you had." She gave a short, curt laugh and gazed through the windshield. "Ironic, isn't it. Our timing has always been off. After Marcy's killer had been caught, I would think of her when I looked at you and knew it just wasn't going to work for us until I'd had some time to put her death behind me. Then when we saw each other four years ago and spent those three days together, I was involved with someone else. That's why I never called you after that. And now you're married."

She looked over at him then, her eyes as moist as grapes. "When you showed up at the house the other day, Mike . . . all these emotions . . ." She made a sweeping gesture with her hand, as if she were trying to pull something from her chest. "These old feelings . . ." Her voice caught; she shook her head and quickly backed out onto the road.

They sped back toward the Pink Slipper in silence. He ached all over inside—for Quin, for Callahan, for himself. He wanted to crawl into a cool space and pull a sheet over his head. She drove into the lot outside the

131

club and pulled alongside Lady. She turned off the BMW. The engine ticked in the silence.

"Let me know what happens with Travis. If you need anything, just holler."

"Thanks. I will."

The words echoed hollowly. McCleary unlocked the door, opened it, then turned back to Callahan and reached for her hand. He squeezed it. Then he fled to his own car, his misery pursuing him like a hungry dog.

14   Fatal Run

HE WAITED FOR Bob Summer on the dimly lit running track which he used six days a week. The dark quavered with early morning sounds—the sweet trill of birds, the echoing din of interstate traffic in the distance, the susurrous whisper of a breeze through the surrounding trees.

The sinuous track wound three miles through a park with posted signs warning that the area was unsafe at night. Signs, he thought, which Summer and several other runners repeatedly ignored. But that would change.

He glanced at his watch. It was 5:32 A.M. The ideal time for the kill was at 5:42, when the moon entered Summer's house of death and turned sextile to Venus in his own house of creativity. He could do it after that moment, of course, but doing it at precisely 5:42 would enhance the effects of the kill.

He crouched behind a bush in his running suit, a thin line of sweat crossing his forehead despite the cool temperature. The scissors in his hand seemed to vibrate with anticipation. His body was releasing generous doses of adrenaline, as if to reward him for his planning. Its ignescent heat thundered through his veins, raced across the surface of his skin, sucked at the saliva in his mouth.

5:34. He parted the bushes with his hand, peering out at the track less than three yards away, looking for Summer. Instead, a man and a woman jogged past, eidolous, surreal, beneath the glow of the sodium vapor lamp. They were regulars. He knew they did the track just once. Right behind them was another guy, on his second lap. Good. The regulars would be gone by the time Summer loped by.

In the branches above him, a pair of doves cooed.

5:38. And here came Summer at a slow jog, his arms curled loosely at his sides, his hair a pumpkin orange in the lamp's glow. As he passed the bush, the man stepped out and began to jog along behind him. The breeze tickled the shells of his ears and slipped around to the back of his neck, chilling him. An abrupt, unexpected chill. *A warning? Is my body warning me?*

Ridiculous. He had calculated the time, he had planned, he was close now. *Close.*

The scissors heated up in his hand.

Adrenaline pumped through him at a frantic rate. Summer was rounding a curve in the path that marked the beginning of a half mile that was the darkest on the track. It was now 5:40.

As he closed the gap between them, Summer glanced around and kept on running. Christ, two minutes to go and by then he would be past the dark stretch, out in the open, and he would have to wait for Summer to go around again, and by then the sky would be oozing light.

He had to do it now or not at all.

No no no, whispered his body. *It's not time.*

But he was less than a foot away from Summer, the scissors were raised, and now his arm was coming down, swishing through the air, and the scissors impacted with Summer's back and sank through his running jacket.

He let out a strangled cry and fell to his knees.

The man yanked out the scissors and was raising them again when Summer suddenly rolled and his legs shot out with astonishing force and slammed into the man's gut, knocking him to the ground.

He gasped for breath, lifted himself up, but Summer was already scampering to his feet, stumbling, falling, getting up again. He had a sudden, terrible vision of Summer making it to the edge of the road and shouting for help. He could imagine cops pouring into the park, fanning out like busy ants, and catching him. This thought shot him forward. He tackled Summer, sent him sprawling into the gravel and dirt, but not before he screamed. Jesus, it ripped through the morning air, that scream, startling doves from the trees, and threw him into a blind white panic.

He sank the scissors into Summer's back. The blades sliced through tissues, muscles and struck bone. Summer groaned. His hands grappled for the scissors, trying to reach them. But the man yanked them out and drove them in again. Again. Power surged through him as Summer's life flowed into him. He opened his arms wide to receive it and felt its heat, its pulse, its reality swelling his insides like a balloon, lifting him up, up, up. He soared. He would touch the sky. Kiss the face of the sun. He would live forever. This was what he had waited for. This ubiquity was the source of his addiction.

Then he realized that a nacreous light seeped through the trees. That blood had stained his own running suit. What the hell good would the kill be if he got caught? He yanked the scissors from Summer's back and slapped the blades against the grass to clean them. He grabbed hold of his arms and pulled him into the bushes. He turned Summer over, felt for a pulse at his neck. There was none.

Move, shouted his body. *Get outa here.*

But he was staring at Summer's ear; he wanted a trophy. Oh God, how he wanted one. The trophy would be the clue. And this would be the first from a male victim; he knew precisely what he would do with it.

His hands twitched.

Go now now now, yelled his body.

The scissors opened. He placed the edges of the blades around Summer's ear.

The files, think about those files of McCleary's.

McCleary knew about the trophies, the sweets. He knew . . .

135

Nothing. Everything was in front of him and still McCleary knew nothing. But he would when it was his turn.

The man smiled and snipped the scissors closed.

PART TWO

Minotaur

15 Portents

1.

A CRY SLASHED through Quin's sleep. She flew forward, blinking hard in the hot gloam, her hands clutching the sheets. Her heart boomed. Her ears rang. Where was McCleary? Hadn't he gotten home yet? What time was it? Had she really heard someone cry out? Why was it so bloody hot in here?

She lifted up on her elbows and glanced at the clock. It was nearly ten. She remembered turning on the heat last night when she'd gotten home and had forgotten to switch it off before going to bed. Now it was probably eighty-two in the shade outside and ninety in here. She threw aside the sheet, swaying a little as she stood, her head aching as if she'd had too much to drink last night. But this hangover had nothing to do with alcohol, she knew. It was the result of anger and frustration as she'd paced the house for an hour and a half last night, waiting for McCleary to get home.

Her imagination, naturally, had conjured numerous scenarios, all starring Sylvia Callahan. The amount of food she'd consumed had increased in direct proportion to the increments in time that she'd waited. Finally, at three o'clock, worn out and stuffed, she'd fallen into bed, into a sleep like death.

She padded out into the hall, the light from the window at the end hurting her eyes. She turned off the heat, then peered over the banister, into the living room, and saw McCleary sacked out on the couch. The afghan was tangled around his waist, an arm was thrown back over his head, his pillow had slipped to the rug. He was murmuring, making sharp, startled sounds deep in his throat. Frowning, disturbed that he'd slept on the couch, Quin went downstairs.

Peace was absent from his face. He grimaced, as if with pain. Then he groaned, cried out, and brought his hands to his face, rubbing at his forehead, scratching it, leaving ugly red marks. He flopped on his side. The afghan slipped to the floor. Hepburn, the Persian, who'd been draped over the back of the couch, now rose, arching her back, and strolled toward Quin. She meowed plaintively.

Quin touched McCleary's shoulder gently, tentatively. "Mac, hey, wake up."

His eyes fluttered open, glazed with sleep. He didn't seem to recognize her. Then he blinked and moaned as he raised up. He rubbed the back of his neck. "God, I feel like I slept on boards. What time is it?"

"Almost ten."

He sat up, dropped his legs over the side of the couch, and dry-washed his face with his hands.

"What were you dreaming? I heard you cry out."

"I did?"

She nodded.

"Someone was chasing me, that's all I remember."

"What time did you get in?"

"After three sometime. You were asleep. I didn't want to wake you."

He didn't look at her as he said this. But even if he had, she wasn't buying it. He knew she was a sound sleeper. There were plenty of times when he'd come in late before and simply rolled into bed without awakening her. Why should last night have been any different?

An image of Callahan spread through her mind like a bloodstain. It translated as guilt. McCleary's guilt. Her stomach twisted.

Stop it.

He'd been doing a job. Playing a role. Just because Callahan's face had pursued her into sleep last night was no reason to take it out on McCleary. She hugged her

140

arms against her. Hepburn leaped down from the couch and rubbed against her leg until Quin picked her up. "So what happened? Did Travis buy your cover?"

He sat back, the afghan draped across his lap, as she settled at the other end of the couch. "Yeah, he did. I told him I'd present his asking price for the club to my client and get back to him in a couple of days. We went to his penthouse after the show. I saw Bean as we left, but you weren't around. What happened?"

Her mind was stuck back on the casual reference to *we*, to him and Callahan. She felt a sudden, truculent urge to say something nasty, to comment on how he had certainly thrown himself wholeheartedly into his role. She swallowed the sardonic words as she might a teaspoon of castor oil and told him about Neal Schloper.

"Interesting. So Schloper's lying, Travis is lying, everyone's lying."

Including you, Mac? Are you lying?

"Do you have the photograph of Joyce?"

"In my purse."

"Fantastic. That's the first solid piece of evidence we've got, Quin."

"But it doesn't mean he killed Joyce. Or Lois Dwight. Or any of those other people."

"No. But it *does* prove that he wasn't honest about his relationship with her. She was one of his porn princesses."

"So if he killed her, what was his motive? Did she threaten to tell his wife about his video sideline business? Or his kids? Or the cops?"

Why are we having this conversation before breakfast? Before anything?

"The cops would be interested only if the videos involved kids. Or were sent through the mail. Or if they're snuff videos."

"You said that's hearsay," she pointed out.

"I figure hearsay is a little like the Bible. They both have a kernel of truth in them."

His acerbic tone made her laugh. "You sound like a heretic."

"You know what I mean." He smiled. It was just a regular McCleary smile, quick, bright, with nothing minatory or dark behind it, and it filled her with a momentary levity.

"I've got to eat something." She got up. "How about oatmeal?"

His head bobbed, but he didn't seem to have really heard her. He was just staring at the rug, his smile buried now. She sensed he had moved as far away from her in time and space as possible without leaving the room.

"Mac?"

"Hmm?"

"You want oatmeal?"

"Oatmeal's fine. Thanks."

"You going to run first?"

"I'm too tired."

Too tired to run? That was the equivalent of her saying she wasn't hungry.

He wrapped the afghan around himself and shuffled toward the stairs. He paused at the thermostat and turned off the heat. Quin watched him for a moment, noting the sag in his shoulders, the way he passed his hand over his hair, the way he moved. Something had happened that he wasn't telling her. Maybe it involved Callahan, maybe it didn't. But she thought longingly of the plane tickets to Venezuela, pinned to the kitchen bulletin board like a reminder of the path not taken.

In her mind, she saw McCleary stepping on the welcome mat.

By the time they sat down at the butcher block table in the kitchen, her anxiety had left a chasmal hunger in her gut. She consumed two helpings of oatmeal smothered in raisins and walnuts, three slices of whole wheat bread, a slice of cantaloupe and one of grapefruit, orange juice, coffee, and a banana. She had also misplaced the butter dish, which she found in the middle drawer of the cabinet, and her car keys, which turned up a little later in the fruit bin in the fridge. McCleary, who usually would have had a comment about such absentmindedness, didn't even seem to notice.

Portents, she thought. The day had just begun for them, and already she was surrounded by portents. They sprouted from the table, where McCleary was perusing the paper, hiding inside it. They were strewn across the floor, where a trail of ants marched with impunity toward the cats' dishes. They swelled inside her head as the silence stretched on and on.

She wanted McCleary to talk to her, but a wall had grown up between them overnight. She wanted to hear him laugh, but she couldn't think of anything funny to say. Mostly, she felt as if he was slipping away from her, slipping irrevocably.

The phone rang. The sound had substance, weight, and seemed to dry the skin on her arms, her face, rubbing it raw. She drew her hands from the soapy water in the sink and answered it.

"Quin? Hi, this is Ross. Ross Young." His voice brimmed with alacrity.

"Ross. Hi. I hope you're still planning on coming Saturday night."

"Wouldn't miss it, Quin. Is Mike there?"

"Sure, just a second." She held the phone out. "It's for you."

McCleary took the receiver. Quin pulled the plug in the sink and watched the dirty water swirl down the drain.

". . . do you have it? Now? . . . Uh-huh," McCleary was saying. His face, Quin noticed, had turned fallow. He scratched at the spot between his eyes. His hunch spot. The spot that had been blazing when he'd brought the jar of honey into the bedroom two nights ago. "Okay, give us forty minutes or so . . . right." He hung up.

"What happened?" she asked when he didn't say anything.

He raised his head, as if just remembering her presence. "Ross just found a videotape in Joyce's attic. He wants us to take a look at it."

"A videotape of what?"

"Of her."

The way he said it told her what sort of tape it was. "I'll follow you in my car."

Young's home, like his office, didn't blend with the landscape so much as grow out of it, like an appendage. It was built into the side of a man-made hill on several acres at the tip of a tongue of land that jutted into the intracoastal. Most of it seemed to have been built inside the hill. But it was difficult to tell for sure because of the tricks he'd performed with color, decor, and the skylight like a sun around which the rest of the house revolved. The place bore the same futuristic imprint as his office. It made Quin feel as if she were glimpsing how people might live in a post-nuclear era.

They sat in a pale blue room beneath the skylight, where a black cat, Joyce's cat, he explained, was perched on the stool at his drawing board. Young, as usual, was casually dressed in jeans, a T-shirt out, and loafers. This morning his socks were lavender with designs on them that looked Mayan.

"I saw Tim Benson yesterday and asked if it would be okay with him if I got Joyce's place cleaned up and started going through her stuff. I'd like to put the house on the market. So this morning I started going through the things in her attic and I found this." His fingers closed around the edge of the videotape on the coffee table in front of him. He held it up. The only identifying mark on it was a label with a Roman numeral one on it. "I'd like you to take a look at it."

"That was the only one you found?" McCleary asked as Young crossed the room and slipped the tape in the VCR.

"Yes."

The screen flickered to life. A slow zoom focused on a

woman—Joyce Young—descending shallow steps to a swimming pool. She wore a scant bikini. She was smiling at someone off camera, beckoning to the person. She paused on the lowest step, slid the straps of the bathing suit off her shoulders, reached around, and unhooked it. The top floated like a water lily on the surface of the shimmering blue water. Joyce slid her hands up her stomach, cupping her breasts as if in offering, her smile strange, almost haunted. Then her hands fell along her sides to her waist and she peeled away the bottom of the bikini, stepping out of it carefully, lazily. Her body seemed to be sculpted of sunlight and water and sky.

Now the camera focused on a man as he swam toward her, only his back, shoulders, and arms visible. His strokes were long, powerful. He disappeared underwater, reappeared, dived once more, his movements as sleek as a dolphin's. The camera zoomed in on his hands as he reached for Joyce.

Behind her, at the edge of the steps, appeared a second man. Only his feet and the bottom portion of his legs were visible. He slid into the water, the camera slicing him off at the neck, and his arms wound like tentacles at Joyce's waist. His hands dipped beneath the water, caressing her, as the first man's hands moved over her breasts.

Quin's gaze slid toward McCleary. He looked acutely uncomfortable. Young's expression was inscrutable, except that the pinched look at his eyes seemed deeper, ineffable. She thought of the photograph of Joyce she'd taken from the club last night and knew it was a still from this video.

"Do we ever see the men's faces?" McCleary asked.

Young nodded. "One of them. It's coming up in just a second."

Quin stared at her knees, wishing the damn thing were over. When she looked up again, Joyce was draped over the side of the pool like a cat, just as she'd been in the photograph. The man with his face against her thighs suddenly lifted his head. It was Neal Schloper.

Young froze the frame. "Now, I may be wrong, but I think the other man is Gene Travis."

Quin and McCleary exchanged a glance that Young intercepted. "You don't seem surprised."

"We're not." McCleary ran a finger across his upper lip, ruffling his mustache. When he began to explain their suspicions about Gene Travis, Quin thought he was going to violate his own rule and tell the man everything. Or perhaps she was just hoping he would because then it would mean he might tell *her* everything. But he told Young just enough to make him aware of what their game plan was, then explained their "death sweet" theory.

Young unfroze the frame and the tape flickered another moment or two to the end. When he spoke, unease inumbrated his voice. "But how can you prove Gene killed these other people?"

McCleary shook his head. "We don't have to. All we have to prove is that he killed your stepsister, Ross. The other killings just give us a pattern to work with."

No, that wasn't quite right, Quin mused. McCleary wasn't *working* with the pattern, he'd become obsessed with it, he was *connecting* with it. The honey, the icons, provided him with a kind of conduit to the killer's mind. It was almost as if he had made love to her the way the killer had to his victims.

A chill snaked along her arms. She absently touched her shoulder, where McCleary had sucked so hard at the skin that by today a bruise had appeared.

The killer bit Lois Dwight's shoulder.

An ache began to throb at her temple. The bruise was another portent, it was . . .

A gross coincidence, one of the small jokes the cosmos tossed out from time to time to keep you on your toes. But suddenly all she wanted to do was get out of the house. Her stomach cramped with hunger. She felt nauseous with hunger.

"Quin?"

She looked over at Young, who'd been saying something to her. "I'm sorry, what?"

"How about some coffee?"

"Thanks, Ross, but I've got an appointment across town." She stood too quickly, drawing a frown from McCleary. "Mac, I'll see you later at the office."

"What time are things getting started tomorrow night?" Young asked.

It took her a moment to realize he was referring to the party. She hadn't even shopped yet. "Eight, how's that? Bring your suit."

He started to get up, to show her to the door, but she gestured for him to remain seated. She had no clear memory of walking from the skylit room through the hall to the front door. But when she stepped outside, the pelagic scent of the air, warm and sweet, soothed the ache at her temple. She cosseted the back of her neck and peered up at the February sky, pendulous with thunderheads.

Please let me be wrong about Mac, she thought, and hurried to her car.

2.

When the coffee was done, McCleary and Young ascended a black iron staircase in the hall that opened onto the top of the man-made hill. They stepped out onto a covered redwood deck that overlooked the canal. There was a wicker table with matching chairs, a low bookcase against the wall stacked with *National Geographic*s and crowned by a phone, and a telescope. A warm breeze spilled through the branches of twin oak trees at either side of the house. McCleary smelled rain in the air.

"Your hideout, Ross?"

Young laughed and drew the wicker chairs up to the table. "Yeah, I guess it is. On clear nights I like to come

147

up here and play around with the telescope. You ever used one?"

"As a kid. My dad's brother had one. He always called stars 'ghost lights.' "

Young set his coffee down, peered through the telescope, and motioned to McCleary. "No ghost lights, but you can get an idea of how powerful an instrument it is. It's aimed at a ketch across the canal."

McCleary looked through it, adjusted it, and an old guy on the deck swam into view. He seemed so close McCleary could see a mole on his cheek and the title of the magazine he was paging through. He swung the telescope right and a dog's snout filled the lens. Farther right and he impaled a kid on his bike on the pier. McCleary laughed with delight. "It's great. If I had one of these things I'd probably never get any work done at all."

Young smiled. "That's how it is on weekends sometimes, especially when the weather's clear. The day the *Challenger* exploded, I was watching. I knew something was wrong before the computers at the space center had registered it. I could see the damn flames."

McCleary sat down again, and for a while they talked about the crippled space program, politics and religion, books, movies, architecture and art, women, philosophy. They disagreed on almost everything, which made Young one of the best sparring partners McCleary had had in years. The man's mind was lightning quick and perspicacious. He seemed to possess a photographic memory capable of retrieving facts like a computer.

Their conversation inevitably became personal and it began with Young's question about Zivia. "What do you think of her, Mike?"

"She's a good investigator. Bright, very capable."

"Is she seeing anyone?"

"I don't think so."

"Good. She intrigues me." He sighed; it was a small, almost lonely sound. "I'm afraid I've spent so much time trying to make a name for myself as an architect

148

that I've cheated myself personally. Or maybe it's just that the closer you get to forty, the more you feel the tug for something permanent."

McCleary nodded; he understood the feeling, all right. But after last night, he also understood the importance of resolving the past if you could before committing yourself to marriage. He said as much, and Young shrugged. "That's fine in theory, but life isn't like a novel. There are always loose ends. Besides, I think it's unrealistic for two people to pledge absolute monogamy for the rest of their lives."

Absolute monogamy: he made it sound like a prison term.

"Suppose I were married," Young went on, "and a man my wife had known before she knew me suddenly came back into her life and she realized she might still be in love with him? Why should I deny her the right to find out if she is? Better that she find out now rather than five years down the road."

McCleary had only been speaking in general terms. He hadn't mentioned Callahan or his own situation, so Young's uncanny hypothesis left him uneasy. He wasn't ready to think about it yet. "And you'd want to know?"

"Sure. I'd prefer things be up front rather than hidden."

"You've never been married, have you?"

He grinned sheepishly and shook his head. "No. But I've been involved in some fairly long-term relationships where similar issues have come up."

"It's not the same." Not the same at all, McCleary mused. Somehow, the license, the ring, the ceremony, altered the rules. He changed the subject. "Did Joyce have any, uh, unconventional sexual habits that you were aware of?"

"I guess I figured she might have some unusual interests, simply because I couldn't imagine how anyone could get involved with a guy like Gene Travis. But I never gave it much thought, really. Like I said, the main thrust of my energy has gone into architecture. Sometimes I feel that if I'd been there more often for her, she

149

might still be alive." He finished his coffee. "Where do you think you'll go with things from here?"

"Aside from turning the tape over to Tim, I don't know."

The phone pealed and Young answered it. "Tim, hi . . . Yes, he's here. . . . Sure, hold on."

He passed the phone to McCleary, and Benson said, "Mac, sorry to bother you. Ruth said you were at Ross's."

"What's up?"

"Uh, would you mind coming down to the morgue to identify a body?"

The skin across his forehead tightened in that now familiar way. "Well, sure, but—"

"I've already gotten one ID that it's a guy named Bob Summer. Isn't that the name of your friend who—"

"Yes," he whispered. *Dear God, yes.*

16 New Leads, New Victims

1.

"MISSY, YOU WORK in dah ladies' houses and you gets to know what's goin' on in dere lives pretty well, whether you wants to know or not, and dat's how it was with her," explained Nelly Brown, Joyce's maid.

"What kinds of things did you find out about her life?" Quin asked.

They were in Nelly's neat little living room in her neat little concrete house in Overtown, Miami's black community. A ceiling fan turned overhead, stirring the warm air wafting through the open windows. Nelly, whose plump shape vaguely resembled an avocado's, shifted on the cushion that sank with her weight, and ran her dimpled fingers over her skirt.

"Things," she said, "dat ah don't think Ms. Y would be wantin' me to go tellin' to no detective." Her obdurate tone weighted the air. "Ah'm sorry, but dat's all ah gotta say. Dese ladies hire me 'cause dey trust me, and ah don't go betrayin' dat trust."

"Joyce is dead, Mrs. Brown. All I'm trying to do is find out who killed her."

Her eyes were as dark and soft as melting chocolate. "Missy, you don't needs to go tellin' me she's dead. Ah found her."

"And you don't care who killed her?"

"Course ah cares." She dropped her gaze, flicked at her skirt again. It had hiked up, cutting her thighs in half and exposing her fat, dimpled knees.

"Then please help me out, Mrs. Brown. What you tell me won't go beyond the two of us."

She considered this. In the silence, the ceiling fan wheezed as it circled, a dog's barks drifted through the windows, the screech of brakes shrieked through the warm air. Then Nelly rose abruptly. "How 'bout a glass of lemonade, Missy?"

"Thanks. I'd love some."

"Be right back."

She waddled into the kitchen. Through the doorway, Quin watched her open the fridge and bring out a pitcher of lemonade. She reached into the cabinet for two glasses, the sacks of skin on her underarms shimmying. "So youse not workin' for dah pol-eese?" she asked as she returned with the lemonade.

"No."

"And what ah tells you is jus' for you?"

"You have my word."

"Who hired you?"

"Mr. Young."

"Den dat means you gotta tell him everything ah tells you?"

"No. He hired my husband and me to find her killer, that's all. How we do it is up to us."

"Uh-huh."

She passed Quin a glass, and the cushions sighed with her weight as she sat down again. "Well, ah shuda known he'd hire someone. Dat's just dah sort thing he'd do, all right. If he'd paid more 'tention to her when she was 'live, maybe she wouldn't be dead. But ah don't s'pose he ever thought of dat."

"You don't like him?"

"Ah'm not sayin' whether ah like or don't like him, Missy. Don't go puttin' words in mah mouth. What ah'm sayin' is dat if he'd paid more 'tention to her, she wouldn't 'ave gone and got herself in trouble with dat

Travis man. Now *he* ah don't like, not one bit. No siree, you can look in dat man's eyes and see he's bad.''

"So he was at her house a lot?"

"Shore was. One day ah come to work and dere he is, takin' movie pictures of Ms. Y while she's swimmin' in the pool. She didn't have no clothes on, neither. Well, dat's fine with me, wasn't none of mah bizness. Ah jus' went about mah work and pretended nothin' was goin' on. But den he comes in dah house later sayin', 'Morning, Nelly, smile pretty for my camera,' and ah done tol' him what he could do with his camera." She nodded quickly and snorted like a horse. "Ah did, all right. Ah tol' him ah knows 'bout his bookstores and his Satan club; ah told him he was gonna burn. He jus' laughed, and later ah heard him tellin' Ms. Y that she oughta fire mah ass, that's jus' how he said it, too. Fire mah black ass."

Quin sipped at her lemonade. It had so much sugar in it she nearly gagged. What she really wanted was a piece of fruit. Several pieces of fruit. And an English muffin. "Did Joyce ever mention her relationship with Mr. Travis to you?"

"Sometimes." Her eyes dropped to her lap once more.

"What'd she say?"

Nelly squirmed, worried her hands in her lap. "Well, one night she had a party and ah came to help her with the servin'. We was in the kitchen and ah could tell she'd been drinkin' already. She tol' me Mr. Travis wanted her to be in a movie. Well, ah knew what kinda movie she meant, and ah tol' her it was a sinful thing to do. She started to cry. Well, Missy, ah can tell you ah don't like to see a grown woman cry. And it was worse with Ms. Y 'cause she didn't really have no friends. Not close friends she coulda talked to. Ah was her friend like dat. Ah felt awful bad, so ah puts my arm around her and pats her like her mama woulda if she'd been alive." She stopped, sat forward, back, crossed her legs at the ankles, uncrossed them, sipped from her glass.

"And?" Quin prodded.

She rolled her lips together, dabbed at her moist face with a hanky she pulled from her pocket. "And ah . . . ah tol' her ah understood why she was doin' dese things and dat someday she'd find a good man, a man who deserved her."

Quin frowned. "Why *was* she doing these things?"

" 'Cause she loved Mr. Y and he didn't love her."

"Why wouldn't she love him? He was her stepbrother."

Nelly's soft brown eyes ossified. "No, she *loved* him, Missy. Wasn't natural, was Satan's work, ah knows it was, but she loved him like a woman loves a man, not dah way a sister loves her brother."

"She'd told you how she felt about Ross? About Mr. Young?"

"She didn' have to tell me. Ah could see it in her eyes every time he came by dah house. Dat's why she married dat Mr. Slurper." The way she pronounced Neal Schloper's name made it sound obscene. "She married him and then gets messed up with dat Travis fellow just to spite Mr. Y 'cause he didn't like neither of dem."

"How long did you work for her?"

"Long 'nuff to know, Missy. Long 'nuff to know jus' what was goin' on. Ah may not have schoolin', but ah knows people. Ah knows what moves round inside dem."

"How long did you work for her, Mrs. Brown? A couple of months? Years? What?"

"Three years and den some. Ah was workin' for her when she was still married to Mr. Slurper."

"Do you think Mr. Young was aware of Joyce's feelings for him?"

Her eyes pinched at the corners. "Hard to say. He's always been a real gentleman with me, mighty fair. But ah can 'member how dah night of dat party, ah catches him lookin' after her like he knew and like he felt dah same way but dah difference was dat he knew it was unnatural."

"It wasn't really. I mean, they weren't related by blood."

She shook her head. "Dat's true, Missy, but it's still

154

not right. Dey grew up together. Dey grew up like brother and sister, and it's wrong, dat's all. By God's law, it's wrong." She paused. "But dat same night, ah 'member Mr. Slurper was dere, too. He was makin' a big to-do over Ms. Y, you know, takin' her hand and kissin' her on the cheek, and ah could see jus' how much Mr. Y didn't like it. Joyce used to do it jus' to aggravate him, to make him jealous. Ah knows she did."

Why was it, Quin wondered, that clients rarely told you the whole truth? Okay, so maybe Ross was embarrassed by it. She could understand how uncomfortable it would be to spill your guts to a couple of strangers. But it would've made things a little easier on this case.

"To your knowledge did she ever make that movie she'd mentioned to you?"

Nelly wound a vagrant strand of her black hair around her finger and stared down into her glass of lemonade as if the secret of the universe had been poured inside. "Yeah, she done made it. She went away for two days and den she came back and den two days after dat she was dead." Her voice ended in a whisper, and she began to cry, her thick, dimpled fingers covering her face.

After a few moments she yanked two pieces of Kleenex from the box on the end table and blew her nose.

"Do you know where Joyce went, Mrs. Brown?"

"No."

"Out of town? Did she go out of town?"

"She didn't tell me, Missy. But when she got back, she didn't go to her store. She didn't go nowhere. She jus' sat round dah house in her robe. She said ah was s'posed to tell people who called dat she was sick, couldn't talk. She refused to talk or see Mr. Y, Mr. Slurper, or Gene Travis. Ah knew somethin' mighty bad musta happened, so I sat her down, acting like her mama again, and she starts cryin'. The only thing she done tol' me was dat she was scared, scared bad."

"And she never told you why?"

"No."

"Did you know she got pregnant by Mr. Travis?"

She regarded Quin with surprise. "How'd you know 'bout that? Mr. Y never knew."

"Mr. Schloper told me."

"Yeah, he would. Shore. He couldn't get her pregnant, so when she found out she was, she knew it was Mr. Travis'. Mr. Slurper he found out by accident. He answered dah call dah day the clinic phoned to confirm her next 'pointment. Well, things weren't going none too well in dere marriage by den, and dat ended things. He moved out dah next day."

"When was that, do you remember?"

"Shore. Fourteen months ago. Four months after dat, she got dah divorce. By den, she'd lost dah baby. She woulda had a 'bortion, if she hadn't lost it. She was talkin' 'bout a 'bortion. Ah tried to change her mind, but ah 'spect she was 'fraid to do it by herself. Ah told her ah'd know'd plenty who'd raised a family on dere own. But Mr. Travis he was pressurin' her bad to get a 'bortion. Ah tol' her ah'd be dah nanny and all, but she wasn't hearin' none of dat. So she fretted so much, she lost dah baby."

"Mrs. Brown, didn't a Lieutenant Benson speak to you?"

"Shore."

"Why didn't you tell him any of this?"

She wiped her hanky across her throat, then dipped it inside the front of her blouse. "Missy, ah was so upset dah day ah found Ms. Y ah had to take more of mah heart medicine. Ah got high pressure, you know. Ah didn't think of any of dis until a few days later, and ah was gonna call him, but by den ah was sorta 'fraid to. Ah don't know, ah got it in mah head dat whoever had done dis might come after me next."

"Do you think Mr. Travis killed her, Mrs. Brown?"

"Do you?" she shot back, those dark eyes now impatient, annoyed.

"I think it's possible, yeah."

"Well, so do ah, Missy. And ah think it's jus' as

possible dat Mr. Slurper killed her. And dat maybe someone who didn't even know her killed her. Ah think, Missy, dat Joyce bein' the kinda woman she was, bless her soul, dat she mighta gone out to one of these fancy bars and brought a man home with her who killed her."

Swell, Quin thought. "Did she do that a lot?"

"Ah reckon she mighta done it a few times. But the way ah see it, Missy, most everything she did with men was because of dese unnatural feelings she had for Mr. Y."

Which was probably as good an assessment as she would get from a shrink about the mystery of Joyce Young, she decided.

"You got any more questions, Missy?"

"No, I think that about does it. Thank you for taking the time, Mrs. Brown."

Nelly Brown walked her to the door. Quin extended her hand, and it vanished in the other woman's. "You 'member how ah was tellin' you ah knows the darkness that moves in people?"

Quin nodded. Mrs. Brown still held on to her hand. Her skin was softer than a baby's.

"Well, ah knows there's some darkness movin' round in you, Missy."

"There is in most of us," Quin said with a smile.

"True. But ah'm not talkin' about the darkness of jus' bein' human, see. Ah'm talking 'bout a darkness with your husband. Ah sees it in your eyes. The way you talk. The way you moves. Somethin' dere don't settle right with me."

What the hell . . . it shows?

Nelly patted her hand. "Jus' give 'im room to move around, Missy. Dat's what all dese men need. Dey gotta do what dey gotta do, jus' like we women folk, and when it's done, dey usually comes back better than before."

Righto, Nelly Brown. I'll keep that in mind.

157

Doc Smithers, Dade County's coroner for longer than McCleary could remember, was a rotund man with a head as bald as a radish, except for a sprout of hair above each ear. He was wearing a white lab coat and spectacles, which rode low on his nose. McCleary thought he looked more like an ornithologist or an entymologist than a pathologist. He gripped McCleary's hand in both of his as he entered the office.

"Mac, good to see you again. How's Quin?"

"Fine, Doc, thanks." McCleary glanced at Benson, who had stopped pacing and was standing there with his hands in his pockets. "Hi, Tim."

"Thanks for coming, Mac."

"Well, let's get this over with and hope to God he isn't the Bob Summer you know," Smithers said.

"Where was he found?" McCleary asked as they walked down the hall.

"On a running track in the park on Floresta Street. He didn't have any ID on him. One of the joggers found him," Smithers replied.

McCleary's heart sank. Summer lived two blocks from Floresta Street.

They descended into the bowels of the building, where the gelid air smelled sharply of alcohol and cleansers. The wall of body drawers gleamed in the fluorescent lights. The aluminum autopsy table in the heart of the room chilled him. Smithers opened a middle drawer, and McCleary moved toward it on wooden legs. Smithers carefully peeled back the sheet, and McCleary stared into Bob Summer's face. *His* Bob Summer.

His left ear had been cut off.

McCleary's fingers closed over the edge of the drawer to steady himself. Blood surged like high tide in his ears. Hot tears stung the corners of his eyes. Waves of heat, then cold, swept through him. It was several moments before he could speak, and then all he could muster was a whisper.

"It's him."

He touched the back of his hand to Summer's cheek. The skin was cold, like wax. Quick memories fluttered through his head: Summer six years ago when they'd met and he'd helped McCleary on a homicide; Summer making one of his vegetarian meals for him and Quin, his arms lost to the wrists in bean sprouts. Summer, dead.

The skin across McCleary's forehead turned hot as he moved Summer's head to the side and stared at the crusted blood where his ear had been removed. *Scissors, like Joyce.* Smithers drew the sheet back over Summer's face and closed the drawer. McCleary leaned into the wall.

"Any sweet found on him?" His strained voice sounded unnaturally high, shrill, like the call of a wounded bird.

Benson nodded. "Yes. A small candy cane. In the pocket of his running jacket. The sweet, the mutilation . . . Summer must've been a health nut if he was out jogging and—"

"And he belongs to the Grove Fitness Club, and he was born in May. He's a Taurus." *Like me, a Taurus like me.*

Benson's mouth was moving, but for a distended moment McCleary couldn't hear what he was saying. The pulse in his ears was too great. The skin between his eyes burned terribly. He could feel it blistering, turning black, and in the next breath or the next it was going to burst and something grotesque, something living would crawl out. He pressed the heel of his hand to the spot, pressed until the burning seemed to diminish. Sound returned to his world. Benson was saying, ". . . it's the same guy, Mac."

"I *know* that. But is Bob dead because he was a friend of mine or because the killer had chosen him already?"

The question hung in the cold, still air and seemed to echo. Smithers cleared his throat. "It could be either. The point is that Summer was killed by your death sweet man."

A dull ache spread through the back of McCleary's

159

head. "No, that's not the only point. Don't you see? If this guy went after Bob because he was a friend of mine, then who's to say he won't go after someone else I know?" *Like Quin.*

Benson ran a hand alongside his jaw. "When was Quin born?"

"The latter part of June."

"Then if this guy follows the pattern he's on, it's more likely that he'd go after you, as a Taurus, than after Quin."

"Is that supposed to be a comforting thought, Tim?"

"Wait. Let's backtrack for a second," Benson said. "Mac, was your place broken into before or after Summer came by with his computer equipment?"

"After."

"Then I think it's likely he'd already chosen Summer. We suspect this guy follows his victims before he kills them, so maybe he was following Summer the night he came to your place."

"Maybe," McCleary conceded.

"And you said you felt the files on your den floor had been gone through, so he figured out that Summer had provided you with some vital links to his behavior patterns and so on which gave him an added impetus to get rid of him."

"That's a fine explanation, and I don't doubt that some of it's valid, but it doesn't tell us why he stole one of my paintings."

Smithers leaned against the edge of the aluminum table and folded his arms at his waist. He peered at McCleary over the rim of his spectacles. "I've got a theory on that, but you may not want to hear it."

"Tell me."

"Well, we've got a guy who takes trophies from his victims, right? So the stolen painting is a trophy *before* the fact. In some ways, it would be like voodoo, where a shaman takes fingernail clippings or strands of hair from his chosen victim to establish a connection."

"Voodoo?" Benson snorted. "Aw, c'mon, Doc."

"I'm not saying this guy's going to be sticking pins into Mac's picture, just that in his own mind it helps establish a link between them. It works on the same premise as crucifixes, religious icons, rosaries."

Like the honey, McCleary thought uncomfortably. He'd been trying to do the same thing with the honey, and he just hadn't had a word for it.

"I think you should drop this business with Gene Travis, Mac," said Benson. "I don't like any of it. If he's our guy, he's just leading you into something. And if he's not our man, no telling what the hell might happen."

"You're assuming he's made the connection between me and Mike West. Maybe he hasn't." His gaze flitted toward the drawer where Bob Summer lay, then darted back to Benson's face. "I'm seeing it through, Tim," he replied, then explained what had happened last night at the club. He removed a copy of the videotape Ross Young had given him from his pocket and passed it to Benson. "You may want to take a look at this. I suspect Travis had something to do with it. It's a soft porn number starring Joyce and Neal Schloper and another guy whose face you never see."

"And Schloper was at the club last night. Great," Benson muttered. "I knew there was something about that guy that didn't set right with me. Do you think Travis bought your story?"

"Callahan seems to think so."

"I still don't like it, Mac. I don't know how the hell you expect to find evidence this way that he killed Joyce Young."

"I sure won't find it sitting around on my ass. Maybe I can beat him at his own game."

"Or die trying," Benson said quietly.

3.

The woman who'd brought the paternity suit against

Travis looked like a Suzi with a Z-I. Quin guessed she was probably in her early to mid-thirties. But her countenance was that of a woman ten years older: a desert of blond hair dried from overbleaching, the dark roots a badge testifying to her bad taste; puffy bags under the faded gray eyes; a persistent sniffle that hinted at a coke habit; obesity that seemed to contradict a fondness for coke and that she tried to hide with loose clothing.

They sat in her cluttered living room in her beachside condo. Suzi's hand kept dipping into a bowl of potato chips as she reeled off the travails of single parenthood. Suppose her son, who was now three and going to nursery school four times a week, turned out queer? Or worse, suppose he turned out to be a pervert like his father? Quin seized on this opening and ran with it.

"You think Gene Travis is a pervert?"

"Bet your ass." She munched noisily on another potato chip. "Anyone who's into porn is a pervert in my opinion." Then her cheeks flushed with color. "Including *moi*, when I was into porn."

"That's how you met Gene?"

She flicked at crumbs in her lap. "I wasn't always fifty pounds overweight, you know. I was pretty damned attractive, I can tell you that." Her hooded eyes suddenly opened wider, revealing an inviolate belief that she had once been lovely. "I was in a couple of Gene's films, that's how we met. You know about his films?"

"You mean his videos?"

She made an impatient gesture with her hand. "Shit. Videos, films, what's the difference. They're both done with cameras." Another potato chip, with dip this time, vanished into her mouth. Her cheeks puffed out like a squirrel's. "It was kinda neat, goin' to these pretty places like Trinidad and Barbados and Puerto Rico. Yeah, after San Juan, I decided I like spic men the best." She laughed, munched. "Listen, you want some coffee? Or maybe somethin' cold to drink?"

"Whatever you've got would be fine."

"C'mon. Let's talk in the kitchen." She shambled

162

across the soiled rug in her bare feet, and Quin followed. The capacious kitchen was as cluttered as the front room. Dishes were stacked in the sink. Crumbs littered the counter.

"I got this condo through the settlement, you know. On the paternity suit. Had me a dynamite lawyer." She filled the coffeepot, brought out a bag of Fritos, and dumped them into a bowl. She whisked out cheese, more dip, set everything on the table. "Gene knew he was the father of my kid. Hell, I even know when I conceived. I could feel it. There we were, in this plushy suite in San Juan, see, goin' at it like there was no *mañana*, and all of a sudden, I knew. My tubes were supposed to be tied, but I'm tellin' you, I knew when that little ole sperm did its trick. Jus' like in that Woody Allen film, *Everything You Always Wanted to Know About Sex*." *A rambler*, Quin thought, and steered her back toward the videos like a tour guide as they sat at the table.

"What kind of video were you doing?"

Her plump hand went for the Fritos. "What kind do you think? It was for one of Gene's special clients."

"Describe it."

Those gray eyes gazed at Quin with a feral intensity. "Gimme that check first."

Quin dug in her purse for the fifty-dollar check. She set it on the table between them. Suzi Mellon shook her head. "That's just for my time. You want extra information, it'll be a hundred bucks."

Quin thought of the $3,500 check Young had given them for *expenses*. "Let's make it two hundred and you tell me about the snuff films, Suzi." Quin had been banking on hearsay, but something—fear?—flittered through Suzi's gray eyes, and she decided to bluff. "Two hundred and some information about the snuff videos, Suzi. Easy money."

The flesh along the underside of her arms quivered and danced as she drew her hand back from the bowl of Fritos. "I think you'd better leave, lady."

"Three hundred," Quin said.

Suzi Mellon had been rising from her chair, and now she stopped in midstream. Quin recognized the concrescence of greed in her face: the tightening of muscles at her mouth, the pinch at her eyes, the slow smile. "Make it five hundred and as long as this conversation is confidential we've got a deal."

"Five, then."

. She sank back into the chair. Quin wrote out the check. Suzi Mellon's fat fingers snatched it up. "You don't have cash?"

"No."

"Shit." She folded the check and stuck it under the sugar bowl. She laced her fingers together. "Snuff films. He does them."

Fear fletched Quin's spine.

"For big bucks. Over a hundred grand a film. Usually chooses beach bums, whores, nobodys for the victims. That way the cops never get too interested. What's one more bum who's disappeared, they figure. The video in Puerto Rico—that was one." She raised her eyes. "When I sued him for paternity for the kid, he wasn't about to mess with me. That's why we settled outa court. He knew that I knew, and he also knew that all I wanted was some money to support myself and the kid in a good style." She flung her arms out. "This is a good style. A beach place, money in the bank . . ." She nodded her head quickly. "He also wanted to keep things copacetic with wifey number two, see. Hey, how would it look if the kids knew Big Daddy was into snuff films?"

"Doesn't he use code names with his videos?"

"Yeah. So I've heard. But I don't know what they are."

"Describe what happened in this snuff video you did."

The fat fingers parted reluctantly and reached for more Fritos. She shrugged a plump shoulder. "A little kinky stuff, then the guy gets killed."

"How?"

"Butcher knife."

164

"Gene was there? Shooting the video?"

She laughed. "You must be kidding. That's shit work. He's got guys who do all his shit work, and *those* guys are hired by someone else who's hired by someone else and on down the line, so it'd take a fucking Sherlock to trace it back to Gene. You got *no* idea, lady, how this man's mind works. Even God wouldn't be able to figure it out."

"But *you* know it's Gene who set the video up."

"So what? You think I want to rot in the slammer?" Her plump finger vanished to the first joint in a fold of skin as she stabbed at her own chest. "I was in on it. That's how he keeps his princesses quiet." She sat back. "Any more information will cost ya an extra five hundred."

"You know what I think, Suzi?" Quin leaned forward, her fingers straying toward the check under the sugar bowl.

"What's that?" *Munch, munch.*

Quin flicked the check out and ripped it in two. "That you don't deserve five hundred bucks,"

Then she stood, grabbed her purse, and started for the door. Suzi Mellon hurried after her with quick, exigent steps. "Hey, we had a deal. C'mon. We had a goddamn deal."

"I had my fingers crossed." Quin slammed the door behind her.

165

17 The Trophy

THERE WAS A certain beauty about it, he decided. It was no longer as pink as a seashell because it was drying up, but the ear's ridges and once-soft curves were still visible. It reminded him of an exotic piece of weathered coral or jewelry. In fact, if he poked a tiny hole in the lobe with an ice pick, it could be hung from a necklace.

For a moment, he imagined the ear hanging around Joyce's neck. He could almost see it, pale pink against the lapis field of a sweater or a blouse. And Joyce's fingers would be touching it absently, the way she used to do whenever she wore jewelry, her touch like a distracted caress.

But Joyce was dead, and he already had a use for the ear.

He pulled on his gloves and carefully picked up the ear from the patch of sunlight where it had been drying out. He set it in a square of aluminum foil and folded the edges of the foil around it. Next, he placed it in an unmarked box that had once contained cuff links and wrapped it in plain brown paper. Like Christmas. A late gift, he thought, and smiled as he pressed the address label to the front, a neatly typed label. This time, the trophy itself would be the teaser.

When the package was ready, he tied a piece of string around it like a bow, and stood there, gazing at it, recalling the kill. Even now, he could taste the vestiges of a triumph that had almost gone sour. Almost.

Summer had surprised him.

But then, his male victims were usually more difficult

than the females. It was part of what made them such great challenges, forcing him to be innovative, to be prepared for the unexpected. But with each kill, male or female, he ferreted out something new about himself. It was as if he were a revolving moon and each kill thrust a different side into light. With Joyce, for instance, he'd learned he was capable of killing someone other than a stranger. With Summer, he'd stumbled upon his apparent capacity to act instinctively, even though the odds might be stacked against him.

With McCleary, he would learn . . .

Well, he would have to see.

He opened a cabinet and brought out McCleary's painting. It was the first time he'd looked at it since he'd taken it, and he was struck by its soft-focus beauty. The curve of the woman's naked back and the way the bourbon stream of her hair followed its contours were enhanced by the color of the light. A dream light, he thought, part pearl, part mist. The light bled along the backs of her arms and spilled into the splendid gold of the field in which she lay.

It was an admirable work of art.

He experienced a visceral shudder deep inside him that was almost sexual in its violence, its abruptness. Tenderly, he brushed a spot of dust from the woman's back, his fingers lingering on McCleary's signature. No grand flourishes, no fantastic loops, just a tight, scrupulous signature so small it was almost diffident.

An instinctive artist, he thought. McCleary was one of those people who, the moment he picked up his brush, tapped into something larger than himself.

He closed his eyes, his fingertips remaining on the signature. After a moment or two, the canvas seemed to heat up against his skin. He could sense McCleary's presence as if the signature created a bridge between them, an inviolate nexus.

Hello, McCleary.

He opened his eyes, and the fingers of his other hand curled around the box with Summer's ear in it. A surfeit of energy surged through him like electricity. By touching the signature and the box, it was as if he were completing a circuit, grounding it. The sensation that infused him was nearly as splendid as a kill—the same white, blinding radiance, the heightened awareness and lightness of being.

Don't get too cocky, warned a voice in the back of his mind. *You were lucky with Summer. It could've been a disaster. You may not be as lucky with McCleary.*

The sensation fled, leaving him utterly deflated.

"Shut up," he hissed, his hands dropping away from the box, the painting. "Just shut up."

And his body, now sated, now as full and fat as a well-fed hog, fell silent.

But he wondered how long its silence would last this time.

18 T.G.I.F.

IT HAD BEEN exactly four hours and thirty-seven minutes since McCleary had shuffled into her office and told her about Bob Summer. He'd uttered it at the end of her tale about Nelly Brown and Suzi with a Z-I Mellon, in a voice flatter than old Coke. Then he'd walked back to his own office, and she knew he'd been there ever since, working through his grief privately, just as he had always done.

She, on the other hand, had immediately raided the fridge in the kitchen. She'd eaten as though food could relieve the shock of Summer's death. But in the middle of a tuna fish sandwich, her sorrow had caught in her throat and she'd started to cry. She'd imagined Summer's ghost standing to her side, clicking his tongue against his teeth as he passed her the box of Kleenex and murmured, *Really, Quin. I appreciate how you feel, but go find the fucker, will you?*

The damnable thing about murder was that it smashed open the safe cocoon of your life like a walnut. Then the effluvia poured in as swiftly and deadly as a radioactive cloud. By the time it cleared, your cells had been seized by the vicissitudes of the radioactivity; you were no longer as you were.

Quin turned back to the computer and finished entering the particulars on the Young case. Her phone buzzed. It was Ruth Grimes, telling her she had a call from Neal Schloper. "You want to take it, Quin?"

"Yes, thanks. Put him through."

The phone clicked. She heard a sound like wind through

a tunnel, then Schloper said, "Hello? Ms. St. James? Uh, this is Neal Schloper. We spoke the other day at the airport?"

Like I could forget. "Yes, I remember. What can I do for you, Mr. Schloper?"

"I've been thinking about our conversation, and there're some things you should know. Could you meet me at the Grove Café tomorrow morning? Around ten?"

"Can't you tell me what it is over the phone, Mr. Schloper?"

"I'd rather not."

She didn't feel particularly comfortable about meeting with Schloper. Considering what she'd seen at the Pink Slipper, it was pretty obvious there was a connection of some sort between him and Travis. But she supposed a café was safe enough. "All right. You'll have to give me directions." He did, and she scribbled them down. "See you at ten, then."

She switched off the computer, then swiveled around in her chair, reached for her purse on the couch, picked up her briefcase, and padded down the hall toward McCleary's office. Most everyone had gone home, and the building seemed peculiarly quiescent, as if the rooms were sighing with relief that another week was behind them.

McCleary's door was open. He was on the phone, his chair turned around, so his back was to the door. Quin started to turn away but heard an odd gentleness in his voice that froze her right where she was. ". . . I understand, really . . . I know what you're saying, Callahan. Just stop blaming yourself, okay?"

Quin walked into the office on weak knees and sat down, clutching her briefcase against her. McCleary glanced around, his smoky eyes heated with a pastiche of conflicting emotions. He managed to smile, a weak smile that cockled his eyes. It was a hell of a lot more than she could muster as Nelly Brown's parting words scampered through her head like hungry roaches. *Just give 'im room to move around. . . .*

". . . right, okay, we'll see you in a while." He hung up and sat back in his chair, lifting his feet to the edge of his desk. "That was Callahan. She wants to meet with us at Studebaker's in Lauderdale so she can brief you on Gene Travis."

"You really feel like doing that after what's happened today?"

He shrugged, dropped his feet to the floor, and folded his hands on his meticulous desk, his eyes glued to them. He spoke softly. "Bob's dead, Quin. There's nothing I can do about it except to try to outwit this guy before he gets someone else."

In the subsequent brief silence, Quin heard the air conditioner click on. A bluejay flitted past the window. A gloam was settling into the room, and Quin reached over and turned on the lamp. Pats of light fell onto the backs of McCleary's hands. She thought of how often those hands had soothed and excited her.

Did they soothe and excite Callahan as well?

"I don't think we should cancel the party tomorrow night," McCleary went on, as if there'd been no pause. "It'd make Bob turn in his grave."

Yeah, it probably would, she thought, smiling in spite of herself. "Okay. There aren't that many people coming, anyway."

His expression suddenly seemed so lost that she rose from her chair and crouched in front of him and slid her arms around his waist, burying her face against his chest. "I'm sorry about Bob, Mac."

He hugged her wordlessly, his chin resting on top of her head. She could feel his pain, almost as if she were absorbing it through her own skin like a sponge. "I wish," he said finally, "that we'd driven to the airport that day, Quin."

"We still can. The tickets are on the kitchen bulletin board."

He cupped her chin in his hand and kissed her softly, tenderly, one of those real McCleary kisses that made her skin leap with desire. Then she thought of his remark to Callahan, about not blaming herself for something, and her desire blinked out like a star. She stood. "If we've got to drive all the way to Lauderdale in five o'clock traffic, I guess we'd better get going."

His eyes followed her up. "Unless you want to head for the airport."

He grinned at her, and she was tempted to grab the opportunity, tempted to say, *Yes, all right, let's go. Now. This minute.* But she turned pragmatic. She, who had known maybe two pragmatic days in her life, said, "Can we afford to refund most of Ross's advance?"

His grin disappeared like a rabbit into a magician's hat. "No."

"I guess that settles it, then."

Studebaker's was one of the many clubs that had sprung up in South Florida in the last year that was a tribute to the fifties. It was set back from Oakland Park Boulevard in an innocuous mall that was mostly concrete. Its pink and purple neon sign was as visible as Venus on a clear night.

The entrance was blocked off with a huge red sign that said VALET PARKING. Young surfer types dressed in shorts, shirts, and bow ties were hopping into cars, screeching away from the curb, and shrieking to a stop in spaces several yards away.

"No way one of those maniacs is parking Lady," McCleary mumbled, and stopped at the road block. A valet opened his car door. McCleary passed him a couple of bucks. "I'll park it myself."

"Right over there, sir."

As they got out of the car and walked toward the entrance, the stillness of the air seemed an odd contrast, Quin thought, to the music pounding from the doorway. Inside, Studebaker's was a cave of raised platforms, bright tiled walls, a dance floor, and people, the T.G.I.F. crowd. They wended their way through the smell of perfume and smoke to a platform in back where a buffet of free food was laid out. Sylvia Callahan, sitting in a booth by herself, saw them and waved. Quin's insides immediately tightened, as if she'd eaten something that had disagreed with her, and that old, familiar worm called jealousy began its slow, painful burrow.

Close up, Callahan reminded Quin of Candice Bergen—the same type of hair, a sultry mouth, pale blue eyes that promised universes. But there was some minute flaw in her face—perhaps in the curve of her jaw or the set of her eyes—that prevented her from being the knockout Bergen was. But why nit-pick; she was still gorgeous.

McCleary introduced them. Callahan's hand was thin and delicate and soft. Not a hand that did dishes, mopped floors, or scrubbed, Quin noted. She greeted Quin warmly, then slid into one side of the booth as the McClearys slid into the other. Her nervous chatter betrayed her cool demeanor and continued until a waitress dressed in a fifties getup came over and took their order.

The music wasn't as loud in this corner, but Quin's temple pulsed to the beat. When their drinks arrived, she sipped at hers gratefully. The sapid taste of the Scotch proved to be a temporary anodyne for the growing stiffness in Quin's neck.

McCleary suggested she tell Callahan about her meetings with Joyce's maid and Suzi Mellon. She went through her stories and noted that Callahan listened avidly, that she had the woman's complete attention. When Quin had finished, Callahan's head bobbed, as if some obscure piece of a puzzle had fallen into place.

"Correct me if I'm wrong, but I gather the point of all this is to get evidence that Gene contracts for murder on video." Her brows shot up. Her eyes darted from Quin to McCleary and back to Quin again.

"*If* that's what was involved in Joyce's murder and *if* he's the killer," Quin replied.

"Okay, then there're a couple of things you can do, Quin, as Mike's client. Gene's got some rather strange ideas about women."

"So I've gathered."

She smiled. "Not all women, just certain types of women. First, you've got to seem totally aloof, unattainable, a woman who's strictly interested in business, in profit. Cold. Classy and cold. Second, the surroundings have got to be believable for a woman with your kind of wealth. Third, he's going to have you checked out—your finances, who you are, and so on. I think I can help you there. Also, when you start talking about the deal, tell him you've heard he has a sideline business that interests you and that you're willing to pay an additional X number of dollars for that. He'll be impressed that you know something about his video thing. Tell him you'd like to see it."

Quin had wanted to dislike this woman; she found that she didn't. She had hoped Callahan was an airhead; she wasn't. She had wanted to believe that McCleary's judgment had been impaired when he'd known her. But looking at Callahan, listening to her talk, Quin understood why McCleary had been involved with her. There was nothing specious about her. Her directness was infinitely appealing. She was bright. Quick. And hey, Quin thought, on top of it she looked like Candice Bergen.

In a moment of lucid insight, she also sensed that whatever had happened between them had never run its natural course. Their affair had been cut short by circumstances. This incompleteness now enhanced the initial chemistry between them, imbuing it with all the tragic elements of a Shakespearean play. But the tragedy had a contemporary twist. Instead of madness or incest or warring families, the binding, forbidden component was the fact that McCleary was married.

Quin had several quick, distressing images of McCleary and Callahan meeting on the sly. She imagined congeries of white lies that quickly became darker, deeper, more tangled. She understood how the secrecy, the sneaking around, would emerge as a player itself in this little drama. And she knew that given the choice, she would rather have it all in the open. She had neither the time nor the inclination to be cast as the poor little wifey in all this. She didn't feel like sitting around, playing the *Is he or isn't he?* game with herself, her paranoia metastasizing, eating away at her like acid. If there was an affair in progress, if McCleary needed to resolve this thing with Callahan, fine, then he could do it with her knowing about it.

"Do you think this meeting should take place with Mac present?" Quin asked.

"Absolutely. I also think you should be wired for sound, Quin. I suppose the cops could help you out on that end. Another thing. There should be some sort of preliminary meeting before the big one. Something casual, in a party type setting, maybe, where you two can check each other out. Gene is big on ritual. What I had in mind—and it's just a suggestion—is a party at my place."

"Whatever you think is best. You're the one who knows him. What bothers me is that *if* he's the one who broke into our house, then he knows Mac isn't who he says he is. That means he's being set up."

Callahan's smile made the blue in her eyes dance. "True. But it's exactly the sort of game Gene likes to play. It's a game he'll think he can win. That'll make him careless. And that's where your strength lies."

Quin looked over at McCleary, who'd simply been sitting back, listening and observing. "When are you planning on a meeting?"

"I'd like to do it as soon as possible."

"Then think about it, pick a date, and we'll go from there," Callahan said.

"Before we decide anything, I'd like to meet with Neal Schloper tomorrow," Quin noted. "Did Mac tell you about Neal's antic at the Pink Slipper?"

Callahan nodded. "It's not too surprising that some of Gene's clients star in their own videos. But then, nothing about Gene surprises me." She sat back, stirring the skewer in her drink, her expression pensive. "We need a fictitious name for you, so I can get a friend of mine to build a financial history in the event Gene checks."

"How about Anise Rochelle?" It was the name she and Bean had chosen.

Callahan's lips moved silently, as she repeated the name to herself. For the next few minutes they tossed out names as if they were placing bets on jai alai players. Or on dogs at the greyhound races. Eve and Ramona, Janice and Annette, Stephanie and Linda. But they finally settled on Anise Rochelle.

With business momentarily concluded, they went through the food line at the buffet table, piling their plates high with casseroles and salads, meatballs and pasta. The din of voices soon competed with the volume of the music. More of the T.G.I.F. crowd poured into the place. A cop McCleary had worked with joined them at the booth. The smoke and the Scotch and the noise eventually got to Quin, and she excused herself and went to the rest room.

As she stepped out into the hall a few minutes later, Callahan was at the cigarette machine, fumbling through her wallet for change. Quin walked over to her. "Need some quarters?"

Callahan looked up and smiled. "Yes, thanks. I've got change, but no quarters."

Quin went through her wallet and they made the exchange for dimes and nickels. Callahan fed the machine, yanked on a lever, and a pack of Winston Lights sailed out. She ripped open the pack, offered Quin one, but she shook her head. "God, I always smoke too much when I go to a bar," Callahan griped, lighting the cigarette, inhaling deeply. "But damn, I enjoy these things. I'm hoping that by the time I've got lung cancer, they'll have found a cure."

Quin laughed.

"Did you ever smoke?"

"For years. Then one morning I woke up with a hangover and I couldn't even look at a cigarette. I think that's what did it. I haven't touched a White Russian to this day, either."

Callahan motioned toward the exit door. "C'mon, let's get some air."

She pressed the bar across the exit door, they stepped

176

outside, and Callahan propped her shoe between the door and the jamb so it wouldn't close. They were in an alley that bordered a housing development. The air smelled clean and sweet. Stars spalled the sky, almost as if someone had thrown handfuls of bleached white pennies across the cold black of space. Quin leaned into the wall, which was cool against her back. "I think I had too much to drink."

"I've got the perfect remedy for that." Callahan brought out a joint and lit it. She passed it to Quin, who inhaled too deeply and coughed until she thought she would gag. It went straight to her head and certainly took care of the alcohol. They smoked half the joint in silence, then Callahan put it out against the wall. "Mike says you've been a private eye for more than ten years."

"Of sorts. In the beginning it was mostly medical malpractice and insurance cases. Now it seems to be primarily homicides, missing people, and background checks for corporations."

"How'd you and Mike meet?"

"A man I was living with was murdered, and he was the investigating officer. It turned out that his partner was the killer. One of life's grotesque little ironies, I guess."

"Robin Peters?"

"Yeah, he told you about it?"

"No." Her left foot, the shoeless foot, slid up the wall. "I read about it in the paper, I think. Yeah, that was it. Homicide officer shoots partner. Some lurid head-line like that." She puffed on her cigarette, then flipped it away from her. Quin followed the glow as it arched through the blackness and sighed against the ground. "I met him because of a homicide too. My sister's."

"I know. He told me."

"It does weird things to your head when someone you love is murdered. Well, you must know. I don't think I was myself until, oh, maybe two years later after Marcy's death."

'Was she your only sister?"

"Yeah. Younger. She had her problems, but hell, she was a good kid. She really was. She didn't deserve what she got."

"They rarely do. Bob Summer sure didn't."

Callahan turned toward her, arms hugging her waist, her lovely mouth drawn in a tight grimace. "Gene Travis is a very tricky character, Quin. If I were you, I'd leave the whole thing alone."

"No, I don't think you would."

The grimace loosened as she laughed. "Yeah, you're right. I wouldn't."

"Are you still in love with McCleary?" Quin blurted and immediately regretted it.

She hadn't intended to ask. She hadn't, really. She didn't want to know.

She wanted desperately to know.

She wished Callahan would go away.

She hoped Callahan stayed.

Now Callahan was gazing at the ground, lighting another cigarette, tilting her head back. "I don't know." The words whispered into the air with the wisps of smoke.

"But you were."

"Yes." She shrugged her thin shoulders. There was something infinitely sad about the gesture, as if she were dismissing something she didn't really want to let go. "We were—still are—from very different worlds. Worlds which, in real life, in day-to-day life, probably wouldn't mesh very well. I was extremely vulnerable when my sister was killed. Otherwise I don't think I would ever have gotten involved with a cop."

"They tend to be bossy sometimes."

Callahan chuckled. "Yeah. Yeah, they do. They also happened to be the bad guys in the game I was playing."

Quin closed her eyes and drifted to the echos of the music from inside. The night air stroked her face. She felt as if she and Callahan had stepped into a separate time zone unequipped for the journey. Were there rules you were supposed to follow in a situation like this?

Guidelines? Her husband had been in love with this woman, might still be in love with her, and here they were, standing in a dark alley discussing him as if he were just any man.

"I really wanted to dislike you," Quin said.

"The feeling was mutual."

They looked at each other. The moonlight silhouetted Callahan's face. Quin imagined McCleary's hand caressing its curves and contours. Oddly, the worm of jealousy remained motionless, silenced.

"But it didn't work out that way," Callahan said.

"I know."

Quin reached into her purse and withdrew a bag of sunflower seeds. She opened it and offered the bag to Callahan. "I get the feeling that things between you and Mac were kind of left hanging."

Callahan passed the bag back to Quin, bit down on a seed, spit out the husk. "Yeah, I seem to be real good at that. Leaving things incomplete." She turned sideways, her fingers picking through a tiny pile of seeds in the palm of her hand. "Look, Quin I haven't been with a man in more than three years. Celibacy tends to warp your perspective."

"*Three years?* Why?"

Callahan made a sound that was supposed to be a laugh but fell pitifully short. "Ridiculous, huh, in this day and age. It's been a combination of things, really. When I last saw Mike four years ago, I was involved with a guy who was really pushing marriage. He was a terrific man, and in retrospect I probably should've married him. But I was still a mess inside from Marcy's death, and I was trying to decide whether or not I wanted to sell my business. Anyway, he broke off the relationship about three months later, and I sold the bar. I think what happened was that I suffered a Callahan version of a mid-life crisis or something, about five years early." She smiled a little and looked up. "Instead of religion or drugs or promiscuity, I just turned off and tuned out."

179

Quin munched on some sunflower seeds, incredulous that she and this woman were even having this conversation. "But I thought you and Mac . . ."

"Had been together?" She shrugged. "I was certainly willing." She paused. "You sure you want to hear this?"

No.

Yes.

Maybe.

What for?

Don't be stupid.

You're asking for trouble.

I've got to know.

"Yes, I'm sure."

Callahan gazed out into the dark alley. "Last night something started and might've been finished if he were a different sort of man. There're a lot of unresolved things between us, things that were never worked out because of circumstances. Stuff that eats away at you. But I don't think he's capable of a clandestine affair, Quin. You two obviously have something very good between you, and he's committed himself to the marriage."

But at what cost? If *she* were in McCleary's shoes, what would she do? What would *he* do? Would he be standing here discussing the situation with his competitor? Would he encourage her to resolve the feelings so they could get on with their lives? If she did that, if she told him to do whatever he had to do, what guarantee did she have that he wouldn't decide he was in love with Callahan?

Which was exactly the point. If she was going to encourage him to resolve things, she couldn't impose conditions. "I appreciate your honesty, Sylvia."

Callahan let out a small laugh. "I must have rocks in my head."

"Then we both do."

"Yeah."

Quin returned the bag of sunflower seeds to her purse. "So what happens now?"

"I don't know. This is as new to me as it is to you."

180

Terrific. She would've preferred an answer as solid as directions to a particular locale. *Go two blocks north and then turn east.* Instead, Callahan's *I don't know* left her stomach in knots.

"I guess we should go back inside."

Callahan nodded, removed her shoe from the door, and they stepped back into the hall, into the other time zone, Quin mused. They made their way through the crowd toward the booth where McCleary and the cop he'd worked with were still sitting. She knew from the expression on his face that he and the other man had been discussing Bob Summer.

"Hey, what happened to you two?"

"Kidnapped," said Callahan. "By Diogenes, seeker of truth."

19 Developments

1.

IN THE DREAM, death sweets circled the floor around him like corpses. They quivered, these sweets, they danced, they rose up on their ends and stumbled toward him, metamorphosing as they moved, becoming bodies. *Hey, Mac*, shouted a sweet that looked like Bob Summer. *Watch this*. And Summer reached for a second sweet that was Joyce Young and they did a soft-shoe shuffle across the floor. Joyce laughed and laughed; powdered sugar rained from her hair like dandruff.

McCleary raced for the stairs that spiraled up through the fusty air toward a glimmer of light. But the steps melted like ice beneath his feet, and when he grappled for the banister, Lois Dwight slid down it dressed in a ballerina tutu smeared with honey. *No, no, Mr. McCleary. You can't leave yet. You're next you're next you're next*. . . . And then a shape appeared at the top of the stairs, holding a giant pair of scissors that it clacked in the air like castanets. *McCleary, I need a trophy*, a man yelled, and the scissors glistened in the dim light and seemed to float toward him, still clacking, clacking, circling his head.

He fell back, his arms pinwheeling, and the scissors came down over his arm, snipping it off at the shoulder. He leaped out of the dream, the sheets tangled around his neck, his waist, his skin as wet as a forest after a rain. Light bled through the curtains. The hands at the clock skipped toward seven.

He untangled himself from the sheet, then wiped his face with the edge of it and lay back against the pillow.

Quin rolled over and lifted up on an elbow. "Is it time to get up? Did we oversleep?" Her voice was husky.

"No. It's Saturday," he said softly. "Go back to sleep."

She flopped over on her side, her arm draping him at the waist, and in seconds was fast asleep. McCleary brushed strands of hair from her forehead, then carefully disengaged her arm and got up. He went into the bathroom to take a shower and made the mistake of glancing at himself in the mirror. He looked like hell. He looked like he'd been on a binge. Dark stubble shadowed his jaw, his eyes were bloodshot, his hand trembled as he reached for the soap, his head ached, his stomach cramped.

Maybe I've got a brain tumor.

It would explain the things that had been happening to him: the incident with Callahan in the car the other night, the headaches that had little to do with his hunches, this pervasive feeling that he was suffering from withdrawal from drugs or something, these compulsions he kept having.

Compulsions. He didn't like the way that word sounded. But it described perfectly how he'd felt when he'd lined up those items in his den that morning, and used the honey on Quin. And last night, after Quin had fallen asleep, he'd felt *compelled* to put on his running suit and drive over to the park where Bob Summer had met his demise.

He'd run along the track, a flashlight illuminating the path, the skin across his forehead blazing. For a few minutes it had seemed that he was connected to the killer again, that he could sense the man's excitement, hear the hammering of his heart. He'd stopped, blinking hard, looking around, fear bristling along the back of his neck. And then he'd fled back to his car. When he'd gotten home, he'd spent another two hours going through the files again, setting up the tools of what Doc Smithers had called 'sympathetic magic': items that represented trophies, teasers, victims, the *pattern*.

When he'd been unable to think about murder anymore, when the very notion became an oppressive weight, he thought about Callahan. And Quin. And then he'd crawled into bed and tried to drive out the memory of Callahan's mouth and the taste of her skin, and his emotions balled up inside him until he felt physically ill.

As ill as he looked now.

He turned on the shower and stepped under the hot spray. How could he still have feelings for Callahan? How could he have feelings for her when he was married to Quin? When he loved Quin? Even when he'd been single and involved with a woman, he'd been monogamous. So why this division now?

The curtain rustled and Quin peeked in. "Room for two?"

He smiled and pushed the curtain back. "Always."

She shucked her nightgown and stepped under the hot spray. "I couldn't go back to sleep." She reached for the soap and her hands moved over his back, his neck and buttocks, and down the length of his legs. He stood with his hands against the wall, the hot water drumming his head. Her hands slid around to his stomach; she kissed his spine, then reached for the bottle of shampoo. She squirted some into her hair and passed him the bottle. She lathered her hair, she rinsed it, she picked up the razor that lay in a puddle of water at the corner of the tub and began shaving her legs. He noticed the rust marks the razor had left on the tile.

Were there rust marks on Callahan's tub? Did her butter dish ever end up in the pantry? Was her nightstand stacked high with books and old letters? Did things vanish under her bed as if they'd been sucked into the vacuum of outer space? Did her closet look as if a twelve-year-old child had arranged it?

Stop it.

He picked up the soap and lathered Quin's shoulders, his fingers kneading the tight muscles in her neck, moving down her arms. She turned and they embraced. The soap and water had transformed her skin to satin. Her mouth tasted like papaya. He rubbed the soap over her breasts, her tummy, and lower.

She giggled. "That tickles," she whispered.

The soap slipped from his hand, and he cupped her chin and kissed her again, kissed her hard, trying to drive out the image of Callahan's face. But it brightened in his mind like a rising sun, brightened even as he lowered his mouth to Quin's breast, as his hands sought the warmth between her legs, as they made love in the sweet scent of lilac soap and steam.

Afterward, as Quin sat at the edge of the tub drying her hair, a fluffy brown towel wrapped around her, McCleary touched the fading bruise on her shoulder.

"My first hickey in fifteen years," she laughed. "They probably don't even call them that anymore."

"He bit Lois Dwight on the shoulder when he came," McCleary said.

Her laughter died. She stood and turned off the hair dryer. "I figured as much." Then she opened the door and walked out into the bedroom.

McCleary followed. "You don't understand what I'm saying, Quin."

"I understand exactly what you're saying. You're . . . I don't know, tied into this guy somehow, Mac, tied in because you've become as . . . as obsessed as he is. It scares me. It scares me worse than your feelings for Ca—" She stopped quickly, abruptly. A funny look claimed her features, as if she'd just swallowed a piece of food and it had gone down the wrong way. "Well, it scares me, that's all." And she turned away and yanked open a drawer of her bureau.

"My feelings for Callahan? Is that what you were going to say?"

He approached the bureau and stood at the side. She pushed strands of her hair behind her ear.

"Quin?"

"Yes. Yes, that's what I was going to say. Your

feelings for Callahan. Right.'' She plucked a clean pair of underwear from the drawer, then a T-shirt and shorts. She untied her towel, it sighed to the floor, and she dressed rapidly, as if she wanted to get away from him. "How about a big breakfast? I'm famished." She said it casually, like they'd been discussing something as impersonal as world politics, and started toward the door.

McCleary stopped her. "That's it? That's all you're going to say?"

She leaned into the wall, arms folded across her breasts, and studied the floor. He stood in front of her, blocking her way, trapping her. "What do you want me to say, Mac?" Her voice was soft, and when she looked at him, her eerie ghost blue eyes coruscated with confusion, hurt. "That she's a jerk? She isn't. You want me to say I'm jealous? Well, I am. Terribly. But I'm not going to slit my wrists if you sleep with her, all right? The hell of it is that when I put myself in your shoes, I can understand why you still have feelings for her. I don't like it, but I understand it. Which really doesn't make anything any easier at all, does it.''

"No."

He ran a hand over his head, wishing now that he hadn't prodded her. He didn't want to have this conversation yet. But it was too late. The Pandora's box had been opened, and the disease was floating out, wrapping around them like tendrils.

"Were you in love with her? Five years ago?"

He nodded. "But it was never a normal relationship. There were never any commitments made."

"Are you in love with her now?"

He hesitated. "I don't know."

It was true. He didn't know. He should have and didn't. Quin lowered her eyes and jammed her hands in the pockets of her shorts. Neither of them spoke. McCleary's insides knotted; he thought he was going to puke. He wanted to wind the clock back fifteen minutes and start over again. Instead of asking Quin what she'd been about to say concerning Callahan, he would suggest going out for breakfast. Or taking a drive up the coast. Or they would make love again.

She looked up. "Mac, if you don't know what you feel for Callahan, then I think you'd better find out." She touched her hand to the side of his face and tweaked the end of his mustache. In a voice which defied that they'd just had a conversation riddled with insinuations about a possible infidelity, *his* infidelity, she said, "Do you want cinnamon rolls for breakfast?"

2.

Most of the Grove Café was a terrace shaded by banyans and black olive trees. Birds trilled from branches, several cats strolled about leisurely, and the air was redolent with roses, gardenias, and nuances of other fragrances Quin couldn't identify.

Couples claimed most of the tables. Couples lingering over coffee, perusing the morning paper, or simply enjoying each other. She spotted Neal Schloper—*Slurper*, as Nelly Brown called him—at a table along the railing, his fawn-colored hair falling across his forehead, his wire-rim glasses perched on top of his head. He was paging through the newspaper, looking as though he didn't have a worry in the world, and didn't glance up until she stopped at the table. Then he stood quickly as she pulled out her chair.

"Hi. How about some coffee?"

My, aren't we friendly this morning. "Thanks, that sounds great." But as she sat down, the aura of coffee and bacon made her mouth water. It had been three hours since she'd eaten breakfast. On top of it, the business with McCleary had stirred her anxiety, and whenever she felt anxious, her appetite grew to immedicable proportions. "I think I'd like a menu, too."

She ordered the house specialty: oatmeal smothered in dates and walnuts and bananas, a basket of homemade biscuits, a baked plantain, and juice. When the waitress walked away, she folded her hands on the table and effected her best *So what is it you wanted to tell me?* expression.

Schloper rubbed his square, obdurate jaw. "I, uh, wasn't entirely honest with you the other day, Ms. St. James."

Oh, brother. Whenever anyone started a conversation like that, alarms shrieked in the back of her head. "About what?"

"About myself and Joyce."

Quin thought briefly of the videotape of Schloper and Joyce that Ross Young had found in his stepsister's attic. "Go on."

"Even though we were divorced nearly a year ago, we continued to have relations."

He made it sound so clinical. "So why lie about that?"

He shrugged. "Because I knew how it would look to the cops. Here Joyce was having an affair with Gene Travis, but she and I were still involved and—"

"Look, Mr. Schloper. It's been my experience that when people lie and then do an about-face, there's a motive. So why don't you tell me the real reason you wanted me to meet you here. It wasn't just so you could tell me you and Joyce were still sleeping together."

His eyes, a puerile blue that seemed to be deepening even as they sat there, crinkled at the corners. A lazy smile claimed his face, a smile that might have sent shudders of alarm along her spine had they not been in a public place.

"Dispense with the bullshit. Yeah, all right." He sat with an arm thrown over the back of the chair, his manner easy now, his body language shouting that he had nothing to hide. "Are you aware that Gene Travis has a, uh, video service for some of his better clients?"

"You just talk, Mr. Schloper. I'll ask the questions."

He didn't like her tone of voice, she could see that, but he continued just the same. "Okay. Sometimes customers make requests for certain types of videos and

Gene finds the people to be in them and hires someone to shoot them. Joyce and I were involved in a couple of them."

"Pornographic videos."

"Yes."

"Was this before or after your divorce?"

"Both."

"Any particular reason?"

"Reason?"

"Yeah. Was there any reason you two decided to be porn stars?"

As Schloper sat forward, an intensity seemed to flow through him again. "Look, I don't know how much you know about Joyce's relationship with Ross, but every goddamn weird and rebellious thing she ever did in her life—including marrying me and her involvement with Travis—was because she was in love with her step-brother. So you wanna talk about weird shit? Talk to him."

He echoed what Nelly Brown had implied, she thought. "At the moment, I'm talking to you. You were telling me about why you two became porn stars, Mr. Schloper." *And while we're at it, Mr. Schloper, does this extracurricular pursuit impair your ability as an Eastern mechanic?*

"It was Joyce's idea. I went along with it in the beginning because the machinists for Eastern were on strike and we were having money problems. I figured it was better than Joyce running to Ross for another loan." His voice had turned taciturn, ugly, moody. "I didn't realize at the time that she was screwing Travis."

The waitress brought over a pot of coffee and Quin's breakfast. She dug into it with relish, and listened as Schloper continued.

"On the first film we earned about five grand. It was easy money, and, weirdly enough, it seemed to improve our marriage."

"Was Travis ever in the films?"

"Only in one of the handful that we did, and I don't think his face was ever shown. It was shot in his backyard, around his swimming pool."

Well, that solved the mystery of the identity of the second man in the video Ross had found in Joyce's attic.

"About two weeks before Joyce was killed, I know she went out of town for a couple of days for a film. When she got back, she refused to see me or take my calls."

Another echo of Nelly Brown's story.

"When I finally saw her again, three days before she died—I think I told you about that, right?"

Quin nodded. "That was when she told you she was afraid of Travis and wanted to try to patch your marriage back together."

"Yes." He paused and sipped at his coffee. "Anyway, I stayed at the house that night. I woke up around three or four in the morning and found her at the kitchen table, her head in her arms, fast asleep. Next to her was a pad of paper where she'd scribbled something over and over. The word 'Minotaur.' I bugged her the next morning to tell me what it was, but she kept saying she couldn't, that if she did and Travis found out, he would kill her.

"Two nights ago, I went to the Pink Slipper to see if I could find out what Minotaur is. I know some of his people pretty well."

An image of Schloper with the two naked women in the basement of the club flashed through her mind. *Pretty well, Neal?* She stifled a smile. "And what'd you find out?"

He no longer looked either easygoing or smug. "That when you say the word, people's faces go totally blank and they stammer 'I don't know' or 'Never heard of it' or 'Don't know what you're talking about.' One woman finally told me that Gene's got names for the different types of videos he does. They're like code names. In other words, if some guy he's never met before comes to him and says he wants an 'Icarus' video, that means the guy's cool and that what he wants is straight porn. Then there's 'Theseus'. That means male-dominant S and M. 'Ariadne' is female-dominant S and M."

"All the names are from Greek mythology?"

"They seem to be."

"And Minotaur?"

He shrugged. "All I know is that it's 'the ultimate,' whatever that means. And that it's what terrified Joyce, what she said Travis would kill her for if she opened her mouth."

"So why tell me all this now, Mr. Schloper? Why not go to the cops?"

"Shit. If I went to the cops my ass would end up in jail. My alibi is already suspicious. That Lieutenant Benson has been bugging me every day since the murder, talking to my neighbors, the people I work with. And now the cops have a tail on me. Ain't that cute?" He jerked his thumb over his shoulder. "The guy's not too subtle. He followed me over here."

Quin saw a dark-haired man several tables away, watching them.

"Where *were* you the night of the murder, Mr. Schloper?" She knew he was about to tell her the same thing he'd told Benson, so she held up her hand. "And no bullshit, okay? Otherwise we're just wasting your time and mine."

He sighed deeply, a cloying sound that said more, perhaps, than anything he'd actually vocalized. "I was doing a video for a multimillionaire on Miami Beach. *With* her, actually. And no, Travis wasn't there. This was something that was, uh, set up privately, you might say."

"Privately? How?"

"My name's gotten around." He leaned toward her, his unctuous smile filling her with a creeping malaise. "There are some *mighty* rich and lonely women in South Florida, Ms. St. James, who have some *mighty* peculiar needs for which they are willing to pay some *mighty* hefty bucks."

"What makes you think I won't go to the cops, Mr. Schloper?"

"Be my guest. They still can't prove anything."

"Wouldn't it be a lot simpler to just give them this woman's name as your alibi?"

191

He laughed. "Right. You know how fast my name would become mud among the rich and lonely women of Miami?"

Quin finished the last of her oatmeal, which was cold. "How do you know Joyce was in love with her stepbrother?"

"I was married to the woman long enough to know, for Christ's sakes."

"How'd he feel about her?"

"Jesus, who knows? The bastard is so mute about everything. But considering how much he *didn't* like me —or Gene, for that matter—I would say there was some jealousy."

"Were they ever lovers?"

"I don't know."

"I'm still a little unclear on why you decided to tell me all this. I mean, it would have been just as easy to keep it to yourself."

For the first time since she'd sat down, an umbra of fear turned Schloper's eyes a deep, deep blue. He lit one of his black and skinny More cigarettes, rubbed the side of his neck, seemed to be wrestling with himself. "When I saw Lieutenant Benson yesterday, he told me about some woman who got cut up bad in her house. Lois Dwight. He told me some weird shit about honey and the powdered sugar that was found with Joyce and . . . and how this guy has killed some other people. And he told me about what was found in the health club locker and . . . well, other stuff. And it scared the piss outa me, I don't mind telling you that. I just want Travis off the streets."

Quin wanted to believe him, but it seemed so . . . well, so pat. Suppose Schloper was one of Travis' sycophants? One of his no doubt numerous lackeys? Suppose Travis knew who McCleary was and had deduced who his fictitious client would be and was, through Schloper, setting her up?

She murmured, "I see," then thanked him for his time.

192

"You don't believe me, do you?"

Quin stood. "I don't know. But I *am* sure of one thing."

"What's that?"

"I won't ever fly Eastern again."

20 Saturday Night

1.

MOONLIGHT VARNISHED THE pines and citrus trees in the backyard. It splashed around the swimming pool, where people chatted and laughed and drank. It puddled along the poolside bar, tipping bottles of booze and plates of steaming hors d'oeuvres. Jazz drifted out through the open windows. Now and then, as McCleary strolled restlessly from one group of people to another, an image of Bob Summer would surface like flotsam at the heart of his thoughts. He would see Summer supine in the steel box in the morgue, Summer minus his left ear. Then he would wander back to the bar and pour himself another Scotch-on-the-rocks and wash the image away.

By nine-thirty he was feeling no pain.

By ten he was noticing the sweet curve of Callahan's hips as she strode across the yard with Ross Young and Zivia, and wondered, *What if?*

By ten-thirty his guilt was a dark, colubrine shape at the forefront of his brain, and he was pacing a thin line between inebriation and sobriety. He switched to coffee. He felt particularly uxorious toward Quin as they re-filled the plates of munchies. He wanted to explain to her what had happened that night in the car with Callahan, but his throat constricted, choking off the words. He finally wandered back outside, drawn inexorably toward the thicket of trees, the darkness, the isolation.

He knew the path by heart and ended up at the goldfish pool that Grant Bell had built shortly after he and Quin had bought the house. He sat at its edge, dipped his fingers in the cool water, then scooped up a handful of pebbles. He lined them up like ducks in a shooting gallery, tagging them: *Tupperware container, powdered sugar, honey, scissors. . . .* He waited for the telling twitch, the slow burn that would indicate he was immersed in the killer's psyche again, but nothing happened. He named them aloud. But still he felt nothing. It was almost funny. For days, his intuitive grasp of the killer's psyche had bordered on obsessive, and now he was as empty as a child's piggy bank.

He heard footsteps behind him, the murmur of voices, and was relieved when they veered off in another direction. He studied the pebbles again. Music from the house meandered through the stillness. Now and then a peal of laughter reached him. He shut it out, all of it, and sank into the stones as if into water.

"Hiding or just seeking refuge?" asked a voice behind him.

He looked around to see Callahan emerging from the trees, ghostlike, her pink silk blouse shimmering in the moonlight, her white slacks rustling as she lowered herself to the edge of the pool. "Both, I guess."

Moonlight and shadows bled across the promontories of her face. She smiled and gestured toward the pebbles lined up between them. "Target shooting with your slingshot, right?"

He laughed. "Yeah, something like that." He touched a finger to the first pebble. "This represents the killer's trophies." His finger slid to the second pebble. "This symbolizes his teasers—the clue he left on Joyce's bedroom wall and the other one in the second Tupperware container found at the health club." He pointed at the third pebble. "This is the death sweet. . . ."

Callahan shook her head, scooped up the pebbles, and knelt in the grass as she arranged them in a circle. Then she chose the two largest and smoothest pebbles, handed one to him and kept the other for herself. "We'll have to improvise, but I've found that a good game of marbles usually clears the head. You first. Whoever knocks the most pebbles out of the circle wins. We alternate turns. We have to call which pebble we're shooting for."

McCleary laughed and got down on the damp grass and sat back on his heels. "How far away do I have to be when I shoot?"

She showed him, then drew a line on his side of the circle and a second line on her side. "We have to shoot from behind the line. Crossing it means an automatic loss. Also, if you think you can hit a second one with the first, you have to call it beforehand."

"Fair enough." The light wasn't great, but there was enough so he could see the circle. "Okay, I'm going for the one directly in front of you. At twelve o'clock."

He got lower to the ground, positioned his shooting pebble against his thumb, aimed, and let her fly. It smacked the target and knocked it out of the circle. He grinned and looked up. "Your turn."

Her tongue moved languidly across her lower lip as she studied the circle and named her target. She chose the pebble directly opposite her—and closest to him— then called a second pebble as well.

"If you default on the second pebble, you lose," McCleary said, grinning mischievously.

"You're changing the rules midstream," she protested, gluing a hand to her hip.

The rules always change midstream, he thought. "C'mon, Callahan, you called your target, now shoot."

"Wicked," she murmured. "You're wicked and without mercy. If I get it, I win another turn."

"Okay, okay, just go."

She took careful aim, her hair falling around the sides of her face. The pebble shot from her hand, slammed into its target, and it in turn smacked the second pebble. Callahan let out a whoop. "Ha. I told you. Now I get a second turn."

"Cheater," he mumbled.

"You're just a poor sport, Mike."

She took aim again—and missed.

He shifted slightly and called his shot. As he aimed, he felt the cool dampness of the grass seeping into his slacks. The thick humus scent of the air triggered an image of Callahan from the other night, and his shot flew wide of the mark.

"I told you you'd be sorry," she teased.

His fingers tightened over his kneecaps, clutched them so he wouldn't lean across the circle and touch her face. He stood, quickly. "I'd better get back to the house."

Callahan's smile faded. She looked as guilty as he felt as she got to her feet and brushed off her slacks. "I shouldn't have come tonight. I shouldn't even be involved in this case. I ought to just march my ass on outa here and . . ." Her voice cracked with the nimiety of an emotion he understood well. Too well. She turned away, but McCleary caught her hand, pulled her against him.

The scent of her hair, her skin, her body crushed against his, all of it brought back the past. Against the template of memory, he saw them embracing like this one night five years ago, when she'd told him things weren't going to work out between them. They wouldn't work, she'd said, because when she looked at him she thought of her murdered sister.

He tilted her head back, smoothed hair from her cheek. Her eyes shone with tears, with the ache of a nameless something that tore him apart inside. He opened his mouth to say something, but she shook her head and touched a finger to his mouth. "Don't make it harder," she whispered. "Please. We had our chance and we blew it." Then she broke away from him and hurried through the trees. He watched her, watched until the dark seized her.

A schism ripped open in his chest and bled as brightly as a wound.

Quin saw Callahan fleeing from the trees in the backyard as though she couldn't get away fast enough. She
saw McCleary emerge several minutes later. A wave of
anger swept through her, and on its heels, hurt and
resentment. A hole yawned open in her stomach that
demanded to be filled. She turned away from the kitchen
window, where she'd been stacking dishes, dipped her
hand into a mound of peanuts, and jammed them in her
mouth. Slices of an orange followed quickly. Then several grapes, seeds and all. Next, she scooped a piece of
cauliflower into a container of onion dip and bit down
on it. The nerve, the goddamn nerve.

*But you told him to find out what he felt about
Callahan*, chided the voice of reason. An irritating voice
like a persistent itch.

She stuffed more peanuts into her mouth.

Tears bit at the corners of her eyes. She felt callow
and stupid, estranged and betrayed. To approach this
intellectually was one thing. To deal with it emotionally
was quite another. Yes, indeed, she was certainly a
contemporary liberated woman, wasn't she. Sure thing.
She was an infinite well of compassion. *So go find out
what you feel, McCleary*. Hey, yeah, she'd sanctioned
it. Marvelous. She'd sanctioned it, and now she felt like
shit. Now she was waist deep in the consequences of her
magnanimity.

"Quin, where do you want this stuff?"

She whipped around. Ross Young stood there with a
tray swamped with dirty paper plates, glasses, bowls.
Young in khaki slacks and bright red socks. Santa Claus
socks. She started to laugh. She laughed until tears
rolled down her cheeks. Young smiled, hesitantly, not
understanding what was so funny.

"There," she gasped, pointing at the already jammed
counter. "Just put everything there."

"My socks, huh." He chuckled and tugged at the side

of his pants, exposing his right sock. It had a white cotton ball that bobbed from the top. "K Mart specials. Zivia hates them. They embarrass her."

"I love them. Really." She wiped at her eyes, feeling absurdly better now. "People are starting to leave. Why don't you and Zivia stick around and I'll make coffee?" *Please stay. Please.* She didn't want to be alone with McCleary. Not yet. Not until she was certain she could keep her mouth shut.

"Sure. We'd love to."

In the end, Ross, Zivia, Benson, and Callahan stayed around for coffee, all of them sitting in the kitchen amid the clutter of paper cups and plates, half-empty Coke bottles, discarded cans. The night air spilled through the open window, buzzing with an orchestration of insect noises and a medley of fragrances as Quin, McCleary, and Benson updated Young on the case.

No one mentioned what Schloper had said about Joyce's feelings toward Young. That would be McCleary's department, when the two men could speak privately.

Callahan reiterated her idea for a party at her place, her voice as trenchant as music. Quin kept looking at her, wanting to hate her, blame her because her marriage was stalled in the eye of a hurricane, pressure building up on all sides, the barometer shooting for the stars. Something was going to have to give—and quick.

"Hold it," Benson said when Callahan was finished. "We need to take some precautions." He wore his glasses instead of his contacts now, and looked like a college professor. "What we're trying to do is get Gene Travis to let you in on what Minotaur is. I doubt that he's going to follow Mac or Quin, since he seems to have accepted Mac's story about being a business broker. But just in case, the night of the party, Mac, I think it'd be wise for you to stick around Sylvia's for a while, and Quin, you and Joe should drive to a hotel on the beach for a drink or something afterward just to make sure you aren't being followed. Does Travis have a phone number for you?"

"Just the answering service number we reserve for cases like this," McCleary replied.

"No address?"

McCleary shook his head. "I think he believes I'm staying at Sylvia's."

"Great. Then keep him thinking that."

Thanks, Tim, Quin thought.

"You have a rental plate on your car?" Benson asked.

"I did the night we met at his club, and I will again tomorrow."

"You mean for this party at Sylvia's?"

"Yes."

"I think the party should be moved farther up in the week. Maybe on Wednesday or Thursday or even next Friday. Then the meeting with Quin should take place a couple of days later. That'll give me time to make some arrangements. Is that okay with you, Sylvia?"

"It'd actually be easier."

"Okay, let's see." Benson's fingers drummed against the tabletop. "Quin, you and Bean should have a Mercedes or BMW or something. The department's got a couple of impounded models. I'll see if I can get you one of those to use. And you'll need to be wired for sound." He made notes on a pad of paper he whipped out of his pocket. "Anything else?" His eyes loomed abnormally large behind his glasses, like black moons.

"Just a question," said Young, who'd been quiet during this entire exchange. He was sitting beside Zivia, his arm resting along the back of her chair, his feet hoisted on the edge of McCleary's chair, so his red socks showed. "Tim, maybe I'm obtuse, but if you think Gene Travis is the man you're looking for, why can't you just arrest him?"

"His alibis check out for the night of Joyce's murder and for the night of Lois Dwight's, too. The bite mark on the Dwight woman's shoulder wasn't the kind we could take an impression from. The only thing it told us was that the killer has a slight underbite. We'd have to get an impression of Travis' teeth to establish whether he has one. So at this point if we can establish a possible motive Travis might've had for killing her—which maybe this Minotaur thing will enable us to do—then we've got a shot at an arrest.''

Zivia poked Young in the shoulder. ''The cogs of justice are never fast, Ross.''

''And sometimes they don't work at all,'' added Benson. ''But I think we've got a good chance with this.''

Everyone but Zivia and Ross had left. He and McCleary were outside, putting away tables and chairs, while Quin and Zivia stood at the kitchen counter, stacking dishes, packing up leftover food. What Quin felt most of all at the moment was relief—that Callahan had left, that the evening was over.

''You okay?'' Zivia asked.

''Yeah, just tired.'' Quin ran water in the sink and squirted in dish-washing liquid. She watched bubbles forming, fracturing the light into rainbows. ''Has Ross talked about his stepsister at all with you, Zivia?''

''Yeah, some. Why?''

''According to Neal Schloper, Joyce was in love with Ross.''

''In *love* with him? God, how bizarre.'' She wrinkled her nose, and for a moment juggled three radishes, then four, then five. It made Quin dizzy and she reached out, grabbed one, and popped it in her mouth, breaking Zivia's concentration. ''He hasn't said anything about it. But then, why should he? It's not exactly the sort of thing you'd want people to know, I guess. Sometimes we don't talk much. We practice juggling. We roll around in the hay. We laugh. We eat ice cream in bed. One night he showed me his collection of socks. I can't say that we've ever really discussed his relationship with Joyce in any detail. But then, there is only so much ground you can cover in a week, right? It's crazy, Quin, but we've spent every night this week together and I'm not sick of him yet.'' She picked up a dish of munchies and carried them over to the table. ''C'mon, let's polish this stuff off.''

Quin eased her feet out of her shoes with a sigh and plucked a carrot off the tray. Zivia was spreading dip on a cracker. ''I could fall for this guy, Quin. He's different. We get along well. There's a lot of chemistry.''

''Music to a matchmaker's ears.''

Zivia laughed and leaned back in her chair, hands locked behind her head. Her smile brought a flush to her cheeks. ''Chemistry, like I said. My two ex-husbands couldn't hold a candle to him.''

''I'd like your opinion on something.''

She came forward, arms resting along the edge of the table now. ''Ask away. I feel wise tonight.''

''If you were married, say to Ross, and a woman from his past reappeared and he realized he still felt something for her and you knew that until he got it out of his system your marriage was stalled, what would you do?''

Zivia rolled her lower lip between her teeth. ''It's Callahan, right?''

''Yes.'' She devoured a cracker and washed it down with a sip of what had been iced tea.

''Funny, isn't it, how during the sixties you'd do acid and go off in the woods with some guy you barely knew and screw your brains out just because it was a nice thing to do when you were high and it was no big deal. Then twenty years later, the circle has swung back to this clutchy, clingy thing, this possessiveness, this weird monogamy that's got it's own set of problems.'' She shook her head and popped a cracker into her mouth. ''Maybe the moral of the story is that Leary was right all along. A better life through chemistry.'' She paused. ''Has he slept with her?''

''No.''

''You're sure?''

''Yes.''

''Is he in love with her?''

"He doesn't know." As she picked her way back through the last few days, a pall of unreality clamped down over her. It was as if she were talking about someone else's life, someone else's husband. Now and then she gazed through the window, where McCleary and Ross were hosing down the pool area.

"What do *you* want to do?" Zivia asked when Quin had finished.

"I'm not sure." Quin stared at the plate of food, at the bright red radishes, the squares of cheddar cheese, the blooms of cauliflower. "I keep trying to put myself in his place, Zivia. And I think I would need to find out exactly how I felt. It's tearing him apart. Part of it is this case, the fact that we work together and spend more time together than most couples I know. But the other part is that there's a lot between him and Callahan which was never resolved. God, I sound like a shrink, don't I," she added wryly. "Or a marriage counselor."

Zivia's chin was cupped in the palms of her hands. "I think you just answered your own question, Quin."

"Yeah, I guess I did." She smiled thinly. "But what do I do if he decides he's in love with her?"

"Either way, Quin, it's a risk. But at least by being up front about it you're yanking away all that heaviness bullshit: them against the world."

It wasn't much, Quin thought miserably. But it was better than nothing.

3.

McCleary and Young were sitting by the pool finishing up the last beers in the cooler. Moonlight painted the yard and the pool a soft yellow, like lemons, and splashed through the trees. For the last half hour, McCleary had been trying to figure out how to tactfully approach Young about his relationship with Joyce. Under other circumstances, whether she'd been in love with him might have been a small point, irrelevant. But in a homicide investigation, even the most minute facts often proved vital. There didn't seem to be any diplomatic way to pose the question, so McCleary just leaped in.

Young's reaction was one of acute embarrassment. His face sagged at the jowls, he ran a hand over his blond hair, and energy seemed to hiss from him like air from a balloon.

"Yeah, it's true. I suppose Schloper told Quin."

"Yes." McCleary shifted uncomfortably in his chair. "Look, Ross, you hired us to do a job. It's tough to do it unless you're completely honest with us. I realize it's not the sort of thing that's real easy to tell people, but it's important. Is there anything else about her or your relationship with her that you haven't mentioned?"

He shook his head.

"Were you ever lovers?"

"No. Although maybe if we had been, she'd still be alive because she never would've married Neal or gotten involved with Gene Travis." He raised the can of beer to his mouth. As he swallowed, his Adam's apple bulged against his throat like a tumor. "Since she died, it seems like I've been replaying everything that happened, going over how I could've done things differently, treated her differently. But it doesn't change things."

Overhead, a scythe of clouds impaled the moon, then gobbled it up, plunging the heart of the yard into darkness. The only light came from the open kitchen windows, where McCleary could see Quin and Zivia silhouetted at the kitchen table.

To his right, Young pushed up from his chair. "It's late, Mike. We should get going. Keep me posted on things, all right?"

"I will."

They walked toward the house. A breath of cool air slipped past him on the left. It brought goose bumps to his arms and a sudden rawness to his face, as if the air possessed a siccative substance that scraped against his cheeks like steel wool. A quick, intense heat sprang across his forehead. He felt a wrenching in his gut. His mouth went dry. A part of himself seemed to stretch through the moonless night, through the sinewed paths of time and space, connecting with the killer. *He's hungry, he's stalking, he's ready.*

And just as quickly as the sensation had seized him, it released him, leaving him as hollow and dry as a gourd with the innards scraped out.

21 A Test

1.

IN THE SIX days since he'd killed Summer, he'd been thinking of this, a little test for McCleary. He would be clement with him, at least for tonight. He only wanted to see how well he performed under stress. It wasn't a usual component of his surveillance. But the grooves of his addiction had deepened, and his body had begun urging him in new directions, toward greater, more parlous challenges which would, he knew, ultimately sweeten the kill.

He stepped into the men's locker room at the Grove Fitness Club. It was late, twenty minutes before the club closed for the night, and the place was nearly empty. He could hear the drumming of a single shower, a locker clanging shut, a couple of guys talking loudly about the stock market. He moved like a shadow past two rows of lockers, careful to avoid being seen, and watched as McCleary shuffled off toward the sauna, a towel wrapped at his waist, his burly shoulders slumped as if with fatigue.

Yeah, he had plenty to be tired about. *Too bad, pal, about your problems*. He knew about the major glitches that had developed in McCleary's life. He'd been privy to them through the marvel of electronics—specifically an infinity transmitter hooked to his phone which enabled him to eavesdrop on the McClearys simply by dialing *their* number. An electronic oscillator silenced the bell on their phone when it rang and opened the mike, and *voilà*, out came voices as limpid as streams.

There were, however, certain problems with this system. It worked only in the rooms where they had phones —the bedroom, kitchen, and den, which was where their most intimate and also their most mundane conversations took place. So while he'd discovered the McClearys' marriage was tottering like a toy boat in an unexpected storm and that McCleary himself was suffering from nightmares, he had also found out other less useful facts. The wife's penchant for chocolate chip cookies, for instance. And that the cats were fed moist food twice a day and Friskies at night. And that the armies of ants were back. But he'd listened to everything, big and small, with a crescive fascination at the multitudinous details that composed the geography of a single man's life.

A geography he would eventually destroy.

He saw the red light blink on outside the sauna, indicating someone was inside. He smiled. Now he would see what McCleary was made of. He started across the locker room toward the sauna, but just then the shower went off. He heard the guy inside whistling, a strange, disjointed tune, and he stepped quickly back behind the wall and waited.

Stay in there, McCleary.

Now the man from the shower was opening his locker, reaching for his clothes. *C'mon, c'mon, buddy, hurry up.*

Footsteps resounded in the hall, accompanied by another noise which took him a moment to identify. It was the janitor's mop bucket, rolling along the tile floors. Great, just great. He didn't want to hurt ol' Sammy, but if he came in here, what the hell choice would he have?

Keep on truckin', Sammy.

"Hi, Sammy," called the guy from the shower. "Be outa your way in a minute."

"No problem. Still got ten minutes till closing. Anyone left in here?"

"A guy in the sauna."

Sammy's bucket clanked on past. The guy from the

shower slammed his locker shut and, whistling again, strolled out into the hallway.

He waited, expecting him to return because he was the type who would. He was the type who'd get halfway down the hall and realize he'd forgotten his wallet or his keys or his jockstrap. But after thirty seconds, his truculent need was greater than his apprehension, and he darted toward the sauna door.

The red light continued to glow like a cat's eye in the dark.

He picked up the metal chair against the wall and carefully fitted it under the door handle. Then he stepped back, smiling to himself, the visceral rhythms of his body becoming music—frantic drumbeats in his chest; a trumpet's high notes dancing in his blood; a banjo's quick staccatos in his toes.

New directions, greater challenges. Yes, he believed that. He did. And he believed that this preliminary test would sweeten the kill when it happened. But right now, this moment, his addiction was a shriek in his head. It rarefied the air around him, as if he were perched at the pinnacle of a ten-thousand-foot peak, and made him so dizzy that black spots swam in front of his eyes.

No, not yet.

But soon, he thought. Soon.

He turned and hurried into the hall. He let himself out the back door and sprinted along the running track, through the redolence of gardenias, pine, the penetrating humus odors that intoxicated him like a sapid wine. He climbed over the gate and slipped soundlessly into the alley.

Good luck, McCleary.

2.

Since the night of the party last weekend, the sauna had become a punctuation mark at the end of each of McCleary's days. When he stepped in here, into the thick odor of cypress, the hot stones hissing as he poured water over them, it became the world, unsullied, simple, stripped to elementals.

He was stretched out on the hard bench, a towel bunched under his head. Sweat poured out of his skin, sweeping away the day's effluvium. He dozed. Hypnagogic images flitted across the inside of his lids like butterflies: geometric designs that melted into Quin's face, then Callahan's; iridescent orbs that wobbled as uncertainly as baby birds, then caved in on themselves; evanescent bits of light as elusive as dreams. An effeteness settled into him, infecting his blood, his bones. Voices warbled through his head, triggering a lazy slew of questions that were as imponderable as riddles. Why had the killer remained so silent? How much longer could he and Quin move through their lives as if nothing were different? Did he love Callahan? How was he ever going to know without risking his marriage? How the hell had he gotten into this mess? And where oh where the hell were his hunches?

Every day after breakfast and at some point during the evening he'd been lining up his little icons, studying them, puzzling over them, waiting for that ineluctable tug of his compulsion. But there'd been nothing, zip, *nada*. It was as if the killer were dead. Or hiding.

He sat up, wiping his face and chest with the towel, and realized it was nearly eleven. His head hurt from the heat, but the sauna had relaxed him tremendously, and the only thing he wanted to do was go home and crawl into bed. But when he pushed on the heavy cypress door, it wouldn't budge.

He leaned into it.

Nothing.

He threw himself against it and it didn't give, and now he banged on the door with his fists and started to shout. Sweat sheathed his skin. It rolled off his face and from under his arms. Even his feet were perspiring.

"Hey, someone," he yelled, kicking at the door, slamming his fists against it. "Hey, I'm locked in here. Someone!"

He pressed his ear to the wood. He couldn't hear anything. He grabbed hold of the end of the bench and slammed it against the door. The goddamn thing splintered like a toothpick. "Someone!" he screamed again, and pummeled the door with the bench once more. This time chips flew.

He had to pause. He couldn't breathe right. The heat was an esurient beast, sucking him dry. He puckered his lips, trying to draw saliva into his mouth. He wiped his face with the towel. His pulse had soared, hammering inside his ears, and he forced himself to take long, deep breaths until it calmed somewhat. Then he shouted some more and banged his fists against the door, and then he started in with the bench again.

Ten minutes had passed.

Panic had rooted inside him.

He stepped back, clutching the end of the bench like a kid with a toy, and slammed it against the wooden door handle. It snapped off. He shouted again. His mouth felt as if it had been stuffed with cotton, his throat pulsed with rawness, with pain, and just as he was about to shout again, he heard a voice.

"Hold on jus' a second and I'll get ya out."

A noise reverberated outside the door, then it swung open and cool air rushed around him. McCleary sucked at it as he stumbled drunkenly forward and fell to his knees in front of a small black man.

"Shit, oh shit," the guy murmured, kneeling beside McCleary. "Hold on, son, let me get you some water. Don't you go movin' none. Be right back."

He didn't move. Couldn't move. He just kept inhaling the cool, sweet air as steam rolled out of the sauna door, licking his back. By the time the janitor returned, McCleary was shivering. Violent shudders fled up and down his spine. The janitor draped a dry towel around his shoulders, then pressed a glass of tepid water into his hands. "Sip that very, very slowly, son. Easy does it . . . that's right. . . ."

McCleary rocked back on his knees. He had stopped

trembling. It was a moment before he could speak. "Thank God you were around."

"Someone done pushed a chair up under the handle, son."

He stared at the old man with his coriaceous face and his kind eyes and he thought, *Here, the bastard was here, and he was testing me.*

"C'mon, lemme me help you up."

McCleary leaned into the old man. "I think I'm okay now."

Just then, a man appeared in the doorway. "We're about to close and . . ." He realized something had happened and frowned. "Something wrong, Sammy?"

"Someone done—"

"No, nothing's wrong." McCleary silenced the old man by touching his shoulder. "I just slipped and Sammy helped me up."

"You all right?"

McCleary could see he was thinking lawsuits.

"I'm fine, yes."

"Good. Well, we're about to close."

"Right. I'll get dressed."

He left, and the old man said, "You shoulda told him."

"Wouldn't have done any good. But thanks for your help."

"Jus' glad you're okay, son."

McCleary dressed like a madman, wanting only to get out of here. Away. Home. Into bed. Asleep. *Dream. Forget.* In the hall, Sammy was mopping, and McCleary stopped. "Did you see anyone in the locker room before you found me? I mean, like twenty minutes or a half hour before?"

"Jus' Mr. Lafferty. He'd jus' gotten outa the showers and was on his way out."

"What's he look like?"

Sammy described him. It wasn't anyone McCleary knew. He reached into his wallet and withdrew all the money he had—a little over fifty bucks. He slipped it in the janitor's pocket. "Thanks again."

"Hey, wait a minute, son, I—"

"Please," McCleary said quietly. "Keep it. If you hadn't been out here, I'd be dead."

The temperature outside was in the low sixties. The night air had never smelled as good, as fresh. A plump moon hovered like the Goodyear blimp in the black sky. Beneath the glow of the street lamp, Lady's hood gleamed. Everything he looked at, in fact, seemed to possess a preternatural clarity, an almost painful clarity, as if he had risen from the dead.

He unlocked the hatchback, dropped in his bag, and walked around to the driver's side. The riddle of the killer was a Fibonacci coil, he thought. Each of his acts was the sum of its two predecessors, spiraling crazily downward toward greater depravity. He wanted to pursue the thought, play with it, but his fatigue was too extreme.

As he inserted his key in the door, he realized it was already unlocked. He opened it slowly. His eyes fell on the dashboard. Roosting there was a piece of candy and a tiny box wrapped in brown paper.

He got inside the car, slammed the door, and locked it. He reached for the candy, his fingers working at the blue paper that encased it. *A Parfait mint.* He popped the candy in his mouth. *Never figured I'd do that, did you, fucker?* Then he picked up the box, shook it. His flesh crawled, it burned, he nearly swallowed the candy and choked.

"Jesus."

He started the car and slammed Lady into gear and tore across town toward Benson's.

3.

She would play a game with herself.

She would not look at the clock. She would continue to lie here, reading, and she would not look at the clock and she would not imagine McCleary en route to Callahan's.

She glanced at the clock. It was eleven-fifty.

So much for her game.

Quin threw back the covers and sat up, disturbing all three cats, who were curled in their various niches on the bed. She stared at the phone. *Ring*.

It remained silent.

She went downstairs and opened the fruit bin. She helped herself to an apple and then went back upstairs and ate it in bed. It drove McCleary nuts when she ate in bed, but he wasn't here, so tough. If he couldn't be considerate enough to call her, then she would eat an apple in bed and maybe she would even eat crackers and then sprinkle his side of the bed with the crumbs.

She looked at the phone again. *Please ring please please*.

He was with Callahan. He was making love to Callahan. Maybe he was even smearing honey on Callahan's mouth.

She squeezed her eyes shut. *I can't live in limbo anymore*.

The irony, of course, was that McCleary said he hadn't seen Callahan since the night of the party; she believed him. She believed that there had been no clandestine meetings, no passionate paroxysms of pleasure, no declarations. And that was somehow worse because even a clandestine meeting would've been a thrust forward, Quin thought, would've ended this ersatz life they were moving through.

The phone pealed. She reached for it, then let it ring twice more because she didn't want McCleary to think she'd just been sitting here, waiting, biting her nails, eating in bed. Even if it were true.

"Hello."

"Quin, it's me. I'm at Tim's." He sounded shaken. "I'll be home in a few minutes."

"What happened?"

"We found Bob Summer's ear."

An hour later, Quin lay in the dark, unable to sleep because whenever she closed her eyes she saw McCleary being steamed like shrimp in the sauna. *Travis or Schloper? Eenie, meenie . . .*

"Mac?"

"What?"

She rolled on her side and reached for his hand. "I've been thinking things over."

She felt him stiffen.

"I wish you'd go ahead and do whatever you're going to do with Callahan so we can get on with our lives. Even if they're separate lives. I mean, even if that's how it ends up." Her words rang out in the dark, echoing for a moment, then fading like a cripple's dreams of walking.

"Is that what you want? Separate lives?"

"No." The word caught in her throat. "But I don't like things like this, either. And it'd be worse if you felt you had to sneak around. Just do what you feel you have to do."

Another silence now, deeper, darker than the first.

"Do you want me to move out?" he asked finally.

"No." It was barely a whisper. "Unless that's what you want to do?"

"No." He just continued to hold her hand. Then he rolled onto his side, his arm in the curve of her waist, and kissed her mouth and ran his fingers through her hair. She ached all over inside and began to cry. "Please don't cry," he whispered. "Please, I can't stand it when you cry. I can't stand it when I've hurt you. I love you, Quin, I do. I just feel . . . I don't know . . . I—"

She touched a finger to his mouth, hushing him. They made love with a wordless passion larger and sweeter than language. To this single act of love, they brought all of their knowledge of each other—and themselves, and she knew that if he could find more than this with Callahan, then so be it.

She slept.

22 Preliminaries

1.

IT WAS ZIVIA'S idea. It was Zivia who said, "Bloom-ingdale's," as if it were a magical word, an abracadabra word that opened doors, universes, the cosmic riddles. So here they were, at the only Bloomie's in South Florida, fifty-three miles from Miami straight up the coast in Boca Raton. Mouth of the Rat. According to one survey, every forty-third person in Mouth of the Rat was a millionaire, and *all* of them, Quin thought, were in Bloomie's this Saturday morning.

But Zivia was oblivious. Zivia floated from rack to rack, aisle to aisle, touching, picking, sampling outfits as if they were dishes at a buffet, looking for the *perfect* raiment for Quin's new persona, Anise Rochelle.

Zivia had the practiced eye of an inveterate shopper. She was quick. Quin, on the other hand, was one of those shoppers who lingered, who couldn't decide, who tried on three dozen outfits in every department and walked out with nothing at all or with nothing that matched because she got fed up and disgusted with the whole thing.

Quin watched Zivia drape more clothes over her arm. The pile had grown in just five minutes. Reds and lavenders, blacks and whites, silk and crepe and cotton that wrinkled like a ninety-two-year-old face. Even after she'd found an outfit, she would need shoes. A purse. Jewelry. New perfume. New underwear. New makeup. A new face. The last time she'd gone shopping with

Zivia, she'd charged over $400 worth of clothes and accoutrements, and when McCleary had seen the bill, he'd scrawled *Quin's day with Zivia* across the face of the receipt.

The difference was that this time Ross Young would get billed for it.

"Okay. Let's go try this stuff on," Zivia said in her impatient shopper voice, urging Quin toward the dressing rooms. "I've got everything from conservative to punk. There should be something for Anise Rochelle in between, don't you think?"

"I'm not exactly the punk type," Quin replied.

She tried on skirts and blouses, slacks and sweaters, suits and dresses. For the party tonight, the *perusal* party, they finally settled on a simple cerulean blue silk dress. It was not something that Quin, had she been by herself, would've bought in a million years. But as she gazed at herself in the hallway mirror in the dressing room, turning slowly, as the chatoyant blue seemed to shimmer, to hug her in all the right places, it astonished her that she looked good—and not like herself at all.

"Well?" she asked Zivia's reflection.

"Perfect. Buy it."

She sought the price tag. It was $220. "No way. I can't justify sending Ross a bill for this."

Zivia supplicated the ceiling with her eyes. "He gave you a check for expenses, right? Well, this is an expense. Look, I already warned him I have expensive tastes."

Quin laughed. "That's understating the case a little, but okay, you twisted my arm."

"All right, now something for the *real* meeting. Try this on. It's a little more conservative." She held up a tailored black suit with a pale salmon silk blouse. "It's about the same price as the dress."

"Maybe I can lease this stuff."

"Sure, Quin."

An hour later, Ross was nearly $700 poorer and Quin and Zivia were riding the escalator to the top floor of

Bloomie's for lunch. Over chef salads, soup, and coffee, Zivia said, "I asked Ross about his relationship with Joyce. Neal Schloper was right. She *was* in love with him, but they were never lovers."

"Yeah, I know. Mac spoke to him."

"He's smothering me, Quin," she said quietly.

"Oh c'mon, at the party a week ago you were talking like this guy walked on water, Zivia."

"I still feel the same way, don't get me wrong. But my God, Quin, if I don't see him one evening, he sulks about it. And when I do see him, he practically grills me on what I did that day. When I told him we were going to Bloomie's to go shopping today, he acted like I'd just announced I was seeing someone else." She pushed her bowl of salad away and sat back. "I seem to have this penchant for men who are either indifferent to me or they try to own me. For once, I'd just like something in between."

"So tell him."

"I have. And then I always feel like a heel afterward." She made an impatient gesture with her hand, then picked up her fork and began a second tour of duty on her salad. "But here I am going on and on and you haven't said a thing about what's happening with you."

"Status quo, that's all."

"You and Mac haven't even talked about it?"

"Yeah, we have. I told him to just do whatever he's going to do because I'm tired of feeling like my life's on hold."

"And?"

"I don't know." She paused to stab at the remaining tomato in her salad. "He's going up to Callahan's sometime this afternoon just to make sure he's there when Travis arrives."

"You don't seem too upset about it."

Quin shrugged. "What's the point? It's not going to change anything."

"I think . . ." She stopped, her gaze fixed on something over Quin's shoulder, and color bloomed in her cheeks. "Shit, it's Ross. I can't believe he'd do this."

Young strolled over to the table and greeted them both effusively. His blond hair was windblown. He looked casually dapper and, somehow, younger. He planted a kiss on the top of Zivia's head and seemed totally oblivious to her chilly reception. He pulled out the chair next to her and sat down, gesturing toward the packages piled high in the chair to Quin's right.

"A jackpot?"

"Absolutely. Thanks to Zivia."

"I thought I'd take you ladies to lunch, but I guess I'm a bit late," he said as Zivia's cheeks became progressively more erubescent. "But I know a great French restaurant here in town where we can go for dessert."

"I really can't, Ross," Quin said quickly. "I've got to get back to Miami."

"So do I," Zivia added.

It was difficult to read his expression. He might've been deeply wounded—or angry. But after a tense, uncomfortable moment in which Quin fidgeted in her chair and Zivia stared at her hands, Young said, "I'll drive you back, Zivia."

"I'm going back with Quin, Ross."

His mouth twitched. He glared at Zivia; she didn't look at him. Quin was tempted to hurry off to the rest room or something, and probably would have except that she felt a surge of annoyance toward him. Didn't he have anything better to do than cruise fifty-three miles up the coast in pursuit of Zivia? Why wasn't he designing buildings? Homes? Why wasn't *he* out looking for his stepsister's killer? *Her* marriage was unraveling at the seams, *her* husband was obsessed, had nearly been fried in a sauna, was being stalked by a maniac, for Christ's sakes, but here was Ross, looking as fresh as crisp celery. He had butted in here with his smile and his undoubtedly good intentions, and why should she accommodate him by excusing herself from the table so he could argue with Zivia?

She remained seated. No one said anything. The waitress came over to the table and asked Young if he wanted to order. He shook his head, and Zivia requested the check. As the waitress dropped it on the table, Young picked it up. "I'll walk out to the car with you. Here, Quin, let me help you with those packages," he offered as they stood.

"Thanks."

At the register, Zivia drew Quin aside. "I'm going to ride back with him, Quin."

"Are you sure?"

"Yeah." She sounded resigned. "You can say a lot in fifty-three miles without getting distracted by sex."

"He's like an exuberant kid. He means well," Quin replied, not so sure she believed it.

"Maybe."

Young turned around, flashing one of his quick, winning smiles. "All set."

"Quin's going to go on," Zivia said. "Why don't we go sample that French dessert you mentioned."

He grinned, obviously delighted with this turn of events. "Great."

They descended four flights through Bloomie's, down through housewares and lingerie, stationery and perfume, and Young chatted the entire way. The lower they went, the more crescive became Quin's aggravation.

By the time they reached the parking lot, she felt like telling him he could take this case and stick it. *We're resigning from the case, Ross, and going to Venezuela like we should've done in the beginning.*

Except that it was too late for that. Too late because other elements had entered the picture. They should've driven to the airport that day instead of stopping by Young's first. They should have and they hadn't, and here they were.

He put her packages in the back of her Toyota and wished her and McCleary good luck tonight. *Good luck?* she wanted to shout. What'd he think this meeting with Travis was, anyway? A sales meeting? Good fucking luck. Right. *Hey, yeah, thanks, Ross. We appreciate your concern.*

She murmured a terse, "Thank you," and fumed all the way back to Miami.

2.

The boom of a departing Eastern 727 rattled windows as McCleary approached the hangar. Instinctively, he winced at the intrusive propinquity of the sound, and for a moment felt its weight, its mass. Then it lifted into the blue morning, and his eyes followed its graceful ascent.

A frisky breeze, tinged with the faint smell of oil and gasoline, whipped dried leaves and dust across the asphalt desert between him and the hangar. Electric cars pulling platforms piled high with cartons hummed around him. He spotted Neal Schloper standing with another man at the mouth of the hangar. He was dressed in blue pin-striped coveralls like train engineers wore, and they were spotted with grease.

For most of yesterday, McCleary had followed Schloper, trying to get a sense of the man. But his life, like most people's, seemed entrenched in routine. He had driven from his home to the airport and had spent eight hours working in an Eastern hangar. Afterward, he'd driven to Wynn Aviation and had given flying lessons until six. Then, according to Bean, who had taken over the surveillance, he'd spent another three hours puttering around the aviation hangar, refurbishing an aerobatic plane, and had gone home.

Hardly unusual.

Schloper started to step into the hangar with his companion when McCleary called his name. He glanced around, dropped his cigarette, and brought the heel of his shoe down over it as the other man continued on inside. "You again?"

"Could I talk to you a minute?"

"If you make it quick."

"Tell me about the porn, Mr. Schloper." Schloper slowly pushed his wire-rim sunglasses back into his corn-colored hair. The corners of his mouth plunged. The derision in his voice when he spoke vexed McCleary.

"Look, man, I already told you everything I know. In fact, I probably told you and that other detective more than I should have. So I got nothing to say."

He turned away. McCleary caught his arm. "You either talk to me or to the cops, Mr. Schloper."

He yanked his arm free. He rocked forward on the balls of his feet, his eyes skewed with anger. "Listen, pal. I haven't broken any goddamn laws. In case you haven't heard, porn is legal. So what I—"

"Tell me more about the code names, Mr. Schloper. About Theseus and Icarus and especially about Minotaur. Yeah, I think Minotaur is what I want to hear about. The 'ultimate,' isn't that how you described it?"

"Not how I described it. How it was described to me. There's a difference. And like I told the lady, I don't know what Minotaur is. I don't know what the hell the 'ultimate' would be to someone like Travis."

"How about snuff films, Mr. Schloper? How about if Joyce was in a snuff film shortly before she was killed? How about if that's what terrified her so much? Huh? Do snuff films sound familiar?"

His mouth, a rather generous mouth with wide lips, twitched and fussed. Color trickled from his face until the skin was as white as bleached flour. "I don't know anything about any snuff films. And I doubt that Joyce, as screwed up as she was, would've been in one, Mr. McCleary. Now if you'll excuse me," he finished, and hastened toward the hangar as though salvation lay within its yawning depths.

Maybe he's telling the truth.

"And maybe not," McCleary murmured.

When McCleary drove through the black iron gate into the courtyard of Callahan's mansion at three that afternoon, the place had been transformed. Hedges had been clipped, Japanese lanterns decorated the branches of the giant oak, the pale gold Mercedes 240SL had been brought out of the garage, and everywhere he looked there seemed to be people. A gardener, men removing stuff from a catering truck, a maid, someone else waxing a BMW that was half in and half out of the garage, another guy cleaning the pool.

He spotted Callahan standing at the seawall, gesticulating to someone on the dock. She wore shorts that showed off her long, shapely legs and a blouse tied at the waist. Her short, wheat-colored hair was pulled back from her face with a bandanna, and a breeze from the river flattened several vagrant strands against the sides of her cheek.

She saw him and motioned him over. "Mike, meet *Someday*," she said, and pointed below at the dock. A forty-foot ketch was anchored there, its twin masts reaching for the thin blue sky like slender arms. A shirtless guy with a hirsute chest was carting the sails up toward the yard.

"*Someday?*" He laughed. "What kind of name is that?"

"As in someday I'll hop aboard and just keep on sailing. Want to take a look?"

"Love to."

The boat, like Callahan, possessed certain idiosyncratic touches: furniture that folded out of the walls; an illuminated nautical map that had been laminated onto the pine floor; a galley equipped for gourmet cooking; a bedroom at the stern decorated in flamingo pink, blues, and grays. Callahan opened a door off the bedroom. "My real pride and joy." The ovoid-shaped tub inside dominated the bathroom. Light streamed in through the porthole, spilling over small clay pots of billowing ivy, sliding down the tiled wall to the blue tub. "It also doubles as a Jacuzzi. I figure that when I *do* sail away, and if I started running low on money, I could always rent out the Jacuzzi."

They stepped back into the bedroom, Callahan so close to him that McCleary could smell the fragrance of her skin. In the close confines of the cabin, it was a cloying, seductive scent that brought an ache to the backs of his eyes. She slid open the long, wide window and they leaned out into the afternoon. The sea air cleared his head. Callahan removed the kerchief from her hair and the breeze tousled it. She inhaled deeply.

"Some nights I just come down here to sleep. Because the air smells so good."

"Where all have you gone?"

"Just to the Bahamas. And only a couple of times." She shrugged. "I don't like sailing by myself. It's too dangerous. And not much fun. C'mon, let's go have some coffee and figure out the details for tonight."

To the right of the swimming pool was a staircase that led to an apartment over the garage. It was decorated in grays and blues with wicker furniture and chrome and glass tables. The air was cool and still and smelled faintly of coffee. "Just in case Travis gets snoopy, I made this place look lived in," Callahan explained, leading him through the kitchen, where the table was set for two, into the living room. There was a leather briefcase open on the coffee table, a pair of men's bedroom slippers in front of the couch, a jacket over the back of a chair. In the bedroom, a suitcase stood against the wall, and the closet was hung with shirts, slacks, and jeans.

"Where'd you get the clothes?"

"My gardener."

He laughed. "I'm impressed, Callahan. I really am."

"Good. Let's hope Travis is, too, if he's inclined to look around."

They had coffee in the neat little kitchen and went over the details for tonight. Callahan returned to the house, and McCleary brought in his clothes from the car. He showered, then padded into the bedroom with a towel at his waist and called Benson and Bean. He dialed the house, but Quin wasn't home and he got his own voice on the answering machine. *Quin and I aren't available at the moment . . .*

The rituals of marriage, he thought, stretching out on

223

the bed. *Quin and I . . . we . . . the McClearys . . .* He closed his eyes and drifted off and dreamed he was in the sauna again, only this time he didn't get out. This time steam breathed from the cypress walls and he banged his fists against the door until his hands turned raw and bloody. The heat sucked so much water from his body that his skin began to shrink and his bones turned brittle and his eyeballs dried up in his head, and when they found him he was nothing but a pile of dust. Except that he could think. He was a pile of dust with consciousness.

Someone swept him up and poured him into a jar, and now and then a huge eye would appear in front of the jar and a giant hand woud unscrew the top and sprinkle powdered sugar on him. He came awake with a start, his mouth drier than flour, his eyes aching with dryness, the membranes in his nose like tissue paper. The light in the room had shifted, dimmed. He rolled onto his side and saw Callahan standing there, watching him, just watching him, her blue eyes like melting ovals of ice.

She sat beside him and ran a cool hand along his arm, leaving behind a trail of heat. He watched while both her hands moved across his chest, as if she were blind and reading him through the musculature of his body. *Stop it now*, he thought. *Stop it while you still can.*

But he didn't move.

His body felt like it was sinking into a giant feather pillow. It cradled him, this pillow, but did nothing to abrade the raw sensation of Callahan's fingers tracing the curve of his jaw, the shape of his mouth.

A spasm coursed through his fingers as he touched his hand to hers. "No." It lacked credibility, that small word, that ridiculous word, that perfunctory negation. It lacked power because his body was saying *yes*, because the inchoate yearnings of the past impaled him against the bed like a moth. "Callahan, I—"

"Please," she whispered, her eyes sheened with tears, desperation, hunger, need, emotions so intense that she seemed fragile, vulnerable. "Please, Mike," and her fingers worked at the knot in the towel and the towel fell open and she stroked him with her hands and then with her mouth. McCleary's arms wrenched from the bed, and he wound his fingers in her hair and groaned as her tongue slid up over his stomach and chest to his mouth.

He kissed her. Desire shuddered through him as she yanked at the tie that bound her blouse and unfastened the buttons and peeled it off. The fabric grazed her nipples, and she sucked at the air as if with unbearable pleasure. McCleary suddenly understood that Callahan had not been with a man for some time. Perhaps a long time.

I can't.

But he was.

"I . . ."

She shook her head and reached for his hands and brought them to her breasts. "Please," she whispered. "Please."

Her skin was softer than an infant's. It leaped beneath his fingers, against his tongue, his mouth. He urged her onto her back, unzipped her shorts, slid them off her. The opaline light painted her: hipbones sharper than Quin's, legs not as thin, breasts that were larger. A different continent, yet one he remembered in exquisite detail, and oh God, how he wanted her, he did, he couldn't help himself.

His mouth lingered against hers, a mouth as soft as the rest of her, a mouth he could melt into. She clutched at him so hard, clung to him so desperately, that it startled him. He gently disengaged her arms from his neck, caressed her cheek with the back of his hand, whispered that they had time, plenty of time, hating himself even as he uttered it. A lie, it was a lie because time had never been on their side, time had been an albatross, a division. But he rocked back, ignoring the inner voice that told him to stop as his hand cupped her breast, as his tongue caressed it more delicately than his fingers had.

His hand trailed across the silk field of her tummy and limned her hip. His fingers lingered in a patch of sunlight that dimpled her knee like a smile, slipped to the inner part of her thigh. She made soft, startled sounds and lifted her hips. She threw off waves of heat. Her body grew damp and slippery. A fever gripped his head like a vise as they rolled, parted, came together again, a fever that seared new afferent pathways through his being. He touched her with his mouth, and she gasped sharply. Quin flashed through his mind, Quin and the honey, and a dim thought coiled like smoke in the back of his mind. *This isn't me.* He wanted to believe that. He wanted desperately to believe this case had altered his cells, his blood. But Callahan clutched at him, effacing the thought, and their bodies seamed.

Guilt rode him, tore him apart even as she drew him inside her. Time turned inside out as the past filled him, inundated him, overwhelmed him. They were on that beach in Pensacola, the hot sun beating against their backs, the surf pounding in his ears, the reaving, bone-white sky sagging above them. His awareness shrank to a small orb of sentience in which pleasure and pain melled, in which the matrix of his life split down the middle.

He strummed her like a fiddle. She played him like a harp. And just when they found their rhythm, he couldn't hold back anymore, he was swept up in the raw, frenzied pounding of emotion.

Afterward, Callahan cried and McCleary held her. The light turned caliginous, as though the sun were rising, not setting. His eyes burned. Distantly, he heard a boat whistle on the river, its sound so piercing, so lonely that it struck a corresponding chord in him. What had he done? This hadn't simplified or clarified anything. He knew what he had always known—that he loved Quin, that he loved Callahan, but that the disparity between their worlds still existed. Would exist forever. And more, he felt as if he'd betrayed both of them. And most of all, that he'd betrayed himself.

23   Anise Rochelle

SHE DIDN'T LOOK like Quin. She didn't feel like Quin. Even her body didn't seem to be *her* body. It was as if she'd ingested a drug that had divided her like a continent, split her soul as neatly as an atom. *Jekyll and Hyde. Quin and Anise.*

As the BMW whispered through the gates of Sylvia Callahan's island home, Bean let out a slow whistle. "No one told me the lady was *this* rich."

"You're supposed to be unimpressed, Joe." She dropped her chin and slid her hand under the collar of her dress, bringing the pin on it closer to her mouth. Its gold leaves enfolded a tiny bugging device. "Testing, Tim. Got that? Joe's impressed with Callahan's moola."

Bean made a face, and pulled up next to a shiny blue Mercedes. He and Quin started up the walk. Lanterns glowed from the branches of a huge oak tree in the courtyard and from the hibiscus hedges that bordered either side of the walkway leading to a patio and swimming pool. A murmur of voices and soft chords of music floated through the air. Quin's gaze swept through the crowd and zeroed in on McCleary like radar. He was sitting by himself on the seawall, looking out over the river, lost to the crowd. Then, as if he sensed she were nearby, he drew his eyes toward her and Bean. He got up and strolled over.

Everything about him seemed as peregrine to her as she did to herself: the jacket and tie he wore, the way he nodded toward Bean then touched her shoulder and brushed her cheek with his mouth, the way he said,

"Nice to see you, Anise. Joe." The momentary coolness of his mouth on her skin connected with something inside her, and she knew immediately what had happened here this afternoon. It was a direct knowing, as if the knowledge had leaped from his skin to hers. He'd been with Callahan.

She braced herself for the first wave of dismay, hurt, betrayal, anger. A part of her consciousness seemed to step outside of itself, observing, waiting to see her reaction. But nothing happened, nothing except for a sharp, biting sting somewhere in the vicinity of her heart that abated in moments. Either an iron curtain had slammed shut on her emotions or she was actually viewing this philosophically. After all, McCleary had taken a first step toward discovering what he felt for Callahan. A step meant a forward thrust. It was better than being stalled in their marriage, going nowhere.

As she followed him and Bean toward the bar along the wall, she heard a peal of laughter. She gazed over Bean's shoulder at Callahan standing with Gene Travis near the pool in a puddle of light. Now that she saw him closer up like this, he reminded her of David Letterman. He was older, his mouth was different, but the resemblance existed.

McCleary's hand touched her back; she felt its warmth through her dress. "C'mon, I'd like to introduce you to Gene, Anise."

How exotic her new name sounded when he pronounced it. *Anise*, as if it were a new kind of Swiss chocolate. Delectable. She felt like she was moving through a peculiarly lucid dream, a dream in which she knew she was dreaming, but that seemed as real as life. Her senses had sharpened. The trenchant scent of the river, the sweet fragrance of gardenias, jasmine, innerved her. She was going to pull this off. She was going to find out what Minotaur was. She knew she was.

McCleary made the introductions, beginning with Callahan. The other woman's hand was soft and cool in Quin's. She'd done something different with her hair, drawing it up, away from her face, revealing the long, smooth whiteness of her neck. Her pale blue eyes seemed to glow like damp moons. *Three years of celibacy ended in a flash*, Quin thought. She waited for an ache of resentment or jealousy or even a wave of vitriolic dislike toward Callahan. Instead, her stomach twisted with a pang of hunger.

This isn't normal. I should feel like slapping Callahan's face. Or slugging McCleary.

"Anise Rochelle and Joe Bean . . . Gene Travis," McCleary said.

His hand was large, slightly damp. His smile was generous. "Mike's been telling me quite a bit about your club, Mr. Travis."

"Gene, please call me Gene."

Effusive.

"I was quite impressed with your floor show."

"Oh, you've seen the club?"

"The other night. I like to see a place for myself, on my own terms, before I meet the owner. It's like the difference between taking a guided tour of a country and hoofing it on your own."

Travis smiled. His deep gray eyes shone like hot stones in his cheeks. "Why don't we sit over here on the seawall," he suggested, and she nodded and they moved away from the others.

She felt McCleary's eyes on her back.

She hoped Benson, stuck somewhere nearby in a boat on the river, was getting this.

They sat on the seawall and Travis brought out a pack of cigarettes. He offered her one and she shook her head. "I really had no intention of selling the Pink Slipper until Mike told me he had a client interested in it. What I'm a little unclear on is why you would want to own a topless club."

Quin laughed. "The same reason you do. It's a tax shelter. It's profitable. The land is valuable." She paused and sipped at her drink. "Let's face it. Regardless of what happens politically or how many fundamentalists

229

rant and rave about morality, a club like yours will probably stay in business. It's as permanent as alcohol during Prohibition.''

"It just strikes me as an odd business for a woman to own, that's all," he remarked.

"My money, Mr. Travis, has the same thing written across it as a man's.''

He laughed, but she sensed a wariness behind it. "Mike said he's given you all the figures on the number of employees and the revenue generated each year, as well as my asking price. You're welcome to inspect the books, of course.''

"He didn't elaborate about payment terms.''

"A quarter up front and the payments spread out over the next three years.''

"And if you were paid in cash?" She was looking at the river as she said it and now drew her gaze back to him, a smile taunting the corners of her mouth.

"In cash? Yes, I suppose that would change things somewhat. I would be prepared to drop the price by a quarter of a million.'' He smiled. "Keeping it away from the IRS is worth at least that much.''

"Would the sale include any sideline businesses?''

"Sideline businesses?" His gray eyes went as smooth as glass.

Quin touched his arm and leaned toward him. "Gene,'' she said quietly, "let's not bullshit each other, all right? I know you've run a check on me and you know I've run a check on you, independently of Mike. I'm particularly interested in the video service you offer. Specifically, Minotaur. I have some clients with rather exotic tastes, and I'd be prepared to offer you your asking price, in cash, if Minotaur is included.''

He was the quintessence of innocence. "I'm afraid I don't know what you're talking about, Anise.''

Her eyes lingered on his for a long moment, then she smiled politely and stood. "Then I guess we don't have anything more to discuss.''

She walked off through the crowd, hoping Travis would

take the bait, and stopped at the buffet table opposite the bar. She went through the line, heaping her plate with munchies. Not ordinary munchies, but exotic ones like smoked Alaskan salmon and shish kabobs and raw oysters. Pig heaven, for sure.

"Anise?"

She turned around. McCleary smiled and held up a drink. "I got you a refill."

"Thanks."

They moved toward the courtyard, where there were fewer people. "What happened?" he asked.

She told him.

"He'll come around. Just give him a little while."

They sat on the low wall that embraced the oak tree. McCleary handed her the drink, and she sipped and nearly gagged. "God, what's in this?"

"Vodka. The guy at the bar makes strong drinks. How did he act when you mentioned Minotaur?"

"I already told you." She didn't feel like expatiating on what Travis had said, and it irked her that McCleary was prodding her.

"His expression. What was his expression like?"

"He acted like he didn't know what the hell I was talking about. I implied you didn't know anything about it."

She polished off the salmon and dived into the oysters. Forgetting that she was wired for sound, that just a while ago she'd felt an acute absence of jealousy or resentment, she now said, "I don't think you should come home tonight." Then, like an afterthought, she added, "Mike."

"Quin, I . . ."

"Don't," she whispered, certain she was about to cry.

"Let me explain."

"There's nothing to explain," she replied, cutting him off short and instantly regretting it. *Stop it. You can't push him out the door with one hand and yank him back in with the other.* She had suggested he find out what he felt for Callahan, and now he was doing it, and the least she could do was zip her mouth shut. She speared the remaining oyster on her plate with a toothpick. She couldn't look at him, was afraid that if she did her imagination would run wild with speculation. *Was it good, Mac? Do you know now what you feel for her? For me? Did she cry? Scream? Did you do it in the shower?*

She felt sick.

She wanted to go home.

She wished McCleary would disappear.

She wanted to press her face into the curve of his shoulder and cry.

"Here comes Travis," McCleary whispered.

She looked up and smiled. Travis stopped in front of her. Light from the lantern bled into his hair, highlighting the gray. "How's the food?" he asked.

"Scrumptious," she replied.

"May I speak to you for a minute?"

McCleary, acting on cue, stood. "Talk to you later, Anise."

He walked off, and Travis claimed the spot McCleary had vacated. "What you mentioned earlier," he began.

"About Minotaur?"

"Yes."

Got that, Benson? "What about it?"

His hand flicked at his slacks. "It would have to be done on a, uh, leasing arrangement. I've established several contacts who would prefer to remain anonymous."

"I understand. I'm sure a lease could be worked out." Her heart waltzed across the inside of her chest.

"It would take a little while to set up."

"How long?"

"Several days."

"All right."

"I'll have to contact Mike with the details."

"However you want to do it. And then we can both think about things and go from there."

He stood. His smile was strange, eerie, and brought

232

goose bumps to her arms and raised the hairs on the back of her neck. "It's been a pleasure talking with you, Anise."

You, too, pal.

"We're in," she said to Bean as soon as they were inside the car, rolling through the iron gates, away from Callahan's. The night air swept through the car, rich and cool.

Bean looked over at her, grinning like a Halloween pumpkin. His teeth shone in the dark. He snapped his fingers, clapped his hands once, and let out a whoop as they crossed the bridge that connected the island to the mainland. "Goddamn, Ah-niece," he laughed, pronouncing each syllable of her new name. "I still think we should play it safe and do what Benson suggested about going somewhere for a drink just in case we're followed."

"Yeah, okay."

"What I'd like to know is how Travis can stand there acting like he and Mac are good ole buddies when last night he nearly turned him into sautéed clams."

She wanted to say, *Because he's a maniac*, but it seemed too pat, too simple, and most of all, wrong. Gene Travis was shrewd, he had lurid interests, he was eccentric, but he was not a maniac. He had evaluated the pros and cons of what he believed to be a possible business deal, and he had reached a logical conclusion: cash up front was a hell of a lot better than payments out of which the IRS would take its considerable cut.

No. He wasn't a maniac, and that bothered her. But perhaps Travis was a true Jekyll and Hyde, a man divided, a Janus whose madness surged like a black tide in his blood.

But even this didn't seem quite right. Flummoxed, the most she could concede was a *maybe*.

They sped west on the Seventeenth Street Causeway, past Pier 66, rising against the moonlit sky, sleek as a silo, over the intracoastal canal, winding like the gold road toward Oz.

No Oz for you, Anise Rochelle or whoever you are.

She had not spoken to McCleary again after their brief conversation by the tree.

He would not be home tonight.

The house would loom as empty as a waiting coffin, and she would pace and eat, eat and pace, her solitude a mounting pressure in her chest, her groin, her head.

She knew how it would be.

And she wondered if there was something wrong with her for not feeling what she was supposed to feel.

Who says what you're supposed to feel? asked the voice of reason.

She had no response to that.

She felt wounded but not angry, lonely but not indignant or betrayed. This was preferable to having the whole thing occur clandestinely, where one day McCleary might simply walk into the house and announce he was in love with another woman, that he had, in fact, been involved with the woman for some time.

At least now, if he decided he was in love with Callahan, it wouldn't shock her. It wouldn't rip apart the foundation of her life. It wouldn't—

"Hey, Quin," said Bean, his eyes fixed on the rearview mirror. "Is that a van behind us?"

She eyed the side mirror on her door. "I think so. The headlights are pretty high. Why?"

"It's been following us since we turned out onto A-1-A."

"Can you lose him?"

"Maybe. But why don't we let him follow us to wherever we're going to get a drink?"

Twenty-five minutes later, Bean slowed as they approached the Carlyle Hotel on Miami Beach. It was part of the Art Deco rehabilitation project on the beach, one of Ross Young's babies. There were no parking spaces in front, so they went around the block and pulled into the parking lot. As they got out of the BMW, a strong breeze from the ocean teased the hem of her dress and filled the night air with the odor of salt. She could hear the pound of the surf, a steady, truculent beat.

The van trundled past as she and Bean walked along the side of the hotel toward the entrance. The moment it rounded the corner, he said, "C'mon, let's get back to the Beamer and lay low and see if he pulls into the parking lot. That way we can get a look at him."

They hurried back to the parking lot. Bean unlocked the door, angled himself inside the BMW, and leaned across, unlocking her door. They slid down low in the front seat, waiting.

A few minutes later, headlights swept through the lot. "It's the van," she whispered, her eyes fixed on the side mirror.

A gangly man with curly black hair got out and hurried toward the hotel. Quin knew there was something familiar about him but couldn't place it. They waited until he'd moved around the corner, then got out and followed him inside. The dance floor was in the center of the room, and around it were elevated booths and tables, sparges of bright colors against the pink and blue walls. The man strolled through the archway into a small bar. Quin and Bean claimed one of the paisley booths and ordered drinks.

She could see him from where she sat. He straddled one of the bar stools, his eyes sliding around the room, evidently looking for her and Bean. The sense of familiarity he evoked in her suddenly clicked into place. The night at the Pink Slipper when she'd followed Schloper into the bowels of the building, this guy had been the cameraman.

She told Bean. "Now what, Joe?"

"Let's play him. See that hall there?"

Quin followed his eyes. SERVICE ELEVATORS, REST ROOMS, EXIT. She nodded.

"Now here's what we're going to do, lady."

Ten minutes later, as the band started playing a rumba and couples were kicking up their heels on the dance floor, Bean left cash on the table for their drinks. They got up and strolled toward the hallway. Quin could feel the man's eyes on them. The moment they were in the hall, they fled toward the EXIT sign and pushed through a door into a stairwell. The only illumination came from the floor beneath them, and it was negligible. Bean punched the button for the service elevator, calling it down to their floor, then scampered up the four steps directly in front of them. The dark devoured him. Quin flattened herself against the wall to the left of the door.

She reached into her purse for her .38.

They waited.

The elevator arrived, the doors whispered open and then shut again a moment later.

She could hear the rumba music, the pounding of feet on the dance floor. And then she heard something else, a small sound like a mouse scratching at the door. It creaked open. She pressed against the cool wall. The door opened wider, and the cloying smell of after-shave thickened the air. Suddenly Bean was hurtling toward the man, hurtling faster than light, his body as flexible as rubber, and knocking the guy to the floor. He grunted, rolled, and he and Bean grappled for a weapon. Quin delivered a swift, hard kick to the man's ribs, he yelped, Bean scrambled to his feet, and Quin leveled the gun at his chest.

"Don't move, friend. I've got a real nervous trigger finger."

The man was clutching his side. He scooted toward the wall. "Jesus, you got lead weights in your shoes?" he gasped.

Bean shoved his head forward, whipped a pair of handcuffs out of his pocket, and secured the guy's hands behind his back. "All right, m'man," drolled Bean, "how about tellin' us who you are and why you've been following us for the last hour?"

"Go fuck yourself," the man spat.

"He has a very nasty mouth, Joe," Quin said.

Bean grabbed him by the arm and pulled him to his feet. He hit the elevator button, the doors opened, and he pushed the man inside. Quin punched the third-floor button and the elevator began a slow, creaking ascent. When they were in between floors, she pushed the STOP button.

"What're you doing?" His voice held the incipience of alarm.

"Shut up," Bean growled at him, then reached into the man's pocket for his wallet. He rifled through it as Quin kept her weapon aimed at the man's chest.

"Well, well. Depending on which ID we use, he's Jimmy Vincent, Bob Franklin, or Steve Wicker. Good WASP names, buddy. Now which is it? Jimmy or Bobby or Stevey?"

The man said nothing.

"Okay, we'll call you Jimmy. Now, you are pissing me off very bad, Jimmy m'boy. And since you don't wanna talk . . ." He brought out a handkerchief and gagged him. "Now let's see, what else? Oh, right. How could I forget." He unfastened the buckle on Jimmy's slacks, unzipped them, slid them down his legs. "Okay, step out of them."

Another grunt. His eyes widened. Quin pressed the gun hard against his temple. "You heard him."

Jimmy kicked off his slacks, and Bean draped them over his shoulder. "Sit, Jimmy."

He slid down the wall.

Bean tied his ankles together, removed his sneakers, and patted down his shirt pockets. The man looked pathetic, Quin thought, with his skinny white legs, like a flamingo's, protruding from under his shirttails, and his knobby knees pressed closely together.

Bean plucked a business card from Jimmy's shirt pocket and made a clicking sound with his tongue against his teeth. "Designer Videos. My, my. Your employer wouldn't be Gene Travis, now would it, Jimmy?"

He shook his head frantically and grunted.

"I think Jimmy has something he wants to tell us," Quin commented.

"That so?" Bean asked.

Another grunt and now his head bobbed like a fishing float. Bean rolled the gag out of the man's mouth and Quin cocked her gun.

"Be careful with that thing," Jimmy said hoarsely, eyeing Quin's gun with unease.

"Just say your piece," she snapped.

"He—Gene—just hired me to follow you," he said, looking at Quin.

"And who am I?"

His look was bemused, it shouted, *You don't know who you are, lady?* "Anise Rochelle. The lady in blue. That's what he told me. I was supposed to follow the lady in blue and the black dude. That's all he said. I swear to God, that's all I know."

Bean's weapon slipped to Jimmy's crotch. "Now why don't you tell us the rest of it, Jimmy. It'd be a shame to blow your nuts off."

He blurted, "You're . . . you're going to buy Gene's club."

"Very good, Jimmy," cooed Quin. "Now why don't you tell me about this special video service Gene has. I already know you shoot some of the soft-porn stuff. But why don't you tell me about the *other* stuff. Like Ariadne and Theseus and Minotaur. Otherwise you're going to find yourself out of a job when I take over."

Quin recognized Jimmy's momentary stuggle: allegiance to his old boss or to the new one? The gun at his crotch helped sway him toward her, but not without skepticism. "If you're gonna buy the club, then you'll find out this stuff from Gene."

"Gene is holding out on me. He wants to lease the video part. I want to know what's involved."

"I . . . I only shoot straight porn."

"You mean the sort of stuff Neal Schloper's keen on."

The fact that she knew Schloper's name seemed to strengthen her position. "Yeah. Right. Straight porn, a little S and M. But no Minotaur stuff. No way." He shook his head.

238

"And who shoots that?"

"I . . . I don't know. Only Gene deals with those customers."

Bean pressed the gun harder into Jimmy's crotch and Jimmy winced. "Okay. Okay. Sometimes I deal with them. Sometimes I take the orders."

"From who? Who orders the most Minotaur videos, Jimmy? Who gets wasted? Where're they shot? That'd do for starters." Bean's face had turned petrous, mean.

"Look, man, the only thing I know is the . . . the Minotaur orders come from maybe five, six people. That's it. Sometimes they're shot outside the country. I've never done one."

"So you or Gene take the orders," Quin said. "The stars are chosen, a site is chosen, then what? How's payment made?"

"Depends on the customers. Some come to the club and pay in person. One customer Gene's never even met. That's always a drop—for both the money and the film."

Quin's gaze met Bean's over the top of Jimmy's head. "A drop? How do they communicate?"

"Computer. All in code."

"C'mon," Bean said irritably. "More. Tell us the goddamn code."

Drops of sweat trickled along the sides of Jimmy's face. "Daedalus."

Quin rapidly flipped through her paltry knowledge of Greek mythology. The only thing she knew about Daedalus was that he was the father of Icarus, who tried to escape the island of Crete on wings made of wax and feathers. He'd flown too near the sun and the wax had melted.

"We call him Big Daddy," Jimmy added.

"How many Minotaur films has he ordered?" Bean asked.

"I think three. Yeah, I think there've only been three. For seventy-five grand apiece. Gene gave him a discount. 'Cause he ordered three."

A discount for murder: she felt ill. "And no one's ever met him?"

"No. Like I said. It's done by computer."

"How's Gene know he isn't a cop?"

Jimmy shook his head. "I don't know. I guess because he keeps paying, and he can't prove it's Gene behind the films any more than Gene can prove who Daedalus is."

It made a warped sort of sense, she supposed.

"I'll tell you what, Jimmy," said Bean. "You've been *so* cooperative with us that when Ms. Rochelle here takes over Gene's club, you'll receive a fifteen percent bonus on any business you bring in. Fair?" He removed the gun from Jimmy's crotch, which made the man very agreeable.

"Sure thing."

"And I'm sure you've got enough sense to keep our little talk to yourself, don't you, Jimmy?" added Quin, leaning close to him.

"Hey, Gene never offered me no fifteen percent bonus. He pays me three fifty a week and *maybe*, just *maybe* he gets generous around Christmas."

"Really. Then I suppose I can afford to be a little generous now. Joe, why don't you unlock those cuffs."

He did, and she reached into her purse. Ever since her meeting with Suzi with a Z-I Mellon, she'd been carrying a lot of cash. She counted out eight hundred-dollar bills. "I pay for my information." *And maybe now you'll keep your mouth shut.* "You cooperate with us, Jimmy, and there's more where that came from."

As Jimmy counted out the money, grinning like a loon, Quin disengaged the elevator's STOP button.

"Can I have my pants back, man?" he asked as the elevator jolted once, then descended as nosily as a ghost wearing chains.

Bean laughed. "No problem, m'man. No problem at all. We're just glad we all understand each other."

Amen, brother, Quin thought, stifling a laugh. *Amen.*

24 Ocular Movements

1.

HIS BOAT CRUISED out of the inlet, through the navy yard, across the New River toward Callahan's place. The house no longer glowed like a witch's lair. The guests were gone. The party was over. Now the fun would begin.

Through the miracle of optics—an infrared zoom lens on his camera—he had watched two maids carting food back into the house. He had seen McCleary helping them take down the long buffet table. He had tracked McCleary and Callahan through the courtyard to the seawall, where they had sat for a long time, talking. He had watched them embracing, had heard Callahan's soft laughter ringing out over the river like music. It had brought goose bumps to his skin, that laugh, and he had entertained himself with thoughts of what he would do to her. Then he had seen them walk off toward the garage, and an hour or so later Callahan had come back across the courtyard alone, as evanescent as a ghost, and vanished inside the house.

There was no traffic on the river at this hour. He cut his engine when he was nearly on the other side and paddled to Callahan's dock. His bones yodeled. His body was a litany of anticipation, excitement. Blood pounded through his veins, expanded his arteries like air in lungs.

He tied the boat to the post, stepped onto land, his bare feet sinking against the cool, moist grass. From his back pocket he withdrew gloves, which he put on, and a nylon stocking, which he pulled over his head. *Just in case*. The stars, after all, hadn't been exactly encouraging for this little venture. But maybe it was time to dispense with the hieroglyphics of astrology, the mumbo jumbo as Joyce used to say.

Joyce. The thought of her here, now, rising to the surface of his mind like detritus from a storm, dismayed him. He paused at the top of the scarp and leaned into the seawall, his knees oddly weak. Around him, the night danced with sounds: the chirr of insects, the splash of fish, the sorrowful ululations of a dog somewhere along the river. An image of Joyce kept insinuating itself in his mind, and he shoved it away again and again until it finally diminished to just a spicule of light inside his eyes, a spectral light.

The dead walk, McCleary. Don't ever let anyone tell you different.

He felt stronger now. He was ready. He slipped over the wall, into the yard that paralleled the garage. From his pouch, he brought out a handful of carrot candies, little gold sweets shaped like pyramids and striated with ribbons of orange. He hadn't used them since . . . well, he couldn't remember. He sprinkled them around the yard and then behind him as he moved silently toward the house.

In the backyard, he passed a detector around the edges of the doors and windows to see if the burglar alarm system was on. It wasn't. He didn't know what he would've done if it had been. A calculated risk. Next, he jimmied the lock on the sliding glass door, opened it ever so quietly, and stepped into the house. The cool darkness soothed him. He moved through a wide, spacious living room toward the stairs.

It was so quiet, he heard someone cough at the end of the downstairs hall. *The maid?* Had to be. The lady of the house certainly wouldn't have a bedroom on the first floor. He took the stairs slowly, a pulse quickening at his throat, his mouth turning glutinous, the banister cool and firm against his hand.

At the top of the stairs he paused, his excitement so extreme now that for a moment a terrible dizzines seized him. *Hello, Callahan. Fancy meeting you here.*

He moved past open doorways, a bathroom where a night-light burned, and then he was at *her* door. He knew from the scent in the air, a lovely almost overwhelming fragrance of bath oil and perfume and something duskier, deeper. *Guess what, Callahan. I'm going where McCleary's been.*

He brought out two strips from a nylon stocking, which he tucked in the waistband of his jeans. He stopped at the side of her bed. A sliver of light bled through the crack in the curtain, too little for her to ever get a good look at him, especially with this stocking over his head, but enough to see that she slept on her side. He pressed a gloved hand over her mouth, and when she grunted, when she started to struggle, he held the tip of a knife to her throat. She got the picture and immediately went as limp as a sacrificial lamb.

"Hold up your wrists," he whispered huskily.

She did, and he bound them to the headboard with one hand, tying the stockings securely, and kept the knife at her throat with the other. Then he gagged her. She had little mobility in her legs, because from the waist down she was snugly under the covers, like a caterpillar in a cocoon. So he carefully peeled the covers off her and drew the tip of the knife down the front of her nightie. He kept it against her stomach as he secured her ankles with the second strip of stocking. Then he let the tip of the knife slide upward, gently, moving the nightie from her thighs past her pubis, up, up until it was bunched at her neck like a collar.

Her head was twisted to the side, her eyes squeezed closed. He could feel the frantic hammering of her heart against his palm when he rested it between her breasts. Such lovely breasts. Such a pretty Callahan. He drew the knife lightly down the length of her. When she began to whimper, he let the tip of the knife nick her pretty, flat white tummy.

With his left hand, he reached into his pouch once more and took out a carrot candy. He set it in her navel. There was a symmetry about it that pleased him, the beautiful gold and orange candy poking up from the flat terrain of her tummy like a tiny mountain. From his pocket, he brought out a handkerchief and blindfolded her. *I've got more tricks than Houdini, Callahan. What do you think of that?*

Now he stepped to the foot of her bed, removed his glove, and touched her. Such opprobrious behavior, he thought with a smile, enjoying the hot dampness of her flesh against his hand. But she didn't move, didn't make a sound. He touched the knife to her stomach and kept it there as he knelt over her, as he unzipped his jeans.

And then he went where McCleary had been.

2.

The TV flickered in the dark. The house sighed and burped, speaking in a babble like an infant's. The cats, curled at various spots on the bed so they seemed to form a protective circle around her, purred and twitched. Quin stared at the television without seeing it, listened to the sounds without hearing them. She was wide awake, despite an orgy of food, three glasses of wine, a long, hot bath, and all the usual soporifics. The problem, of course, was that when she closed her eyes, an image of McCleary and Callahan danced across her lids.

She would see them coupling. Dancing. Talking. Touching. Laughing. Swimming. She would see them driving through a soft autumn light, see them as if she were perched on the hood of McCleary's car and peering in at them through the windshield. And when her imagination tired of them, she would be back in the elevator with Joe Bean and Jimmy what's-his-name, the gun tight and cold against her damp hand. Or she would be sitting on the seawall with Travis or with Zivia and Ross Young at Bloomie's. The images erected from her mind like lava from a volcano; she didn't have to summon them. It was as though her brain were sweeping everything out and away in a violent and early spring cleaning.

She finally threw back the covers and walked downstairs. She stood in the doorway of McCleary's den, the distinctive smell of the room bringing a warm ache to her chest. She hit the switch. The lamp in the corner flared. She opened the closet and gazed at the icons, lined up on the lower shelf. She brought them out and set them carefully on his desk. She sat down and studied them. She got out the files they'd put together from Bob Summer's computer stuff. She sped through them, her eyes telescoping the more important events, her mind absorbing them like a sponge did water.

She read about the Capricorn in Atlanta, the Aries in Melbourne. She read about the death sweet victims. She immersed herself and tried to attach a face, a name, to the dark, sullied mind that had done these things. She hated him. She hated him not only because he had killed with impunity, but for stalking McCleary, for tossing Callahan back into his life, for the disintegration of her marriage. She hated him and she blamed him and suddenly she couldn't stand looking at the icons anymore or the files and she swept them off McCleary's desk with a vehemence that frightened her, that reduced her to tears.

She leaped away from the desk, swiping angrily at her runny nose, and flew into the kitchen to check the back door. The windows. She rushed around the house, making sure everything was locked, rushing as though she were fleeing, rushing until she stopped dead in front of the telephone.

Her eyes flitted to the pad beside it where Callahan's number was printed neatly.

She reached for the receiver. Picked it up. She would say . . . she would demand . . . she would. . . .

No way.

She set the receiver softly back into its cradle. She stepped away from the phone. She would not call. She would not rant. She would not humiliate herself.

She would eat.

In the kitchen, she retrieved a package of whole wheat muffins from the freezer and popped two halves into the toaster. She got out the strawberry jam, a bottle her sister had sent her, homemade. Her sister was one of those women who made everything—bread, jams, cakes that melted in your mouth like communion wafers. She, on the other hand, never cooked, never baked, had never sewed and had, in fact, flunked home ec. Why was it that everyone who meant something to her was her complete opposite? *Why?*

She searched for the butter dish.

She found it in the pantry. Troops of ants swarmed over it. She grabbed it, the ants scurried up her arms, and she heaved the thing against the wall as a sob of frustration hurtled into the air.

The ceramic shattered. The butter squashed, then oozed down the wall, over the baseboard, and puddled like sunlight on the floor. She stared at it. She yanked a glass from the counter and threw it and shards of glass rained down over the kitty dishes, and then she slammed the heel of her hand against the faucet and plunged her arm under the stream of water, washing away the ants.

She watched them swirl down the drain and the tiny corpses became her marriage, became everything she had ever loved and lost, and she doubled over the edge of the sink and cried until she couldn't breathe, until her self-pity disgusted her.

246

Then she took a final look around at the kitchen, at the ruin, and realized only one thing was missing. She found a package of Saltine crackers and squashed a stack between her hands, ripped it open and dumped it on the floor. Then she leaned into the counter and laughed and laughed. She had misplaced her mind just as she had misplaced the butter, but hey, so what? Who'd she have to answer to? Who the hell but she was going to notice? For that matter, if mold grew at the edges of the sink and inside the toilet, who would know? If the lettuce rotted in the vegetable bin, she would just toss it out. She wouldn't make a big deal out of it like McCleary did with his gloomy talk of ptomaine poisoning. She would shop for more. She would subsist on yogurt and fruit and veggies like she had when she was single. Was it really all that bad?

She turned on her heel and slammed the door on her way out. She went back upstairs and crawled into bed, exhaustion claiming her the moment her head sank into the pillow.

3.

McCleary skimmed the edge of sleep, his dreams not fully formed. They were like wisps of memories, of faces, each a single color. Quin shimmered in an indigo lake and Benson floated in celery green. Callahan pulsed pale yellow; Ross Young glistened in white, as if he were covered with snow; and Gene Travis trembled in lavender. He, McCleary, raised his paintbrush and dipped it into each of these colors. He faced a canvas as blank as an egg and then flicked the brush. A spray of color leaped against the canvas and the colors oozed and melted together, then quivered with life.

Quin's hands folded out of the canvas, beckoning. Callahan's mouth unfurled like the petals of a flower, then yawned open in a chasmal darkness into which Young strolled. Travis' lavender feet protruded from the canvas, then he leaped out, as moist and naked as a newborn, and Benson stumbled after him, green dripping from him that was as stringy as spinach. They knocked McCleary down and he tumbled out of the dream, arms pinwheeling.

He sat bolt upright, staring at the opaline blot that was the window, identifying where he was. The apartment, okay, he was in Callahan's garage apartment. Where he didn't belong. Anxiety looped his throat and squeezed like hands. The skin across his forehead burned, and his arms tingled as if he'd slept on them wrong. Air, he needed a breath of air.

He slipped on his jeans and a shirt and padded out into the apartment kitchen. He unlocked the door, trotted down the steps to the yard. The swimming pool swelled with starlight. A cool, damp breeze licked at his face and arms. He curled and uncurled his toes in the grass. He filled his lungs with the humus odors of the night, the river, this small jungle. If he'd had his jogging shoes here, he would've taken a three-mile run. He felt the need for familiar habits, for the structure of the life he'd built with Quin, and yet only a few hours ago, for the second time today, Callahan had left his bed.

It had been a slow, lazy lovemaking punctuated with soft talk, remembrances, confession. The umbra of the past had cradled them like a cocoon, and he'd felt as though they were unraveling the skein of inchoate yearnings that had plagued them from the beginning, five years ago. But now and then a breeze had rattled the windows, reminding him that beyond the room time still marched ineluctably forward, that Quin was home alone, that he was married, that he did not belong here. She, sensing it, had left and gone to the house.

Get it together, McCleary.

He started to turn back toward the apartment, but a blur of movement at the side of the house caught his eye. A spasm of apprehension twitched in his chest, his hunch spot blazed, and he stepped quickly back into the

248

shadows at the edge of the garage, waiting. Then he saw the figure clearly, sprinting away from the house toward the seawall. He wore dark clothes and something—*a stocking?*—over his head. McCleary sprang from the shadows like a rapacious animal and tore across the yard, past the pool. The man saw him coming and flew over the seawall. McCleary followed, jumped the wall seconds later, and half slid down the damp hill. Just as the man reached the dock, McCleary hurtled himself forward, tackling the guy at the knees.

They both went down, smacking the hard wood. The man wiggled free, turned, and an instant before his knife sliced through McCleary's shirt, he saw the gleam of the metal and feinted. But he wasn't fast enough. The blade sank into his upper arm. The agony flared white hot, molten, bone deep. He clutched his arm, doubled over with pain, blood seeping through his fingers as the man scrambled to his feet.

McCleary's left hand shot out and manacled the man's ankle. He expected his opponent to fall, but he didn't. He spun, spun with the grace and discipline of someone well versed in karate. His other foot, *a bare foot*, impacted with the side of McCleary's face with such force he was knocked almost senseless. Stars exploded behind his eyes. Pain flashed through the lower half of his cheek. He tasted blood. He spit out blood. Blood streamed out of his arm. The night blurred and shifted around him. He shook his head to clear it, but it was too late, the boat had sputtered to life, leaped away from the dock, fled across the dark ribbon of the river, spewing water.

Callahan.

McCleary stumbled to his feet and weaved like a drunk toward the side of the house, then around back, where the man had exited. He threw open the sliding glass door and shouted Callahan's name. Lights flared in the hallway, illuminating a trail of candy across the living room and up the stairs. "Oh Jesus," he whispered, blinking hard, sucking at the air. Then the maid sailed out of her room and into the hall, questions fluttering from her mouth like moths. McCleary told her to call the police and raced up the stairs, turning on lights, clutching his wounded shoulder, shouting Callahan's name again. There was no answer.

The moment he reached the bedroom doorway, he knew she was dead. The stench of death inspissated the air, infected it, made him gag. He groped for the light switch and stared at Callahan, lying in a pool of blood, arms bound with strips of nylon stockings to the headboard, ankles tied together, a gag in her mouth, her eyes blindfolded. She'd been cut open from end to end.

I did this, she died because of me, she . . .

A vertiginous horror clamped down over him, and then he was toppling forward, falling in slow motion, tumbling head over heels toward a blackness softer than feathers and as final as death.

PART THREE

Daedalus

25 Backlash

1.

"THAT'S ALL HE does? He just sits out by the pool?"

The incredulity that punctuated Wayne O'Donald's question disturbed Quin. She followed his gaze through the kitchen window, where McCleary was stretched out in a lounge chair by the pool. "And he sleeps. For the past week, he's been sleeping ten, twelve hours a day."

O'Donald's expression was that of a concerned friend, not a shrink, as he drew his eyes away from the window and cupped his hands around his coffee mug. "Has he gone into work at all?"

"No. He's done some stuff over the phone. He's left the house only once since Sylvia Callahan's murder."

It had been eight days since Callahan's death. Eight long, interminable days, Quin thought, in which McCleary had sunk like an autistic child into his own silent world. Her attempts to draw him out had miscarried and had only driven a deeper wedge between them.

"Sometimes he shuts himself in his den and studies those icons. Did Tim tell you about them?"

"Yes."

Quin glanced at McCleary again. It hurt her to look at him there by the pool in his swimming trunks and sunglasses. The knife wound had required thirty-two stitches; he wore the bandage on his right shoulder like a badge. "The second day after Callahan's death, he had a security alarm company come out to the house, and now this place is as impenetrable as the White House.

Yesterday he went out and bought two guns. Around midnight last night I came downstairs and found him in the family room, slamming cartridges into them. And then this morning he calls you."

O'Donald nudged his glasses back onto the ridge of his nose. He sat forward in his chair, his dark eyes seeming small and luminescent behind his thick glasses. "Has he talked to you about what happened?"

"No, not really. Nothing more than what he told the police. Except that last night he said this was all his fault, that he was a harbinger of death—first Summer, then Callahan. I told him it was exactly what the killer wanted him to think."

O'Donald nodded. "Did he, uh, give you any indication what he wanted to talk to me about?"

"No."

"He wants me to hypnotize him, Quin."

"*Hypnotize* him? Why?"

"To take him back to the night of the murder to see if he can remember any specifics about the killer."

"You think that's a good idea?"

He shrugged. "If that's really why he wants me to do it, I think he can do it himself through his painting. Art can bridge the gap between the subconscious and conscious mind just as well as hypnosis. And at least with painting there would be little or no risk of the trauma hypnosis might set off."

"You honestly think he's forgotten something about that night?"

"Sure, it's possible. Anytime there's trauma, the conscious mind can censor certain details. It's a protective device. But the subconscious absorbs everything like a giant sponge, so it's still in there somewhere." He tapped his temple. "I just think it'd be safer for him to try to dig it out himself by painting."

Quin nodded.

"Where do things stand with Gene Travis at the moment?" O'Donald asked.

"Travis called two days after Callahan's death to offer

his condolences, and Mac said he'd get back to him in several days to set up this next meeting.'' She brought her fingertips together, as if she were praying, and touched them to her mouth. ''Tim feels that with the tapes he got the night of Callahan's party, we'd have enough evidence to arrest Travis. But he thinks Travis would beat the rap.''

''Because the tapes aren't admissible evidence?''

''Yes.''

O'Donald looked disgusted. ''Figures.'' He pressed his hands against the edge of the table and scooted back. ''Let me go talk to him. You going to be around?''

''I wasn't planning on it. I've got five million things to do that should've been done yesterday. But I'll stick around if you think I should.''

''No. I think it'd be better if you weren't here.''

''Will you let me know what happens?''

''You bet.''

Quin stood and gave O'Donald's hand a quick squeeze. ''Thanks.''

She started out of the room, but O'Donald called her back. ''One other thing, Quin. You don't have to answer it if you don't want to, but it might help me understand some things.''

''What's that?''

''How've things been between you and Mike?''

He phrased it delicately, but she knew what he was actually asking. ''Not so great. He's been sleeping in the den.''

''Okay.'' He opened the back door and stepped outside.

2.

The hot light weighted McCleary's eyelids and illuminated the inside of his head, so there were no shadows, no cupolas of darkness from which death might spring. It was the light that made the days safe for dozing, and the absence of light that made the nights intolerable.

When he did manage to sleep at night, it was only with a lamp shining in his face. Even then, his slumber was sporadic because he would invariably sink too deep and the nightmare would begin.

It was almost always the same, this nightmare. He was fighting on Callahan's dock with the killer and the knife slid into his chest with the ease of a blade through a melon, and impaled his heart. He actually felt the knife puncturing his left ventricle. Blood spurted from his chest. But he didn't die. He grabbed for the stocking on the killer's head and yanked it off, and always the face was that of someone he knew. Quin or Callahan. Benson or Ross Young. Wayne O'Donald or Gene Travis. Zivia or Bean. As soon as he knew the killer's identity in the dream, he toppled forward into the river and heard the person cackling as the dark waters closed over his head.

Instead of drowning, he drew water into his lungs through gills that had sprouted just under his armpits. He swam through the underwater silence into a labyrinth where Gene Travis was making videos. Travis aimed the camera at him, mouth opening in a taunting grin, and laughed, *When you figure out who Daedalus is, let me know.*

Daedalus, Ariadne, Theseus, Minotaur, Icarus—a parade of mythological heroes who symbolized exotic sexual tastes. Terrific.

"Mike?"

It was an effort to lift his head at the sound of O'Donald's voice. McCleary sat up slowly and dropped his legs over the side of the chair. The concrete warmed his bare feet. A mockingbird trilled from a nearby pine tree. "Hi, Wayne. Thanks for coming by."

O'Donald pulled over a chair and clipped some plastic shades to his glasses. "How's the arm?"

"It aches sometimes and it's stiff, but other than that, I suppose I'm lucky the bastard didn't cut it off."

"I read the statement you gave to the Broward cops." O'Donald's intractable eyes made McCleary squirm.

He reached for the towel draped over the back of his chair and wiped his face with it. "And?"

"Seems to me your memory's pretty intact. I don't see any reason for playing around with hypnosis. I think it'd do you more good to get off your ass and go back to work, Mike. Unless you've decided to retire."

McCleary started to interrupt, but O'Donald shook his head. "Let me finish. Look, I know you feel like you're responsible for Bob Summer's murder and for Callahan's. But that's precisely what this guy wants you to feel. You're playing right into his game. It's almost like he's grabbed you by the shoulders and steered you into an emotional chasm, and now you're mired in it. So the way I see it, you've got two options—either drop the case or get on with it and beat this bastard at his own game."

For a long moment, McCleary just stared at O'Donald. Then anger broke his torpor. "You don't know what the hell you're talking about."

"Oh, don't I? Then allow me a little psychiatric license, Mike. What I see here is a man who's rapidly approaching middle age. He's a Type A personality, a compulsive overachiever, a goddamn perfectionist. He couldn't just be a good homicide detective, he had to be the best, so he became head of the homicide department. Then he got burned out. Understandable. It happens to cops all the time. Even to the best ones.

"Now three years down the line, I see him getting burned out as a private eye because he brought these same Type A personality traits into the business with him. Because of the nature of this particular case, he calls on an old lover for help. This is where I'm a little unclear on what part Callahan played in all this, Mike. Did you realize there were some unresolved things between you? Is that it? Did it start interfering with your marriage? Did you do something about it? Because I'll tell you right now that what I see in front of me is a man who's being consumed by guilt that's coming at him from several angles.

"Now if you want to capitulate to guilt and go the way of some of the better cops I've known, fine. That's your choice. But just remember there isn't a damn thing you can do about what's happened. You can't change any of it. And guilt is a waste of energy. Lighten up on yourself, Mike. You're human, just like the rest of us. You make mistakes. So what. The best thing you can do is pick yourself up and dust yourself off and move forward."

The words had hurtled toward McCleary like white-hot rocks, striking him in the chest, the head, around the face. Now, in the subsequent silence, he felt bruised. His bones ached. He wished he had the energy to spring toward O'Donald and tighten his hands around his neck. But all he could manage was a terse, "That was some speech, Wayne."

O'Donald ran a hand over his balding head. "Wore me out. I guess I've been wanting to say those things to you for a long time."

McCleary sat back in the chaise lounge and closed his eyes. *Go away, Wayne.*

But he didn't. Shrinks were as tenacious as sharks once they'd sunk in their teeth, and police shrinks were by far the worst of the bunch. He heard O'Donald's chair squeak. "You can't hide out by the pool forever, Mike."

"You really think I'm Type A, huh?"

"Classic."

He said it as if a classic Type A didn't stand a chance for a longeveous life.

"You had any more of those weird hunches of yours?"

"Yes, but nothing specific. Why? You think hunches are detrimental to my mental health or something?" *C'mon, Wayne, tell me about hunches. Tear them apart. Shred them.*

"No. But I think that by shutting yourself up with your icons, Mike, you're trying to force intuitive leaps. Why not try some painting?"

Annoyed, McCleary sat up and pushed his sunglasses

258

back on top of his head. "Painting? What the hell's that got to do with anything?"

"It's right-brain. That's where intuition originates. For that matter, that's what hypnosis taps. Right-brain, Mike." He tapped his right temple as if to underscore the point. "You want to try to clarify what happened that night? Then paint."

McCleary didn't say anything.

"How long's it been since you've painted?"

"Eons."

"Well, if I were you, I'd get started."

"Art therapy for the bereaved and the fucked up. Right, Dr. Freud?" McCleary smiled thinly as he said it, but the smile didn't fool O'Donald.

"My, aren't we testy."

"You bet your ass I'm testy," McCleary exploded. "You come waltzing in here with your textbook theories like I'm some sort of fruitcake locked up in a mental ward, and then proceed to tell me I've got my head screwed on backward. Testy? Yeah, you'd better be—"

He stopped suddenly when he saw the slow smile playing with O'Donald's mouth and realized he'd fallen right into his game—just as he'd played right into the killer's game. His fingers tightened over the edge of the chair.

"Very good, Mike," O'Donald said evenly. "Anger's a good beginning." He stood. "Give me a call if you need anything else."

"Like what, primal scream therapy?" McCleary called after him as he strode toward the back door.

O'Donald laughed, waved his hand in the air, and kept on walking.

3.

A bell jingled as Quin stepped into the shop. The odor of perm and hair spray, shampoo and nail polish covered the air like a thin membrane. Cat Stevens crooned an

259

old tune from the wall speakers. Quin spotted Terry Travis standing behind one of her customers, coaxing strands of the woman's hair through holes in a plastic cap that covered her head like a second skin. Nothing much had changed here in the several weeks since Quin had met Terry. But in her own life, everything had changed.

Terry caught sight of Quin in the mirror. "Hi, hon."

"You have a second, Terry?"

"Sure thing." She told her customer she'd be back in a jiffy and strolled over. "News?"

"Is your offer about Gene's secret closet still open?"

Terry combed her fingers through her red hair, a smile dimpling a corner of her mouth. "You bet. Let me get someone else to do that frost job and we'll go have coffee."

Twenty minutes later, seated in a coffee shop two doors down from the beauty salon, Quin explained what she'd discovered about Terry's ex-husband's video operation—and how.

Terry's eyes gleamed with astonishment. "Jesus, hon. You got more guts than me, that's for sure." She blew a pother of smoke into the air. "Did Gene buy your cover?"

"Apparently."

"And that same night of the party this Sylvia Callahan was killed."

"Yes."

"I read about it in the paper, but I don't remember anything in there about your husband."

"There was just a statement by a Mike West. That was him."

"So what do you have in mind?"

"Well, first, do you know a guy named Jimmy who works for Gene?"

She rolled her eyes. "Yeah, I know him. He's slime. He was just getting in real thick with Gene when he and I were married. Is he the one who told you about Minotaur?"

"Not initially, but he's the one who told us how the

ordering and delivery works. Does Gene have a computer at home?"

"Sure. Real fancy thing. Some of his video orders come in over the computer."

"You know how to work it?"

Terry laughed. "Hon, what I know about computers would fit on the tip of my little finger." She leaned toward Quin and dropped her voice. "But the one thing I *do* know might be what you're looking for."

"What's that?"

"The password for the video program that gets into his records and stuff. It's named after my son. Sean. Or at least, it used to be, when we were married. He might have changed it, but it's someplace to start." She stabbed out her cigarette. "Now, tell me what you've got in mind."

4.

McCleary fumed for a while at the pool, hurling mental invectives at O'Donald. He tried to concentrate on the February vignette of thin blue sky, frail wisps of pearled clouds, the flatness broken only by the trees. He listened to the distant din of traffic, the sounds braided, tangled, indistinguishable from each other. Then frustration shoved him to his feet.

He paced in corybantic agitation, through the holts of pines and citrus trees, the earth and grass cool against his bare feet. He plucked stones from the garden and tossed them with a vengeance at the fence. They pinged against the old wood and seemed to echo like gunfire. He finally stormed through the house and into the garage, where he kept his art supplies. He got out his sketch pad, a blank canvas, his easel, his paints and brushes. The first whiff of paint hissed into his nostrils, touching off a parade of memories as fleeting and insubstantial as pen and ink sketches.

He set his stuff up outside, where the light was best.

He straddled a stool, picked up his sketch pad, his charcoal, and experienced a brief but sharp panic when his hands refused to move. *What're you going to sketch, hotshot? The pine trees? The sun?*

Yeah, great. He could see it now. He would end up with a sketch pad of doodles.

He closed his eyes, letting himself drift back to the night at Callahan's. *Stepping outside . . . the seawall . . . the smell of the air . . . the courtyard and the house on the other side . . .* He opened his eyes and let his hand move across the page. Wide, jerky arcs, smooth curves, sharp angles, yes, he had it now, the rhythm, the fluvial currents between now and that night. He rode the tide, rejoiced in it, only dimly aware that his connections were also with a part of himself. At some point he skipped from sketch pad to canvas, his brush dabbing, darting, swirling until the picture had been quartered like a cut of meat. There, the struggle on the dock, the killer wearing a stocking over his head. And here, a trail of candy from the dock to the house, a trail like bread crumbs. Now, in the left-hand-corner, the killer alone, wearing dark clothes. Here, in the upper-right corner, the killer's boat and . . .

McCleary stopped, his hand suspended in midair, and stared at the name on the boat. He'd seen it, perhaps only for an instant, but it had burrowed down into his subconscious as relentless as a mole, and he had coaxed it out. Remembered it. A name meant it could be traced. Then he looked closely at the name, frowning. *Minos.*

Another Greek hero.

26   Instant Replays

HE NEEDED TO hear their voices. He needed it bad.

All day, he had thought about their voices, particularly McCleary's. His need had rooted in him, possessed him in the same way that the notion of a drink tantalizes a reformed alcoholic. And now his hand trembled as he dialed their number. He waited for the hollow hum that indicated the mikes in their phones were open. He waited for the flurry of house sounds. Instead, he heard nothing.

He slammed the receiver down.

They had unplugged their phones. Or his equipment had malfunctioned.

A sharp pain bit ferally into his gut, and he doubled over, gasping for breath. *Feed me,* demanded his body.

But he couldn't. Not yet. The stars said . . .

Oh, Jesus, it had nothing to do with the stars. It was Callahan's fault. She hadn't acted the way she was supposed to. She'd made him kill her. If she'd only behaved, if she . . . He hadn't wanted to kill her, at least not then. He had only wanted to go where McCleary had gone. *Like the Starship Enterprise.* He laughed, a loud, almost hysterical laugh, and slapped his hand over his mouth.

She had started to struggle, and it had inflamed him, blinded him. His body's needs had claimed him, and at the end, when he was released, he saw that she was dead. And then the fight with McCleary.

He could have killed him then, on the dock, because he'd had the advantage. But it would have been a quick, unsatisfying kill. It would have robbed him of all the elements he had planned for so carefully. His scrupulous attention to details would have been wasted. Besides, he'd wanted McCleary to suffer, to experience the creeping paralysis of terror.

He grabbed for the phone and dialed the McClearys' number again. Nothing. The same goddamn hollowness. He shoved the phone away from him. Knuckled his eyes. A pain sliced through his chest. He clutched the front of his shirt, rose unsteadily, and veered toward the closet where he kept his collection of tapes. A Minotaur tape. A false fix. Sometimes it worked. He prayed that tonight was one of those times.

In moments, he'd inserted the tape into his VCR and sat back, watching. There, Joyce as lovely as a goddess, strolling into view of the camera. Now a long shot of her white, perfect thighs, her buttocks, and a peek over her shoulder at the woman on the bed. A woman bound, gagged, struggling, as a man approached to the left of the bed.

He froze the frame. He stared at the ice pick in the man's hand. A beautiful weapon, slender as a shadow, deadly. He smiled and unfroze the frame.

The camera zoomed in on Joyce's face, eyes glazed from whatever drug she'd ingested—*barbiturates? smack?*—her steps measured, slow, strangely graceful. She sat at the edge of the bed and touched the back of her hand to the woman's face. Her other hand reached for the man's as he sat down.

He felt a tick of jealousy in his chest. *Jealousy, now?*

"Ssshh, don't struggle," she cooed to the woman, trailing her fingers across her chest, down to the boundary of her tan.

The woman's wide, startled eyes filled the screen.

A rush of adrenaline coursed through him. He clenched and unclenched his hands. He waited with bated breath.

The man let go of Joyce's hand and caressed the bound woman's jaw, her throat, her breasts. "See how

264

nice we can be when you don't struggle?'' whispered Joyce, slurring her words slightly.

And then the man raised the ice pick above his head, high above his head where the bound woman could see it. The camera captured the absolute terror in her eyes, the way the cords of muscles stood out in her thighs, her arms, as she struggled impotently. The camera cut to the ice pick, to a spicule of light that gleamed at its tip like a single drop of water.

It swooped through the air, like one of those high divers from the rocks in Acapulco, and hit home in the center of the woman's chest. His bones convulsed. His body rioted. A weight like gravity impaled him against the chair. His breath came in long, ugly pants, worse than a dog in heat. Sweat broke out on his face like a sudden case of rash or acne. The inside of his mouth turned to cotton.

His fingers sank into the armrests of the chair.

Sated.

For now.

The screen went snowy. He stared at it, feeling as if he were inside one of those little glass paperweights that snowed when you shook it. *I'm sorry, Joyce, it was the only way*. She knew. She had to die for what she knew because otherwise she would have cracked, and eventually she would have gone to the police, and that would have been that.

He got up, popped out the tape, turned off the set.

His body purred.

27 Coming to Terms

QUIN HAD SPENT several hours in the library, gathering books on Greek mythology, and now she was sequestered in her office with the heroes and heroines. They played coy at first, their essences eluding her, annoying her. They were like spoiled kids reveling in their incestuous stories, their histories as layered as onions. But as she peeled and plodded, their lives became fenestrated perches from which she could observe the similarities between the ancient Greeks and contemporary man.

Once, someone had said to her that there were only forty dramatic situations in life. If that was true, the Greeks were onto all of them. But they twisted the dramas so the plots divagated like nomads, then joined, becoming grander and stranger than the original concept. Take Theseus, for instance, regal son of Aegeus, king of Athens.

His various exploits included: killing the infamous robber Procrustes, who stretched or amputated the limbs of travelers to make them conform to the length of his bed; battling the Amazons and the Centaurs; attempting to abduct Persephone; and killing the Minotaur, the beast that was half human, half bull, and housed in the Cretan labyrinth.

Theseus was married to Phaedra, daughter of Minos, the king of Crete, and of Pasiphaë, who mated with a white bull her husband owned and gave birth to the Minotaur. So, technically, Quin mused, Theseus had killed his brother-in-law when he slew the Minotaur.

Minos, upon learning of the abomination his wife had borne, ordered Daedalus, an Athenian inventor, to build the labyrinth in which the Minotaur was imprisoned. Until Theseus killed it, the Minotaur was annually fed seven youths and seven maidens from Athens.

The postscript to this gross little tale was that Daedalus was later betrayed by Minos, who threw him and his son, Icarus, into the labyrinth. To escape, Daedalus built wings for himself and his son made of wax and feathers. Icarus, as the legend went, flew too near the sun, the wax melted, and he fell to his death into the sea.

These Greeks, Quin decided, had outdone anything Gene Travis could conceive. But it was no wonder he'd chosen Greek names for his special videos. The question was what connection, if any, did his prime snuff video buyer—Daedalus—have to any of this? It couldn't be coincidental that the buyer used a Greek code name. So did that mean the man was someone within Travis' organization?

Who?

"You look like you're studying for your MBA."

Quin glanced up. McCleary leaned into the doorway, hands in the pockets of his khaki slacks, a package tucked under his arm. His blue shirt blended with the color of his eyes and hid the bandage at his right shoulder. He looked different somehow, rested, as if he'd been suffering from a disease that suddenly had gone into remission.

"Not an MBA. Just a little education in Greek mythology. So how'd it go with Wayne?"

"Okay."

What's that mean? Okay great? Okay so-so? Okay bad? What? Patience, she told herself. She should have learned by now that McCleary could never be rushed. She sat back, rubbing an eye, realizing for the first time that twilight swam in the window. "What time is it?"

"Six-thirty." He plopped into the chair across from her desk, cradling the package on his lap. "Ross called and wanted to know if we'd like to meet him and Zivia for dinner at eight-thirty."

"Sure." She gestured toward his package. "What's that?"

He smiled. "I thought you'd never ask." He dug into the bag with all the zeal of a kid on Christmas morning. "First . . ." He drew out a small square package and set it in front of her. "I'd ordered it for your birthday, but I think I want you to have it now."

Quin unwrapped it, raised the lid, and was struck mute. Inside was a gold rope chain from which hung a gold heart with a sapphire in its center. She picked it up. On the back of the heart was inscribed, *I love you. Mac.* A lump rose in her throat. "It's beautiful." Her voice cracked, the tight ball of tension that had taken up residence in her chest broke loose, and tears rolled down her cheeks.

"Quin, I'm sorry." He spoke softly. "For everything. I know an apology doesn't make up for what happened, but . . ."

"It's not just your fault." She swiped at tissues in the box of Kleenex and blew her nose. Her hands were clenched on top of her desk, and she stared at them, at the erumpent tendons, the tiny hills and valleys that her knuckles made. She wanted an amelioration without accusations, without blame. So she chose her words carefully. "I sometimes think we put ourselves in situations to test our limits." She raised her eyes. "Not just you and me, but people in general. Maybe we needed something like this so we could learn to appreciate each other again."

"You think we were taking each other for granted?" A pair of lines on his forehead slid upward; the blue of his eyes deepened.

"Sometimes." Her fingers touched the cool gold of the heart; the sapphire caught the last bits of twilight and winked like an eye. "Maybe it's inevitable when two people are together as much as we are."

"You'd rather we worked separately on cases?"

"No. Would you?"

She was relieved that he shook his head.

"A couple of times," Quin went on, "I wanted to shout and stuff like they always do in the movies, you know?" She shrugged. "But then I would stand in front of the mirror and try to imagine myself doing that and I felt like an ass. It just didn't . . . oh, I don't know, it just seemed so . . . so undignified." She paused. "Suppose our situations had been reversed, Mac? How would you have dealt with it?"

"I don't know. Probably not as well as you did."

She wasn't so sure she'd dealt with it at all, much less dealt with it well, but she kept that to herself. McCleary leaned toward her, elbows on the edge of the desk, his chin resting in the palm of his hand. Miniatures of herself appeared in his smoky eyes. "I found out what I already knew, Quin, that I didn't belong in Callahan's world, and that I wanted to be with you."

The words hung there like a thick fog.

"Even if my side of the bedroom is always a mess?"

He laughed, and the fog dissipated. "It's no worse than walking into a den that's so neat even God would get bored."

"Maybe we could each learn to be a little less—me a little less *dis*organized and you a little less organized."

"Sort of borrow from each other, you mean."

"Yeah, I could learn to think before I blurt and you could learn to blurt before you think."

"And sometimes I could be on the one who leaves the butter in the pantry. Or in the drawer."

"Right. And sometimes I could be the bossy cop."

"And it'd be okay for me to leave the cap off the toothpaste," he countered.

Neither of them was smiling now. The air had gone deadly still. Her chest began to tighten again. But this was the first time she could remember that they'd both aired their grievances without argument. Petty grievances, yes, but day after day they'd accrued like interest on an unpaid debt and had eaten away at the marriage in small, subtle ways.

"I think," he said, the banter gone from his voice now, "that maybe it'd be easier if we just accepted each other as we are."

"We haven't been able to do it in three years, Mac."

Why had she said that? They'd been doing just fine, and then she'd spoiled it. She'd shoved the conversation toward the yawning black hole of unpleasant truths.

"We haven't tried."

Was it true? She didn't know. All she could think of was McCleary's critical streak and her own defensiveness, the two elements imbricated as tightly as shingles, joined at the hips like Siamese twins. A pattern. They had fallen into a behavioral pattern with its own peculiar MO, she thought.

He touched his hand to the back of hers. "I want this marriage to work, Quin."

She had a sudden impulse to ask him why it had taken him three years and a romp in the hay with Callahan to figure out that the marriage mattered. She felt like telling him what it had been like that night alone in the house. In fact, every erratic emotion that had moiled inside her for the last few weeks ruptured like a boil. What would have happened if Callahan hadn't been killed? Would he have continued to see her? Sleep with her? Would he have tried to divide his life between his wife and his mistress? Or maybe she and Callahan would have become close friends, sharing McCleary like a couple of Mormon wives married to the same man.

Sick.

Blood rushed to her cheeks. She opened her mouth. And then a familiar something flitted across McCleary's eyes, a vulnerable quality that sucked at her anger, robbing it of impetus, power. He had tried to deal honestly with the situation, openly, and his probity had cost him dearly.

"Quin?" Anxiety etched deeper lines in his forehead.

"I want the marriage to work too, Mac." The tip of

her finger circled the gold heart. Her body felt heavier than iron, her ears rang. She picked up the piece of jewelry. "Would you fasten it for me?" The request itself sealed something between them, and he understood it as well as she did.

He came around behind her, lifted her hair, fastened the chain. Instead of moving away, he slid his arms around her and buried his face in her neck. She stood, turned, and hugged him, loving the musculature of his back beneath her hands, the smell of his skin, the rightness. It was going to be okay now. It would be. They would restore the equilibrium of their lives. They would burrow back into the safe niche the murder of a woman they'd never known had squashed like a pea.

After a bit, he stepped away from her and eagerly returned to the package. "This is something Wayne suggested." He brought out a canvas. He stood it on end and peeled off the plastic sheet that covered it. The canvas had been divided into quarters, and each quarter depicted a different scene. But Quin's eyes were drawn to the one in the upper right-hand corner. A speedboat with *Minos* written across the back of it.

"The name," she exclaimed.

"Any connection to Daedalus?"

"Minos was the king of Crete and the guy who instructed Daedalus to build the labyrinth where the Minotaur was imprisoned. The Minotaur Theseus killed."

"And Daedalus is one of our man's best snuff video customers."

"Whom he's supposedly never met," Quin added.

"Just because this Daedalus character is Travis' best snuff character doesn't mean he has anything to do with these murders. That's what bothers me." He covered the painting again and they both sat down.

"I know. But it's too coincidental that his code name is also out of Greek mythology."

"Maybe Daedalus is Travis. Maybe he's concocted an imaginary customer for some reason."

"Or Travis isn't the killer, Mac."

"Maybe," he conceded. "But then who is? Schloper? Jimmy the videoman? Someone Travis has hired?" He shook his head. "The evidence points toward him, Quin. I know he's involved, but we just need the link."

"So we'll check around to see if he owns a boat called *Minos*, and in the meantime I've got a couple of ideas to bounce off you."

McCleary caught the twinkle in her eyes and laughed. "I hear trouble."

"C'mon." She stood. "I'll tell you about it on the way to dinner."

Outside, a breeze brushed clouds over the moon; a curious peace settled through her. It defied the blaring of horns on the interstate several miles away, the shriek of brakes a couple of streets over, the relentless, tacky noise of this concrete peninsula. It underscored the abnormality of life in general in South Florida and of her life in particular. She and McCleary should've been headed for divorce court, not dinner.

But on second thought, dinner was certainly the more interesting option.

They reminded Quin of Zelda and F. Scott Fitzgerald. There was Zivia with her blond hair and her quick laughter, looking as lovely as a flapper, and Young with his wide, refulgent smile and bright green socks, a man in an ascending spiral of fortune. They seemed untouchable, Quin thought, or blessed, and a continent away from the unpleasantries at Bloomingdale's that day lifetimes ago. Some small miracle had obviously taken place between them while she'd been wrestling with the tumults in her own life.

The miracle turned up halfway into the hors d'oeuvres when the waiter brought over a bottle of champagne. He uncorked it with a flourish, poured glasses for each of them, then twisted the bottle into a bucket of ice. As he walked off, Ross said, "Since you two introduced us, we thought you should be the first to know." He smiled at Zivia, whose cheeks flushed. "We're getting married."

It was as if they'd just announced they were joining the Moonies. Quin and McCleary both stammered congratulations, then they all toasted the occasion.

"I hope that doesn't mean we're losing an investigator," McCleary said.

Zivia shook her head. "No way."

"Only for a three-week honeymoon," Young interjected.

"And that won't be until June," Zivia added, then held up her left hand and flashed a diamond the size of a small walnut. "I've been wearing it two days, can you believe that? And in an office filled with private eyes. I thought detectives were supposed to be observant. The only person who noticed was Joe Bean, and I swore him to secrecy under the threat of death."

They had more champagne, and it bubbled through Quin's blood until she felt lighter than Ivory soap. When the pianist inside began to play, the music drew them all to the dance floor, where Quin ended up in Young's arms. He was a regular Fred Astaire, guiding her expertly, gracefully.

"I'm glad you and Mike could join us. Zivia told me he hasn't been at work since Sylvia's death."

She hoped she was imagining the accusation in his voice. "Between her and Bob Summer, he was pretty wrung out, Ross."

He drew back, looking at her, strands of his wheat-colored hair curling like punctuation marks against his forehead. His eyes seemed a deeper blue than she recalled. "I didn't mean it that way, Quin. I'd be the last person to blame either of you for bowing out of this case. Here I am, the guy who hired you, and two of *your* friends have gotten killed in the process and Mike got wounded."

"I think the killer chose Bob Summer. He fit the criteria. But Sylvia was a mistake."

"I got the impression this guy didn't make mistakes."

"Maybe 'mistakes' is the wrong word. He got careless. He raped Callahan without any protection. Also, there was nothing about her except her age that fit the MO except the sweets, Ross. I think all he intended to do was use her as a means of further terrorizing Mac. Something went wrong and he killed her. Did Benson tell you they've finally got a blood type on this guy?"

"No, he didn't."

"He's A-positive. From the bite on Lois Dwight's shoulder, we know he's got a slight underbite. Not enough to show just by looking at him, but something a dental impression would pick up. He's also missing his eye teeth. Then there's his knowledge and use of astrology, his preference for scissors and knives, the death sweet element, and this compulsive edge to his personality. Actually, when you think about it, we know an awful lot about the guy, including the name of his boat."

"His boat?"

"The one he used the night of Callahan's murder. It's called *Minos*."

He sounded out the name like a young student testing a word phonetically. "It seems like it should be Spanish."

She smiled. "Yeah, I guess it does. It's from Greek mythology."

He waited for her to elaborate, and when she didn't, he said, "So you're saying Gene Travis has an interest in Greek mythology? Christ, who ever would've guessed."

The number ended, and Quin detoured to the ladies' room before returning to the table. The rest room was empty, and she opened the window and leaned out into the night, bothered deeply by something she couldn't name. Distantly, the wail of sirens warbled in the air, echoing against the unremitting concrete. Her mind flickered to useless questions: would the Florida peninsula eventually sink beneath the weight of all the concrete? How many condominiums on a four-mile strip of beach did it take to create a transgression? If Florida sank, would it cause Atlantis to rise? Had there ever been an Atlantis? Had she known McCleary there? Had he known Callahan?

The thing that bothered her coated her insides like

lacquer. But she couldn't reach it to chip away at it, so she left it alone.

Zivia came in a few minutes later, while Quin was standing at the mirror, running her comb through her hair. She held up her hands before Quin could even open her mouth.

"I know, I know. Here I am, headed for husband number three, and you're thinking I've got pea soup for brains, right?" Her brows peaked, and Quin laughed.

"Not that bad. But considering what happened in Bloomie's, I am kind of curious."

"Curious, yeah. I'm a little curious about all this myself. Me. Engaged for the third time. Ridiculous." She leaned against the sink. "It's like this. When it's good between us, it's very good. And the very good makes marriage worth a shot. That's my story. Now what's yours? I haven't seen enough of you this last week to even ask you how Mac's been."

"I think things are going to be okay now. But what I really want to know is if you're free the night after next."

Zivia, her mouth forming an O in the mirror as she applied lipstick, nodded. "Sure. For what?"

"A job."

"A dark-clothes-and-hush-hush-job?"

Quin smiled. "Just a little ole B and E."

28 Preparations

1.

GENE TRAVIS WAS prompt, McCleary would give him that much. Exactly at nine-thirty the next morning, he appeared on the Grove Fitness Club jogging track. Instead of the gray running suit he'd worn the first time McCleary had seen him, he was garbed in navy blue shorts and a white and blue sleeveless top that revealed the mounds and hills of his biceps. McCleary thought briefly of the white-hot agony of that knife searing through his shoulder the night at Callahan's. *Arms powerful enough to do that.* He felt like grabbing Travis by the hair and throwing him against the wall and beating him to a pulp.

Instead, he smiled and greeted Travis like an old friend and thought about how sweet it would be to nail this sucker *legally*, so that even his big bucks and a fancy attorney wouldn't be able to get him off. *Humpty-Dumpty, pal. That's you.*

They started off at a comfortable pace on their three-mile run. "How's the arm?" Travis asked.

"A lot better than it was nine days ago."

"It was quite a shock, I can tell you, opening up the paper and seeing the story right there on the front page. I used to tell Callahan that she should've had a body-guard living at the house with her. Or at the very least a Doberman." He glanced at McCleary, his gray eyes sheened with what was supposed to be sympathy. "I guess it's been tough on you."

276

Tough: you got no idea, buddy.

"I'd known her a long time," he said finally. "I didn't do anything but lay low for a week. That's why it took me so long to get back to you."

He made a gesture of understanding. "Me, I probably would've stayed drunk for two weeks." They rounded a curve in the track, marking the first mile. Travis, he noted, wasn't the least bit winded. *Tip-top shape, aren't you, Gene my boy?* "I noticed you were barely mentioned in the paper. You were lucky. The less the hyenas in the press know, the better."

"There're some details about the murder the cops are keeping to themselves. Otherwise my photograph would probably have been smeared all over the front page."

Actually, Mike West's part in the story about the murder of Sylvia Callahan had been almost painfully brief, McCleary thought, considering what had happened. He had Benson to thank for that, Benson who had maneuvered him through the Broward County bureaucracy like a pro.

"Anise has been called out of town on business, but she instructed me to go ahead and arrange a meeting with you as soon as possible. At your convenience."

The only sign that Travis found this change in plans unsettling was in the twitch at his mouth. "She, uh, told you about Minotaur?"

"She mentioned it, yes."

"And?"

"And what?"

"What do you think about it?"

McCleary smiled. "Morally? Professionally? Personally?"

"Any of the above. All of the above."

"Whatever turns a profit, Gene. I'm just supposed to observe, talk to you about details, and make an offer based on that and what you two have already discussed."

He felt, for a moment, like an IBM executive versed in the lexicon of industrial espionage. *For this bit of information, we are prepared to pay . . .*

"She told you the service would have to be leased?"

"Yes. I'm a little concerned about the safety factor."

"Don't be. I've had no problems at all with the law."

And that's about to change, pal.

"How about tomorrow night around ten-thirty or eleven? I'll give you the address."

"That's fine."

They were headed down the last stretch of the track now, where branches tangled overhead in an integument that provided thick shade. Travis suddenly stopped and crouched down to tie his shoe. "There is one other thing, Mike."

"What's that?"

"I'll need a token of intent from Anise."

"Nonrefundable?"

"Only if she doesn't buy."

"How much?"

"Seventy-five."

"Make it fifty and we have a deal."

"Sixty."

His gray eyes rolled up from his shoe to McCleary's face, eyes like the plump belly of a pigeon, eyes that waited patiently for an answer from business broker Mike West. "Sixty. All right." Travis stood and they shook on it.

Honor among thieves.

As they jogged the remaining distance to the end of the track, McCleary wondered where the hell he was going to get sixty thousand.

He wasn't sure what tipped him off—the fact that the car was a van and a van had followed Quin and Bean the night of Callahan's party, or just that he'd expected something like this from Travis. But as he headed north out of the Grove along Biscayne Boulevard, the blue van hugged his tail as if it and Lady were connected through a tractor beam, *Star Trek* style. When he sped up, the van mimicked him. When he turned, it turned. When he slowed, it slowed.

Okay, sucker.

McCleary pulled onto I-95 and drove north in the right-hand lane, holding a speed of sixty. The van cruised along two cars back. McCleary tried to imagine the driver, sitting back, popping a Bruce Springsteen tape into his tape deck, tapping his fingers against the steering wheel in rhythm with the music. Right about now he was probably lighting a cigarette and wondering where McCleary was going.

Shopping, pal, that's where.

At Ives Dairy Road, McCleary exited east. So did the van. He sailed through the entrance of the 163rd Street Mall, slowed, and parked in front of Burdine's. As he reached the front door, the dark glass captured the van driving into the lot. A predictable sucker, this one. Good.

He stepped inside Burdine's and stood at the window, watching as a guy about five-ten, with curly black hair, got out of the van. As he neared, McCleary saw that he was wearing jeans and a blue western-style shirt. The acne that scarred his thin, rapacious face matched Quin's description of Jimmy the video cameraman.

McCleary strolled over to a rack of men's shirts and feigned interest, his fingers stepping through them, sliding hangers to the side. A few minutes later, Jimmy the Shadow—evidently feeling secure in his anonymity—stopped at a rack to McCleary's left. McCleary walked away, out into the main corridor that led past cosmetics and perfume, women's handbags, and shoes, and stepped onto the escalator. He rode it to the second floor. He walked back through housewares, stopped in the stationery section, and found what he needed. He paid for the items at the register and moved on toward the rest rooms and pay phones. He stole a glance over his shoulder and spotted faithful Jimmy dawdling over a display of crystal vases.

Keep following, sonny.

He paused at the water fountain, and Jimmy entered the hallway. He hesitated momentarily, as if taken aback that McCleary wasn't where he was supposed to be—in the rest room. He couldn't exactly turn around and leave without seeming suspicious, so he continued forward into the men's room. McCleary reached inside the bag for his purchases. He slipped a roll of duct tape into his jacket pocket, then brought out a five-by-seven Post-it notepad. He opened it and across the top one printed OUT OF ORDER. He stuck it to the door of the rest room and waited a few moments to see if anyone exited. An older man strolled out, and McCleary went in.

Jimmy stood at one of the four urinals, a sole pisser in a room which probably wouldn't be empty very long, despite McCleary's note on the door. He looked up, then turned back to more important business, giving McCleary a chance to come up behind him, as if he were going into the stall. Instead, he pulled his .38 from his shoulder holster and stuck it into the small of Jimmy's back.

"Don't even breathe too hard, buddy."

The man sucked in his breath and stammered, "You m-mind if I, uh, zip up my fly?"

"Yeah, I mind. Raise your hands. C'mon, fast."

He did, and McCleary patted him down. Strapped to the guy's ankle was a snub-nosed number—small but lethal. McCleary dropped it in his jacket pocket. "Turn around."

As he turned, his dark eyes widened with distress. "My money's in my wallet. Go on, take it."

"Look, we both know you've been tailing my ass since I left the health club. So let's cut the bullshit." McCleary aimed his .38 at the man's limp cock. "Start talking and make it fast. Why'd Travis have you follow me?"

"Dunno."

He cocked the .38. Blood rushed out of Jimmy's face, so the scars on his cheeks stood out in stark relief. "He . . . he doesn't think you're who you say you are."

"C'mon, what else?" McCleary snapped, pressing the gun against Jimmy's wilted member.

His breath eructed from someplace deep inside him.

Sweat popped out on his forehead, across his upper lip. "Jesus, I . . ." His eyes slid hopefully toward the door.

"Don't count on it, buddy. There's an OUT OF ORDER sign on the door. You've got to the count of five. . . ."

"I'm supposed to follow you, keep tabs on you. If . . . if you're not wh-who you . . . you say you are, then he's gonna . . . gonna set you up tomorrow night." He spoke in a breathless rush, as though he couldn't get the words out fast enough. "If I . . . I was you, I'd call the whole thing off, mister . . . he . . . he isn't a man to fuck with."

"Tell me about this place we're supposed to meet. You *do* know where it is, don't you, Jimmy?"

"Yeah. Sure, I know. It's a warehouse way the hell west of town. Practically in the goddamn Glades. It's where . . . where Gene does some of his films."

"His snuff films, Jimmy?"

His face turned whiter, milkier, and as thin as tissue paper. "Yeah." It was barely a whisper. He blinked. His eyes dropped to McCleary's .38. "You're a cop, huh."

McCleary ignored his question.

"How many snuff films has he done?"

"Dunno exactly."

"Who's his best customer?"

"Dunno the guy's name, except that he's called Daedalus."

"You got any ideas on who Daedalus is, Jimmy?"

He shrugged. "Shit, no. Really, man. I got no idea."

"And the orders come in over Travis' computer?"

"She told you, didn't she? That Anise woman."

"I'll ask the questions. Was Joyce Young in one of these snuff films, Jimmy?"

He looked down at the gun. His head nodded so slightly, it might not have been a nod at all. "Yeah."

"And who was that film for?"

"Him. Big Daddy Daedalus."

"You the man who shot it?"

"No. No fucking way. I don't know who shot it. Don't wanna know."

Oddly, McCleary believed him. "Take off your jeans."

His eyes swept to McCleary's face. His tongue darted into the corner of his mouth, chasing an orb of sweat that had trickled down his cheek. "Oh c'mon, man, I—"

"*Do it.*"

Off came Jimmy's jeans.

"Now the shorts."

Off came the shorts.

"Move into the stall."

He covered himself with his hands and backed into the stall.

"Lower the seat and sit down."

He did.

McCleary removed a pair of handcuffs from his jacket pocket and cuffed Jimmy's hands to the toilet paper dispenser.

"You can't *do* this to me, man," Jimmy wailed.

"It won't be long. I promise. But I can't have you making noises, now can I, Jimbo?" He dropped his gun back in his shoulder holster and reached into his pocket for the duct tape. He tore off a generous strip and taped Jimmy's mouth shut. Then he scooped up Jimmy's slacks and underwear. "I'll just take these with me. Don't worry about a thing, Jimbo."

He grunted. He struggled to free his hands, the cuffs rattling against the toilet paper dispenser.

McCleary locked the stall door and scooted out beneath it. On his way out of the rest room, he stuffed the man's clothes into the wastebasket.

Just outside the mall, he used the pay phone to call Benson. "Tim, it's Mac."

"Hey, buddy, where've you been? I've bombarded your office with messages. What happened this morning with Travis?"

"First things first," McCleary replied, and told him about Jimmy the videoman.

Benson's reaction fell somewhere between laughter

and a groan. "I'll get a car over there pronto. At the very least, we can get him for indecent exposure."

"Just keep him out of my hair until tomorrow night. Tim, I'm going to need sixty thousand cash for this deal with Travis."

"Sixty grand?" Benson whistled softly. "Shit, Mac." McCleary could almost see him, raking his fingers through his hair, pursing his mouth, shaking his head.

"And why don't you mention to Ross what we've got in mind. I think he needs a boost from the cops, Tim. Quin and I had dinner with him last night. He said he feels like he's been cut out of all this."

"How much do you want me to tell him?"

"Just enough so he doesn't feel left out."

"Okay, I will. Now look, about the sixty thou. I can check with Vice and see what we can raise from their drug impoundments. I'll have to get back to you. Where're you going to be?"

"Looking for *Minos*. I'll call you in a couple of hours."

2.

Quin stood in a phone booth a block from Travis' financial consulting office in the Grove. Sunlight the color of lemonade poured through the glass, baking her like bread. The din of traffic on the main street behind her was muted. She dialed his office number, then pinched her nostrils shut as a receptionist answered the phone.

"Good morning, Travis Consulting. May I help you?"

"Yes. Is Mr. Travis in?" Quin's voice sounded as if her adenoids had been shoved so far up her nose, they were resting against the forefront of her brain.

"I'm sorry, he won't be in today. Is there someone else who could help you?"

"No. No, I don't think so. Thank you."

"Would you like to leave a message?"

"I'll call him back. Thanks."

She hung up and hurried back to her Toyota. She

drove the block to the building where Travis Consulting was located and parked in the guest lot in back. She plucked her briefcase off the passenger seat, locked the doors, and walked around to the front. As she neared the entrance, she eyed her reflection critically. Her umber hair was pinned up, off her shoulders, with strands falling loosely around her face. Her sunglasses were huge and round. The designer's initials, engraved in the lower corner of the left lens, were an annoying blind spot. But the glasses went along with her flowered designer skirt and silk blouse—conservative enough so that she wouldn't be remembered, but not so conservative that she seemed severe.

The Spanish-style building that housed Travis' cover financial consulting business was pink as salmon and built around a plant-filled courtyard. Birds sang from the branches of black olive trees. Butterflies flitted between gardenia bushes and honeysuckle. Her shoes clicked against the tile, as rhythmic as the pulse of passing time, lulling her into her new persona. *You are a dental insurance salesman. You will get the information you need.*

She sailed through the front door, her body vibrating like a hummingbird's. Her shoes sank into the plush plum-colored rug. Her gaze swept across the expensive but simple furnishings, the eggshell-white walls covered with Japanese prints, and came to rest on the receptionist behind the desk.

"Morning," she said cheerfully. "Is Mr. Travis in? I have an appointment for eleven-thirty."

The woman wore Benjamin Franklin glasses that rode low on her nose. She peered at Quin over the rims, her gray hair as perfectly motionless as Ruth Grimes', Quin noticed. "I'm afraid you must be mistaken. Mr. Travis won't be in today."

Quin allowed her face to sag. She pushed her sunglasses back into her hair. "I'm *sure* it was today. Could you check? My name's Prudy Charles. With Dita Dental Insurance."

The woman consulted an appointment book and shook her head. "No, I'm sorry, he didn't have you down."

Quin leaned on the counter. In a voice that just begged for commiseration, she said, "Would you mind if I went through my speech, just the same? I need the practice. This is only my second day on the job. And I've *got* to account for my time on my sheet."

The woman smiled. "I used to sell real estate, sweetie. I know exactly how you feel."

"Well, first of all, we have several group rates you can choose from. Each rate covers between sixty and eighty percent for *major* dental work like crowns and root canals and oral surgery. The going price for a crown these days is about three hundred and fifty dollars, so that means a savings of two ten to two fifty *just* on a crown, for instance." She dropped her voice. "You're supposed to ooohhh and aaahhh."

The woman laughed, and Quin knew she had an ally. "Aren't there only certain dentists you can choose from in a given area?" she asked.

Quin could've kissed her; she'd led her right into what she'd come here for. "Well, yes, there are." She retrieved a brochure from her briefcase—one that had been given to her and Mac by the real Prudy Charles when they'd purchased dental insurance for the firm. "Okay, let's see here. Would you know offhand who Mr. Travis' dentist is?"

"Sure. I make his appointments. Dr. Charles Kruger on Miami Beach."

"Kruger, Kruger." She drew her finger down the list and shook her head. "He's not on here. But that's okay. We have thirty-five dentists and specialists on our list who . . . Listen, instead of boring you with all this, why don't I just leave you the brochure and my card?"

"That'd be great. I'm not sure when Mr. Travis will be in, but I'll give it to him."

Quin sighed. "Thanks. And I really appreciate your listening to my spiel."

"You did great. A lot better than I did on my second day in real estate."

Bless you, honey chile.

The plaque outside Kruger's office said: CHARLES KRUGER, DDS, PA, MSD. Quin had no idea what all the initials meant, except that Kruger was probably expensive.

She had to wait half an hour to see him. That meant thirty minutes of music intended to soothe the frayed nerves of traumatized patients in the waiting room. But the music was so changeless, Quin nearly fell asleep.

She was finally ushered into Kruger's office. He was eating what looked like a peanut butter and jelly sandwich, and paging through a magazine. He was a short, adorable little man who looked like an artist's conception of an absentminded professor: absolutely white hair, wire-rim glasses as round as his black eyes, a quick smile that revealed a spot of peanut butter on his front tooth. He rose and shook her hand, then gestured for her to sit.

"So what can I do for you, Ms. St. James?"

She got out her ID and passed it across the desk. "I need some information on one of your patients, Dr. Kruger."

He examined her ID and handed it back to her. "Concerning what?"

"A homicide. Several homicides," she added, and picked her way carefully and selectively through the murders of Joyce Young, Lois Dwight, Bob Summer.

He listened attentively, his hands on the desk, one on top of the other, his partially eaten peanut butter and jelly sandwich forgotten. When she finished, his bushy white brows came together in a frown, forming an erratic straight line across the bridge of his nose. "And you believe one of my patients may be this man?"

"Yes."

"Who?"

"Gene Travis."

He sat back, pensive, the rete of wrinkles at his mouth

286

elongating, shooting along the sides of his nose. He picked up his phone and dialed a number. "Sara, could you please bring me the file on Gene Travis? . . . Yes, thanks." He hung up. "Let's take a look, Ms. St. James."

A woman in white appeared a few moments later, set a file on Kruger's desk, and left. He opened it and spent several long minutes aahhing and sighing. "He's got a slight overbite."

Her heart fell. "What about his blood type?"

"Let's see now. Blood type. Okay, here we go. He had oral surgery last year, so we typed his blood. A-positive." He looked up. "Anything else?"

"Yes. Does he have his eyeteeth?"

Kruger returned to the file, unclipped an X-ray, and held it up to the lamp. "Yes."

Strike out on the bite and the eyeteeth.

"Does that help?"

"Perfect match on the blood type, but not on the bite. The killer supposedly has an underbite and doesn't have his eye teeth."

"And this was something gleaned from a bite on the woman's shoulder?"

"Right."

That pensive expression took hold of his face again. "Was she a thin woman? Maybe like yourself?"

"Yes, I think so."

"Now I'm sure you could ask a dozen dentists and get a dozen different opinions on this, Ms. St. James. But based on my forty-two years in dentistry, I think it would be impossible to prove without a doubt from a bite like you've described whether a man had his eyeteeth or not. With a bite on a fleshier part of the body—like the buttocks, for instance, as in the Ted Bundy case— then yes, it would be possible to prove. But not this. Not on a thin shoulder. Absolutely not." Then he looked down at his partially eaten sandwich, as if just remembering it. He picked up the untouched half with his napkin and held it out. "Could I interest you in this half?"

She eyed the sandwich, then glanced up at Kruger. "I'll split it with you."

29 In the Hangar

DARK CLOUDS LACINIATED the evening sky as he parked in front of Wynn Aviation. A nacreous light bled from the clouds and spilled down the sides of the sky. He smelled rain in the breeze that whipped dried leaves through the nearly deserted parking lot. Rain that would cleanse after the kill.

A pulse fluttered in his throat as he walked around to the side of the hangar. Adrenaline spurted through him. His blood rushed through his veins with the heat of a summer day. But the anticipation of this kill affected him in much the same way as watching the tape of Joyce had. It was a filler, a substitute for the real thing, because he would not be using the knife or scissors.

In the distance, he could see the small planes in the tie-down area, the waning light tipping their wings, gleaming from their propellers. Daedalus knew about flight, he thought. His only mistake was having a son like Icarus who stupidly flew too near the sun so the wax on his wings melted. But Daedalus learned from his son. He escaped that fatal plunge into the sea.

Just as I will.

His sneakers moved soundlessly across the black asphalt. He would have preferred doing this barefoot, but you never knew what sorts of things might be strewn across the floor of a hangar: nails, screws, bits of glass, slivers of metal. Perhaps shoes, he thought, were part of this new direction his body was pushing him in. A direction that no longer included the crutch of astrology. He hadn't computed the odds for this kill.

He could hear music from a radio somewhere, but he saw no one in the vicinity of the hangar. The flying school at Wynn closed at six every evening, except on weekends. The hangar, however, was open, because this was where Neal Schloper puttered in the evenings, changing spark plugs, rebuilding engines, refurbishing old planes.

At the mouth of the hangar, he stopped. The planes inside all looked wounded: an aerobatic plane minus a propeller, a Cessna 150 with a flat nose tire, a Piper Cub with its cargo door hanging by a thread. Schloper was huddled over the open cauling of a twin-engine plane, a bright work light illuminating the area as he worked. From a radio on the floor behind him, the Fleetwoods crooned one of their golden oldies, *Mr. Blue.*

He entered the hangar with the stealth of a thief, his weapon at his side, crowned by a silencer. *A new modus operandi.* "Hello, Neal," he called over the din of the music.

Schloper lifted his head out of the cauling so fast he banged his head on the edge of it. He spun around, rubbing it, grimacing, a wrench in his right hand. "What're *you* doing here?"

"Just paying you a little visit, Neal," he replied, and lifted the gun. Schloper's eyes, usually so hooded, so somnolent-looking, opened wide. "I should've done this a long time ago, you know. For what you did to Joyce."

"What *I* did?" His voice rang out as shrill as a hungry parrot's. His eyes remained glued to the gun. "What about what *you* did, you bastard?"

"I loved her, that's all I did."

"And you killed her, too, didn't you. And you killed that other woman. And that—"

"Very good, Neal." He wished he could feel a magnanimity toward this man, an affection like he so often did for his other victims. But he couldn't. Schloper had been nothing but a pain in the ass. "Too bad you weren't born in May. Then you'd fit neatly into the scheme of things. But . . ." He shrugged. "A man has to be ready for the unexpected, don't you think?"

In the surfeit of bright light from the work lamp, he could see sweat glistening on Schloper's brow.

"You won't get away with it."

"Why won't I? There won't be anything to connect your murder to the others. Nothing at all. Different weapon, Neal. Different method. They call it an MO. The police are big on MOs, did you know that? They're looking for a crazy who mutilates, who takes body parts as trophies, who leaves sweets, who—"

Schloper's right hand rose abruptly, releasing the wrench. It grazed his shoulder, knocking him back just as he fired his weapon, and the shot zinged off the windshield of the plane. Schloper leaped past him, headed toward the mouth of the hangar. He spun like a dancer, took careful aim, and fired. Schloper gasped, his knees buckled, and he fell to the floor just as the DJ on the radio said, ". . . remember this one by Neil Sedaka?"

Neil Sedaka, Neal Schloper: what ironic twists the universe tossed out, he thought, walking over to where Schloper lay.

A dark stain spread across the back of Schloper's T-shirt. He crouched next to him, touched his fingers to his carotid artery. Nothing. "Too bad, Neal. You should never have gotten in the way. And that's what you always were, you know. In the way."

He turned Schloper over, gazing down at him dispassionately. Then he raised his gun again and aimed at Schloper's face, that face he had hated for so long, and fired.

30 Facts

1.

JIMMY THE VIDEOMAN, whose real name was James Paul Kitt, had a rap sheet as long as McCleary's arm. He'd been arrested fifteen times in six different states, mostly for petty theft. Thanks to plea bargaining, he'd never done more than six months in a county jail. But four years ago he'd jumped bail in North Carolina on a stolen car charge, and now he was ready to sing his miserable little heart out if Benson would 'cut him some slack.'

They were sitting in an ugly, practically barren room on the first floor of the station. There were no windows. The harsh overhead light made Jimmy's acne-scarred cheeks look like the surface of a ruined planet. He kept wringing his hands and glancing from McCleary to Benson as he waited for the verdict on his snitch plea. Benson, peering at Jimmy over the rim of his glasses so that he seemed professorial, said, "Whatever slack I cut you, buddy, is going to depend on what you can tell us about Gene Travis. So start talking."

"I . . . I need more than that. I . . . I need your word that you'll help me if I help you," Jimmy stammered.

Benson's benign demeanor developed fissures. He whipped off his glasses and leaned toward Jimmy, grabbing him by the collar. "Listen, you shithead. You're not in a position to get a promise from Satan, got that? Now unless you want to find your ass on a bus bound for North Carolina tonight, you'll tell us what you know about Gene Travis' video operation." Benson let go of his collar suddenly, and he flopped back in his chair and began to blubber.

"He'll kill me if he knows I've snitched on him," he sobbed, sniffling noisily. "He'll fucking kill me."

"He'll have to find out first, and if you play along with us, he won't ever know," McCleary said. "Does Travis keep copies of his snuff films?"

Jimmy wiped his arm across his nose. He seemed to be struggling with himself, weighing the odds for and against snitching. He finally nodded.

"Where?"

"I dunno. I jus' know he does because sometimes a client's video will break or something and Gene's always got a copy."

"Tell Lieutenant Benson what you told me today about the video Joyce was in shortly before she was killed, Jimmy."

Jimmy stared at the table and ran his hands over his jeans repeatedly, as if he were trying to scrape something off his palms.

"Well?" Benson snapped.

"She was in . . . in one of Big Daddy's videos."

"Big Daddy. That's your name for this Daedalus guy, right?" McCleary said.

"Yeah. Big Daddy, Dildo, Big Dick, we got a bunch of nicknames for him."

McCleary and Benson exchanged a glance. Benson said, "Who is this guy, Jimmy? You ever seen him? Talked to him?"

"No. I told him . . ." He jerked a thumb toward McCleary. "I told him how it's done. The order comes through the computer. A drop's made. That's all I know." He patted his shirt pocket for his cigarettes and lit one. He dropped the match into the Styrofoam cup in front of him. It hissed as it hit the remaining coffee inside.

"So tell us about this warehouse," McCleary said. "Are they actually going to be shooting a snuff video in there tomorrow night?"

"Before Gene got suspicious, they were. Now I

dunno." He raised his dark eyes. They'd shrunk into his scarred cheeks like raisins. "But I can tell you one thing. If I don't come back to him with a report on you as Mike West, there won't even *be* a tomorrow night. You guys'll be pounding sand."

What do you think, Mac? Benson's eyes inquired.

Let's play him a little more, McCleary's shrug replied.

"Who was this film supposed to be for?" Benson asked.

"Big Daddy."

"Who's in it?" Benson asked.

"Dunno."

"Hey, Jimmy," McCleary said, and pointed at his own mouth. "Watch my lips. Who . . . is . . . the . . . victim . . . supposed to be . . . in this film?"

"I dunno. I swear. I dunno." His voice trilled with incipient hysteria.

"How do they get rid of the bodies?" Benson barked.

"Different ways. They're almost always bums, people no one would miss. So sometimes they throw 'em in canals or lock 'em in the trunks of abandoned cars. Or bury them. Stuff like that."

Sweet Christ, McCleary thought. How many unidentified bodies found around Dade could be traced back to this snuff operation? "But sometimes the videos are shot outside the country, right?"

"Yeah. It depends on the client."

"You think it's possible that Daedalus is actually Travis?" McCleary asked.

Jimmy wasn't as stupid as he looked.

"I dunno. But anything's possible. Gene's a weird dude, there's no telling what he might do."

"Does Gene own a boat?" McCleary had been drumming his fingers against the tabletop, thinking about his futile search today for the owner of *Minos.* Now his fingers paused and Jimmy looked over at him.

"A boat? Fuck no. Gene's chickenshit when it comes to the ocean. He's got a what d'ya call it, a phobia, yeah, he's got a phobia about the ocean."

A phobia? "You sure?"

"Yeah, I'm sure. 'Bout two years ago we were over in the Bahamas doing a job and Gene he was out swimming, and he's not a very good swimmer, and the sea was real rough and he got tugged under. Nearly drowned. He's been scared shitless of water ever since. Oh, he'll swim in a pool, but not in anything bigger than that."

Then either Travis wasn't their man, McCleary thought, or he'd hired someone else to kill Callahan.

Benson stabbed his thumb toward the door. McCleary nodded, and they both pushed away from the table. "Be right back, Jimbo. Don't go away."

"Yeah. Sure. Real funny," Jimmy mumbled.

McCleary and Benson stepped out into the hall. "*Now* what?" Benson rolled his lower lip against his teeth. "Do we go through with tomorrow night or not?"

"Yeah, but with our boy's help."

"You're gonna trust that asshole?"

"I don't think we have any choice."

"Then I'm gonna have a backup at that warehouse."

"No, we don't want to scare them off and come up with nothing. I have a better idea." And he explained.

Just as they were about to go back inside the room, a cop with dark hair and deep bags under his eyes hurried into the hall. "Hey, Tim. Isn't one of your suspects in that Young murder a guy named Neal Schloper?"

"Yeah, what about him?"

"He's dead. Shot through the back and face in a hangar at Wynn Aviation."

2.

It was 10:00 P.M. and Quin and McCleary stood at a chalkboard in their kitchen where for the last hour, they'd been diagramming their investigation. It reminded her of poorly structured English lessons. Nouns and verbs were connected by lines, not conjunctions. Crime scenes were described by clipped phrases such as "tied to bed," "Floresta Park running track," "mutilated corpse." Even the names of the victims had been abbreviated, as if their importance did not extend beyond the two-dimensional rendering on the board.

VICTIMS

J. YOUNG
1. teaser
2. trophy
3. death sweet
4. killed in bed
5. Taurus
6. scissors
7. porn films
8. health nut/club

L. DWIGHT
1. death sweet
2. killed in bed
3. knife
4. condom used?

B. SUMMER
1. death sweet
2. trophy
3. teaser
4. health nut
5. killed while jogging
6. Taurus
7. scissors

S. CALLAHAN
1. death sweet
2. rape
3. no condom used
4. knife
5. killed in bed
6. boat connected to death: *Minos*

N. SCHLOPER
1. *No* death sweet
2. *No* trophies
3. *Gun* not knife
4. health club member
5. ex-hubby of Joyce Young
6. did films for Travis

KILLER
1. astrology buff
2. may have slight underbite
3. A-positive blood
4. may be missing eyeteeth
5. some "random" kills
6. compulsive/obsessive personality
7. above average intelligence
8. observes "chosen" victims for period of time before killing them
9. prefers knives or knifelike weapons
10. according to psych. report from O'Donald, he may be motivated by a need to kill, as well as a need to pit himself against police, perhaps to prove his superior intelligence
11. would be incapable of prolonged relationship with a woman
12. owns/uses a boat called *Minos*
13. access to or belongs to Grove Fitness Club, like two of victims

GENE TRAVIS
1. A-positive blood
2. operates video service for "special" clients which includes snuff films
3. code system for video service based on Greek mythology
4. Minotaur is code word for snuff films
5. Daedalus is supposedly his best Minotaur customer
6. was Joyce Young's lover
7. got her and Neal Schloper involved in his porn films
8. has lackey, Jimmy, who may have filmed snuff videos
9. one divorce, separated from second wife, settled paternity suit with Suzi Mellon out of court
10. password for computer system connected to video service: *Sean*
11. belongs to Grove Fitness Club/ a runner
12. knew McCleary was staying at Callahan's night of her murder
13. might have water phobia

"It's the same guy, Quin," McCleary said. "I'm sure of it. He just changed his MO, that's all."

"Hey, you don't have to convince me." She picked up a piece of cheese from a platter of munchies on the table and sandwiched it between two crackers. "The thing is, we've still got only part of the picture, especially if what that video guy says is true. About Travis being terrified of water."

"I don't know how much I believe of anything he says."

"Look, maybe we should forget this plan Terry Travis and I concocted. I'll go with you tomorrow night as Anise Rochelle. She got back in town. She wants to see the Minotaur operation for herself."

"No, then he's really going to smell a rat. Besides, you may find something we can use."

"Even if I do, we can't use it in court."

"But we can pass it on to Benson, who can get a search warrant."

Why was it *she* had to break a law to nail someone like Gene Travis, whose iniquities should've landed him in prison long before Joyce Young's murder? And who was to say that even if they found the evidence they needed against Travis that he would go to jail? He had money, lots of it, enough to hire someone like F. Lee Bailey, enough to buy off a judge. What the hell, the drug kings did it all the time. It had almost become a standard practice, like plea bargaining. Her sense of impotence against the criminal justice system had become a gnawing hunger in the pit of her stomach, and she turned away from the chalkboard to replenish the plate of goodies.

The doorbell rang.

"I'll get it," McCleary said.

From the living room, she heard Ross Young's profuse apology for barging in so late, but what was going on, anyway? He'd just heard about Neal Schloper's murder on the radio, and he'd tried to call Benson but he wasn't in, and did McCleary know anything about it?

They came into the kitchen, and Young went through his apology again. Despite his obvious agitation, which had brought blooms of color to his cheeks, he looked as dapper as an actor on audition, except for his gray socks with sparkles on them. His blond hair shone salubriously beneath the gleam of the kitchen lights, and there was no trace of that pinched look at the corners of his eyes that had been there the day she and McCleary had met him. He was dressed up and explained he and Zivia had been out to dinner and he'd heard the news about Schloper on his way home.

McCleary told him what he knew about Schloper's death, and Quin brought glasses of cranberry juice over to the table. Young's eyes, she noticed, kept darting from McCleary's face to the chalkboard.

He finally interrupted. "I had no idea you'd amassed so much information."

"Unfortunately, we've still got some missing pieces," McCleary said.

"Who's O'Donald?" Young gestured toward the chalkboard.

"The Metro-Dade department shrink."

"And he thinks Travis is of above-average intelligence?" He gave an indignant snort. "Then I certainly question *his* intelligence."

"*If* Travis is the killer," Quin reminded him.

"I don't think there's any question," Young opined with a certainty that irritated her. "You've got a perfect match on blood type and—"

"And Travis *may* have a water phobia," McCleary said, "which raises doubts that he killed Callahan."

"I thought the police had a tail on him."

"They did," McCleary replied. "But he evidently knew it and lost the guy sometime this afternoon. Tim can't question him without blowing my cover, so until tomorrow night, his hands are tied."

"I hope to God you're at least going to have police backup," Young said, as if he knew all about police backups.

"Just Tim Benson."

Young sipped thoughtfully at his juice. "I don't like it, Mike. This warehouse is out in the middle of nowhere. You said it yourself. Anything could happen."

"It's not your problem, Ross," Quin pointed out, wishing he would just leave. "That's why you hired us."

Something flared brilliantly in his blue eyes when he looked at her, something she thought was going to come out as a curt retort. Instead he said, "Which is exactly why I'm worried. I . . . I feel like I've done nothing but bring you two bad luck."

Hey, guess what, Ross. I feel the same way. But she didn't say it, couldn't have said it even if she'd wanted to, because why fuel the man's guilt? The only thing worse than a nosy client, a client who kept tabs on you like a fretful mother, was one riddled with guilt.

McCleary, she noted, deftly steered the conversation away from death, from murder, into safer areas. By the time Quin got up twenty minutes later, the two men were sparring about politics. She hoped he would get the hint and go home.

But when the soft explosions of rain against the windows awakened her at midnight, she could still hear McCleary and Young downstairs.

3.

At one, McCleary was still awake, irked that Young had stayed so long. He listened to the patter of rain against the window and the tick of the clock on the wall, marking off the seconds in his life. *Seconds Neal Schloper is no longer worried about.* Or Bob Summer. Or Callahan. He turned on his side, trying to find a more comfortable position, and one of the cats padded toward him, purring loudly. It was Merlin. Only Merlin had a purr like an overheated engine.

"Hi, ole boy," he whispered, stroking the animal.

He'd retired to the den because he didn't want to disturb Quin. He was oddly pleased that Merlin had stuck around. He'd been Quin's cat before they'd gotten married and had not exactly taken to him when he'd moved into the house. But over the past week Merlin had divided his loyalties between upstairs and down. Last night, when McCleary finally returned to the big bed upstairs, Merlin had settled at the foot like a guardian angel.

He moved to the side, away from the spring sticking into his back. It was time to replace this old thing. On this convertible couch he and Quin had first made love. Funny, how he could trace the landscapes of that night in such intimate detail. It was as if his memory had seized on the event and magnified it over the years so that now he could hold the memory in his mind's eye and turn it slowly like a magnificent jewel. Whenever violence brushed his life, it seemed he turned first to this memory for perspective.

As if on cue, the faces of the dead slid like smoke through the interstices in the memory, clamoring for his attention. Joyce Young, Lois Dwight, Bob Summer, Callahan, and now Neal Schloper.

The rain was coming down harder now. Gusts of wind exploded against the glass and blew through the den, making the blinds dance. The door squeaked. He closed his eyes and willed himself to sleep. But lightning filled the room, and a moment or two later thunder rumbled overhead like a 747 in a world of trouble.

"Mac, you awake?"

Quin's voice whispered through the room so softly that at first he thought he'd imagined it. Then he lifted up on his elbows and saw her dark silhouette moving toward him. "The storm wake you?"

"No." She sat at the edge of the bed. It was a moment before she spoke. But once she'd opened her mouth, the words poured out as if they'd been stacking up in her mouth like poker chips begging to be played. "I thought Ross was still here. Then I looked outside and didn't see his car, and I kept waiting for you to come up and you didn't and I thought . . . I don't know." A flash of lightning exposed her, the odd tilt of her head, the way she gathered her hair at the back of her head with her hand. "Did Callahan tell you she'd been celibate for more than three years?"

"No." But it explained a lot of what had happened, he thought.

Quin lifted her legs onto the bed and leaned back against the pillow. "I was lying up there thinking that despite everything that happened, I couldn't have resented either of you even if she'd lived. I don't like to think about what would've happened if she *had* lived, about what you might've decided, but I'm sorry she's dead because I liked her." She paused and looked over at him. "I was just wondering if you'd mind if I crawled in bed with you, because I sure hate sleeping by myself."

He reached out, touching her face, drawing it toward his own, and kissed her. Merlin, squashed between them, protested loudly. They laughed and moved apart so Merlin could get away, then she rolled in beside him. She hooked an arm across his waist and rested her head in the crook of his arm. He stroked her hair as they talked quietly in the dark, the rain pounding with misspent fury beyond them.

They spoke of small things—the deep humus scent the rain released, the 10K race McCleary wanted to enter next month, the tickets to Venezuela, still pinned to the kitchen bulletin board. The old familiarity between them crept back into the room like a prodigal child, uncertain at first of its welcome, then drawing them together as swiftly as bits of metal to a magnet. He kissed her long and hard, short and soft, and when they made love, it was as if he'd come home after a long and painful absence. Nothing had changed, yet everything had changed because they were no longer quite the same people they had been before.

For the first time in days, his slumber was dreamless.

31 Countdown

1.

LAST NIGHT'S RAIN had left the air as clear as glass and a crisp blue sky unsullied with clouds. It was the sort of day, Quin thought, that read like a good horoscope forecast in the newspaper. *Everything you touch today will turn to gold. Nothing will go wrong.* But at 11:00 A.M., that was precisely what started to happen.

It started with a visit from Terry Travis just an hour before Quin and Zivia were supposed to meet with her. She flew into Quin's office with her red hair an explosion of curls around her face, spouting words like a speed freak. "It's off, the whole thing is off. Today that dipshit Suzi Mellon calls me up—at *seven*, for Christ's sake, I don't even have my eyes open at seven—and starts screaming that it's all my fault that Gene has cut off her paternity payments. *My* fault, right? I don't even *know* the stupid woman, met her once, that was all, just once, and suddenly it's my fault that Gene's not paying her. So I hung up on her. And at nine when I opened the shop, there she was, sitting on the porch, waiting for me."

Quin patted the air with her hands. "Slow down, okay? Have a seat. You want some coffee, Terry?"

"Coffee. No, thanks. If I had a cup of coffee I'd be so wired I'd do something I'd regret. I know I would." She sank into the chair, the light from the window striking her face and melting into her lap. She clutched her purse against her like a teddy bear. "What I'd really like is a joint. Or a Valium. But I don't suppose you have either of those, huh.''

"Sorry."

"Yeah, I didn't think so."

"What's Suzi Mellon got to do with anything?"

She flipped her sunglasses back into her hair. "She's got a big mouth, is what she's got. Apparently she called up Gene and told him a private eye had come to see her, asking a lot of questions about him. You must've pissed her off. She had *nothing* nice to say about you."

Quin thought of the check for $500 she'd ripped up, and smiled. "I'm not surprised."

"Anyway, she couldn't remember your full name and couldn't find your card, so Gene told her that he wasn't going to pay her for March until she could remember. I guess he thought she was holding out on him."

It wasn't difficult to figure out what had happened to her card, Quin thought. It had slipped into one of the messy piles in Suzi with a Z-I's messy condo and, like light in a black hole, had been lost forever. "So why should she blame you?"

"She saw us sitting together in the coffee shop the other day. She was at the bakery two doors down. At the bakery, right? A bimbo like her at the bakery. God. So she saw you come into the shop. She says if I don't come up with her March payment, she's going to Gene to tell him we know each other. That means I can say adios to my visits with my kid, Quin, and nothing's worth that."

"Not even getting back the video he's been holding over your head all these years, Terry? With that, you can sue for custody for Sean and he won't have anything on you. Besides, by then he's going to be in jail, if things work out the way we're hoping."

Terry dipped her hand into her purse for her cigarettes. She tapped the pack hard and a cigarette flew out and landed in front of Quin. She passed it to Terry, who lit it and inhaled deeply, with the relish of an ex-smoker lighting up for the first time in months. "I don't know. I just don't know if this is worth it."

"Your son's spending the night with you tonight, right? Like we planned?"

"Yeah. Gene's dropping him off at four because he says he's going to be too busy to do it later. So the house is going to be vacant. What I'm afraid of is that dipshit Suzi has already said something to Gene and he's gonna call my place every hour on the hour or something just to make sure I'm there. I mean, he's already suspicious because I asked to have Sean during the week, and it just *happens* to fall on the same night he's got this thing going down with your husband."

"Tell him you two are going to see a show or something and ask Sean not to answer the phone while you're out."

"We're going to a show at eleven o'clock at night? With Sean having school tomorrow?" She shook her head. "Uh-uh, he wouldn't buy it. If we're going to do this, Quin, it's got to be earlier than we planned. Like around seven-thirty, eight o'clock. And we'll use Sean's key to the house, that'll make it a lot simpler."

Simpler? Quin almost laughed. A key would make this whole thing a breeze. "Okay, that's fine. Let me get Zivia in here so you can meet her. She's going to drive the car for us."

Zivia strolled in a few minutes later, looking like Aphrodite. In her black pantsuit and pearl silk blouse, she struck an odd contrast with Terry, who wore a full skirt with wild purple flowers on it, a pearl-colored blouse and saddle oxfords with ankle socks.

"I *love* your hair. Who cuts it?" Terry exclaimed once the introductions were over. She ran her red lacquered nails through Zivia's blond locks. "Great cut. Absolutely fantastic."

"Actually, Ross trimmed it for me."

"Ross? Is that like *Vidal*, *dahling*?" she drolled, and they all laughed.

"Ross Young. Joyce's stepbrother. The guy who hired . . ." Quin began.

"Hon, my memory's bad, but it's not *that* bad."

"Zivia's engaged to him."

"Really? Quin introduced you? How neat. Well, if you're going to be the driver, we should all meet at this convenience store about three blocks from Gene's in the Gables. We'll do a trial run, then you'll let us off and pick us up at a prearranged time. What kinda car you have, Zivia?"

"Datsun 240Z."

"New? Old?"

"New."

"Quin?"

"Toyota Celica. Not very new, and worn out."

"Yeah, like my Honda. Okay, I guess the Datsun is it. How about if we meet at the convenience store around seven?"

"I thought we were doing this later tonight," Zivia said.

As Quin explained there'd been a change in plans, she experienced an unpleasant flutter in the pit of her stomach. Although earlier actually suited her better, because she could then help Benson track McCleary, it was a bad omen to alter plans at the last moment. Okay, so it was a superstition every bit as silly as the one about the welcome mat. But look what had happened when McCleary had trod on the mat three weeks ago.

For a moment, it seemed that all of the warmth in the room was sucked away, leaving a chill like death in the air.

2.

McCleary sped south on I-95, where sunlight beat the asphalt without mercy. The interstate wasn't too bad when traffic was moving, he thought. You could ignore the fact that the landscape was treeless, as if the area had been strip-mined. And the abundant signs advertising everything from Christ to Coppertone passed in a dazzle of color. You could even ignore the crazed bastards who rode your tail like kamikaze pilots. But when it all screeched to a halt because a lane was closed for construction, when you had to turn off the air conditioning and roll down the windows so your radiator wouldn't blow, I-95 became McCleary's version of hell.

He was stalled in a logjam that snaked off into the afternoon light like a necklace of loose beads. Dust from the construction coated Lady's hood. The jerk in the car next to him had his radio turned as high as it would go, and drumbeats pounded the air. The line inched forward. McCleary glanced at the clock on the dashboard. He was supposed to meet Benson in ten minutes.

He drummed his fingers on the steering wheel and debated about an alternate route he could take when he reached the next exit. But it was like trying to solve a calculus problem in his head. He finally opened his glove compartment and brought out the cop light Benson had given him. *For emergencies, Mac.*

Well, this was an emergency. He had to use the bathroom.

He slapped the light on Lady's roof, swerved onto the shoulder, and whipped southward, spewing pebbles and dust, the blue light swirling.

The fourth-floor conference room in the Metro-Dade station had once been McCleary's office. The darkly tinted window that ran from floor to ceiling was like the bow of a ship, riding high on the waters that were the city of Miami. At the moment, the city bathed in a pearl light that blurred the usually trenchant silhouettes of cars and interstates, buildings and neighborhoods. It was as if he were viewing the city through a soft-focus lens or the eyes of Monet. It seemed oddly calm, preternaturally calm, and disturbed him at a level deeper than language.

Something is gonna go wrong tonight.

"Okay, here we go," said Benson. McCleary watched his reflection in the glass, bopping into the room, swinging a satchel.

"All of it?" He turned and walked over to the table.

"Down to the last bloody dollar. Every bill is marked, too, just in case." He set the satchel on the table, opened the mouth, and tilted it so McCleary could look inside. There were stacks of bills. Mountains of bills. More greenbacks than McCleary had ever seen in one place at one time in his life. "Mike West's down payment for a peek at Minotaur." He slapped the satchel closed and flipped open a side pocket. He reached inside and drew out an electronic bug. "It goes on the fender of your car, Mac. We'll never be too far away."

"Just make sure you're far enough away so Travis can't smell you, Tim."

Benson gave a perfunctory nod. He brought out an amorphous gizmo about the size of a flattened golf ball that vaguely resembled a protozoan in a feeding frenzy. Its color was that of anemic flesh, and it was made of lightweight plastic. "This is taped to your chest. It monitors heartbeat, respiration, sweat, you name it. When those things increase by fifty percent, it emits a shriek on our end. That's when we move in."

"And the first time Travis checks me out with an electronic detector, Tim, I'm dead. You keep it."

"Mac, this thing is impervious to detectors. It's real spy shit, buddy. Now, another little nifty thing."

Like Houdini, Benson reached into his bag of tricks and brought out another item, a watch. "This is my favorite. We've used it on a couple of drug deals. It's got a miniature recorder inside."

McCleary secured it to his wrist. It looked, he thought, like an elegant Seiko watch. "Anything else?"

"Yeah, several things. The watch has a tracking device in it, just like the bug on your car, so we can track you once you're out of your car. Two . . ." And this time he reached into the other pocket on the satchel and brought out a pair of shoes.

McCleary burst out laughing. "Maxwell Smart? Is that what we're playing here?"

Benson's mouth fussed with annoyance. "No phone

on the bottom, Mac. Just hold on, will you?" He turned one of the shoes over and pointed at the back of the heel. "Think of this as a pressure point. Now watch." He brought the heel down hard against the table and a blade popped out of the sole at the toe.

"Jesus, Tim. What're you doing with these things, issuing them to rookie street cops?"

"Vice uses them. They have to do something to keep up with the damn dopers." He smacked the heel a second time and the blade vanished. "Try 'em on."

McCleary sat down and removed his tennis shoes. He slipped his foot into one of the shiny, chestnut-colored loafers and wondered dimly if this was how Cinderella had felt. "Perfect fit."

Benson beamed like a proud father.

3.

Spasms of excitement wrenched at his stomach, in his groin, in the back of his head as his feet pounded the hard-packed dirt along the club's running track. Sweet, sweet pain, he thought, pain that would transmute itself as if through some alchemical process. Base metal into gold: presto, chango, abracadabra. This kill, which would be his best, would turn back the hands of time, of aging—not forever, but enough so that he wouldn't have to indulge in random kills anymore. He would return to his annual or biannual kill in different cities. He would be in control of his addiction again.

As he ran at a clipped pace, through circles of sunlight and long ribbons of afternoon shadow, he ruminated on the weapon he'd chosen. It was a hunting knife that had belonged to his father—curved at the tip like a saber, with jagged teeth beginning two inches below the handle. A weapon, he thought, powerful enough to kill a bull and ideal for his last Taurus kill.

He glanced at his watch and smiled.

Six hours and counting.

32 The Secret Room

THE PORN KING'S home in Coral Gables was barely visible from the road. It was set back behind the ancient banyans whose spidery branches reached out like supplicating arms toward the moonlit sky. A black iron fence surrounded it. The yard was a trimmed, neat forest of plants and bushes. A sidewalk wound through it and led, Terry explained, to a second iron gate that guarded an inner courtyard.

"We're going to go in the side door, through the utility room," she said, leaning forward from the back seat.

Zivia shifted into second gear as they cruised past the house. The driveway was empty. The windows were dark. Only a porch light shone through the trees. "What time do you want me back here? My watch says seven-thirty on the nose."

Quin glanced back at Terry. "Forty-five minutes? Will that give us enough time?"

"If we don't run into any problems. But let's make it an hour just to be safe."

"Suppose you're not out front then?" Zivia asked.

"Circle a couple of times, I guess," Quin said. "And if we still haven't shown up, head back to the convenience store and we'll meet you there."

"Right."

She went around the block once more, drew up in front of the house, and Quin and Terry got out, their flight bags slung over their shoulders. The fence seemed more formidable up close. It was at least seven feet high, with its vertical slats ending in points as sharp as stakes.

"Gene's a little paranoid, huh," Quin whispered as Terry inserted the key in the lock.

"Hon, Gene defines the word 'paranoia.' Thank God the neighbors aren't nosy."

The gate creaked as it swung inward. It was like stepping into a secret garden, Quin thought as they hurried into the yard. The air smelled damp and sweet. Bits of chalky moonlight splashed through the braided branches overhead. A faint breeze stirred the leaves as Quin followed Terry around to the side of the house.

"This place was a lot better when I was living here," Terry said softly, looking for the right key. "The yard was a shrine, and the inside of the house was heavenly, all blues and whites and pale golds. Real peaceful-like, you know? Then when Gene married Lenore, she swept through the house like a tank. Wait until you see it. Blacks, browns, it'd be like living in a morgue, for God's sake." She giggled and slipped the key into the lock. "But I got to hand it to her, splitting for the Bahamas with their kid when she heard about him and Joyce. She was smarter than me that way. . . . There."

The door opened. Quin dug her flashlight out of the flight bag. The beam illumined the corner of a washer, a dryer, then a hillock of shirts and slacks and underwear spilling out of a clothes hamper on top of the washer.

"Through here," Terry said, motioning for Quin to follow.

They moved into the kitchen, where the cool air held scintillas of dinner smells. *Chicken? Beef? Fish?* What did a man like Gene Travis eat for dinner?

They traversed a spacious living room which, even in the calcareous glow from the flashlight, seemed as dismal as a funeral home. "You see what I mean?" Terry made a disgusted sound.

Now they were moving through a hall, past open doorways, a bathroom where a light shone, and finally into the den. Quin turned on the desk lamp, figuring it was safe since the room faced the back of the house. "This is where the king does his stuff," Terry said, hands on her hips as she glanced around.

The room was huge. There was a separate sitting area with a wicker couch and matching chairs that faced a TV—but no VCR, Quin noted. Filing cabinets and bookshelves took up two walls, and a computer and printer were perpendicular to the desk on a teak stand. The closet was directly to their left, its French doors made of cypress.

"Through here to the secret room," Terry said, hitting a light switch on the wall and flinging open the French doors. Quin shone the flashlight inside. The closet was deeper than it was wide, with shelves from floor to ceiling. Quin ran her fingertips along the edges of the shelves, then under, seeking ridges, notches, buttons, secret pressure points, anything that would indicate the existence of a panel or door.

"Where's this secret room supposed to be?"

"In here. Sean swore it was in here."

Terry crouched, switched on her own flashlight, and inspected the lower shelves as Quin stepped past her, into the deepest part of the closet. She pressed the heels of her hands against the shelves at eye level. She lifted folders, tipped books forward, patted the wall, liking this whole thing less and less. Maybe Terry's son had an active imagination. Maybe he'd dreamed seeing his father in a secret room. Maybe there wasn't any secret room.

She glanced at her watch. Ten minutes down and fifty to go.

Quin worked her way around to the front of the closet again, her flashlight skimming, darting, pausing, and that was when she saw it. A reflector of some kind on the inner ridge of the doorjamb that glowed like a bloodshot eye. She pressed it. A sharp click rang out in the closet, and the shelves she was leaning against began to creep inward.

"Bingo!" yelped Terry, scrambling to her feet.

When the door had opened all the way, Quin reached inside, patting the wall for a light switch. A moment later, a dim bulb flared overhead, revealing a narrow corridor that twisted off in front of them like a labyrinth. They followed it a short distance, their flashlight beams impaling an occasional roach brattling the bare concrete walls. The corridor opened into a cozy niche Anne Frank would have envied. Gone were the bare walls and floors. The King Tut of porn had a hideaway replete with thick gray carpeting, paneled walls that appeared to be soundproofed, a queen-size bed elevated on a platform, a couple of leather chairs on coasters, venetian blinds that simulated windows, and a door that led to a tiny bathroom. In front of a wall of books rose tall stage lights on metal contraptions that looked like leafless trees. A video camera stood ready to roll on a tripod, and next to it were a TV and VCR.

"Jesus," Terry whispered. "I lived in this house five years and I never knew any of this existed."

"I bet the second Mrs. T doesn't know about it either, Terry, so don't feel bad. What I'd like to know is how he got all this stuff in here. It sure didn't come through that closet in the den. And where're the videos?"

"Hey, Quin, look." Terry had lifted one of the venetian blinds, revealing a panel that resembled a circuit breaker. She threw the red switch and the light in the room went out. She quickly hit it again, the light flared, and this time she popped the blue switch to the left and the wall between the two ersatz windows began to rise, silently, slowly, like a curtain at the beginning of a play. Halfway up, Terry stopped it, and they both crouched to look at what lay beyond it.

It was the family room. "That explains how he got all this stuff in here," Quin said.

Terry's pallor vanished by degrees as her cheeks turned pink with anger, indignation. "And *he* got custody of Sean? Fuck that. Let's find those tapes, Quin."

She slammed her hand against the blue switch and the wall descended.

They began examining the books on the shelves to make sure they were actually books. *Erotica in Art. Darlene Does Dallas. The Joys of S and M.* Wonderful, Quin thought. *The Joy of Sex* wasn't good enough for Gene Travis, apparently. "Hey, look at this number." Quin closed her fingers over a phallic-shaped bookend. She tried to pick it up, but the thing seemed to be cemented to the shelf. She pressed her hand against it, pushing it forward, and the middle section of the bookcase opened inward. It was like a scene from an old Boris Karloff film. The cool air smelled fusty, a couple of roaches scurried out, and Quin almost expected to hear Karloff's weird, spine-chilling laugh. She and Terry looked at each other.

"I think we just solved the riddle of where the videos are," Quin said, and they stepped inside.

The room was small enough to make a claustrophobic person nauseous. There was a desk with a computer on it, disk storage boxes, and four shelves climbing the wall that were jammed with videotape storage cartons. Quin nearly shouted with glee when she saw that each of the boxes was labeled: Ariadne, Theseus, Icarus, Persephone —a veritable parade of Greek heroes and weirdos that ended with Minotaur.

Her hand trembled as she reached for the box. She opened it. Inside were half a dozen videotapes. "And here's my baby," Terry whispered, plucking the box labeled Persephone from the shelf.

"We should check them first to make sure they're what we want."

"I'll check, you do whatever you have to do with the computer."

Quin glanced at her watch. "We've got twenty-two minutes."

"Right."

Terry hurried into the other room, and Quin sat down at the computer. Her fingers stepped through the disks.

There were at least a dozen programs, and most of them she'd never heard of. She chose one at random and booted up the computer. It was an inventory program for Travis' two adult bookstores. She tried a second disk: employee records for the Pink Slipper. She looked up James Paul Kitt, noted his Social Security number and his salary, then switched to a third disk.

Her heart somersaulted as the Greek code names scrolled across the screen, followed by the client's name, the price paid for the video, the delivery date. Under Minotaur, she found ten names, four of them female. They included a prominent Miami neurosurgeon, a well-known philanthropist, the owner of a chain of liquor stores in South Florida, an actor, two filmmakers, three names she didn't recognize—and their old friend, Daedalus.

She made a backup of the disk, slipped it into her flight bag, then requested additional information on Daedalus.

Enter password, please.

Sean, she typed.

One moment, please . . . Proceed.

At least the password hadn't changed. *How many videos has Daedalus ordered?*

Four.

What types of videos?

Minotaur.

Prices paid?

$75,000 each for first two, $85,000, $95,000.

So Jimmy Paul Kitt wasn't fully informed, she thought. *Where were these four videos shot?*

First in Cayman Islands; second in Bahamas; last two in Miami.

Contact number for Daedalus?

None.

How is contact made?

Through modem, by him.

Who is Daedalus?

What followed was a lengthy bio of Daedalus according to Greek mythology. As Quin started reading through it, Terry suddenly flew into the room, her face white as milk, and hissed, "Quin, a car's just pulled up outside and someone's coming up the walk. I got the light in the den and shut the French doors to the closet, but you've got to help me with the door between the closet and here. I can't get the damn thing shut."

Quin leaped up and they ran down the hall. They shoved at the door, threw their weight against it, pushed, but it was stuck. Quin reached through the opening and jammed her finger against the red glowing button. Nothing happened.

Through the slats in the French doors, Quin heard noise in another part of the house—a door closing, footsteps. Surprises: that was what happened when you changed your plans at the last minute. She should have listened to the mutterings of her superstition.

"Let's get back to that computer room," she whispered.

They swept down the corridor again. Terry paused at the VCR, popped out the tape, and tossed it and the others into her flight bag. She turned off the light, and they hurried into the smaller room. This door, fortunately, closed easily.

Quin extinguished the light, switched off the computer, and they sat down and waited.

In the subsequent quiet, she heard water gurgling in pipes, a door slamming shut, more footsteps, someone coughing. Cool air hissed into the cubicle.

"You have a gun, don't you?" Terry asked. In the absolute dark, her words floated toward Quin like tiny balloons filled with chilled Jell-O. Oh, Christ, but she was hungry.

"It's in my lap."

"Well, I hope you know how to use it, because if that's Gene out there, he's going to shoot first and ask questions later."

How encouraging. "I thought he was going to be out."

"So did I. That's what he said. Shit, maybe he just set me up right from the start."

"Look, he's gotta leave by eleven, because he's supposed to meet Mac."

"Unless he's setting him up too, Quin."

Something chivvied at the edge of her mind, something she'd read or heard and wasn't remembering. It was the same feeling she'd had when she'd leaned out the rest-room window at the restaurant the night she and McCleary had met Zivia and Young for dinner: a sense of exigency about dredging up this vital something that eluded her.

What, damn it? What?

She tried to draw it closer, but it remained as obdurately hidden as she and Terry were.

"Did you look at those Minotaur tapes?" Quin asked.

"Yes."

"And?"

"Joyce Young's in one of them."

"You sure it's her?"

"If it's not her, then it's the twin of the woman who was in the paper."

Quin squeezed her eyes shut and rubbed at her temple, which throbbed. It was as if the thing she couldn't remember were pounding like a fist against the side of her skull, begging for release. *Something about Daedalus . . .*

The wait stretched into forty minutes, then an hour. Terry squirmed and sighed, squirmed and sighed, her ennui like that of a child in church. Quin's stomach growled. She tried not to dwell on what McCleary was doing about now, but images insinuated themselves: McCleary taping the monitor to his chest, securing the bug to Lady's fender, fastening the watch to his wrist, slipping on those lethal shoes. She should've been *there*, not here.

"I think he's left," Terry whispered.

"Let's wait a little longer just to be sure."

"Quin, my son's at home alone, he—"

"And my husband may be walking into a trap," she snapped.

Another twenty minutes slipped by.

Suddenly, the world beyond their dark confines exploded with sounds: shattering glass, something being smashed, a door slamming.

"God, what . . ." Terry stammered.

Quin hushed her. She patted her way toward the door and pressed her ear to the wood. The flesh at the back of her neck tightened like the skin of an apple. *He's in the den. Don't open the French doors. Please. Don't.*

She cocked her .38. It clicked loudly in the quiet. She didn't realize she'd been holding her breath until a savage wave of violence erupted in the other room. It sounded like the person was attacking the room with a club as if it were something living. It had finally happened. Gene Travis had flipped out. Quin could almost see him swinging madly at the walls, the tall stage lights, the TV screen, the VCR. In her mind, she saw glass exploding, the lights toppling like trees struck by lightning, books being squashed, torn apart, killed.

Quin backed away from the door, the inside of her mouth as arid as dust. She turned on her penlight and saw Terry crouched on the far side of the computer table, hands pressed to her ears, her face buried against her thighs. Quin scooped up their flight bags and shoved them in the space under the console. Then she stood to the left of it, so that if the door suddenly swung open, she would be hidden by it.

The noise stopped abruptly. In its wake, the quiet quivered with uncertainty, then there was one final blow and the door began its inward trek, creaking, sighing, protesting its abuse.

"What the hell," said a voice. A woman's voice that sounded as if her nose were stuffed with gauze. "What the bloody hell is this . . ."

Through the crack in the door, Quin saw a slight woman with blond hair. *One of Travis' girls? Another airhead like Suzi with a Z-I Mellon?* Quin saw the woman raise the baseball bat she clutched in her hand. *Go away, lady. Please, please, go away.*

But she didn't go away. She kept inching farther into the room, raising the bat higher. Higher. She muttered to herself, she shook her head, and before she turned, Quin took one giant step forward and brought the handle of her .38 down over the back of the woman's head, wincing as it made contact.

The woman folded up like a beach chair. Quin caught her and eased her gently to the floor, praying that she wasn't dead, that her skull wasn't fractured. Her fingers slid to the woman's neck, checking for a pulse, and she nearly wept with relief when she found it.

"Is she dead?" Terry squeaked.

"No. Get the light, will you?"

Circles of illumination melted across the floor, and Terry hurried over. "Oh, shit, Quin. It's Lenore. It's Gene's wife, Lenore, who was supposed to be in the Bahamas."

"Terrific. C'mon, get your stuff and let's get outa here. She'll be all right. But I don't want to be here when she wakes up."

In the larger room, clusters of glass grew from the rug like a new art form. The stage lights had been toppled, and the metal on one of them was as twisted as a pretzel. The TV looked as if it had been run over by a truck. The video camera was worse off than Humpty-Dumpty.

"Lenore's revenge," Terry murmured, as they stepped through the debris and fled down the corridor and out into the den.

And that was when Quin heard the wail of sirens. She guessed that a neighbor, having heard the ruckus, figured a madman was loose in the Travis household and had called the cops. Visions of herself and Terry being arrested, led away, and charged with a lot more than breaking and entering catapulted her forward, with Terry stuck to her heels like glue.

They flew out the sliding glass doors in the family room, down the steps of the porch, and into the blessed dark of the back yard. The screech of sirens ballooned in the air, closer now, as they tore through the jungle of plants and trees toward the black iron fence.

There was no gate back here, no way out except over the top. The fence was cut into thirds by two horizontal bars, one about three feet up and the other closer to the top. Both women grabbed hold of vertical iron slats, pulled themselves onto the lower horizonal bar, then up again to the higher bar.

Quin paused, clinging to the fence, feeling vulnerable and exposed in the wash of moonlight. She was eye level with the top of the fence, where the ends of the vertical slats seemed as insidious as daggers. *One false move and you're history.*

The sirens shrieked more closely now, propelling her over the top of the fence and down, down into the ebony smudge on the other side. Quin dropped the last three feet, then looked up and saw that Terry was still at the top, the flap of her jacket caught on one of the stakes. The sirens had stopped. Through the trees, Quin saw the swirling, ghost blue lights from police cruisers. "*C'mon,* Terry," she hissed.

Terry yanked at the jacket and it ripped, leaving a swatch of material flapping on the stake like a flag. She scampered down, and they ran for the nearest hedge, pushed through it to the other side, and hit the ground.

It was a moment before Quin caught her breath and another moment before she lifted her head from the damp grass. They were in the corner of an L-shaped hibiscus hedge that bordered a yard behind the Travis house. Through the branches, Quin saw the light of the police cruisers clearly—three cars and probably half a dozen men, fanning out from the front yard to the side of the house.

"Let's get to the street," Quin whispered. "Then we just walk normally."

"I may never walk normal again in my life."

They slid back on their stomachs, then scrambled to their feet and raced toward the road. Adrenaline thundered through her. Her stomach cramped with hunger.

Her head pounded. The thing that had been nagging at the back of her mind earlier was being shaken loose. She could feel it working its way up through her consciousness like a splinter of wood through skin.

They stumbled out onto the walk on the next block, looking as disheveled as bums, and hurried east, past sprawling homes like slumbering giants. They cut through a shopping center. Posters of exotic places decorating the windows of a travel agency reminded Quin of the Venezuela tickets. The hopeful, clean-cut face of a young man stared back at them from a Marine recruitment office. Eight-by-ten photos of opulent homes plastered the window of JASPER & McCLEAN, ARCHITECTS.

"I'm beginning to feel normal again, Quin," Terry said.

Quin stopped, backtracked to the architects' office.

A deep chill circled her throat like fingers and pressed down hard.

"Quin, what's wrong?"

Terry's voice reached her like a murmur in a dream. She blinked. "Oh God." Her head jerked around as she looked about frantically for a phone. She saw one ahead and tore toward it. *Don't let me be too late please please please.*

She knew now.

She knew who Daedalus was.

33 Daedalus

AN EERIE QUIET clung to the air like adhesive as McCleary turned into the industrial park. The gloam of the sodium vapor lights bled across the warehouse rooftops and into the deserted streets. He felt as if he were driving through the back lot at Paramount, a ghost on an abandoned set. But he couldn't shake the sensation that any second now, lights would flare, cameras would roll out from between the buildings, someone would shout, *Action! Let 'er roll*, and Gene Travis would leap forth, shooting.

He wondered where Benson and his men were.

He wished he'd consented to a backup.

At the end of the block, he turned left. This street backed up to a canal. The air was so still he could smell the briny water, and between the buildings he saw dark clusters that were overhangs of brush and trees.

He slowed as he approached the warehouse where he was supposed to meet Travis. There didn't seem to be anything particularly unusual or threatening about it. Like its neighboring clones, its reddish hue seemed washed out in the moonlight, like faded rust. Travis' car and a van were parked in front. McCleary drew alongside the van, turned off the engine, and sat there a moment, not liking the quick, ignescent tightening of the skin between his eyes.

His fingers absently touched the center of his chest, where Benson's gizmo was taped. He could feel its protrusion through his shirt, a lump like a large wart. He reached down and checked the weapon in his ankle holster.

Then he got out of the car with the satchel that contained the sixty grand.

His shoes tapped against the asphalt, the noise acuminating with every step, as if his footsteps were being amplified. He knocked at the door, allowed his hand to fall to the knob, and turned it slowly.

It wasn't locked.

He knocked again, dropped his head back, and scanned the upper part of the warehouse, looking for windows. There were none. He removed the weapon from his ankle holster, turned the knob, and nudged the door open with the tip of his loafer.

A ribbon of pale light slanted through the crack. It widened as McCleary opened the door farther. He stepped inside, into a small reception area with a desk, two chairs, a typewriter, and a wire basket with a couple of files in it. The room looked like something you'd find in an employment agency or on a used car lot that could be disbanded with a minimum of fuss.

He checked out the files in the wire basket. They contained résumés and photographs, presumably of some of Travis' recruits. A memo attached to each one spelled out the applicant's suitability, and the letterhead bore the name of the corporation that owned the adult bookstores.

He glanced around, noting that there were only two doors. The first led to a bathroom, and the second into a carpeted hallway lit at either end. The paneled walls were bare. The three doors in the hallway opened into offices as identical as triplets: bare metal desks, a pair of wooden chairs, papers stacked in each of the wire mesh baskets.

Bad news, Mac.

He would go to the end of the hall and see what lay beyond the door.

Do an about-face, buddy.

Just a little farther.

You're gonna regret it.

He was armed, he wore more monitors than an astronaut, what the hell could possibly happen?

He stopped at the door. *Beyond this lies . . .* An atavistic fear gripped him, paralyzed him. In his mind, he saw Bob Summer snuggled into his metallic coffin in the morgue, Callahan splayed out like a dissected frog, himself being fried alive in the health club sauna that night.

He looked back down the hall.

There's the distance you've come.

His fingers closed over the knob.

His fingers twitched as if the metal had burned him.

Once you're in, you can't turn back.

He'd waited too long for this opportunity. He had a score to settle.

The door swung open into a blackness as thick as soup, then swung shut behind him. A white-hot flame burned between his eyes; his heart boomed in the silence. He slung the satchel over his shoulder and reaching into his pocket, brought out a dime. He tossed it into the dark. It pinged against something a moment later. Metal? Maybe a filing cabinet? A desk?

He moved along with his back against the wall, apprehension cockling his bowels. He considered leaving. But if this was the Porn King's way of testing him, then the whole operation would be blown.

He would wait a few minutes.

He would work his way toward the end of the wall.

He sidled left. His right shoe sank into something as squashy as a sponge. He lifted his foot and the stuff, whatever it was, came with it like a huge wad of gum. He slid down the wall, intending to scrape the goo off the bottom of his shoe, but the moment his fingers touched it, his pulse shot for the moon.

Soft candy. Jesus. A gob of soft candy.

He leaped up and two things happened very quickly. The wall ended, and a barrage of hot, bright lights exploded around him, lights like a dozen suns going nova, lights that dived through his eyes, his retinas, temporarily blinding him.

McCleary threw up his arm to cover his eyes and something smashed against his head from behind. He gasped, his gun clattered to the floor, he clutched the back of his skull as an agony as white and hot as the lights seared through it. Then he felt his knees buckling, and distended slivers of blackness swam across his eyes, fattening like hogs until they gobbled up the terrible light. He sank, sank as swiftly as a block of concrete into dark waters.

11:00 P.M.

He stood over McCleary, smiling to himself, feeling like a Viking. Or Genghis Khan. Or Napoleon. Or an ancient Greek.

"Wait until you see the wonderful show I've prepared for you, Mike. Just wait. You'll love it. You'll appreciate it."

But first things first.

He crouched next to McCleary's body and patted him down. He removed the holster from his ankle. He unbuttoned McCleary's shirt and studied the thing taped to his chest. He unbuttoned his own shirt, then quickly removed the contraption and taped it to his own chest. This done, he emptied McCleary's pockets, looking for other weapons. He found none. He took a close look at the watch he wore. Written on the face of it was SEIKO. No problem there.

His fingers now stepped through McCleary's hair, inside the collar of his shirt, then down along his inner thighs and groin, looking for other detection devices. Finding none, he slipped off McCleary's shoes and dragged him across the floor, through another door, into an open area like an arena. He had to stop to catch his breath, then he slipped his arms under McCleary's armpits and hoisted him into a chair.

With nylon rope, he secured McCleary's ankles to the legs of the chair, then lashed each wrist to the armrests.

This done, he stepped away, admiring his handiwork. This kill would be the artistic achievement of his career, a paragon of perfection.

Nothing would go wrong.

11:02 P.M.

The dispatcher hadn't been able to patch Quin through to Benson because he was on "special assignment" and wasn't in a vehicle with a police radio. Quin had debated telling the woman to send cruisers out to the warehouse address, but realized that if cops stormed the place, McCleary might die. So she'd hung up and she and Terry had raced the remaining block to the convenience store parking lot.

She saw Zivia pacing the length of the awning, hands in her jacket pockets. Quin shouted. Zivia's head jerked up and she ran toward them. "*What* happened? My God, it's been . . ."

Quin could barely breathe. A crescive dread had sprouted in her chest like broccoli. It was an effort to speak. "Zivia, where's Ross tonight?"

"What?"

"Where's Ross?"

"At home."

"Call him."

"Now? Why?"

"Just *do* it." Quin took her by the arm and led her to the phone. "Call him. And hurry. I'm betting he isn't there."

Zivia fed a quarter into the machine and dialed the number. As it rang, she covered the receiver with her hand. "What's going on? What—"

"You remember Daedalus?"

"Daedalus. The Greek. The snuff film customer. Yeah. So?"

"Daedalus was an architect, Zivia."

Just as hearing was the last sense to go when a person was dying or in a coma, so was it the first sense that sparked to life as McCleary came to. He heard music—a scratchy but somehow haunting recording. He heard footsteps, a voice or perhaps several voices, and laughter that echoed as if it were rising from within canyon walls. Then he became cognizant of the scalding pain at the back of his head and the light burning through his eyelids, and he groaned and tried to move and realized his hands and legs were bound.

"Turn down the goddamn lights," he shouted.

The recording clicked off. The lights dimmed to a dusk that was tolerable, but it did nothing to diminish the throbbing in his head. A voice amplified and distorted through faulty speakers said, "Welcome, Mike, to the Minotaur's museum."

Then suddenly the floor his chair sat on began to move, to revolve like a bar at the top of some fancy hotel, McCleary thought. The lights dimmed more, more, until he was nearly in total darkness again. A comforting thing, this darkness. He didn't mind it. He stared dully at the floor, trying to think, to plan, but the pain in his head kept inspissating until he thought for sure his skull would explode.

He concentrated on shoving the pain aside.

He visualized the pain dissipating, dissolving.

He realized his shoes had been removed.

Benson's gizmo was gone from his chest.

He still wore the watch, but the only thing that would tell Benson was that he was still in the warehouse.

So much for all the hardware.

He lifted his head as the stage stopped revolving. The echoing voice said, "Now we're going to see the end of a little drama, Mike."

Only two people he knew called him Mike. Gene Travis and Ross Young, and he suddenly knew which man it was. *A obessive/compulsive personality*: Young was a compulsive buyer of socks.

The lights blazed, but not on him. They illuminated a stage about four feet from him. It was lined with mirrors. It took several seconds for him to realize what he was seeing, for a synapse in his brain to connect with the image in his eyes. Even then, his conscious mind denied the truth as surely as Saint Peter had.

A king-size bed claimed the center of the stage and was cloned in the mirrors. At either side of the bed was a video camera, mounted on a tripod. On a stool behind the right camera sat Jimmy Paul Kitt. The poor dumb bastard's throat had been slit. Dried blood covered his shirt like a bib. On the bed, surrounded by a Halloween cornucopia of sweets, lay a man and a woman McCleary had never seen. The woman's limbs were tied to the four posts and the man lay alongside her, an arm thrown over her waist. They were both dead, but there was so little blood, McCleary knew they hadn't been stabbed.

The lights blinked out, and the blackness swam over him like a cool tide. He struggled to free his wrists, but the ropes held fast. They were cutting off circulation in his hands.

"Hey, you can cut the theatrics!" he shouted.

His voice echoed in the cavernous dark. He heard a grinding noise, then a spotlight fell in the center of the stage, where the king-size bed and the video camera and the corpses were sinking into the floor. A few moments later a platform that would have been the equivalent of the orchestra box began to rise. In its center was Gene Travis, tied to a chair like McCleary, and gagged. He made muffled, strangled sounds; his eyes, bulging with terror, skittered around in his head.

Now, from stage right, stepped Ross Young, wearing jeans, a black shirt, purple socks, and no shoes. In his right hand he clutched a small hatchet. Fastened to his waist was a knife of some kind that curved at the end. "Welcome to my version of a Greek play, gentlemen." He bowed deeply at the waist. "Do you like my warehouse?'' He threw out his arms; the blade of the hatchet gleamed in the light. "It's not listed under my name, of course, but isn't it convenient that Gene happens to lease it? He liked the mirrors, didn't you, Gene?"

Travis grunted.

"To get in here, you have to go through a neat little maze of mirrors, like a funhouse. Very artsy, really.'' He threw his head back and laughed. "I just love the little surprises life throws our way sometimes, don't you, Mike?"

Beads of sweat jeweled McCleary's brow.

"Now," said Young. "You might think of the next scene as the twist at the end of Act Two. You, Mike, will be Act Three." He walked over to Travis and touched his shoulder. Travis jerked the upper half of his body and screamed into his gag. "Really, Gene," admonished Young. He strolled up to the edge of the stage, the hatchet cradled in his arm like an infant. The mirrors duplicated him from every conceivable angle.

"I suppose you have some questions, Mike. And it's only fair that I answer them to the best of my ability, just as I did for Gene here, before we, uh, get on with business." He smiled magnanimously. "Unfortunately, Gene screams a lot, so I had to gag him. But you're not a screamer, are you, Mike?"

"You lousy fuck."

The bright spotlight bleached his blond hair almost white. "There are things involved you don't understand, Mike."

"Like what? That you obviously have a taste for your work?"

Young ran a hand down his jeans. "Of course I enjoy my work. I've made an art of murder. Can you appreciate that?"

A slow panic crawled at the back of McCleary's mind. He slammed a door on it. *Keep him talking*.

"Why hire detectives to investigate a murder you committed?"

"You mean you can't figure that out? I thought you

were a real bright man, Mike.'' He shook his head as if to say that McCleary was as stupid as a child. "I guess I'll have to spell it out for you. It's an integral part of the hunt. And the hunt, Mike, has to be an integral part of the work of art. Oh, it wasn't like that in the beginning, but you might say I developed a conscience about it later on.'' He paused, walked back over to Travis, and gave him another pat on the shoulder. "Long before Gene and Joyce were involved with each other, he and I were doing business. He didn't know it was me, of course. I heard about him through a client. More and more often, I'm struck by life's ironies.

"I mean, here I heard about Gene through one of *my* clients, and then later on he begins screwing *my* stepsister and even gets her to be in a snuff film that I ordered.'' Another pause, longer this time, as he touched his fingers to the blade of the hatchet. "Joyce suspected, though; that was the problem. I had to kill her. She would've eventually figured it out, and I knew she'd go to the police.'' He shrugged. "And being a Taurus, she fit nicely into the scheme of things. As you do. I was sorry about her, I really was.'' He looked over at Travis again. "She was awfully good in the sack, wasn't she, Gene?''

Travis tried to leap to his feet; his mirrored clone seemed to leap a second later. His chair toppled sideways, slamming against the stage. He grunted; he screamed into the gag. Young chuckled and rested his foot on Travis' back.

"Look, Ross, even if you kill both Travis and me, someone's going to put things together,'' McCleary said.

"I doubt it. With the main suspect—Gene—dead, the case will just close. Unless your wife starts nosing around. And if she does . . . well, I'll just have to give her some of the same medicine Callahan got.'' His face clouded. "She shouldn't have struggled, you know. That's why she died. Callahan was my one grave mistake.''

Travis was weeping, but with his mouth gagged, it sounded as though he were strangling on his tears. Young kicked him swiftly in the side and he groaned. "Be quiet, Gene. Please. I'm trying to explain things to Mike here."

Sweat oozed down the sides of McCleary's face. His heart hammered. *Talk, say anything. . . .*

"You left a trail, Ross. The trophies, the teasers, the death sweets. Except for Neal Schloper, the MO is consistent enough to eventually hang you. And Zivia's going to piece things together sooner or later."

"I'm really not worried, Mike." He spoke casually, as if they were two businessmen discussing the rise and fall of stock prices over a deductible lunch. "Zivia's going to provide me with stability. She loves me, you know. It would never occur to her to think of me in a disparaging light. And as far as anything else . . . well, you told me yourself that Benson and his guys would move in only if your vital signs went haywire. Which won't happen because that thing that was taped to your chest is now taped to mine. So once you two are dead, I hop on my boat in the canal out back, and when I'm far enough away, I toss the monitor overboard and then the cops show up and find the carnage but no evidence."

McCleary laughed; it was a harsh, ugly sound. "You, pal, are deluding yourself. Any moron can kill a defenseless person. Where's the art in that? Any jerk with a cock can tie a woman to bedposts and rape her and then slice her open. It doesn't take imagination to do that. Hell, it doesn't even take courage."

Something subtle shifted in Young's expression, and McCleary knew he'd struck a nerve. He rushed on. "Any asshole can assault a jogger in the dark or shoot a man who's alone in a hangar or lock someone in a sauna. So what. All that makes you is a fucking coward, Ross."

He swung the hatchet the way a child might swing a picnic basket. His mouth went as flat as a hyphen. "You don't know what the hell you're talking about."

"C'mon, Ross. Let's see what you've got in you.

Untie me and we'll finish things right here. Just like gladiators.''

But he didn't take the bait. He laughed. "*You're* the one at a disadvantage, not me. I don't have to prove anything to you. I've been doing this a long time, Mike, and no one's ever figured it out." He clasped the neck of the hatchet with one hand and the base with the other. "It's something I need to do now, can you understand that? It's . . ." He paused, his tongue slipping slowly along his lower lip. "Well, it's something my body needs. Like a fix." His gaze wandered lazily toward Travis. "What's your opinion on all this, Gene?"

Travis made more pig noises. Young set the hatchet aside and righted Travis' chair.

"Now, what were you saying, Gene?"

While Young's attention was on Travis, McCleary focused on drawing all his strength into his hands. He imagined blood rushing into the muscles, the tendons, a concrescence of blood thicker than syrup, blood with enormous weight, power. The skin at his wrists throbbed. But the ropes didn't loosen.

"Hey, Mike, Gene's going to speak for himself," Young called, and removed the gag from his mouth. He gasped, he wheezed, he sucked at the air like a dying man as Young taunted him. "Now what did you think of Mike's little speech, Gene?"

Spittle flew from Travis and smacked Young's forehead. "Fight both of us, you bastard," he shouted.

But Young didn't seem to hear him. A frown dipped between his brows. He touched his fingers to his forehead, then looked at the spittle smeared on his fingertips. "You shouldn't have done that, Gene. You should never spit at a person. It's a very nasty thing to do, spitting. A way to spread disease. I'm afraid I'm going to have to punish you for that."

He jammed the gag back in Travis' mouth. He picked up the hatchet, circled the chair, watching Travis, tapping the flat side of the hatchet against the palm of his hand as he moved. The tapping became a monotonous rhythm, a ticking like time. "What'll it be first, Gene? Your hand? Your foot? An arm? A person can live quite awhile with an amputated limb. It's not very pleasant to bleed to death, you know."

Travis shrieked into his gag.

McCleary continued to manipulate his wrists.

"Or I could just chop off your head. That'd be quick."

"And cowardly," McCleary shouted.

Young stopped behind the Porn King's chair. "Who asked you, Mike?" He brought out the knife at his belt. It looked like a saber, only it was shorter, fatter. He cut through the ropes that bound Travis' left hand; it jerked up, trying to hit Young, who laughed and with his foot toppled the chair. He slipped the saber back into its sheath and walked over to where Travis lay and pulled his arm away from his side and stepped on the upper part of it, holding it in place.

"This is gonna smart," he murmured, and Travis screeched again as the hatchet lifted, lifted, then descended and slammed against Travis' wrist.

The impact sent the hand flying several feet across the stage. The fingers contracted. They twitched. They seemed to pull themselves along the stage. Travis' muffled screams exploded in the air as blood spurted from his stump.

McCleary's head jerked to the side and he got sick.

For the first time since he'd walked in here, he did not think he was going to get out alive.

34   Maze

QUIN HAD PARKED the Toyota between two buildings at the end of the block. She'd retrieved some items
she needed from the trunk, then she and Zivia had
sprinted toward the warehouse. Now, in the alley that
separated it from its neighbor, they stopped. Quin stared
at McCleary's car. In the wash of moonlight, it looked
like a beached dolphin. Next to it was a van. She didn't
know who it belonged to, but she was taking no chances
with it—or with the front door.

"Let out the air in the tires," Quin whispered. "I'm
going to check the front door."

"Gotcha."

She darted toward the door, pressed her ear to the
wood, listening, but heard nothing. She tried the knob.
The door was locked. She told Zivia she was going to
look for another entrance and would meet her around
back.

Quin slipped along the side of the warehouse toward
the canal at the back, her purse riding her hip, fear like a
smoky collar at her throat. *Please be alive, Mac. Please.*
The cacophany of insects, a wilderness sound, a sound
she associated with the Everglades, exacerbated her sense
of isolation. Maybe she should've asked the dispatcher
to send out cruisers. Or the SWAT team. Or God.

She paused at the back of the building and frowned as
she detected a dark shape bobbing in the canal's gentle
currents. She hurried over to it and her heart fell like a
stone toward her toes. *Minos.* Her fingers worked at the
rope lashed to a wooden post. It slipped free, Quin

plopped down on the seawall, pressed her shoes against the edge of the boat, and shoved it out into the canal. Then she scampered to her feet and trotted back to the corner of the building where Zivia was now waiting for her.

"His boat?" Zivia whispered.

"Yes."

Half a dozen emotions vied for dominance in Zivia's face, in her tristful eyes, but she said nothing. She'd already said it all on their way over here. "C'mon, let's find that entrance."

The back door to the warehouse was barely visible in the dusky light. It looked as if it had been sewn into the wood. The lock, corroded through the years by the salt in the air, gave way quickly to Quin's deft manipulations with a screwdriver. The door squeaked as she nudged it inward. She winced and they squeezed through the opening.

They were in a dimly lit, dank and cool hallway. Air streamed from a vent. She heard water dripping. To their left was a spiral staircase. In front of them was a doorway. Quin could hear Young's voice, rising and falling in an eerie cadence, echoing, loose as old clothes one moment, tight as a guitar string the next. She also heard other sounds—muffled sobs, feet stomping against wood, then Young's laughter.

He sounded as mad as Rasputin.

Chills dampened her arms. She cocked her .38, wishing she had a rifle or McCleary's .357, and moved toward the stairs. The iron felt cool against her palm. The back of her throat seemed dry, thick, as if she were coming down with a cold.

Light spilled through the opening at the top of the spiral staircase, and so did sounds. She heard McCleary's voice, and it filled her like music, filled her until she felt as if she might simply float through the opening like Peter Pan. *Alive. He's still alive. That means we have a chance.*

Quin peeked out over the top of the staircase. It

opened on a narrow half-moon balcony bordered by a railing with thick, vertical wooden slats. Because of the slant of the stage lights, it was layered with deep shadows.

She crawled through the hole and huddled at the railing, peering through the slats. Several things were immediately apparent: McCleary was lashed to a chair, as immobile as a mummy; she could not shoot Ross Young at this distance with a .38 because if she missed, he would reach McCleary before she could fire again; she was going to be sick.

She squeezed her eyes shut and buried her face in her arms, struggling against a wave of nausea. Beside her, she heard Zivia gasp, and when Quin lifted her head, Zivia clamped a hand over her mouth, her eyes were flooded with tears, and she was scooting back toward the wall.

You will not be sick you will not be sick . . .

She forced herself to look again. Her eyes swept over a maze of mirrored corridors astonishing in their complexity. Dead ends, corridors that emptied out into the heart of the warehouse where McCleary sat, corridors that fed into cupolas of shadows. It was like a house of mirrors at a circus. Daedalus' labyrinth. She followed the twists and turns from just below where she and Zivia were, to McCleary. There was no way she could get to him without Young seeing her.

Unless she could distract Young somehow so that he would leave the stage. . . .

The thought was cut off sharply when she saw Young lift his hatchet, when she saw it falling, falling toward the bloodied body on the stage. The body that was Gene Travis. She pressed her face into her arms as the hatchet hit its mark. *Whack, whack.* The horrible sound echoed, rose and fell, rose and fell. Bile lumped in her throat. She swallowed it, she inhaled deeply and drew in the scent of her own skin. Her torpor was as debilitating as polio.

The sound went on.

Zivia whimpered. It might've echoed, had it not been

for the whacking sound. Quin scooted over to Zivia and urged her toward the staircase. She shook her head, her shoulders shuddering even as her hands patted the air: *I'll be okay*, said this Morse code.

Her shiny blue eyes shrank into her cheeks.

Quin wanted to yell at her. Slap her. Instead, she took hold of Zivia's arm and pulled her toward the staircase. She yanked her arm free and crawled of her own volition. When they were halfway down the stairs, she covered her face with her hands and began to weep again.

Quin shook her by the arms. "Please, don't crack up on me. I need your help, Zivia."

Her hands dropped away from her face. Comprehension flickered in her etiolated blue eyes. She nodded. "Okay. I'm okay." She hugged her arms; her nails sank into the skin. "Jesus. That maniac made love to me. He . . . he . . . Jesus, Quin, he killed his own stepsister, he—"

"Stop it." Quin took hold of Zivia's jaw. "Please. Stop. He's going to kill Mac unless we do something fast."

Zivia ran her hand across her nose, bit at her lower lip, sucked in her breath. "Tell me what to do." A plea.

Quin reached into her purse and brought out a bundle of firecrackers. She pressed them into Zivia's hand. "Here's what I want you to do. . . ."

12:11 A.M.

The hatchet slammed down through Travis' left elbow. McCleary could actually hear the bones shatter and the blade embedding itself in the wooden stage.

Dizzy with nausea, dizzy with the knowledge that once Young finished hacking up Gene Travis he would be next, McCleary kept working his ankles, trying to free them. He had given up on his wrists because the rope had bitten into the soft undersides until they'd bled. At least his socks offered the skin on his ankles some protection, and the muscles in his legs were stronger than those in his arms because of his longtime running.

He would do it.

He would free his goddamn ankles even if it was the last thing he ever did.

The noise onstage stopped. Young's deep sigh was somehow more terrifying than the hacked-up body of Gene Travis. It was a sound people made after a full, satisfying meal, after a Thanksgiving dinner in which they'd stuffed themselves to the gills.

Young raised his head.

He smiled.

12:12 A.M.

His body yodeled.

His bones purred.

He opened his arms wide, allowing the life of Gene Travis to seep through his pores. He lifted his arms high, reaching for the spotlight, the cathedral ceiling, the sky, the moon.

Now, his body whispered. *The final kill.*

12:13 A.M.

Quin scurried through the corridor she had memorized from the balcony, a corridor she knew would weave forever through her dreams, her heart pulsing in her ears, her mouth, reverberating against her teeth until they chattered. Very little light spilled in here, but she could still detect the blurring passage of her reflection in the mirrored world. She was almost afraid that if she peered into this alternate world of shifting shadows she would lose herself in it. Or pass through it to an alternate universe.

The corridor twisted, curled, twisted, curled, as if she were an ant working her way along the inside of a giant

Möbius strip or along the inner spiral of a doughnut. She finally had to inch sideways, with her back against one of the mirrored walls to root herself. She focused her eyes on only one reflection at a time. But now and then her peripheral vision betrayed her and her breath caught in her throat because she thought the image belonged to someone else.

The concatenation of her reflections were a dozen shadow dwarves, she thought, come to life, filled out, given meat, substance.

The corridor twisted inward again, toward the center of the labyrinth. The Minotaur's labyrinth. And no one knew it better than Daedalus, its architect. But in real life, Daedalus was also the Minotaur, the monster. And the man responsible for everything that had happened to her and McCleary the last few weeks. *You killed Bob, Callahan, you . . .* For a long moment, her hatred consumed her, distracted her. She began to tremble. *Stop it. Concentrate.*

She glanced at her watch. Fifty seconds to go before Zivia set off the first firecracker, and she wasn't close enough. She hurried along the corridor, her back barely touching the mirrors. Now the glare from the spotlights onstage seeped over the tops of the partitions.

Closer, she was closer.

Twenty-eight seconds.

The corridor narrowed, and the spotlights came into view, two of them, suspended fifteen feet or more above the stage. She couldn't see Young because of the partitions, but she could see the lights. See them clearly. They glowed like twin suns.

Twenty seconds.

She lifted her arms and aimed the .38 at the light closest to her.

Two good shots, that was all she needed.

Eighteen seconds . . .

". . . so, Mike, I guess it's time for the Third Act," Young was saying.

Suddenly, the firecrackers exploded in rapid succession and Quin squeezed the trigger of her .38 once, twice, three times. The lights overhead burst, sizzling like pork chops on a hot griddle, sparks leaping even as the warehouse was plunged into darkness.

12:15 A.M.

The instant the lights went out, McCleary jerked his left leg hard, loosening the ropes enough to wiggle his ankle free. He lifted up on one leg like a flamingo, the chair stuck to his back, as relentless as a monkey demon, and threw himself and the chair against the nearest wall. Pain sang through his left arm, shards of glass sliced through his shirt and into the skin, the watch was crushed. But his arm was free. He clawed at the rope on his right arm, wiggled his limb loose, then worked at the rope that secured his right leg. Before he got it free, he sensed Ross Young rushing toward him.

He pivoted with the grace of a dancer and felt the chair impacting. Young cried out, and McCleary heard the hatchet clatter to the floor. He hopped as far as he could, then slammed the chair against another wall.

The leg snapped, and he yanked his right leg free and lunged forward, arms outstretched.

"No!" yelled Young.

A barrage of firecrackers exploded in the air, lighting the dark like the Fourth of July, and McCleary saw Young racing after him, swishing the saber like a pirate, bellowing as if he were in pain.

The dark bit down again. McCleary collided with one of the walls, and as he fell back, heard the saber swish over his head. Glass shattered and crashed against the concrete.

A greasy bubble of panic burst from his throat as he scrambled to his feet and threw himself forward, blindly, into the corridor again. *Daedalus' labyrinth:* a spiral like the DNA helix, like water swirling down a drain, like a coil, like nebulae. He would be trapped in the spiral forever, trapped like a character in an existentialist play.

And then the lights on the warehouse ceiling blazed. Replicated in the maze of mirrors, they were amplified tenfold and blinding. Oh God, how they blinded, slicing through his eyes, burning into the back of his brain, relentless, cruel.

"Ross!" shouted Zivia. *"Nooo! Stop it!"*

Her voice echoed in the warehouse, and McCleary couldn't tell which direction it was coming from. When he could see again, it was only by squinting, and there was no sign of Zivia. In fact, the first thing he saw was Young, lifting his hatchet, Young with the look of the damned in his eyes, and then just beyond him McCleary saw Quin. But because of the mirrors, the lights, the tricks of illusion, he didn't know what was real. The flashing images, lined up like cutout dolls, were joined at the hips, the shoulders, the feet.

In this illusion of light and glass, he saw Quin aiming her weapon. He saw the hatchet fall. He didn't move quickly enough, and the blade sliced through his reflection's skull and a bullet ricocheted against the mirrors, finally slamming into a wall of glass. A rete of cracks flew out from its center.

McCleary tore away down the corridor, turned, and it dead-ended. He spun, a reflection within a reflection, all of it like a mirage, a hallucination, a dream within a dream, and ran back toward the image of Young. By the time he realized it was not a reflection, that Young was in the same corridor he was, it was too late.

Young grinned, his face ghastly in the terrible light, and he swung the hatchet. McCleary leaped to the side and the hatchet crashed into a mirror. Shards of glass sprayed them both.

McCleary swooped for the hatchet, missed, and jumped back as Young advanced, his madness a raw truculence that distorted his features so that he did indeed look as monstrous as the Minotaur. He grabbed the hatchet, raised it. McCleary darted sideways and stumbled into another corridor.

He heard more shots. He looked over his shoulder

and saw Young racing after him. He panted like an animal. McCleary dimly understood that this seemingly civilized man with the white and blue office, this man of such exquisite artistic tastes, had surrendered to some primal center of his brain, the same center that ruled his compulsion about socks. Sex. Death. Killing. McCleary stopped, turned with the same dexterity and grace Young had possessed that night on Callahan's dock, and his right foot lashed out and connected with Young's solar plexus.

He went down, groaning. The hatchet flew from his hand. McCleary threw himself toward the hatchet, but too late. The other man had gripped it, and was scrambling to his feet again as Quin appeared. She fired. The bullet zinged against the mirrors and whistled away, as elusive as a thief.

Young's head jerked right, left, giving McCleary the opportunity to leap forward. His body slammed into Young's knees. The man went down hard, but he gripped his hatchet just as tenaciously as politicians clung to their lies, his arm drawn back as Quin aimed her .38 at him, her stance indicating that she meant business.

"Don't, Ross. Set it down nice and easy."

McCleary rolled away. His body shook. His teeth chattered. The sutures in his arm had ripped, and his shoulder blazed with agony. Young's eyes shifted from Quin to McCleary as he pressed his fingers against the floor, trying to push himself to his feet.

"Don't make me kill you." The words were a sibilant hiss.

Quin's face gleamed with sweat.

Young's arm twitched, and McCleary would never know whether he intended to let go of the hatchet or fight with it. He would never know because Quin pulled the trigger and Young's face exploded in a spray of blood and bone.

35 March 1

"CHECKLIST," SAID QUIN.

McCleary consulted his notepad. "Hot water off?"

"Yes."

"Cats at the vet." McCleary scratched through it. "Doors locked?"

"Check."

"Burglar alarm on?"

"Yes."

"Timer connected?"

"Yes."

"Mail hold?"

"Yup."

"Newspaper hold?"

"Yes."

"Answering machine on?"

She thought a minute. They were sitting in the car, their bags in the back seat, the plane tickets on the dash in front of them. She couldn't remember if she'd turned on the answering machine. "I'd better go back inside and check."

"Don't forget to lock the door again," McCleary called after her.

Quin hurried up the walk, her stomach fussing with hunger, her thoughts fastened on escaping Miami. They were going to do it this time. They were. She unlocked the door and swung through the kitchen for a piece of fruit to take with her. Just as she was washing it off, the phone rang.

She winced.

"We're not home," she murmured, padding into the living room where the answering machine was. She reached out and turned the switch to ANSWER CALLS. The ringing stopped. The red light glowed. She bit into the apple as the recording clicked on. Then a woman's frenzied voice said, "My name is . . ."

Quin backed out of the room with her teeth holding the apple and her fingers stuck in her ears, the drone of the woman's voice pursuing her. She hastily locked the door and sprinted to the car. She slid inside and slammed the door.

"All set, Mac."

He shifted Lady into reverse and they rolled out of the driveway, into the soft morning light. "I thought I heard the phone ring."

"Wrong number."

He smiled. "You've always been a lousy liar, you know."

"If it's important, they'll call back. Besides, we're not the only investigators in town."

They looked at each other and laughed. "To Caracas," he said.

"To Caracas," she echoed.

And they drove.

About the Author

T. J. MacGregor lives in South Florida. Her first two novels in the Quin St. James/Mike McCleary series were DARK FIELDS and KILL FLASH.